CRASH POINT

A DI FRANK MILLER NOVEL

JOHN CARSON

DI FRANK MILLER SERIES

Crash Point
Silent Marker
Rain Town
Watch Me Bleed
Broken Wheels
Sudden Death
Under the Knife
Trial and Error
Warning Sign
Cut Throat
Blood from a Stone
Time of Death

Frank Miller Crime Series – Books 1-3 – Box set

MAX DOYLE SERIES

Final Steps
Code Red
The October Project

SCOTT MARSHALL SERIES

Old Habits

CRASH POINT

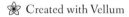 Created with Vellum

DEDICATION

For my wife, Debbie

ONE

Monday

'Do you want to know why I killed him?'

The words rang sharp in Frank Miller's head as the car skidded on the snow-covered road outside the hotel, the headlight beams bouncing off a patrol car. He left the warmth of the car and slammed the door, going as fast as he could up the icy steps to the hotel, the driving snow blinding him. He thought about Neil McGovern, serial killer. Locked up in a psychiatric hospital to rot away the rest of his life. Which turned out to be all of two weeks.

McGovern's taunt had been the first thing on Miller's mind for many sleepless nights afterwards. Tonight he hadn't been given the chance of a sleepless night. His team were on-call and nobody had been to bed yet. They'd been to a fatal domestic stabbing, and were just wrapping up, when Miller got a call from control at 2:56 am. Normally, his Monday morning wouldn't start for another four hours, but they were requested to attend a locus where there was a "possible life extinct". A dead body. Not officially dead until the doctor said so.

1

He was shivering inside his overcoat as he pulled his collar up against the driving snow, noticing the hotel was clad in scaffolding, covered by green netting with a sign declaring they were still open for business.

After the patrol crew confirmed it wasn't a hoax, or a prank, he'd sent an advance team ahead while he wrapped up the first scene

Then he'd taken the call from DS Tam Scott: *Bring your tub of Vicks. It's a go.*

There was a uniform at the door as Miller entered the hotel. Inside, there was a buzz of activity, as if somebody had pulled the fire alarm. Uniforms were herding guests down the stairs, into the bar where they could be watched and statements taken.

Detective Sergeant Tam Scott was already wearing plastic over-shoes, waiting for Miller by the lift doors. Miller brushed the snow from his hair as they rode the lift up to the fifth floor. A sign was taped above the buttons: *No Admittance To Level 5*.

'What have we got up here, Tam?' Miller asked, rubbing Vicks under his nose.

'It's bad, boss.' Scott wasn't far away from retirement, and it couldn't come quickly enough. 'It's like before.'

'You mean...?' Miller didn't want to come out and ask the question, knowing he didn't have to. Scott nodded.

'Fuck.' Miller looked at his watch: 3:45 am. He'd had no coffee, but the buzz of adrenaline was doing the same job.

Scott fumbled in his pocket and held out his hand to Miller.

'What's this?' Miller asked.

'Breakfast,' Scott said, dropping the stick of gum into Miller's hand. Then he tapped the paper sign. 'The hotel's being refurbished. Starting with this floor. That's why guests aren't allowed up here.' The lift jolted to a halt.

'Nothing to stop them hitting the button to come up here though.' He unwrapped the gum and rolled the stick into his mouth, careful to put the wrapper in his pocket.

'There is now,' Scott said, as the lift doors slid open. A burly uniform was standing right at the doors.

'Morning, sir,' he said to Miller, as he stepped aside.

Miller nodded to him. Planks of wood were laying on the floor, along with various other pieces of detritus from the building site.

This floor was barely lit. Miller heard the noise coming from the room, bodies going about the crime scene with exercised efficiency; loud voices, radio chatter and the sound of a camera shutter letting images of the dead seep onto a digital card.

Another uniform stood outside the room and nodded to the two detectives.

'Old Doc Shields confirmed life extinct just before you got here,' Scott said. 'Although everybody could see that for themselves. Rules are rules, though.'

'You been in there yet?'

Scott nodded. 'It's a mess, boss.'

'Who found him?'

Scott looked at his notebook. 'The manager, Donald Goram. He said he thought he heard something up here, so he came to have a look. Melinda, the night auditor, says he comes up here for a sly fag.'

A tech at the doorway made them take off their overcoats and suit up before they went into the room. People were moving about and lights were flashing. Identity Branch staff and detectives. The quick strobe of a flashgun.

One of the techs was standing, dusting the window frame for prints. Another tech was moving around the bed for a better angle, crouching, and snapping off another photo. Miller saw Detective Sergeant Jimmy Gilmour talking with the forensics boss, Inspector Maggie Parks. Another of the older detectives, DS Andy Watt, was looking at the bed.

'Hello, Frank,' Maggie said. 'I hear it's been a busy night for you.'

'It certainly has.'

The room looked like it hadn't been used in a long time, and Miller could understand why the place was being refurbished. The décor was old and the furniture had seen better days. Nothing a can of petrol and a box of matches wouldn't take care of, he thought. It didn't seem as if anything was out of place. The tech with the camera was standing at the side of the bed, blocking his view. He approached the back of the white suit and the young man moved out of the way.

Miller took a deep breath through his nose and held it for a few seconds. He'd been to many crime scenes in his twelve years as a copper, and too many murder scenes in his seven years with Serious Crimes, but this rammed into his gut like a cold, steel fist.

He let out his breath, keeping his composure, and looked at the disembowelled corpse lying on the bed.

In life, the man had started going bald on top, the remaining hair black, with a hint of grey. The nose was thin but looked like it had been broken more than once. The mouth was open, as if he'd been screaming when he died.

They just stood looking down at the corpse.

Miller looked at Scott. Spoke the words nobody else wanted to. 'We got it right, Tam, didn't we?'

Scott looked right back at him. 'I hope we did.'

'Of course we did,' Watt said. His usual philosophy was, *"Don't fuck up, and if you do, don't get caught."*

'It has to be a copycat,' Miller said to Scott. He was starting to feel warm now. Although this floor was being refurbished, the heating was still on, to prevent any pipes from freezing. McGovern had died in the psychiatric hospital. Now Miller was standing looking at a man who'd been killed in the same way as three other people.

'It can't be anything else. McGovern's dead, so it can't be him.' Miller looked back at the pale, waxy face, a spark of recognition punching him in the guts. He looked at Watt.

'So you recognise him, boss?' Watt said.

'That I do, Andy. That I do.'

It was Colin Fleming, ex-police officer.

'Morning, folks,' pathologist Julie Davidson said from the doorway.

They turned round at the sound of her voice.

'Hi, Frank. Good to see you again.' She was already suited up, ready to go to work.

'Hi, Julie. How have you been?'

'I'm fine, Frank.' She put a hand on his arm and gave a small smile that seemed reserved for people who are talking in the wee hours and have been dragged out of bed. 'What do we have here, then?'

Julie was in her mid-forties but looked ten years younger. She was an attractive woman who looked after herself. She was also Frank Miller's sister-in-law. He hadn't seen her much since her father's funeral.

'*Who* do we have here?' Miller said. 'Colin Fleming.'

She looked at Miller. 'Is that the same Colin Fleming who my dad worked with? The one who went to work with Robert Molloy?'

'*The very same.' Robert Molloy. Gangster. A scumbag who'd been giving bribes to serving police officers, most of whom had been caught, including Colin Fleming.*

They stood back as Julie did a preliminary examination. Probing. Poking. Looking. They chatted amongst themselves and looked around. Miller walked over to the window where the tech had stood and held up his hands to the glass without touching it. Creating a dark spot so he could look out. It was still snowing heavily. The worst winter weather in fifty years and Miller caught it when he was on-call.

After a while, Julie stood up straight. 'He had his throat cut, obviously, but he was opened up shortly afterwards, while the heart was still pumping. Otherwise there'd be no spatter. Probably severed an artery.'

They heard a fuss from outside the door. Norma Banks walked in. The procurator fiscal. Detective Chief Inspector Paddy Gibb followed her. Both of them were suited up.

'I wanted to say "Good morning" to you all, but it's not a good morning when I get a call from control reporting the murder of an ex-police officer. I haven't had a coffee, I've had three hours sleep and I'm not happy.' She looked at Gibb. 'Make sure nobody rides that lift up here.'

'We already have uniforms on that, ma'am.'

Banks walked over to the bed and looked down at the corpse. 'I'll have to make changes to this "Let's-get-the-PF-out-of-bed" protocol.' Then she looked around the room. 'Can I have your attention, everybody?'

The techs stopped what they were doing, and the detectives all looked at her. 'We all know DI Miller here caught the man who killed both Harry Davidson a couple of months ago and three women previously. For some reason, somebody's taken it into their head to go and copy what he started. This is not his work, obviously, but that of a copycat. So, it's all hands on deck. I'll be talking with the justice minister later this morning. Then we'll get as many officers as we need, and there won't be a constraint on our budget. We'll put in for as much overtime as we need to catch whoever did this *as soon as*. And there's a media blackout on this for the moment. I don't need to tell you which body parts will be hurting if I find out any of you spoke out of turn to the press.'

She looked at Julie. 'Can you tell a TOD from this?'

'Preliminary time suggests between four and five hours ago.'

Banks shook her head. Looked at Gibb. 'Any word on who owns this hotel?'

Gibb looked at the other detectives.

'Alamo International,' Jimmy Gilmour said, flicking through his notepad. 'Which in turn is owned by—'

'Robert Molloy,' Miller finished for him.

'Has anybody spoken to him about this?' Banks asked.

'Not yet, ma'am,' Miller said.

Banks looked at him. 'Go and wake the bastard up.'

TWO

Robert Molloy's neighbours were used to seeing police cars pull up outside his house, but nobody ever complained. None of them wanted to come home to find their house on fire.

Miller pulled the car to the side of the road, reluctant to leave the warmth that was just starting to build up. The drive had taken fifteen minutes in the snow, a journey that would have normally taken five in dry weather. The hotel was only a stone's throw from Molloy's house on Heriot Row, an upscale enclave in Edinburgh's New Town.

The snow was still coming down as Miller turned the engine off. They got out and walked up to the front door, careful not to slip on the steps, which hadn't been cleared of snow. Miller rang the doorbell, keeping his finger on the button.

They heard a door inside being opened and then the front door being unlocked. Robert Molloy swung the door open. Fully clothed. 'About fucking time,' he said. Then he saw Miller and Scott.

'Detective Miller,' he said, 'what can I do for you?'

'We're not disturbing you, are we?' Miller said.

'Well, now you mention it...'

'We need to come in, Molloy. We need to talk to you.'

Molloy gritted his teeth and shook his head, anger spreading across his face.

Beyond the door was the vestibule, and beyond that, the hallway. A woman stood looking at them, her arms wrapped round herself as she braved the cold draught. Miller had seen her in Molloy's club. Sienna Craig, one of his security staff.

'Before we freeze to death would be nice,' Miller said, prompting the older man.

'Come in, then.' Molloy stood back, and they walked into the vestibule. It was a small reception area, where Molloy insisted they take off their jackets and hats. He looked at the woman. 'Could you do us some coffee?'

'Sure.' Sienna looked to be in her late thirties, with a slim build. She wore jeans and a tight sweater.

Molloy led them through to the back, where one door took them to the living room. The woman went through the other to the kitchen. A gas fire was burning in the large room, and the heat felt good after being out in the cold.

Molloy walked over to an Olde Worlde globe, which sat on a stand, and opened the lid, splitting the Earth in two. 'Want one?'

Miller looked at his watch. 'It's five am. Bit early for me.'

'Bit late for me,' Scott said.

'I see,' Molloy said. 'You two *do* want coffee.' He poured himself a Scotch. 'Find yourself a seat.'

Robert Molloy was in his early sixties, and still had a thick head of hair though at his age, the black colour had to come from a bottle. Miller had to admit the older man looked good, but that's what money did for you. Molloy could afford the best of everything.

Miller and Scott sat on chairs near the fire, Molloy on a settee facing them.

Miller looked at him. Despite it being early, Molloy looked composed and refreshed. As if he'd slept like a baby. Or hadn't been to bed yet.

The woman came back in with two cups of coffee on a tray, with cream and sugar. She set it down on the coffee table, between Molloy and his guests. Miller thanked her.

'So, what can I do for you?' Molloy said, sipping at the whisky, and dismissing the woman with a look. There had been no attempt to introduce her.

'It's about Colin Fleming,' Miller said, sipping at the hot coffee.

'Who?'

'Colin Fleming,' Scott said. 'You know, the copper you used to give handouts to.'

'I'm sorry, sergeant, but there are so many of you, I have trouble keeping up with the names.' He glared at Scott. 'Anyway, what about him?'

'He's dead,' Miller said.

'What?'

'He was murdered in a hotel room last night,' Miller said. 'The one you own in South Learnmouth Gardens.'

'How was he murdered?'

'I'm afraid we can't say right now.'

Molloy took a bigger gulp of the whisky before slamming the glass down on the coffee table with a bang. 'And, I don't suppose you have anybody in the frame for this?' His voice had a hard edge to it now.

'"Frame" is not a word we use, Molloy,' Miller said. 'And no, we don't. It's only been a few hours and the techs are going through the room. I need to know what he was doing there.'

'How would *I* know?'

'It's your hotel, and he worked for you. That's how you'd know.'

'Do you know anybody who'd have a motive for killing him?' Scott asked.

'No. I don't know anybody who'd have it in for him. But there's a lot of fuckers out there who'd have it in for me! Wouldn't you agree?' His narrowed eyes zoned in on Miller's face, as if daring him to argue.

Miller left it alone. 'I also need to ask you where you were tonight.'

'Oh, fuck off. Really?' His voice was full of barely contained anger. 'I was at the club until one o'clock, give or take. Then I came home with Sienna. But I have to say, if I'd wanted to kill the bastard, I wouldn't have left him in a hotel room, especially one of mine.'

Scott looked at Molloy. 'Where *would* you have left him?'

'This conversation is over, gentlemen. Any more questions, I'll call my lawyer. If you need a list of witnesses who saw me earlier, I'll have one of my staff type up the names.' His breathing was faster now.

'Do that, Molloy,' Miller said, standing up. He had no doubt the list of witnesses would include Lord Lucan and Santa Claus.

'We'll see ourselves out,' Scott said.

When they left the living room, Sienna was standing at the top of the stairs. Watching them.

'He knows alright,' Scott said, when they were back in the car. Miller watched as the wipers batted the accumulated snow away. 'You see his face when you told him what had happened to Fleming?'

'I did indeed.'

'Colin Fleming died the same way our boss did nine weeks ago,' Scott said, shaking his head. 'I don't trust Molloy.'

'I know, Tam.'

Miller's phone rang. He fished it out of his pocket. Listened to the voice of the procurator fiscal on the other end, occasionally acknowledging her words, before hanging up.

'That was Norma Banks. She wants me to do something for her. I'll drop you off at the station and meet you there later.'

Scott nodded. Thought about putting his feet up in Miller's office.

Forty-five minutes later, Miller was riding the lift up to his flat on the sixth floor. The building was beginning to stir with life, although he didn't meet any neighbours on his floor.

He let himself into his flat and stopped. He heard a noise coming from the living room. As he cautiously walked down the hall, a woman suddenly stepped out and pointed a gun at his head.

THREE

Miller was marksman trained and knew how to handle a gun. By the way this woman was holding hers, so did she. She was young, maybe late twenties, with short blonde hair pulled into a ponytail. She wasn't wearing a jacket, but a black polo neck, black jeans. And a shoulder holster.

'The TV's not worth much, but it's yours if you want it.'

She took her finger off the trigger and holstered her weapon. 'Sorry about the dramatics, but I couldn't take a chance, Frank.'

He pulled off his hat and shoved it into a pocket. Took his overcoat and jacket off.

She relaxed a little. 'You don't know me, but my name's—'

'Dr Kim Smith.' He hung his jacket on one of the wall hooks.

She smiled. 'I don't normally let myself into somebody's place, but it was cold outside.'

If she could use a gun, Miller had no doubt she was a dab hand with a set of lock picks.

'Norma said you'd be meeting me this morning, I just didn't think it would be this soon,' Miller said, walking through to the living room. 'What's with the gun?'

'I'll explain in a minute.'

She followed him from the living room through to the kitchen, and put his coffee pot on.

Outside the kitchen window, he could see the next round of snow coming down from the dark sky. It was even heavier now. His cat, Charlie, came over and wrapped himself round Kim's legs.

Miller found the whole scenario surreal; first this beautiful woman pointed an automatic gun at him and now she was petting his cat.

'He's a nice cat,' she said.

'Yeah, my wife picked him out.' Just saying the words made him feel cold inside. DS Carol Miller had been his wife for six months. He'd thought they'd grow old together but the driver of the stolen car had cut his plans short.

Miller poured two coffees and they sat down at the small bistro table. His father lived with him, and normally Jack would be bustling about before getting ready to go out. Retirement suited him just fine. He and his cronies hung out all day, doing... what? He wasn't even sure what his father did all day. He'd stayed overnight with one of his buddies again.

'Again, I'm sorry for pulling the gun on you.'

'Don't worry about it.' He gave her a tired smile and drank some coffee, feeling it burn its way down his throat. 'I'd hate to be the guy who stood you up.'

She took a sip of her own coffee, and smiled back at him. 'Oh, I only resort to my gun if they cheat on me.'

'I bet they don't do it twice. You want some toast or anything?' Miller wasn't sure what the "or anything" would be since his father had probably eaten all the bacon again.

'No thanks. I don't eat much bread. Too many carbs. You go ahead though.'

He popped in two slices and they made small talk until it popped up and he buttered it. He sat down again. 'Why do you need to carry a gun anyway?'

'I'm a medical doctor. I could be a GP, or work in a hospital, but I like this job better. So I have to carry a gun.'

'What's your job?'

She looked at him, and smiled. 'I work for the government. Witness protection.'

'And you're here to protect me?' he asked.

'I've been seconded to work for the procurator fiscal's office as an investigator.'

'Investigating what?'

She paused before answering. 'Your boss's death.'

'You're kidding me.' Miller looked at her like she was crazy. He was still tired, waiting for the buzz of the caffeine. Harry Davidson's murder was still fresh in Miller's mind, like it had happened only yesterday. 'What is there to investigate?'

Kim took another sip of coffee and a deep breath, as if she'd been rehearsing the next part. 'Neil McGovern was put away in the psychiatric hospital for killing Harry.'

'I know. I arrested him.'

'Neil McGovern died in the psychiatric hospital a fortnight ago, after being incarcerated for two weeks.'

Miller nodded. 'I read the briefing they sent us. Nobody's going to lose any sleep over the bastard dying.'

Kim drank more coffee. 'I know that, but you don't understand; Neil McGovern wasn't who you thought he was.'

'What do you mean?'

'Neil McGovern didn't murder your boss that night.'

'What?' He shook his head. 'I was there. I saw what he did. He was lying near Harry.'

Kim's face had become serious. 'He didn't kill Harry; he was working with him. Neil was one of us.'

Miller looked at her blankly, as if waiting for the punchline. 'One of you lot?'

'Yes. He worked for my department. He wasn't there to kill

Harry, but to get information from him. That wasn't the first time they'd met.'

Miller shook his head, not quite believing what he was hearing. 'He *confessed*. He asked me if I wanted to know why he'd killed Harry. Now you're telling me he didn't kill him?' Miller couldn't believe it. Neil McGovern was innocent? He watched as Kim got up from the table.

'Hold on, Frank, I have something to show you.'

Miller drank more coffee, desperate for some caffeine.

Kim came back into the room with a folder and sat down. Laid the folder on the table and opened it. 'Neil said you'd have a hard time believing it, so I took the liberty of having some files sent up from London. Here, take a look at this.'

She passed over a sheet that showed a photo of a man's head and shoulders. Neil McGovern. It was a blow-up of a security pass issued by the government. It listed a department name, ID number and some other sort of code.

Kim brought out more papers, each one showing McGovern to be a government operative. 'It's okay to be sceptical, Frank. I understand Harry Davidson wasn't just your boss, but your father-in-law too.'

'Harry said he knew who'd slaughtered those three women two years ago.' He felt tired now.

Kim reached out and put a hand on his. 'I know, but the man who killed him is still out there. I'm here to help, Frank.'

'You know my wife's been gone for over two years?' he asked her.

'Yes, I know.' She took her hand back.

'I still don't know for sure who killed her. Now I don't know who killed her father, when all along, I thought his killer was six feet under.'

'I won't pretend to understand. I'm divorced. I haven't experienced losing a spouse, so I won't patronise you. I want to help you get the answer you want.' She pulled out another piece of paper. 'You know I'm genuine, Frank. I'm working with Norma Banks. It's not like I just walked in off the street.'

Miller looked at the paper. It was a short list of telephone numbers. 'What's this?'

'Those are departmental numbers in London. Call anyone you want and the person will verify who Neil was. Or have them checked out if you like, just to see they're genuine.'

Miller knew he wouldn't have to have them checked out. If what this woman was saying was true, then they were fucked. They didn't get their killer after all. 'Why didn't somebody tell us this nine weeks ago? We could have still been hunting for the real killer.'

She took a deep breath and looked at him. 'It's not as simple as that. My department was looking for Harry's killer. Nobody else could find out. It was important the guy thought Neil had taken the fall for it. That gave us breathing space.'

'It gave *him* breathing space, more like.'

Kim nodded. 'I know it's hard to accept. Neil was working the case with Norma Banks. The PF didn't want to involve you until we'd extracted Neil from the hospital, but as I said, he died before that could happen.'

'So that's why you're here now?'

'Yes. The reason I had the gun out when you came in, is because we now know who the real killer is.' She looked at him.

'And he's coming after you.'

FOUR

There was silence between them for a few moments. Outside the kitchen window, the wind threw some snow against the glass as if trying to break it.

Miller had his hand round his coffee cup. 'So who is it?'

'His name's Raymond Cross,' Kim said, sipping more coffee. 'It was a name Harry whispered to McGovern.'

'How do you know he's coming after me?'

'Harry told Neil. He said you were in danger.'

Miller thought about the name. It didn't register. 'Should I know who this guy is?'

'No. His name will mean nothing to you. It would mean something to your father though.'

'How would Jack know Cross?'

Kim held up a finger, wanting Miller to wait. She got up from the small table again and came back a moment later with a second folder. Passed it to him. Miller flipped it open and started browsing as she spoke.

'Twenty-five years ago, Robert Molloy opened a hotel outside Edinburgh. There was an opening party. His son, Michael Molloy, invited a lot of his friends, including Raymond Cross. Cross worked for Molloy. That night, Cross and his girlfriend, Moira Kennedy, were in his car in the car park of the hotel. Just talking apparently. He went inside to get a couple of drinks. When he came back out, Moira had been stabbed to death.

'There were already police officers nearby, keeping an eye on who was going into the hotel. They were on the scene after they got a tip-off. They caught Cross at the car. He had blood on his hands, literally, but he said he was just feeling for a pulse. He was arrested by three detectives: DI Harry Davidson, DS Colin Fleming and DC Jack Miller.'

Miller looked at her before flipping through some more of the pages. 'I'm assuming they took him to High Street station to process him.'

'Yes. He was put into an interview room. Davidson and Fleming interviewed him, and then they got a request from the Met. They asked if one of their detectives could come and talk to Cross. They had a similar unsolved on their hands; a girl murdered in the same way. So he came up the next day. Went in to interview Cross. When Harry Davidson went into the room, both Cross and the Met detective were gone.'

Miller looked at her. 'Gone?' He shuffled some of the papers, saw a few sheets with the Metropolitan Police logo on top. Saw a few words. Interview. Detective Chief Inspector Dick Bingham.

'They were gone. Vanished. There was no sign of either one of them. Ever again.'

'Let me guess; the detective didn't exist.'

Kim drank more coffee, feeling the hot liquid heat her up inside. She was starting to feel a little shaky as the adrenaline kicked in. 'Right. Phone calls to London came up with nothing. Despite him having proper identification and paperwork, it was all false.'

'And now Cross has come back and reinvented himself as a serial killer twenty-five years later.'

FIVE

After making a phone call, Miller went for a shower. He had the temperature up high and the needles of hot water battered against his skin. The shower radio was on, but he was listening to the conversation he'd just had with Norma Banks, playing over and over in his head.

Yes, Inspector, it's true. Neil McGovern was indeed working for us. We couldn't let on until now. I'm sure you understand. I've called Paddy Gibb and told him to get the team going through the Moira Kennedy murder. How do I know you can trust Kim? She's my daughter, Inspector.

The PF's daughter. Great. When it all went belly up, it would be Miller they'd hang out to dry. However, he didn't have a choice in the matter. She wanted to meet them in a little while. Miller had been expecting to go to her office, but had been surprised by her choice of location.

He towelled off and dressed quickly. Kim was waiting in the living room, playing with Charlie, making him chase a mouse on a plastic pole. Daylight had made an appearance and there was a break in the snow. Rush hour was getting into full swing.

'I need to ask you something,' Miller said.

Kim stopped playing with the cat and looked at him. 'Anything.'

'When you came in here, did you look around? I mean, I'm not suggesting for one second you were snooping or anything.'

'Yes, you are.' She smiled at him. 'I didn't look around, I promise you.' She put the cat toy down and stood up. 'I'm going to be working with you, and I want there to be trust between us.'

'Fair enough. Oh, and Norma told me she's your mother.'

'Oh, she did? I *was* going to tell you.'

'You just thought I'd had enough surprises for one day?' He gave her a small grin and walked across the living room and back into the kitchen. Opened the fridge and popped the tab on a small can. God bless Red Bull, he thought as he swallowed it down.

'You ready?' he said, as he came back into the living room, but Kim already had her jacket on.

'I guess you are,' he said.

They rode the lift down. 'I need to call my partner, Tam.' He excused himself for a moment and stood in the entrance of a newsagent's while Kim stood stamping her feet and clapping her gloved hands together. He called Scott and explained he was on an errand for the procurator fiscal. 'You still at the station?'

'Yes, I am. Gilmour just got in. The body was taken away to the mortuary.'

'Can you meet me at the car, Tam? I need you to come with me.' He gave him a quick rundown about Kim. Asked him for a favour.

'What will I tell Gibb?'

'That he's ugly and drinks too much.' He hung up.

Kim looked at him. 'You trust this guy?'

'Tam? With my life. Somebody tried to stab me in the back in a pub one night. Tam broke his arm. I'd trust him more than my father. Tam's an old-school detective, like my dad was before he retired. Not many of them left now.'

'Good enough for me.'

The pavements were slippery with the fresh coating of snow.

Kim held onto Miller's right arm, despite the fact she was wearing boots, and not the kind you'd find on a catwalk. 'If I'm going down, I'm taking you with me,' she said.

St Giles' Cathedral sat up on their left, just past the station, large and imposing, looking like a ginger bread house that had been coated with frosting.

'Down here,' Miller said, turning right into Cockburn Street, an old road that connected the Old Town to the New Town.

'So, in theory, Raymond Cross could be anywhere right now. Even waiting across the street,' Miller said, as he climbed in behind the wheel. He'd love to meet the bastard.

'Basically, yes.' Kim fiddled with the heater switches, producing only a blast of cold air.

Tam Scott opened the back door, holding a coffee in a throwaway cup. He got in the back seat, his eyes moving to Kim.

'Tam, this is Dr Kim Smith,' Miller said. 'She works for the PF. She's working with us just now.' He briefly explained Cross was now a suspect.

They exchanged pleasantries as Miller pulled away.

'So where are we going, boss?' Scott asked.

'Back to the place where we found Harry Davidson dying.'

SIX

The catacombs in Warriston cemetery.

Looking at them from the front, they could have been a castle, with three large entrances and a wooden fence on top where once a stone balustrade had been. The crypts were built into the side of the top part of the cemetery, and ran deep underground. Two of the entrances were bricked up, leaving only the central wrought-iron gate, now covered in corrugated iron sheets to keep the vandals out.

Miller turned off the engine. Looked across at Kim, who was sitting staring out the window. 'This place brings back memories.'

She turned to look at him. 'I just wish Neil had called me sooner that night. I might have been able to help him.' She got out and trudged through the thick snow towards the main gate.

Miller and Scott followed. A wind shot through the cemetery, disturbing the snow and throwing it in the air as if the place was haunted.

They all heard the car crunching along the snow-covered drive-way, heading in their direction. It was a small German sedan with all-wheel-drive.

'Here's Norma now,' Miller said. 'Oh, and one other thing, Tam;

she's Kim's mother.'

'What? Oh, now you fucking tell me.'

The car pulled up behind Miller's pool car. He walked over to the driver's door and opened it for her, feeling the heat from within escaping.

'God awful weather,' she said, stepping out and pulling the collar up on her overcoat. She looked at Miller. 'Thank you for meeting me here. I didn't actually come here the night Neil McGovern was attacked. I wanted to see the scene for myself, now Harry's killer's resurfaced.'

'No problem, ma'am.' He noticed she was wearing trousers and snow boots.

'When it's just us, you can call me Norma.' She locked the car with the remote and nodded to Scott, walking past him and up to her daughter. 'Hello, Kim.'

Kim turned. 'Hey, Norma.'

The gates were padlocked, a thick chain snaking through a hole in the corrugated iron sheet, wrapping round the vertical bars. 'I had my assistant get these from a council keyholder.' Norma handed a set of keys to Kim.

'Are you going to tell me why we're here, boss?' Scott said.

'In good time, Tam. I don't want to bombard you with details just yet, but apparently Neil McGovern didn't kill Harry Davidson.'

'What?' Scott's face showed his incredulity. 'I was there with you that night. I saw what he did to Harry.'

'It's true,' Norma said, turning round to look at him for a moment.

Scott looked angry but kept his tongue in check.

The lock sprang open.

'Let's go up to the crypt where Davidson was,' Norma said.

The open gate threw a shaft of cold daylight inside. They took out the torches they'd brought with them. Miller gave Scott the spare he'd brought. 'Here, Tam, take this.'

Scott took it and switched it on, swinging the beam of light around in the darkness. The light bounced off the lawnmowers the gravediggers used in season. Tools with dirty, wooden handles were strewn around in a haphazard fashion, as if they'd just been thrown in.

'I wonder what this place looked like when it was new,' Miller mused, shining his own torch around.

'This place was probably an exclusive club,' Kim said. She shone her own light in the opposite direction. More grass-cutting machinery. More gravestones lying about, probably in contravention of some Health and Safety law. 'You just had to die with a lot of money to get membership.'

The place smelled the same as it had that night, nine weeks ago, but back then, the passages had been lit by oil torches, as if somebody had been expecting visitors. Maybe Harry had lit them, or McGovern. *Or Raymond Cross.*

Kim took a step towards Miller, and for a second, he thought she was going to draw her weapon again and he tensed.

'Tell me your story, Frank. Tell me what happened that night. Then I'll give you my version.' She put a hand on his arm and squeezed. First her smell, then the feel of her hand through his overcoat. It had been too long. He relaxed.

They all walked a distance up the main passageway. It should have felt warmer in there, away from the wind, but if anything, it was so much colder, like they were standing inside a giant fridge.

'I'll hold onto your arm, sergeant,' Norma said, grabbing hold of Scott. 'I don't want to fall on my arse and have you lot have a good laugh about it in the office.'

'We wouldn't do that, ma'am,' Scott said, his face going red.

'You're so sweet, but a terrible liar.'

Miller stopped. 'I got a text message from Harry. "*I need to talk to you urgently,*" it read. "*I know who killed those three women. Meet me in the crypts in Warriston cemetery.*" I left the flat, picked up Tam and it took us maybe fifteen minutes to get here.'

He looked past them into the darkness, pointing his torchlight like a lance. 'I was standing right there...'

SEVEN

Nine weeks earlier.

Miller heard his feet thump the hard-packed earth as he ran up the passageway, the flames from the oil torches on the wall throwing his shadow around. He was technically underground now, as the catacombs ran beneath the old cemetery. The walls were made of thick stone, cut from a quarry hundreds of years ago to hold back the dead as they lay in their final resting places. The stone was covered with algae in places, the green streaks running like blood.

'You sure this isn't a mistake, Frank?' Scott asked, as they both stopped for a second.

'No, there's no mistake, Tam.' Miller wondered who'd lit the oil torches. 'Harry's in here and we need to find him.' His breath was ragged and a cold mist escaped his mouth as he spoke.

'Didn't he say exactly where he was?' Scott's voice bounced off the walls.

Miller looked up for a moment, shining his torch at the stone ceiling, as if expecting it to come crashing down at any moment. 'No he didn't, but it sounded urgent. Come on, Tam, let's get moving.'

Miller ran the words from the text message through his mind again: "I know who killed Carol."

There were a lot of flaming oil sconces burning all the way up the passageway. Somebody had gone to a lot of trouble to light this place up. The flames flickered in the dark, fed by unseen draughts, causing shadows to be animated.

'Harry!' Miller shouted, knowing the time for stealth had come and gone. If Harry was in here, then there was no need for a covert entrance. If somebody else was in here with him, then that person would already know they had company. His voice echoed round the long passageway.

No reply.

His own flashlight picked out old, abandoned gravestones, which had been piled in the hallway, reminiscent of a scene from a horror movie.

'Harry!' Scott shouted. All the crypts along the passageway had rusty gates on them, and were closed, sealing off the rooms of the dead.

He stopped suddenly, feeling his ribs ache, his breathing getting faster now as his lungs gulped in the air they needed. He moved forward, cautiously. Saw one of the gates open.

'Look at this, Tam.'

Scott looked at him. 'Looks like we found what we came here for.'

They entered the crypt. A smaller passageway led away to the right. Miller walked into it, expecting to be attacked and preparing himself for a fight. Nobody was there. It was darker in here, but more light was coming from the left at the end of the passageway. 'Harry!' Miller shouted. Nothing.

They stepped round at the end, into the crypt. It was a large room, about thirty by thirty and twelve feet high. A sarcophagus sat in the middle of the floor. The walls were lined with the final resting places of this particular family. The air smelled damp and musty. More torches burned.

'Jeez, it smells bad in here, Frank.'

Miller nodded. They both recognised the smell of blood.

Two figures were lying on the floor. Harry was on his side, his jacket open and his shirt covered in blood.

Miller ran over to him and knelt down. 'Harry! Can you hear me?'

Scott shone his torch around the large, cold room. It picked out a shovel lying on the dirt floor close by. Another man was sitting with his back against a wall, looking dazed, with blood running down his face, coming from his hairline. Scott took the blood-covered knife away and handcuffed the man's hands behind his back.

Miller held Harry's chin in one hand, forcing him to look into his eyes. 'Harry, hang in there. We'll get you help.'

'Keep your eye on that other guy, boss, I need to go out to get a signal.' Tam ran outside, needing to get some bars on his phone.

'Stay with me, Harry!' Miller shouted, feeling the panic rising inside him, but Harry couldn't hear him. He was already gone.

Norma Banks was pale. This place was enough to creep anybody out, but knowing this is where somebody was murdered only added to the horror.

Miller shone his torch at Kim. 'The rest, I'm sure, you already know.'

Scott shone his torch around the cold, dank passageway, imagining pall-bearers carrying a coffin up here a hundred years ago. Water dripped somewhere off in the dark, plonking into the puddle it had created.

Miller said, 'So, when we arrived, it looked as if a fight had broken out, Harry having hit Neil with the shovel, then Neil stabbed him. That's how it was meant to look?'

'That about sums it up.' Kim looked at the two detectives, and started to shiver.

'Tell me what happened to you that night,' Miller said.

EIGHT

Robert Molloy stood in the office of his club and looked out at the traffic below. The snow had stopped but the traffic had still ground to a halt. His son, Michael, was sitting behind the desk.

'So what happened, Michael?' Robert turned from the window and looked at the back of his son's head.

Michael swung the chair round to face his father. 'What's this? Being pulled into the head teacher's office for a dressing down? You wanted this job done, not me. I arranged things, it went belly up, end of story.'

'That's it? The job went belly up. That's your fucking answer?'

'So you lost some cash. A hundred grand is a drop in the ocean to you.' He swung the chair back round. End of conversation.

Robert grabbed his son's hair and pulled him back, the office chair tipping alarmingly. 'Listen to me, sonny,' he said, 'we're a family. We work together. I want you to start caring about things, or it's going to end badly for you! Understand?' He twisted his son's hair harder.

'Yes! Now let go of my hair!'

Robert let go, and Michael shot forward. He jumped up. 'Are you insane? You do that again and I'll—'

'You'll do what, Michael?' Robert stepped round the chair and stood in front of his son. He felt tired now, having grabbed only a couple of hours sleep after Miller left his house.

'Nothing.' The fight had gone out of Michael as usual. He'd take anybody on, but when it came to his father, he was all steam and no train.

'You need to find out what went wrong last night. You were supposed to take care of Cross. So what happened?' Spittle flew out of his mouth as he raged at his son.

'Nobody saw anything. I don't know what you want me to say.'

'Cross is playing a dangerous game with me.' Robert Molloy gritted his teeth.

Michael looked at his father. 'I told you we shouldn't have trusted Fleming.'

'Don't start blaming him.' Now Robert was pointing a finger at him, his eyes wide.

'I'm just saying.' Michael didn't make eye contact. 'What about his missus? Maybe she fucked off with the money. She's young enough to start over again.'

'Toni wouldn't do that to me. I've known her a long time.'

'Know her well, do you?' Michael said, with a sneer.

'I swear to God, I'll have somebody smack the shit out of you, even though you're flesh and blood. Try thinking with your big brain for once.'

'Well, nobody knows where she is. So there's a good chance she stuck it to her husband and now she's on her way to the Bahamas with your dosh.'

'I'm waiting on somebody getting back to me now but I don't think she'd be so stupid. Besides, we both know who's behind this. I don't know why he didn't just take the money and go.'

Robert turned again and looked out at the grey sky. February sucked. Ten months 'til Christmas, cold every day, people skint and not going out, which saw their profits drop. Robert hated February.

He wondered what George Street would have been like to live in

29

a couple of hundred years ago. It had been fancy houses back then. Now it was known for its shops and boutique hotels. What was a boutique hotel anyway? Snow lined the pavements like nature's death trap, while cars and buses sprayed the slush onto parked vehicles. St Andrew Square Gardens had been opened up to the public, creating a thoroughfare, and now anybody could walk through them. What was the world coming to? He knew he was old-fashioned, but he was proud of it.

Robert turned round and looked at his son. Back in the day, they'd be pulling in all their contacts, and smacking a few people around, looking for answers.

Somebody had to have heard from the man they were looking for. You don't just reappear after twenty-five years and nobody knows about it. Raymond Cross. A ghost from their past, back to haunt them. Except this ghost was all too real.

'I don't have the answer to that, Dad. When we find him, he's history.'

Robert walked over to his son and stood in front of him. 'Find him soon. I want the fucker dead.'

NINE

Nine weeks earlier.

"I need to see you now. I'm in the crypts with Harry Davidson. He knows who their killer is."

Kim read the text message on her phone again as she walked into the crypts, the gate swinging open easily.

She started walking. Oil torches were hanging from the wall, the flames dancing as if music was playing. Gates lined the walls. She wondered where Neil was, and then she saw an open gate, with light coming from behind it, down a narrow passageway.

She walked down and turned left, into the crypt. An oil sconce lit this room, so she put her torch in her pocket. A man she didn't know was lying on the floor. Harry Davidson, she presumed. He was bleeding from a stomach wound, the blood seeping into his suit and his shirt, which was open. Neil McGovern was sitting with his back to the wall, holding a blood-soaked knife. A thin line of blood ran down his face from his head.

Neil was barely moving his right hand at her. Waving her over.

She rushed over to him, pulling out her mobile phone, and knelt down beside him. Then he was looking over her shoulder. She heard his words, barely a whisper. 'Behind you.'

She turned round just as the man with the mask and hoodie on swung the shovel at her head. She brought her arm up, the gun swinging round, but before she could get a round off, the shovel connected with her forearm, sending the gun spinning through the air. She lashed out with her right foot, tripping her attacker up. Down he went, dropping the tool. Kim kicked out at him, but hoodie got up and started running out of the room. She dropped the shovel, grabbed her gun and started running after him.

Out in the passageway, she watched hoodie charge round a corner, further down on the right. She slowed as she approached, and poked the gun round the corner first and followed it. Stopped and listened. She took out her torch and switched it on, knowing she was making herself a target, but unable to see anything without it. She stood with her back to the wall and pointed it. This was another passageway, running at right angles to the one she'd just come down. There were dozens of old gravestones in here, so old she couldn't read the faded inscriptions. Then she saw another passageway off this one, on her left. She heard a noise. Somebody running.

She ran to the corner and pointed her torch. At the end of this passage, she saw a pair of legs disappear into the ceiling. She ran on, her torch lighting the way. Old gravestones had been piled into makeshift steps, leaning against the wall, three feet high. Above her head, was a semi-circular ventilation shaft and she could see the stars in the sky. As she was about to climb the gravestones, she looked up and saw a grate falling over the opening. It was hinged, and banged into place. She didn't see by whom. Now she had a choice; go after him or go back to McGovern. She decided to go back, knowing McGovern would need her help.

She ran back the way she'd come. Nobody had moved. She checked Harry Davidson for a pulse and found a weak one. By the look of him, she knew she couldn't do anything. She went over to McGovern who hadn't moved. 'Let's get you out of here,' she said, grabbing his arm.

She stopped when she heard a voice, shouting. 'That's Frank Miller,' McGovern said, his voice low. 'Go now. I can't move. Just go. We'll deal with it later.'

She knew it was pointless to argue with him, and quietly left the crypt, running as softly as she could along the passageway, back to the overhead grate. She climbed the gravestones and heaved up on it. The metal was old and rusty and what was once paint began to flake in her hand as she pushed as hard as she could. Finally it moved. She threw it open and it landed on the snow-covered grass.

Then she was out. Her car was where she'd left it, on the upper level. She got in and drove away.

Kim blew out a breath. Felt shaky.

'He obviously saw you were a fighter,' Norma said. 'You would have been dead if you couldn't fight.'

'I know. Come on, I'll show you where we went.'

She led them back out into the main passageway, and they turned left, heading further away from the main entrance.

Norma Banks held onto Scott's arm for balance.

'The passageway ends in a sort of T-junction here,' Kim said, stopping. The only sound was dripping water, echoing lightly somewhere out of sight. 'He turned right. I saw him going round here.'

'More crypts?' Miller said.

'Yes,' Kim said. 'They go way back.' They followed her. She walked on, all the time her beam moving around like a light sabre.

'Left here,' Kim said, turning a corner. It wasn't as dark here. Daylight fell from the roof at the far end. More gates lined the walls here. She pointed out the metal ventilation grate set into the roof.

'He could have been up there waiting for you.' Miller didn't want to think what Cross would have done if he'd overpowered Kim.

'He was gone. Like years before, Raymond Cross had just vanished.'

TEN

Outside in the cold, Miller thought about what he'd been told; a man who'd disappeared twenty-five years ago killed three women two years ago, then came back and killed Miller's boss and set McGovern up to take the fall. Now he was killing again, and Colin Fleming had been at the top of his list. Harry also said he knew who'd killed Carol. Did he mean it was the same guy?

'How can you be sure McGovern was telling the truth?' Miller asked Kim.

'There's one more thing I need to tell you; you knew him as "Neil McGovern" but I knew him as "Dad".'

'He was your father?' Scott asked.

'He was your husband?' Miller said, to Norma.

'We all have different names. I kept my maiden name for professional reasons, and Kim was married. Neil was her father. He wasn't your killer. That bastard is still out there, and now he's back in business.'

'He's certainly not messing about,' Miller said.

'That's why my daughter's working with you,' Norma said. 'I need to be kept in the loop, and she knows all about the case.' Her cheeks

34

were rosy red now, and she was starting to shiver. She unlocked the car with the remote. 'Keep me posted. I want to know everything. And this time we'll get him, Frank. You're not the only one who wants to know what happened to Carol.'

Miller's phone rang as Kim started the car. The engine rattled as she pulled away. Miller nodded a few times, and thanked the caller before hanging up.

'We still don't have an address for Fleming, but at least we know where his office was: West End Yards.'

They headed up the back roads through the New Town and drove down Magdala Crescent towards Haymarket, the old Donaldson's school for the deaf on their right, looking majestic. It was a building Queen Victoria had once said looked better than some of her own palaces. Miller doubted that would have been the case when it was used to house German and Italian POWs during the Second World War.

Kim turned into West End Yards, a group of relatively new office buildings and pulled into a free parking space. Tossed the keys to Miller.

Inside, the atrium was bright and large. They stopped to look at a directory, quickly scanning it and finding the PI office listed, just below a clown-for-hire's office, and for a moment, Miller wondered what the difference was.

They walked over to the lift, and a few seconds later, were making their way up to the fourth floor.

'These are serviced offices, if memory serves me correctly. Pay by the month, fly-by-night affairs,' Miller said.

They made their way along a dimly-lit corridor. At the end, they came to Fleming's. A window was set into the end wall, and looked down to Haymarket Station. The door was ajar.

Miller pushed the door hard and it swung back on its hinges. Daylight shafted in through the window at the back of the room. He hit the light switch and they all stood and looked, not quite believing what they saw.

35

ELEVEN

This is becoming a habit, old son, Richard Sullivan thought, as he padded out of the en suite bathroom. Tai Lopez was still sleeping under his duvet. He towelled off his hair and slipped his robe off, dressing quickly. He knew the jet lag would get to him later, but right now, he was flying on caffeine and sex.

The office was taking care of itself, under the guidance of his office manager, Gayle. There was just the usual amount of lawyer stuff to be going on with, tasks the other lawyers were dealing with.

This was a perk that came with owning the practice.

He heard Tai moan in her sleep, and watched as the form under the covers rolled over.

Sullivan smiled as he walked up the circular staircase to the living area upstairs. He made coffee, and went through to the living room where he stood at the window that overlooked the Firth of Forth and Fife in the distance. He wondered what his folks would have thought of him; just turned fifty and living in a duplex in what was now a fashionable part of town. The flat bought and paid for. He looked over to Dalgety Bay in the distance, and imagined a line from there, leading up to Kelty where his parents had lived, and where he'd lived until he left for university in the big city.

He wished he'd been on speaking terms with his mother before she died.

'Penny for your thoughts?'

Sullivan turned round quickly, his chest thumping. Tai was standing wearing his bathrobe. She was smiling at him. There was the slightest trace of a Columbian accent in her voice, a legacy from her father who still lived there. She said she got her looks from her Scottish mother.

'I was just thinking about my folks,' he said. 'Here, let me get you a coffee, but we'll have to watch the time.'

She sat down at the table. Looked out the window, past the balcony railings, and watched as more snow fell on Fife, a dry run before it came across the water and pelted Edinburgh. Sullivan came back in with her coffee. Put it on the table and sat opposite her. Looked at the clock on the wall, above the TV.

'Don't worry, I won't be late again.' She smiled, and drank some coffee.

'I don't want Molloy getting suspicious.'

'I'm his restaurant manager. We don't open until twelve. It's only just gone ten.'

'I hate that you even have to go over there.'

Tai worked on the *Blue Martini*. A floating restaurant, bought by Robert Molloy simply because he had a notion when the vessel came on the market.

'It's a job right now, honey. You know how it is. I have to pay the rent and eat.'

'I know, you're right.' Sullivan debated with himself if he should ask her to move in with him, but they'd only been seeing each other for a few months, and he thought it might be too soon.

Or maybe you're worried in case Robert Molloy finds out you're sleeping with one of his staff.

'What are you doing today?' she asked.

'I'm going in late to catch up on some paperwork. Or maybe I'll stay home and play some video games, I'm not sure yet.'

She laughed, and playfully slapped his arm. 'Or maybe we could go back to bed and make love all day.'

'Wait until I've ordered a defibrillator on eBay before we do that.' Sullivan was well aware Tai was ten years younger than he was, and felt athletic at times, but once round the track a day was his limit these days.

'I'm going to shower,' she said, finishing her coffee, and smiling at him.

Five minutes after she'd left the room, the front door buzzer rang. A few minutes later, Geddes Fyfe was standing in his living room. Fyfe was Sullivan's office investigator. A wiry man a few years younger than his boss, he always dressed as if he was about to go out on an SAS mission. Like now, dressed from head to toe in black.

'You heard the news?' Fyfe said, getting straight to the point.

'What news?'

Fyfe shook his head, picking up the TV remote and aiming it at the TV. 'You're playing with fire' he said,

'What do you mean?'

'I heard the shower running downstairs in your bedroom, and unless that's your sister, I guess Miss Lopez spent the night again.'

'I don't have a sister.'

'Exactly. Robert Molloy won't be a happy camper if he finds out.'

'Who cares what Molloy thinks?'

'Maybe you could quote that to him when his men are tying breeze blocks round your ankles at Granton Harbour.'

Sky News was reporting the death of a man in a hotel in the centre of Edinburgh.

'What's this got to do with me?' Sullivan asked. The police weren't releasing the name of the victim until next-of-kin were informed. He saw the police cars outside the hotel, and the grey mortuary van waiting to take the body away after the SOCOs had crawled all over him.

'I had a call from a friend of mine. It's Colin Fleming in the hotel room.'

The colour left Sullivan's face. 'You sure?'

Fyfe didn't take his eyes off the TV. 'Oh yes.'

TWELVE

The woman lay on her back in the middle of the desk.

Her head hung over one end, the angle accentuated by the large slit in her throat.

'Still got your tub of Vicks?' Scott said. For the second time that morning, Miller put some under his nose. Offered it to Kim, who shook her head.

Whoever the woman was, she'd been stripped to the waist and had her abdomen ripped open. Blood flowed over the desk and had dripped over the edge onto the carpet.

Miller angled his head, and looked at the woman's face; she looked like she was in her late forties.

Kim stepped forward, while Scott took in the rest of the room. There was a closet at one end. 'He knew we'd come round to look at Fleming's place of work, so he left her here for us to find,' Miller said. He took his Airwave out and called it in.

Scott pulled the closet open, only to find shelves with not much on them except an old coffee mug and an out-of-date phone book. 'Nothing in here, boss.'

They'd pulled on their nitrile gloves and looked around the office, while Miller picked up the woman's handbag. He took her purse out and looked through it. There was no sign of a driving licence, but there was a name on a bank card. 'Toni Fleming,' he said, holding up the piece of blue plastic.

Scott walked over to Miller. 'That was his wife's name.' He looked at the corpse. 'So Cross killed them both? I wonder if she saw him or something. Witnessed him killing her husband.'

'There's a mobile in there,' Kim said. Miller held out the bag to her and she reached in and took it out. An iPhone, unlocked. Kim brought the screen up and checked the text messages. 'Here's an interesting one from last night.'

Miller looked at it, and Scott came round, craning his neck.

Come to my office. This is urgent. Don't call me. Phone on silent. Don't tell anybody. Danger. Be careful honey.

'It was sent right about the time Colin was being murdered, if Julie's estimated time-of-death is correct,' Miller said. 'Cross probably lured her here.'

Minutes later, they heard the sirens.

Paddy Gibb led the charge, followed by Jimmy Gilmour and Hazel Carter. Uniforms stood outside, in the corridor.

'This is different, Frank,' Gibb said. 'Two on the same night.' He took Miller into the corridor, over to the window that looked down to the car park. 'I spoke to Norma Banks. She briefed me on the Neil McGovern situation.' He looked Miller in the eyes. 'I don't believe this is happening, and I know how hard it must be on you.'

'I'm looking on the bright side, sir. I might get to catch the bastard who killed Harry this time. I thought I had before, but maybe we'll get lucky this time.'

Gibb patted him on the shoulder. 'We all want him, son. Somebody killed one of ours. We'll never stop looking for him.'

They both looked round as the lift announced its arrival. Julie Davidson stepped out. Walked towards them, her face looking grim. She stopped in front of Miller. 'Is it the same as this morning?'

Miller nodded. 'It looks like the same MO.'

She looked at him, her face grim. 'Why would somebody copy Neil McGovern's method of killing? Do you think he was working with somebody?'

'I didn't get that feeling,' Miller said.

Her breathing got a little faster. 'It makes me feel sick, if I'm honest. However, we all worked together to get McGovern, and we'll work just as hard this time.'

'I know.' He reached a hand out and put it on her arm. 'If you need to talk, call me, okay?'

'I will.' She turned, and made her way into Fleming's office, passing Scott as the other detective walked up to Miller and Gibb, holding a diary.

'An entry for yesterday. Take a read.'

Raymond Cross. Dead man.

'So he did know his killer,' Gibb said. 'We've re-opened the Moira Kennedy murder Cross was involved in.'

'Although, technically, it was never closed,' Miller said. He turned to Gibb, as Scott walked back to the office. 'I have to go and see somebody. Can you tell Scott and Kim I'll see them back at the station?'

'Sure I will. I *am* your secretary after all.'

Miller got back in the lift, and wondered when they were going to start telling people about the mistake they'd made with McGovern.

A mistake that was now costing people their lives.

THIRTEEN

Outside, Miller took a deep breath of the fresh, cold air. He felt shaky, the adrenaline still coursing through his veins.

He's coming after you.

That was fine by him. Taking on Harry's killer didn't frighten him one little bit. And if they got him and he wouldn't talk, then all he'd need was five minutes alone with him. No witnesses, no rules. That would never happen, but maybe they could use a little psychology on him.

Or wire the fucker up to the mains.

He left Haymarket, and hit the Western Approach Road, coming off at Slateford Road, opposite the Athletic Arms. Known by the locals as *The Diggers* because it was opposite Dalry cemetery, they eventually had that name put on the façade above the windows. He drove up through Polwarth, and five minutes later, was at his destination.

The flat he was looking for was on the third floor.

'Long time, no see,' Ian Powers said, as he opened the door.

'Get the kettle on, Ian, I've a job for you,' Miller said, as Powers stood to one side.

'Not so loud, Frank,' Powers said, quickly shutting the door.

Miller went through to the living room. It was more like the bridge on the Enterprise. Computers were set up everywhere. Several monitors were displaying programs that were running. The room gently buzzed.

'So, to what do I owe the pleasure?' he said.

'I need you to hack into something for me, Ian,' Miller said.

Miller heard a girl's voice coming from one of the computers. 'You there, Ian?'

'Linda, I have a friend round.'

'That's okay. He a techie?'

'No, he's the polis.'

The girl disappeared as quickly as she'd appeared. 'My girlfriend. Linda. Nice girl but a bit nervous.'

'She in the same line of work as you, Ian?'

'She works with computers,' he said, shrugging.

They walked through to the kitchen in the back of the flat. It was a small room, off the family room. Powers made them both coffee.

'You want sugar in yours, Frank?'

Miller shook his head. 'I don't take sugar, you know that.'

'You look like you could do with some, my friend.' Powers added milk and handed the mug over.

Miller drank some. 'I'm just knackered, that's all. I've had no sleep. We had some chav stick a breadknife into his wife and we had to go round at one o'clock this morning. That was the easy one, though. Now we have a real psycho on the loose.'

Powers stood, looking at him for a moment. 'Wow. That's indeed bad news. I heard on the news you guys found a body this morning in that hotel.'

Miller nodded. Looked at the snowflakes swirling outside the kitchen window. It was almost like a different planet out there now, not at all what they were used to.

Powers shook his head. 'You know I'm at your disposal, Frank. I can't ever repay what you did for me, but I can always be here to help you.'

'Brothers in arms. Sort of.'

'I'd be dead if it wasn't for you. I'm not one of those people who say, call me if you need me, then screen their phone calls. I really do mean it. I knew Carol too. She's the one who saw through all the bull-shit and knew I didn't kill my wife.'

'I know. Neither of us believed it.'

'I couldn't have handled being in prison. I'm not a hard man like you. I would have killed myself.'

'Your brother couldn't do the time either, Ian.' That's why he stepped in front of the eight fifteen Edinburgh to Glasgow at Edinburgh Park, before we could arrest him.

Powers shook himself. Even after five years, it still hurt. 'Now, what's it you want me to do for you?'

'I need help in tracking Colin Fleming's new address. I need it kept quiet. We're trying to find the next of kin.' Miller didn't let on about Toni Fleming. He was hoping to find another family member.

'Is that all? No problem.' Powers went to work, tapping his keyboard and sliding his finger over the trackpad sitting at the side of it. 'The firewalls are pretty good on some of these places.'

'Can you get past them?'

'I helped design some of them,' Powers said. 'It's going to take some time, but you're welcome to stay.'

'As much as I enjoy your company, give me a call when you're done.'

'Will do.'

Miller let himself out, and went back down to the car. Sat and thought about Carol. Thought about Richard Sullivan, the lawyer who'd once worked for Robert Molloy. The same Richard Sullivan who Carol had once arrested. The slimeball had gotten off on a tech-nicality.

It was Sullivan's car that a witness saw that night. She didn't see Carol get hit, but she saw somebody driving like a maniac. She'd had a drink, but she saw a car screaming into The Shore where it almost hit a bus. She didn't see the face, but she got the number of the car. Prostitutes were used to jotting down car registration plates when their friends got into one. Then they'd chalk the number on a wall.

This woman saw Carol's killer that night. She just didn't *see* him.

Sullivan was their main suspect, but he had an alibi and his car had been reported stolen. Miller didn't believe for one minute Sullivan wasn't involved.

Now his wife was dead.

But Richard Sullivan was still alive.

And Miller was going to talk to the man one day soon. Without any witnesses.

FOURTEEN

Miller stood looking at the whiteboard that had been erected in the back of the investigation suite. All the photos they had of their first three victims were back on display, their names written in red marker underneath. Harry was number four.

Another two photos had been added: Colin and Toni Fleming.

All the file boxes were brought out and people were sifting through the paperwork, to see if something jumped out at them.

Paddy Gibb was busy barking orders. Everything they had on the Moira Kennedy murder was to be looked at again.

'Ladies and gentlemen, your attention, please,' he shouted. The room went quiet, each conversation playing out until it died. Then Gibb had centre stage.

'Most of you will know the gentleman on my left, but for those of you who haven't had the pleasure, let me introduce him: Dr Harvey Levitt. He's the psychologist who helped us before, when three women were murdered. I've asked him to talk to us again and to give us a hand.'

Gibb stood to one side, and true to his American sense of show-manship, Levitt stood on a chair, looking down at everybody.

'Ladies and gentlemen, thank you for your attention. As you may have noticed, I'm American, but I've been a psychologist at Edinburgh University for some years now. I am also the psychologist for Police Edinburgh.' He scanned the crowd standing before him as if he was waiting for a heckler. Nobody obliged.

'I've been told our serial killer's back, but for the moment, the press think a copycat is out there.' He took a deep breath and let it out again. 'This is after the procurator fiscal discussed some information that came to light with the commander.'

'So, seeing as Neil McGovern's dead, it seems we got the wrong man,' Andy Watt said, turning to look at Miller for a moment.

'I'll get to that in a minute, Andy,' Levitt said.

He'd taken his jacket off and Miller noticed the pattern on his tie: Smiley Faces. He wondered if the man had been given it as a Christmas present and felt a duty to wear it.

Levitt was in his forties, and had close-cropped hair and a goatee. He had *shrink* written all over him.

'Those of you who worked on the first case, will remember the first victim was Diane Appleby. Aged forty-five. Divorced. No children. She was abducted and then he sent us a note through the mail, giving us a clue as to where we could find her. She was discovered in an old warehouse that was earmarked for redevelopment. She'd been dead for three weeks.'

He looked around the room. 'Then victim number two was taken. Lisa Charles. Aged forty-three. Married, with no children. Her head was left on a walkway in a carrier bag. He was taunting us then, playing games. He was in charge, and he wanted us to know it. Now, with Diane, he sent us a note after twelve days, and we found her remains two days later. In an abandoned house in West Lothian. Again, it was earmarked for redevelopment. Fourteen days, beginning to end. He'd changed his MO and increased the intensity.'

He looked at the photos on the board, focused on Harry for a second, then looked over at Miller. Levitt raised his eyebrows slightly at Miller, barely perceptible. *Are you okay?*

Miller gave a small nod.

Levitt carried on, his eyes constantly scanning the room, as if he was expecting somebody to pull out a gun.

'Doreen Myers. Victim number three. Aged forty-six. Single. She was found on the construction site of a new casino being built in Leith Docks. Timeframe, seven days, from the time she was taken to the time she was found.

'Then we didn't hear anything from him again.'

Miller suddenly felt hot, and he thought he was going to lose it for a moment, so he turned away and walked into his office. Nobody paid any attention. No one could understand what he'd gone through but they gave him space.

Levitt carried on. 'Sometimes serial killers will just stop. This can be for a number of reasons: they get caught, they go to prison for another crime, they die or reach what we in the trade unofficially call a Crash Point. They reach a point of exhaustion and crash and burn. We think this was the case with our killer. Given today's murder, we're pretty sure he didn't die, we didn't catch him, so he either went to prison for another crime or he reached his Crash Point. I think it was the latter. As I said, he accelerated the killings, and this would exhaust anybody. From start to finish, the whole episode took five months. Some guys do it over many years. This guy was on a roll. So he was away for a long time, over two years, before we heard about him again, which can happen. Nine weeks ago, Harry Davidson contacted Frank and told him he knew who the killer was. Unfortunately, Harry went on his own and paid with his life. You got your killer, in the form of Neil McGovern, but as we learned this morning, Neil McGovern was innocent. The media think there's a copycat out there, and no doubt they'll eventually find out it's not a copycat, but until they do, we have to let them think there is. Any questions?'

A hand went up. 'How did Harry find out about the killer?'

'Good question, and the answer is, we don't know. Harry didn't tell Neil McGovern or anybody else. There's no clue as to how he

49

came by that information, but we thought it was McGovern, and he was arrested.'

Another hand. 'Why didn't McGovern tell us he wasn't our man?' A young female detective, who Levitt hadn't seen before.

'Again, that's a mystery. Some of the big names upstairs reckon because McGovern was stunned by the smack from the shovel, it also did more damage inside his head than anybody knew. The wound on his forehead was superficial and he was cleaned up. And to answer Andy's question, he then started saying he was the killer. He had a brain injury and led us to believe he was our suspect, so that wasn't our fault. It wasn't really his fault either. That's what we're theorising anyway. Again, that's something he took to the grave, just like Harry. We might never find out the answer to either of those questions. However, you've been working with the name of a suspect this morning: Raymond Cross. It's a name from the past, so please familiarise yourself with the old case.'

Levitt looked around the room again. 'I'm going to be available anytime while the investigation is ongoing, so if anybody wants to come and talk to me, my door will always be open, either here or at the university. This can be very traumatic, and if you just want to swing by and have a coffee, bounce an idea off me, or just talk, feel free.' He stepped off the chair as the team went back to their work. He walked over to Gibb.

'Let's go and check on Frank, Paddy. This is going to be hard for him.'

'It is, but he knows he's got a lot of support.'

They knocked, and waited for Miller to call them in.

'I'm fine, guys. It's hard, but I need to keep it together.'

'You know I'm available twenty-four seven, Frank,' Levitt said.

'I know. Thanks.' Levitt was the only man he'd ever opened up to. Not even his father had been privy to his innermost thoughts. 'Tell me more about Raymond Cross, Paddy.'

Gibb took a deep breath, and reached for his cigarettes. 'Crack that window a bit, son,' he said, to Levitt. The doctor obliged.

FIFTEEN

'I read about the Met detective coming up to talk to Cross and they both disappeared,' Miller said.

Gibb looked at him. 'There was pandemonium, Frank. A detective comes up, is left alone with Cross for half an hour, and the two of them fuck off out the station, never to be seen again. We had the biggest manhunt Edinburgh had seen in a long time. We came up empty, though. There were never any sightings of them after that. It's as if they just vanished. Probably ended up in Mexico, or somewhere.'

An alarm bell started ringing in Miller's head. 'Who was the last one to see Cross in the interview room before the Met guy went in?'

Gibb looked at him. 'Harry Davidson. Why?'

Miller shrugged. 'Nothing. Just thinking, that's all.' Something didn't feel right.

'We're opening up the case again. We're going over every piece of evidence we have, in case we missed something back then.' He took a puff on his cigarette and blew it out. 'The case was never closed, but he was forgotten about.'

'Until now. Seems he's back with a vengeance.'

Gibb stood up and stretched. 'He couldn't wait 'til I was retired, eh? Bastard. Take it easy, Frank.' Gibb left the office.

Miller suddenly felt tiredness creeping in.

'You okay?' Levitt asked.

'I'm fine.'

'I know it wasn't easy for you. Losing your wife, then two years later, losing your father-in-law.'

'It feels like I let them both down.'

'This wasn't your fault. Any of it. Just remember that.'

'I'll try.' The phone rang, and Levitt excused himself.

'Miller.'

'Frank, it's Julie.'

'Hi. What's going on?'

'Would you like to come down to the mortuary? I have the preliminaries on Fleming and his wife.'

A pause for a second. 'Sure. I'll bring Tam and Kim.' He looked at his watch. 'Say, ten minutes or so?'

'See you then.'

He hung up, and went to find Kim. 'You up for going to the mortuary?'

The City Mortuary was located in Cowgate, which ran parallel with High Street. It was an anonymous grey, two-storey building with only a small sign by the front door that gave a clue as to what it was.

They went in through a door next to the freight entrance. Walked over to a short corridor where Julie's office was located. She was sitting at her desk.

'Frank! Come away in.' She stood up, as Miller and Scott entered.

'You wanted to see me,' Miller said.

'I wanted to go over the report on Colin Fleming.' She looked over at Kim. 'Hello again.'

'Hi.'

Julie turned to Miller. 'Kim and I were introduced this morning in Fleming's office.

Miller felt himself sweating. He'd sat in this very office many times, talking to Julie about Carol and how much he missed her. She said she missed Carol too. Carol had been her only sister and although Gary Davidson was her brother, they didn't see each other much.

'I don't mean to be rude, you two, but would you mind if I spoke to Frank alone for a minute? Just something personal,' Julie said, bringing him back to the present.

I knew this was going to happen, *Miller thought.*

'No problem, Julie,' Scott said, and they left the office, heading upstairs to the break room.

Julie waited until they could no longer hear footsteps. 'I haven't seen you for a while, Frank.'

'I've been up to my ears in it,' Miller said, feeling his cheeks turn red.

'No, you've not. You've been avoiding me. You think I'll go mental that you didn't save my dad. Something like that. Is that about right?'

'No, of course not.'

She smiled at him. 'You don't have to avoid me. I know you couldn't do anything for my dad that night. Why would I be angry with you? If you could have saved him, you would have. So let's not have any more nonsense about you avoiding me, okay?'

He smiled back at her. 'You're right. I just feel useless.'

Julie held a finger to her lips. 'No more talk like that.'

Miller nodded.

'You and Gary are the only family I have left,' Julie said.

'I appreciate that.'

'That's what families are for.' She picked up a folder from her desk. 'I have the preliminaries on Fleming and his wife.'

Miller put down his coffee. 'Apart from being a slimy bastard, what else did you pick up on?'

'He was fit for a man in his fifties, I'll give him that. It was the

53

trauma to his neck that killed him. The knife, or sharp instrument, nicked his carotid. Opening him up would have killed him obviously, the nick just accelerated the job.'

'What about defence wounds?'

'That's what's strange, Frank; there were none. Fleming wasn't a big guy, but he wasn't a wimp either and I'm assuming, as he was an ex-copper, he would have put up a fight, but there wasn't a scratch on him. No marks on his hands or arms. Nothing under the fingernails.'

'Which meant he knew who killed him. He was there to meet somebody last night, somebody he knew, and for some reason that person murdered him.' Miller thought about the name in Fleming's diary: Raymond Cross.

'That's what I would guess. Your lab's running the toxicology, and it won't take them long to find if there's anything in Fleming's blood. If there was indeed a substance that hung around to give a toxicology result.'

'What about his wife?'

'Unlike her husband, Toni Fleming was opened up post-mortem, as if the killer was enraged. Again, there were no defence wounds. Almost like she was taken by surprise.'

'We saw the time on her text messages, and it looked like she died later than he did. Does that tally with your time of death for her?'

'Yes, he definitely died first. That's what the timeline indicates.'

Miller stood up. 'Thanks, Julie. Can you fax us the reports when they're done?'

'No problem. It'll be late tomorrow.' She put a hand on his arm. 'Listen, if you're not doing anything tonight, why don't you come round for a coffee? We can have a chat. We haven't had a good old chinwag for a long time.'

'Okay, I'll do that. Say around seven thirty or so?'

'Great.'

Julie smiled, and watched as Miller left her office.

SIXTEEN

Jack Miller always told his son he was a retired cop, not a retired chef. When he said he'd get the dinner ready, he meant shoving a couple of Fray Bentos Steak and Kidney pies in the oven. Along with a bag of chips.

'Chips are bad for you,' Miller said, as he let the oven door close.

'Don't eat them, then,' Jack said, popping the ring pull on a beer.

'I didn't say I wouldn't eat them. A man's got to have veggies after all.' He grabbed a Coke from the fridge and took a swallow out of the can. 'Where've you been the past couple of days anyway?'

Jack walked through to the living room from the kitchen. Sat on the couch in front of the TV. 'Just here and there.'

'Arsing about with your pals again?' Miller said, sitting in a chair.

'Hardly arsing about.' Jack looked at his son. 'Why? You miss me?'

'You wish.'

'I could have been lying in the gutter somewhere and you wouldn't even notice I'd gone.'

'If you're looking for attention, you're looking in the wrong place. Save that for your dodgy mates.'

Jack smiled, and shook his head. Then became serious. 'I heard about Colin today. Andy Watt called me.'

'He said he'd spoken to you. I was going to wait until I got home.'

Jack put his beer on a coaster on the coffee table. 'I'm not complaining, son. Andy called because he knew I worked with Colin.'

'Did he tell you about the similarities to Colin and Harry's murders?' Miller asked.

Jack nodded. 'It sent a shiver down my spine, let me tell you.'

Miller trusted his father with his life. He didn't doubt for one second he could trust him with any information, but if he came right out and said he knew Neil McGovern didn't kill Harry, then Jack would blow a fuse. So he kept quiet for now.

'Did Andy tell you we think Raymond Cross is back and he killed Colin?'

Jack looked at his son and nodded. 'Yes, he did.' He thought back twenty-five years. 'That was a bad one. That poor girl was butchered in the front of that car.'

'Did you get to sit in on the interview when they arrested him?'

'I was guarding the door. The tension in that room was thick.'

The timer on the cooker rang. Miller got up. Dinner was ready. He dished the pies and chips onto plates and they sat at the same small dining table in the kitchen where he'd sat with Kim that morning.

'Did you see that copper from the Met when he came to interview Cross back then?' Miller asked.

'Yeah, briefly. Looked a bit of a yahoo. He had that air about him.'

Miller cut a piece of pie, added a chip and ate. It was his favourite food. He chased it down with some water. They ate the rest of their dinner, talking chit-chat. Jack's upcoming trip to Spain in the summer with his friends. His reasons why Miller should join them. Miller trying to explain he wasn't seventeen anymore.

'Mickey Hagan's coming. You remember his son, Bruce?' Bruce

Hagan. Miller remembered him well. He'd been a DS in Serious Crimes a few years back before taking a post in Fife.

Later on, after Jack had washed the dishes and Miller had showered and changed, they were sitting in the living room again.

'Do you remember the night Moira was murdered, Dad?' Miller said.

'Of course I do. We were keeping an eye on Molloy's hotel from a distance. Who knew one of Molloy's men would turn mental and kill that lassie? Lucky we were near. He might have got away if we weren't.'

'Tell me more about it.'

Jack sat for a moment, as if making sure he was getting everything in the right order.

'It was a Saturday night, I remember that. Me and your mum were supposed to go out that night, but she came down with the flu. It was winter. A cold night...'

SEVENTEEN

Twenty-five years ago

DS Jack Miller pulled up in the Ford Granada pool car, and parked behind one of two ambulances, their blue lights spinning furiously. Other patrol cars were forming a barricade round the car park. Jack could see it was serious, but his boss wouldn't tell him what it was over the radio.

The cold air hit Jack as he got out of the car. The sky was clear, letting whatever heat had built up to disappear into space. Harry Davidson came striding over to his side. Jack could see Colin Fleming standing, talking to a uniform.

'The hotel's locked down,' Harry said.

'What's going on, sir?' Jack asked, shutting the car door.

Harry shook his head. 'Holy Christ. It's a fucking mess in there.' He turned and pointed to a patrol car. 'We caught this nutter near a car with a young girl in it.' He looked back at Jack. 'She was slaughtered.'

Jack looked at his boss. 'What did he do to her?'

Harry's breath blew like steam into the cold, dark night. 'He opened her up. Sliced her right fucking open, from her neck down to her belly. There's fucking blood everywhere.'

Jack shivered and pulled up the collar on his overcoat. 'Who is he? Do we know?'

Harry nodded. 'Raymond Cross.' He looked over to where a small group of people were hovering, being shepherded by uniforms. 'They said he was Moira's boyfriend. That's the victim. They don't know much about him because she wasn't dating him for long.'

'Who called it in?' Jack asked, as they started walking towards the car. Raymond Cross looked out at him from the rear seat. There was blood on his jacket. Blood on his face.

'Anonymous tip from the phone box inside. Somebody doesn't want to get involved.'

'Man or a woman?'

'A woman.' They stopped. Harry shook his head. 'We were nearby, watching who was coming and going when I got the call on my radio.'

'At least we got the bastard though.' Jack shivered. 'Who arrested him, boss?'

'I did. DI Fleming was with me.'

They took Cross away while the scene was processed and information gathered. Harry Davidson followed the patrol car Cross was in.

When Jack Miller went into the hotel, Robert Molloy was standing in the bar with his son and a group of women. He didn't look pleased.

In the few short years Jack had been on the force, he'd never known anybody to annoy Robert Molloy and get away with it. He didn't envy Raymond Cross one little bit.

'What happened after that?' Miller asked.

Jack looked at the TV, as if the answer lay there. 'Cross was charged with murder. He denied everything at first, then he admitted it. Harry let me sit in on the initial interview they did with him. Harry was part of an Organised Crime Task Force, but us lowly detectives still had to do a lot of the grunt work.'

'What was Cross like in the interview room?'

Jack gritted his teeth. 'A complete bastard.'

'You know you're going to be charged with murder, right?' Harry said.

'Yeah, well, what do you want me to say? Except, where's my fucking lawyer?'

'You shut your fucking mouth, Cross. You'll get a fucking lawyer when I see fit.'

'That's not right. This'll be thrown out of court.'

'I'm not recording yet, you arrogant little bastard. I can say whatever I like to you, do whatever I like to you, and there's no fucking witnesses. Bear that in mind before you mouth off to me.'

There was usually a uniform guarding the door inside the room, but this time it was Jack Miller who was doing the guarding. Cross looked right at him, as if trying to look through him. Jack stared right back.

They'd taken Cross's blood-covered clothes away and put him into a pair of prison jeans and a prison sweatshirt, both dark blue and cheap. Cheap trainers too.

Cross looked at Colin Fleming, who was sitting next to Harry.

'You his sidekick, then?'

Fleming ignored him, and nodded to Harry. 'You better get the tapes running soon, or I'm going to be over this table and kick the shit out of this fucker.'

Cross laughed. Threw his head back, and laughed out loud. When he looked at them again, there was no smile on his face. 'I'd love you to see you try, sunshine.'

Fleming stood up, his chair sliding backwards and tipping over. Jack watched Harry sitting calmly as Fleming leaned down on the table, staring right into Cross's eyes.

'How old are you, sonny?'

'Twenty-five.'

'I'm ten years older than you, and I could still rip your fucking face off.'

'Sit down and shut the fuck up,' Cross said. 'You don't scare me, you big fucking—'

Fleming lifted his right hand off the desk and slapped Cross across the face, knocking him sideways off his chair. He moved round the table and drew his leg back as if to kick Cross.

'Colin!' Harry Davidson was on his feet, and the mere shout was enough to stop Fleming. Jack had seen Fleming fight before, and the older man never turned away from anything. He turned to look at his boss as Cross lay sprawled on the floor.

'You saw that,' Cross said, looking straight at Jack. Both Harry and Fleming turned to look at Jack.

Jack paused for a moment. 'I saw fuck all,' he said, looking right back at Cross.

Fleming smiled. Harry looked at Fleming. 'Pick him up, before anybody comes in, for fuck's sake.'

Fleming was a big man. Worked out with weights and pint glasses. He reached down and roughly grabbed Cross by the front of the sweat-shirt and hauled him to his feet. 'Get that fucking chair up and sit your arse in it.' He waited until Cross was seated before sitting down himself.

Harry put the tapes into the recorder. It would be several years before Lothian and Borders switched over to filming interviews. 'You ready, Colin?' Harry asked.

'Ready as I'll ever be.' He glared across the table at Cross.

'Tell me why you killed Moira,' Harry said.

Cross rubbed his left cheek, where Fleming's hand had connected with it. 'I didn't kill her.'

Fleming turned to look at Harry with a look that said, "Switch that recorder off and give me five minutes with the fucker, then we'll know why he killed her". Harry shook his head, as if he'd read Fleming's mind.

Fleming sat back hard in the chair, seemingly in a huff. Folded his arms. 'You were seen in the car with Moira. You were covered in her blood. A jury will eat you alive. Then we'll stick you up in Peterhead and those bastards will chew you up and spit you out in bubbles.'

'Once again, and for those who are hard of hearing, this announcement will be shouted: I did not kill Moira!' Cross leaned forward and shouted the last few words at Fleming.

'Well, we think you fucking did!' Fleming shouted back. 'That's why we're fucking charging you right now. You're looking at twenty years after the judge sees the photos of the poor lassie lying on the front seat of that car.'

Cross looked like all the life had gone out of him. Looked at Fleming, then at Harry for a moment and raised his eyebrows slightly. Just for the briefest of moments, Jack thought he saw Harry shake his head. Just the slightest of movements, unnoticed by Fleming. Then Cross's whole demeanour changed.

'Okay, then. I admit it. I killed her. Go ahead and charge me.'

So they did.

'What happened with the Met cop?' Miller asked his father.

Jack stared for a moment, as if trying to pluck his thoughts out of mid-air. 'He was an arrogant tosser. Breezed into the station like his shit didn't stink. Harry kept him in his place though. Told him in no uncertain terms if he wanted to talk to Cross, then he had to do it in front of *him*.'

'How did the guy react to that?' Miller's tiredness left him and he leaned forward eagerly.

'He was... indifferent. Tried to pretend he was one of the boys. One of us. We all knew he was a wanker, though. If it walks like a duck and it quacks like a duck, know what I mean?'

Miller nodded.

'Then all hell broke loose. The guy was in the interview room with Cross. Alone. I was on duty that day, and I must say, Harry was acting a wee bit strange. Like he was coming down with something.

Seemed sort of nervous. Next thing we know, the alarm goes off. Everybody ran to the room, thinking Cross had given Super Met a kicking, but when we went into the room, they were gone. Some uniform was standing with his mouth open. Bingham had asked for a cup of tea, and dafty went and fetched it. When he got back, Cross and the DI were gone. They'd just got up and left.'

'And it turned out Bingham was a fake,' Miller said.

'We never did find out what the connection was. Was probably a mate of his or something, but he must have had some good connections to get all the fake papers. There was a manhunt, but we never got him. Then, all of a sudden, it all went away, almost as if somebody swept it under the rug.'

EIGHTEEN

Miller pulled his woollen hat on before he stepped out into the street and walked round to the pool car. Being on call meant he took the car home. He'd be at his destination in less than ten minutes, traffic permitting. The Balmoral Hotel sat on the corner of Princes Street and North Bridge, all lit up and resplendent as if it was dressed up for going out. It had been a stalwart on that corner for over a hundred years, starting off as the North British Hotel, a railway hotel, until it had been refurbished in the eighties.

Just like a lot of things that were changing in Edinburgh. The city was like a chameleon, changing colour every few years, as if trying to reinvent its image. Once known as a city full of heroin users, it was now known as the first UNESCO City of Literature. Yet Miller knew; to the world, Edinburgh appeared to be a supermodel, but only those closest to her saw the needle tracks and the bloodshot eyes.

The snow had stopped for a while but the air temperature had fallen. Pedestrians slipped on the pavements. The slush would harden up overnight, making walking even more treacherous in the morning.

Miller pulled up outside the house he'd headed for. Looked at the lights in the living room, not sure if he should go in or not. Then he climbed out into the cold and dark.

He walked carefully to the door and rang the bell. It was a nice townhouse, with the living room on the first floor, so he knew it would take her a few minutes to get downstairs.

'Who is it?'

'Santa Claus. I couldn't get down your chimney.'

He heard her laughing before the door was unlocked. 'Frank! I'm really glad you could make it tonight.' Julie said. She'd already changed into what she called her "geeky" nightshirt and sweatpants. Her hair was slightly damp as if she'd only given it a brief blast with the hairdryer after her shower.

'I didn't want you to think I was avoiding you again.' He smiled.

'Well, what can a woman say?'

'How about, "Come on in, it must be freezing out there?"'

She laughed. 'Come on in.' She stepped aside, and let him into the warmth.

'I thought about what you said earlier. About me avoiding you. I feel bad now.'

'There's no need. I just wanted to set things straight. Although I must admit, I miss you and Jack at times. You more than anything.'

They walked upstairs, to the living room. The gas fire was burning away, the flames looking inviting. The heat felt good, and Miller shed his overcoat and jacket, then sat on one of the comfortable chairs that faced Julie's flat-screen. A soap opera played out on the screen but the sound was muted.

Julie held up the bottle that sat on her coffee table. 'Can I interest you in one?'

He shook his head. 'No thanks. I'll have a coffee if you have any.'

'Sure. Give me a minute.' She went through to the kitchen.

He sat back and smiled, feeling the tensions of the day ebb away. He liked coming here and had missed Julie. He looked on her as an older sister, somebody he could confide in about anything. Somebody he could talk about Carol with. He'd spent many an evening here, reminiscing. They'd exchanged stories about Carol, neither of them allowing her memory to die. Nobody else in the world would be interested in talking about his dead wife like this.

'I want to ask you a question, Julie,' he said, when she came back in with a mug for him. 'It's work related, and I know you're off the clock, so if you don't feel comfortable, just say so.'

She smiled. 'No, that's okay. Fire away.'

'I was wondering if you'd ever heard your dad talk about Raymond Cross?'

Julie looked puzzled for a moment, searching her memory banks for the name. Then her eyes widened for a moment before she answered. 'Yes. Wasn't he the guy who killed that girl in the car a long time ago?'

Miller took some of the coffee. It tasted good. 'Yes, he was.'

'I remember that case. My dad spoke about it a few times. Cross walked out of the station with another man and they were never seen again.'

Miller nodded. 'My dad remembers him. He worked on the case as well, but Harry was the lead investigator.'

'Why would you ask about him after all this time?' She sipped her wine. Curled her legs underneath her. Put the wine glass down on a side table.

'He's back. We think he killed the Flemings last night. Maybe he was angry with them and wanted revenge, but we don't understand what the catalyst was that set him off now.'

'I appreciate you telling me, Frank.' She took more wine, needing it now. 'Do you have any leads on Cross?'

'Not yet.'

'You know, Carol and I were more than ten years apart, but as we grew older, we connected more, as siblings do. I remember one time...'

Miller was trying to listen to Julie, but his mind was focused on Carol. Smiling, holding hands as they walked along Portobello Beach one summer's night. A magical time...

'Frank?'

Miller could hear Carol's voice, calling to him.

'Frank? Frank, your phone's ringing.'

His eyes snapped open. He fumbled for his phone and took it out of his pocket, not sure how long he'd dozed off for. 'Miller.'

'Frank, it's Matt. From Leith.'

It took Miller a second to process Matt from Leith. Then he smiled. DI Matt Taylor. 'Hey, buddy, what's up?'

'I need to see you, Frank. Can you come and meet me?'

'Okay. Sounds ominous.'

Miller heard a breath being taken in before he heard the words.

'Somebody left an envelope at the front desk. It's got your name on it and it's marked private.'

'Thanks, Matt, I'll come down and pick it up.'

Miller hung up, feeling uneasy. Wondering who'd sent him something.

He'd soon find out.

NINETEEN

Miller was pulling up outside Leith police station, ten minutes after the call. The building sat on the corner of Queen Charlotte Street and Constitution Street. It had been built as Leith Town Hall in the early eighteen hundreds, and a row of Georgian townhouses had been added later on.

Miller walked into the public entrance and recognised the desk sergeant on duty. 'Hey, how's things?'

'Good, sir. Long time no see. How's Jack?'

'He says you and the boys are overdue for a good hooly.'

'We are that. And when I retire, I'll really be off the leash.' He buzzed Miller in.

On the first floor, Matt Taylor was sitting in his office.

'You're working late,' Miller said.

'Just wrapping up an operation.' He got up and shook Miller's hand. 'Thanks for coming, Frank. I have the letter here.' He opened a desk drawer and pulled out the white envelope. It was in a clear evidence bag. 'I don't know what the chances are of getting prints off it...'

'None,' Miller answered, sitting down. However, he was taking no chances. He pulled on nitrile gloves. 'You said somebody left it here?'

'A homeless guy brought it in a bigger envelope with my name on the front. Says a guy gave him a twenty to hand it in. He didn't give a description, except the bloke was wearing a black hoodie and spoke with a local accent. My mail was in my tray but I was on a shout and only got round to opening it just before I called you. Although it's addressed to me, it has your name on the front, so I didn't open it.'

Taylor opened a drawer in his desk and pulled out a flick knife. He sprang the blade and passed it over to Miller, shrugging. 'I took it off some scally in Niddrie. Wee bastard would just have used it on somebody. I use it as a letter opener.'

Miller took the envelope and looked at the front: *Frank Miller*. Then *Private* typed in bold and underlined. He sliced the envelope along the top seam. Put the knife down on the desk and carefully took the letter out. It was typed, on a sheet of white copy paper. He read it over, before reading it out loud to Taylor.

Would you trust David Stuart? He was too late to meet the lovely Mary herself. Three o'clock plus one hour and one minute was too late for him. It's not too late for you, Frank. If you hurry, you can still find what you're looking for.

He looked at Taylor. 'Any thoughts?'

Taylor had picked up a yellow HB pencil and was tapping it against his teeth. 'Not a fucking thing, Frank. You know, we can take down druggies, do all sorts of shit, but when it comes to stuff like this... well, I'm fucked if I know, mate. Sorry.'

'Don't worry about it. One thing I do know is, this is in relation to Carol. It doesn't mention finding who killed her, but whoever wrote this is implying he knows who did it.'

'I feel like a right twat, Frank, but I've never been any good at puzzles. Maybe that's why I can only take down dealers and hoors.'

Miller stood up. 'I'd like to take this. Maybe get it analysed.' He slipped it back into the evidence bag.

69

Taylor put the pencil down. Put the knife away. 'It's yours, Frank. It was addressed to you.'

Miller shook his hand. Outside, he sat in the car, shivering. Took his phone out.

'Kim? I'm not disturbing you, am I?'

'Not at all, Frank. Just watching some TV. What's up?'

'I got a note delivered to Leith police station. I'm here now, sitting outside. It was from somebody who I think knows who killed Carol. I was wondering if you could help.'

'I'll try.'

He read the note to her. 'I know you work for the government, so I was wondering if you'd know anybody who deals with cryptic clues.'

'I do know someone who could help. I can make a call to a supervisor who works at GCHQ. Before I do, take a photo of it on your iPhone and send it to me, so I can send it to him.'

'I'll do that right now. Thanks, Kim.'

Within a minute, the photo was on its way to her. Miller thought he'd sit for a few more minutes. Going home would mean going into the spare room and looking at the files he'd kept on Carol's death. The reports of how a detective was run down by a drunk driver while she was working a case.

He turned his thoughts to Kim. Didn't think the government spy centre would be able to decipher what was really a pile of shite, the mental ramblings of a madman.

His phone rang. Nine minutes and twenty-seven seconds after he'd hung up with Kim.

He saw her name on the screen. 'Hello?'

'It's always a busy night at GC but this supervisor friend of mine was working. He apologised for the delay. He thought it might be a good exercise for one of the new recruits. It took him two minutes and forty-two seconds to work it out, but he's new, so we have to cut him some slack.'

Miller's heart was racing. How could somebody do that so quickly? What kind of minds worked there?

'You there, Frank?' Kim asked.

'Yes.' His own voice sounded shaky.

'Wait at the station for me. I'm in the car and I'll be there in ten.' She hung up.

TWENTY

He'd started the car and the diesel engine was trying its best to warm him up, but not as well as the bag of chips he'd bought from the chippy across the road.

'I hope you didn't get brown sauce on all of them,' Kim said, sitting in the passenger seat. 'Jeez, it's cold in here. Come on, let's take my car.' She fished out a chip without brown sauce on it.

'You wouldn't think I've had my dinner. I only bought these to get some heat.' They moved to her car, which was behind Miller's. It was an Audi TT. 'Nice car.'

'Thanks.' She turned the engine on and Miller could feel the heated seats. As if she'd had them both on driving over here. She took a piece of paper out of the inside pocket of her jacket. Looked at Miller. 'As cryptic clues go, it was really easy, my friend says.'

'I'm glad he could help.'

'It was no problem. He was a friend of my dad.' She switched on her map light, bathing the paper in a sharp light and read the message out loud to him. 'Would you trust David Stuart? He was too late to meet the lovely Mary herself. Three o'clock plus one hour and one minute was too late for him. It's not too late for you, Frank. If you hurry, you can still find what you're looking for.'

'I have to admit I don't have a clue what this means,' Miller said.

'Luckily we have some very smart people working for the government. No offence.'

'None taken.'

'Would you trust David Stuart? They assumed it wasn't going to be the name of a local hoodlum or a nobody, and they were right. David Stuart, the son of the Marquess of Bute. The key word is trust. The National Trust for Scotland. They're connected with David Stuart. Now the time reference. Three o'clock plus one hour and one minute. Could have been sixteen-oh-one, using the twenty-four-hour clock. But three o'clock is fifteen hundred. Plus an hour, is sixty plus one is sixty-one. Fifteen-sixty-one. It's not a reference to time though, but a date.'

Kim seemed to be getting revved up now, ready for the big finale. 'He was too late to meet the lovely Mary herself. Because David Stuart was born in nineteen-eleven. He was three hundred and fifty years too late. Mary Queen of Scots came to Edinburgh in fifteen sixty-one. The Palace of Holyrood wasn't ready for her, so it was rumoured she spent time in Lamb's House, just round the corner. In nineteen fifty-eight The National Trust accepted David Stuart's offer of Lamb's House. It had belonged to his father.'

She looked at Miller. 'The last part of the letter. It's not too late for you, Frank. If you hurry, you can still find what you're looking for. He's sending you to Lamb's House, Frank.'

Remind me not to fuck with the people at GCHQ, he thought, as Kim started the car.

The all-wheel-drive system on the little sports car handled the slick roads with ease. They drove straight ahead at the lights and round Water Street. In front of them, on the corner of Burgess Street, was

Lamb's House. Miller felt a nervousness inside, something he hadn't felt in a long time.

Kim pulled the car to a stop outside the car park. The building was being refurbished. The exterior was clad in scaffolding, covered in green netting. The car park was fenced off, securing the building materials inside, which were now covered with snow.

They got out of the car, and Miller threw the remaining chips into a nearby bin. Kim was wearing a red Berghaus jacket, and pulled the zipper up to her chin. Her blonde ponytail stuck out of her woollen hat.

'I don't see any footsteps in the snow,' she said, pointing to the car park. The two fence panels that acted as gates were padlocked.

'Let's try round the back. There's a wooden gate there.'

They trudged through the slush on the pavement. The air was freezing and snatched their breath away as it came out in clouds. At the back of Lamb's House, which was side on to Water Street, there was indeed a large wooden gate.

It was open.

Miller gently pushed it, wary of a trap. There were footsteps in the snow on the path, but nothing that could be matched to a boot. Any tread had been messed up by the person who'd been walking back here. The walls were covered in scaffolding, like the front, and it looked exactly the same except for one difference; the back door was open.

'Stay behind me,' Miller said to Kim, taking out his extendable baton.

'How about you stay behind me?' Kim replied, bringing out her Glock. She held a small flashlight in her other hand.

'Go ahead.'

She gently pushed the door open further. It was old but solid wood. Miller looked around, to see if he could see anything through the green netting; nothing unusual.

Kim stepped into what had been an old pantry. The door ahead was open and they cautiously edged through it. Miller swung his own flashlight around. They were in the front hallway now, and they saw a small glow coming from a room on the right.

Kim went through the doorway. Miller followed, and they saw the small teacup candle flickering on the old fireplace at the end of the room. It illuminated an object that sat next to it.

They crept forward, still wary of a trap.

'Just be careful,' Miller said, swinging the light around the room. He approached the candle. It was plastic, powered by a battery, the flame a flickering bulb.

Beside the candle, on the mantle, was a little, black wallet. Miller was familiar with the object. His heart was racing again, and he didn't feel the cold. He reached out a gloved hand and picked it up.

'What is it?' Kim asked.

'Have a look for yourself.' Miller flipped it open.

Then they heard the thump from upstairs.

TWENTY-ONE

Robert Molloy sat in the suite on the Blue Martini, a stone's throw away from the derelict house being checked by Miller and Kim. He'd idly glanced out his window and wondered if Raymond Cross was out there, looking back.

A few minutes later, there was a knock on the door.

'Come in,' he shouted.

Sienna Craig walked in. 'I made a couple of calls, sir,' she said.

'And?'

'Nothing. Nobody's heard of Cross, and there's no talk about him coming back.'

'Thanks, Sienna. Care to join me for a drink?'

'I'd better not, sir. I prefer to keep alert.'

'Good answer. No point in my head of security being pished if Cross comes round with a sawn-off.' He laughed. 'You can get off now. Sampson can drive me home.' He watched her leave.

Sienna Craig had come to him by way of an old friend down in London, a guy known as Mr Winston. He had a right-hand man working for him, known as Hammer, a nickname earned by using the tool as a means of persuasion. Hammer had called him out of the blue four months ago, telling Molloy he'd heard in various circles he was looking for some new security staff. He'd escorted her up the next day.

Four months earlier

The wind blew in off the Forth, rocking the Ford Transit van, which was parked at the far end of the deserted lot. A warehouse sat here a long time ago, but had been knocked down by the developer who'd bought it, planning to turn it into flats.

The two men who were sitting in the front, watched as the rented Focus came round the corner. They saw a man and a woman in the front of the car. The passenger in the Transit had a pair of binoculars and zoomed in on the car's windscreen.

'It's them. A woman and that fuck Hammer.'

The driver looked at him. 'Who calls himself "Hammer"? Fuckin' prick. Let's go and give them a Scottish welcome.' The two men stepped out of the van and stood in front of it. The car pulled up facing them and the man and woman got out.

'You Molloy's men, then?' Hammer was in his early thirties, trying desperately to climb up a ladder that would see him run a gang that controlled part of South London.

The driver smiled. 'You better hope so.' He walked forward, past Hammer and ran his hand over the roof of the car. 'This all you could afford to rent, mate?'

The passenger walked past the woman. She looked to be in her twenties. Blonde hair. Wearing a black, leather jacket and black jeans. Black Doc Martens. She watched him as he walked past her. Turned to see what he was doing. He ducked, and looked in the back of the car.

'Pop the boot, Clarence, there's a good boy,' the driver said.

'Only me fuckin' mam calls me that. Scotch bastard.'

'Don't start cryin' like a wee laddie and pop the fuckin' boot.'

'Wot? You need to see me fucking skids? I've only got me suitcase. Big enough to hold a clean pair for the mornin' and a packet of johnnies in case I get lucky.' He winked at the woman.

She glared back at him without answering.

'Got a name?' the passenger asked the blonde.

'Yeah. You?'

The passenger smiled. 'I asked first.' He knew who she was; he'd seen a copy of the photo that had been emailed to Molloy.

She shook her head. 'Listen, boys, I've spent five hours on a train with this fat fuck, listening to his sexist jokes and smelling his shitty breath. So if you don't mind, I'd like to get the interview over so I can either have my stuff forwarded up here, or leave.'

The driver looked at her. 'Clarence here's brokering a deal for somebody else. Our boss wants to know if it's on the up-and-up. So if Clarence here pops the boot and we see there's no fucker in there with a sawn-off, we can start.'

Clarence glared at him. 'Don't call me that again. And what if there was somebody in there with a shotgun?'

The driver pulled out a Glock and pointed it at Hammer's head. 'Then you'll all fucking die.'

Hammer didn't look too sure of himself now. 'Alright, mate, take it easy.' He took the keys and popped the boot. There was nothing more dangerous in it than two small suitcases.

'Where you staying?' the passenger asked, as he reached in and opened one of the cases. A gust of wind blew harder, ruffling their hair.

'None of your business,' Hammer said.

'Why don't you just return today?' the passenger asked, pulling a knife from his pocket and opening the case, picking up a pair of Y-fronts with it. 'I hope they're fucking clean,' he said, throwing them back in.

Hammer glared at him. 'I want to stop over and sample some of the wares up here, if you catch my drift?' He was totally unaware of the third man coming up behind him with a sack. It was pulled over his head and he was dragged down to the ground, kicking and screaming.

The woman turned round, throwing up her left arm. The fourth man, who was about to put a sack over her head hesitated for a second, giving the woman time to throw a punch at his jaw. The palm of her hand connected with the edge of the jawbone, putting his lights out. Just like a champion boxer would. He fell to the ground, dropping the sack.

As the passenger rushed at her, she pulled her own Glock out and grabbed hold of the man barrelling towards her. She spun him, pointed the gun at the side of his head and smiled at the driver.

'Drop the gun and your friend lives another day.'

The man who was holding onto Hammer looked between her and the driver. The driver smiled, still holding his gun. 'Don't be silly. We're just taking precautions.'

'Tell your fucking boss the deal's off. And if that Glock doesn't hit the dirt in the next five seconds, I'll shoot your pal here, then I'll blow a hole in your heart.'

'Just put the gun away, and—'

'Four. Three.'

'Okay, okay, we'll do it your way.' He looked at her with a slight smirk on his face.

'I don't know what you think's so funny. I've just overpowered four men. Not bad for a wee lassie.' She looked from the driver to the guy with Hammer and back again. 'I wonder if your boss will think it's funny. That's who's coming here in that flash Beemer, isn't it?' She nodded to the black car bouncing its way over the dirt towards them.

'I think maybe it is,' the driver said.

They all watched as the car pulled up. The back windows were blacked out. The one on the passenger side rolled down. 'I hope you like lobster, Miss Craig. My personal chef has our lunch waiting.' Robert Molloy smiled at her.

Sienna Craig pushed the passenger away from her, took her suitcase from the Focus, and walked over to the car. The boot lid on the 7 Series powered open and when her case was in the back, it closed back down. She opened the other rear door.

'Fortunately, I love it,' she said, looking over the roof of the car at the motley crew looking back at her.

The driver smiled, picked up his gun and looked at the passenger. 'I told you the boss knew what he was doing. I guess she passed his test.'

'Tell that to Brian there,' he said, nodding to the unconscious man on the ground. He took the sack off Hammer's head.

'He'll live.' The driver looked over at Hammer. 'Get up, Clarence, and get your fucking manky arse out of here.' He threw a padded envelope at the man, then watched the BMW turn round the corner of the old warehouse. Sienna Craig had just been hired.

Present day

Molloy got up from behind his desk. Poured himself another whisky and stood looking out the porthole window at the groups of people coming and going onto his floating restaurant. He watched Sienna leave and hail a taxi. Wondered if she was going back to her flat. Then he thought about the phone calls he'd made. Sienna Craig was a bloody good worker, loyal and efficient. She'd worked for him for four months now. There was nothing wrong with her work ethic, and she was a trusted member of staff. There was only one thing that bothered him.

Up until six months ago, Sienna Craig didn't exist.

TWENTY-TWO

Kim's finger was already in the trigger guard. 'I don't believe in ghosts,' she said, her voice barely a whisper.

'Me neither.' Miller switched the plastic candle off and moved quietly to the living room doorway, staying to one side. Kim was near him. They stood and listened. They heard it again, coming from the next level up. Somebody shifting their weight.

'Let me lead the way,' Kim said, holding her gun out.

'I don't like that idea at all. I brought you here, I should go first.'

'You don't have to be a hero, Frank. I'm a big girl.'

Miller didn't have an answer for that. Kim was more than capable of looking after both of them. She stepped out from behind the door and aimed the gun up the next flight of stairs. Tested the first tread. It took her weight without making much noise. The next one too. She repeated it until she was on the landing, her gun still out in front of her, finger on the trigger. Miller was close behind her. He had his baton out, but didn't expect anybody with a gun to step out.

There were several doorways along the hallway. Planks of wood lay against one wall, with an array of dusty tools near them.

All the doors were closed. Miller tried the first door, shoving it open and Kim stepped into the room, swinging her gun round, the flashlight attached to the rail underneath the barrel, lighting up the room.

Empty.

'Maybe it was a cat,' she said, as they moved to the next room. Same result.

'A heavy cat,' Miller said, his senses sharpened. His muscles were taut and the adrenaline was rushing through him. Fight or flight, and he definitely wasn't running away from this.

Then they heard another thump, this time coming from downstairs.

Kim pointed her gun towards the end of the hallway. 'Shit. There's another staircase.' She turned to look at Miller. 'I'll take that one, you go back down the one we came up, Frank.'

She took off, running, and Miller turned and ran down the flight of stairs, no attempt at being quiet now. Speed was more important.

Down one flight, past the room they'd been in.

As he turned at the foot of the stairs, he heard the scream and then the gunshots.

'Kim!' he shouted.

Then he heard the explosion.

When he reached the main hallway, there was nothing.

He saw the first tendrils of smoke creeping up from another stairway.

He ran down the steps and saw the flames licking round the doorway, backed away from the heat for a moment, then rushed through it, his arm shielding his face.

There was a wall of licking flames in front of him.

Through it, he could see Kim and another figure illuminated by the flames.

Panic gripped him for a split second. Then his training kicked in.

'Kim,' he shouted through the crackling.

Kim was wrestling with a figure wearing a black balaclava and black clothes. He turned to look at Miller. Then Kim was on her back, falling, rolling into the flames. She screamed again as she was rolled into the middle of the fire. Miller rushed forward, grabbing hold of her jacket. Her momentum helped him pull her clear of the fire, her jacket alight.

He yanked it off her and grabbed her hand. Before he started running, he looked through the flames once more, and saw the figure looking back at them. Nothing but the eyes showed through the mask, but he *felt* the evil emanating from him.

He turned and ran through another doorway.

Miller ran in the opposite direction, out the doorway he'd come through, holding onto Kim's hand, pulling her.

Their feet thumped on the stairs as they made it up to the landing, the smoke increasingly thicker.

They ran towards the back door, the way they'd come in.

It was shut. Miller tried the handle but pulled his hand back. 'We can't go out that way.' He knew from the heat of the handle the door had been set on fire and opening it would kill them.

'Here, I'll smash the window,' Kim shouted, over the mounting noise of the flames. Tendrils of flame seeped through the floorboards from the fire Miller realised was directly below them.

'We don't have long,' he shouted.

Kim grabbed a plank of wood and battered the window with it. It bounced off. They grabbed the length of wood between them and hit the glass with all the force they could muster.

The glass exploded out. For a moment, Miller expected flames to rocket in. When they didn't, he picked up a smaller piece of wood and knocked the remnants of glass out. Kim climbed out, holding onto the scaffolding, closely followed by Miller.

They jumped down onto the snow. The back door was well alight, and the fire starting to grip the planks of wood on the scaffolding.

They ran for the back gate, slipping on the snow.

'Where's your gun?' Miller asked.

The popping noise of bullets going off, ignited by the heat, answered Miller's question.

They crossed the road and Miller looked at the windows in the old building. 'The bastard set a trap for us,' he said, seeing the flames dancing behind the glass as the fire took hold.

'The entrance in the front of the building is on a different level,' Kim said. 'That's why we had an extra flight of stairs to come up to get out. He left by the front.' They looked and saw the front door was open.

Then Kim nudged his arm to get his attention. 'Look.'

He looked up the road. Kim's Audi was on fire.

TWENTY-THREE

It was almost like bonfire night all over again, Miller thought as he and Kim watched Lamb's House being consumed by the fire. The fire brigade couldn't get any men inside yet as the scaffold planks were engulfed in flames, lighting up the dark.

'You okay?' Miller asked Kim.

She nodded. The paramedic had wrapped a blanket round her after checking her out. She and Miller had refused medical treatment, saying they were both fine.

'Thanks to you.' Kim looked at him.

'What happened down there?' They hadn't had a chance to talk, concentrating on getting the calls made to bring in the cavalry.

'When I went down, I couldn't see anything. I heard the noise of the petrol being lit and turned round. Cross was there. I mean, just standing there next to me. He grabbed my gun and it went off. We started fighting. I dropped the gun. I tried to get the better of him, but he fought like a madman. Then you came down.'

'That place is a warren of stairways and corridors. I couldn't believe it when I saw those flames.'

'If you hadn't grabbed me, I would have died, you know that?'

'Now you're giving me a beamer,' he said, putting his arm round her shoulders and pulling her close.

'He set you up, Frank. He wanted to lure you in there to kill you.' She looked at him. 'He sees you as a threat.'

Paddy Gibb walked over to them. 'You certainly know how to entertain a lady, don't you, Frank?'

'Not exactly my idea of a fun night, boss.'

'You okay, Kim?'

'I lost my jacket, my gun, my car. Not in that order. But I'm fine, physically.'

Gibb looked at Miller. 'I know you have this thing with Richard Sullivan, so I sent Taylor along to have a word with him.'

'I hope he's not alone.'

'Two of our finest marksmen were with him, but there was no problem. Sullivan was at home with his girlfriend all night. So whoever was in there,' he briefly looked at the burning building, 'it wasn't Sullivan.'

'He could still have hired someone,' Miller said, not believing his own words.

Gibb shook his head. 'Me old Irish gut tells me otherwise. Sullivan might be daft but he's not stupid. Besides, there are easier ways to get rid of somebody.'

Like running them over in the street, Miller thought, but kept it to himself.

'So it seems Cross is still number one on the suspect list.'

'I would say so, son.'

They heard shouts coming from the fire fighters, then a crash as some of the scaffolding came down.

'What were you doing in there, Frank?' Gibb took out a cigarette, then thought it might not be appropriate, and put it away again.

Miller explained about the note.

'And you asked Kim to help?'

'I did. I wish I hadn't now.' He fished around in his pocket after putting a nitrile glove on. Handed Gibb the leather wallet. 'It's Carol's. He used it to lure me here tonight.'

TWENTY-FOUR

In the flat, they heard a voice. Jack talking to somebody.

Miller took off his coat and walked into the living room where his father was on the phone. He hung up when Miller walked in.

'Bloody hell, are you two alright?'

Miller told him they were, as he introduced Kim.

Jack shook her hand. 'Thank God you're both okay. I couldn't believe it when Frank called me. I put the TV on. Sky News are showing live pictures. You want to see?'

'No, Dad, we had a ringside view of it, remember?'

'Of course you did.' He looked at Kim. 'Sit yourself down.'

'Thanks, Jack, but I feel grubby.'

'That doesn't bother us. Sit and relax. I'll make coffee.'

Charlie came into the living room, stretching. Then he ran over to Kim when she held out a hand to him. He rubbed it and jumped onto her lap.

Miller nodded to the cat. 'I think you have a new friend there.'

'I love cats. I don't have one now, but I've had one before.'

Jack came in with the coffees. Went back for a beer for himself.

Miller pulled out the leather wallet he'd put in an evidence bag. Held it out to Jack.

'What's that, son?'

'It's Carol's wallet.' He opened it. 'There's still money in it, along with her bank cards.'

Jack looked at him in silence for a moment. 'Where'd you get it?'

Miller told him about their exploits earlier that evening before walking through to the kitchen, putting the light on. 'No sign of it had ever surfaced,' he said, when he heard Kim come into the kitchen. 'The wallet or the warrant card.' He knew it was Kim by the smell of her perfume.

'You okay, Frank?' She laid a hand on his arm.

Miller gave her a brief smile, but his heart wasn't in it. He felt like he'd been hollowed out. 'I'm fine.' He looked at her standing there. Two and a half years ago, it would have been his wife standing in that very spot, making dinner, or watching him cook. Talking about what they were going to watch on TV, or which bar they were going to have a quiet drink in. What destination they fancied for a holiday.

Then the subject of having children would be brought up. Miller wanted to be a dad more than anything, and had told Carol he was ready whenever she was. They'd decided to try and start a family a few months before she died.

He felt his throat tighten and had to turn away from Kim. Heard her leave the kitchen to give him some privacy with his thoughts. He leant over the sink for a few moments. He'd been to many crime scenes that involved seeing a dead body, but none of them had shaken him up the way seeing Carol's wallet just sitting there had. To know somebody had gone through her pockets and taken something personal from her, made him feel helpless. He couldn't imagine some-body getting so close she wouldn't fight him off. To know she'd been overpowered made him feel angry, but more than anything, it made him feel a deep sense of longing, of wanting to see his wife again. He didn't think he could stand the pain.

He stood up straight and shook the thoughts from his mind. He had to focus more than ever now. He went back into the living room. Sank into one of the armchairs, as if all the life had gone out of him.

'Tell me what happened that night,' Kim said.

Miller drank some coffee and put his mug on a side table. The lamps made the room feel warm, and the muted TV flicked light into the room.

'A ransom drop was going to be made. Guy Fawkes Night. Specifically picked because of all the activity after dark. He wanted Carol. Asked for her by name.

'He wanted to take control, and that's what he did that night. I wasn't happy about it, but Carol insisted she went. A little boy's life was at stake. After a lot of arguing, we decided to go ahead with it. Harry was livid, but Carol told him she understood as her father he'd be worried, but she was a detective and there were risks that came with the job. She said there wouldn't be a problem, as the team would all be out in cars, shadowing her.'

'Why Carol?' Kim asked.

'We're not sure. She was paranoid about Richard Sullivan.'

'You think he was involved?'

'We checked him out, and he had an alibi that night. I talked to him and he said he and Carol had had words outside court one day. That was all. Carol never told me why she thought Sullivan was wanting to do her harm, but she was convinced in her mind. She'd arrested him once, for disorderly conduct. But he took it on the chin. As far as I knew, he didn't hold it against her. Besides, it got thrown out of court.'

'Do you believe he had something to do with her death?'

He shook his head slightly. 'No. I looked through the flames at Cross. It wasn't Richard Sullivan in there tonight. Cross isn't as big as Sullivan.'

Jack put a coat on. 'Tell Kim what happened that night. I'm going to go out for a wee while.'

Miller nodded. Looked at Kim. She wasn't smiling now, but listening intently. 'The first pub Carol was sent to was the White House in Craigmillar. Then he bounced her round a few more. Then he sent her up to the Gauntlet at Broomhouse. That's when everything changed...'

TWENTY-FIVE

Richard Sullivan stood in front of his living room window overlooking the balcony, holding a glass of whisky and looking out through the darkness. He often just had a little lamp on so it wouldn't throw light at the window and he could stand here, or sit in the leather chair with his feet up on the footstool and look out into the world beyond. He was on the top floor, and his view was of the docks, so he didn't have to worry about nosy neighbours looking back at him.

'You're shaking,' Tai said, putting her arms around him and snuggling herself into his back.

He turned round and held onto her. 'I'm just wondering if Molloy found out about us and decided to burn Lamb's House to the ground to send a message.'

Tai shook her head. 'No, my love, I know he wouldn't do that. He wouldn't like the message he'd be sent from my Columbian cousins if he did. I don't think he'd care one way or the other if he found out we're seeing each other.'

Sullivan let her go and walked over to the drinks cabinet, was about to pour another whisky when somebody rang the buzzer from the street door.

'Yes?' he said, into the intercom.

'DI Taylor. Police. I'd like to have a talk with you.'

'You know where I am.' He pressed the entry button and poured himself another measure. A few minutes later, there was a knock at the front door. When Sullivan opened it, Taylor was standing there on his own.

'DI Taylor. Come in.' He stood aside, and watched as Taylor walked in. 'On your own now, I see? I must have been a good boy if there's no entry team with you. Please go through.'

He watched as the detective walked through to the living room.

Taylor nodded to Tai. 'Hello again.'

'Hi, Matt.'

'Can I get you a drink?' Sullivan asked.

'A wee nip wouldn't go amiss.'

Sullivan smiled. 'Glad to see that not all of Edinburgh's finest pretend they don't drink on duty.' He poured two measures and handed one to Taylor.

'Slainte,' Taylor said. 'Besides, I'm not on duty.'

'Cheers,' Sullivan replied, smiling and taking a sip. 'So what can I do for you?'

Taylor swallowed the whisky and put the glass down. 'You know I was round earlier with the armed response because Gibb sent me.'

'I know that, mate.'

'I'm here to let you know a wallet was found in your new property tonight. Before it was set on fire.'

The smile left Sullivan's face. 'A wallet?' Then he realised who it belonged to. 'Carol Miller's.'

Taylor nodded. 'The place had been broken into and her wallet left there for her husband to find.'

'Richard wouldn't do that, Matt,' Tai said. 'You've known him long enough. Known both of us separately for a while.'

Sullivan looked stunned. 'I had nothing to do with that, I can assure you.'

93

'Care to take a guess as to how it ended up in a property you bought?'

'I've no idea. No idea at all.' Sullivan felt shocked for the second time that night, and all signs of over-confidence were gone.

'I believe you, that's why I'm here unofficially. I wanted to ask you if you know anybody you might have pissed off mightily enough to go to such lengths.'

Sullivan took in a deep breath and blew it out. 'I mean, I've won a lot of cases, and made a lot of money, and with that comes jealousy and anger, but nobody jumps out at me.'

'You know how this looks, don't you?' Taylor put the glass down on the coffee table.

'I know; I was seen arguing with her, she's run over with my car and now her wallet's found in a building I bought. If this was the seventeenth century, they'd be hanging me tomorrow.'

'There might be other people out there who won't want to believe you're innocent. Just be careful. And if anything else comes to mind, call me. It might just save your life.' He walked towards the hallway. 'Nice seeing you again, Tai.'

Sullivan poured himself another drink, his hand shaking. He had a feeling they were going to fit him up and he'd go down for murdering one police officer and trying to murder another.

Tai stepped close to him again. 'You never told him about the phone call you got yesterday.'

Sullivan took a gulp of the whisky he was still holding. 'I didn't think it would do me any good to tell him Colin Fleming threatened to kill me.'

TWENTY-SIX

Miller stared off into space for a moment before he focused his attention back into the room.

Kim drank more coffee, guessing this was going to be a long night.

Miller took a deep breath before carrying on. 'Before being sent to Broomhouse, Carol said she asked to speak to the boy, and he was put on, but the background noise was completely different from the kidnapper's. Like the message from the boy had been recorded in a different building, with different acoustics. We didn't know for sure, of course, but Carol had a feeling. When she asked what day it was, the boy was cut off.'

'Then she was sent to Broomhouse?'

'The Gauntlet,' Miller said, 'over on the west side. She was talking to me on the radio...'

The Gauntlet looked like a detached house and was opposite a park area in the middle of the housing scheme. It was the scene of a gang shooting a couple of years earlier. A huge bonfire had been built in the middle of the small park and had been set alight. Guy Fawkes Night was in full flow. A group of onlookers were braving the cold for the chance to see a stray spark float away and burn a housing block down. The wood crackled as it was consumed by the flames. Shadows played around on the grass as she walked towards the entrance. There was a wooden picnic bench outside, waiting patiently for summer to return. Carol was surprised it wasn't on the bonfire by now. Maybe they wouldn't dare.

'I'm going in now.'

The pub was filled with the usual suspects. It was like a carbon copy of the White House. Almost as if the clients were being bused round to each of the pubs Carol was being sent to.

Once again, there was a small corridor leading to the toilets where the public payphone was. The punters looked at her, eyed the bag and weighed up their chances. Nobody moved.

She got to the phone as it rang. 'I'm going to send you to one more pub, Carol. First of all though, I want you to take off your radio kit and dump it in the Gents toilet. Including your mobile phone. There's a mobile phone in the trash bin. Take it and I'll call you on it. Do it now.'

She went into the Gents. 'Frank, I have to take my radio off.'

'Keep it on. We'll have no way of communicating with you.'

'I'll be fine. I have to find a mobile he left for me. She rummaged amongst the paper towels and found the phone on the bottom. 'It's here.'

She powered it up and realised it was a throwaway phone. Password protected. Then it rang. A "restricted call" message came up on the screen.

'Throw the radio away now, Carol, or Terry dies.'

'I've thrown it away.'

'Don't lie.'

She heard the most excruciating scream, followed by sobbing. 'I've just cut off one of Terry's fingers. If I don't hear that radio hit the rubbish bin in the next ten seconds, the deal's off and maybe one day you'll find Terry's body.'

'Okay, okay, I'm doing it.' She held the phone with one hand while pulling out her radio. She threw it in the bin. 'There, it's done.'

'Good. Now go into the second cubicle and feel inside the toilet paper holder. You'll find something there.'

This toilet wasn't the best kept place she'd ever been in. It stank to high heaven and she could only imagine what the men were like who frequented this place. The toilet paper was encased inside a plastic holder, presumably to keep the men from stealing it. She reached her hand in past the industrial paper and found the car key that was in there.

'You were taking a chance, weren't you? What if somebody had found it?'

'It belongs to an old car parked round the corner from the pub. Turn right, then right again. I'll be watching from somewhere close, Carol, so no funny business. The phone has no GPS in it like your phone.' There was a pause. 'When you're near the car, I'll ask you to strip off your jacket and top and turn out your pockets just to make sure you're not carrying the radio. If I see anything suspicious, even if I'm wrong, the deal's off.'

'I thought you wanted the money?'

'I don't want it enough to risk getting caught. Now move. Don't hang up the phone. Keep talking to me. And remember, I'll be watching.'

She left the pub, still holding the bag, still holding the phone. Turned right. There were even more people watching the fire now. It looked like somebody had thrown petrol on it. Maybe they'd burn the unmarked car she'd left behind.

'Stop!' the voice on the phone ordered. 'Change of plan. Turn round. See the first block of flats? Run through to the back of them. Over the fence. Through the garden and into Broomhouse Crescent. Left, then follow the road round. Do it now, Carol. You have two minutes.' He hung up.

He was sending her in the opposite direction now. Carol put the phone in her pocket, turned and ran, watched by some of the people at the bonfire. Nobody moved. She was just another shadow flitting through the darkness. Up the side of the first block of flats. She stopped and took out her own throwaway phone Frank had given her before she left the station. It had been tucked inside her boot, near her knife. He'd told her not to even speak about it in case the kidnapper heard her. She took it out and dialled his number.

'Frank, this is getting dangerous. You heard him make me throw my phone and the radio away.'

'I heard him, Carol. We're sending somebody in to get it now.'

'I have to cut through to Broomhouse Crescent and turn left. Follow it round. I have two minutes, Frank, so I don't have long. I have to get in a car he left. I don't know what it is yet. He'll have to call me back and let me know.'

'Call me and let me know, Carol.' A pause for a moment. 'I love you.'

'I love you too. And one more thing, before I go: I have some news for you, but it'll have to wait until this is over. It's bad, Frank. I'm scared, but you need to know. I have to go now.'

She hung up. Struggled up and over the wooden fence, heaving the bag over first. Then through somebody's back garden, the bag swinging wildly. She didn't know how much time she had left out of the two minutes, but what would he do?

Cut off another of Terry's fingers! she screamed at herself. A dog started barking. She ran faster, feeling herself sweat under her jacket. She burst onto the street and turned left, still running. The road curved round to the right and she followed it, wondering if he was watching from any of the windows of the houses bordering the street. Then she ran past the church and knew where she was.

The phone rang.

'You're late,' he said. 'Fourteen seconds late.'

'Oh well, I'll just fuck off with the money myself then, will I? She was standing at the fence that ran round the public park, out of breath. She peered into the darkness, knowing he was there somewhere, watching her, knowing she couldn't see him.

'Take your jacket off. Empty your pockets. Lift your shirt. You know the drill.'

She did as instructed; there was no radio attached to her.

'Good. The key's for an old Vauxhall Nova SR. Red. You'll see it sitting near the church. It's stolen, so don't bother checking who it belongs to. Now, get in and head out onto the main road. Keep the phone open. I'll direct you while you're moving. Now, go.'

Carol took the key out of her pocket and walked over to where the old car was sitting.

TWENTY-SEVEN

Richard Sullivan sat at his living room window, staring out into the distance. Visits from the police didn't bother him anymore. Maybe they had when he was doing work for Robert Molloy, but those days were a distant memory. Now though, that sort of thing could tarnish his reputation, even though business was booming right now.

There was always a glut of celebrities doing things they shouldn't, and then needing the best lawyer money could buy. That's where he came in.

This place was a far cry from the house he'd been brought up in, in Kelty, a small mining town in Fife.

Sullivan had always been a working-class man, just like his father before him, but that was where the similarity ended. Sullivan had ambition, whereas his father just wanted to work and get pished. He'd been a bus driver, and while Sullivan didn't look down on his old man for that, he didn't want to follow in his footsteps.

His mother hadn't been happy when Sullivan said he wanted to be a lawyer. She'd had a hissy fit and told him he should be working alongside his father. Sullivan ignored her, and spent his youth with his head in a book. He'd made it through law school and worked his way into a law firm.

It was just the small matter of somebody's infidelity and the need to cover it up that gave Sullivan the leverage he needed...

Twenty-five years ago

Farquhar Campbell was of the old school, a strict disciplinarian with his children, a hard taskmaster with his wife and held the belief if you didn't play golf, there was something wrong with you.

Richard Sullivan didn't play golf; he hated it. He told Campbell he wanted to take up the game, but had no intention of doing so. He wasn't any good at it.

What he was good at was looking after himself. And taking advantage of the opportunities life threw at you sometimes.

He got it one night. At a dinner dance. The Edinburgh North Golf Club was more than exclusive; it was sexist, racist and a den of iniquity. Words used by Campbell himself. Something he was proud of.

'I know you like a drink,' Campbell said, 'but we want to make an impression tonight, and one of us has to stay sober. Hope you don't mind.' It wasn't a question. Campbell had smiled and patted Sullivan on the shoulder.

Sullivan didn't mind. He couldn't keep his ears open if he was out of it. So he'd smiled. 'No problem, Mr Campbell.'

The old man had laughed. 'Call me, Farquhar.'

Farquhar. Fucker, more like, he had thought, but smiled anyway.

'I'm going to meet some friends in the members snug, so please feel free to entertain my wife,' Campbell had said, winking. Like he was giving Sullivan permission to shag her. Wasn't going to happen. Sullivan was twenty-five, and Campbell was fifty. His wife could be anywhere from forty-five to sixty-five, depending on how much make-up she'd plastered on.

'Come on,' Monica Campbell said to him, grabbing him by the arm, 'I think they're going to play a foxtrot.'

'My pleasure,' Sullivan said, allowing himself to be dragged through to the ballroom. The golf club had plenty of real estate, both in and outside the clubhouse. Formerly a mansion, it had been added to over the years until it was bordering on the obscene.

After a few dances, Sullivan excused himself. Went looking for Campbell. Not because he particularly wanted to be in his company, but because he knew the old man was up to no good. After listening in on many phone conversations, he knew the old man's repertoire.

Tonight's especially.

Her name was Zoe Alexander. She was a young woman whom Campbell had met at a Law Society bash. Campbell had taken quite a shine to her. She was apparently looking to work in the big city and Campbell had promised to help her.

Sullivan didn't have to look far. Farquhar Campbell was with Zoe in one of the private suites, which could be reserved for special meetings. He opened the door and walked into the room. Both of them were in what Campbell's wife would have called a "state of undress", on a couch, although Zoe had only gotten as far as dropping a few buttons on her blouse.

'Farquhar! What on earth's going on here?' Sullivan shouted as he walked into the room, closing the door behind him.

Campbell let out a shriek and jumped up, pulling his pants and trousers up. 'What the fuck are you doing in here?' he snapped, getting dressed in a hurry.

Zoe made herself decent and stayed on the couch.

Sullivan smiled, walked over to the table and picked up the champagne bottle. 'I asked first.' He drank from the bottle.

'You're finished at my firm. Your career's over, Sullivan. I'll ruin you. Get out.'

'Oh, I don't think so, Farquhar. In fact, I think the best working day of my life is today, don't you?'

'Who the fuck do you think you are?' The old man was trying to cover his embarrassment with anger.

Sullivan looked at him, the smile gone. 'Your worst fucking nightmare just came true; you got caught shagging around. Now sit down before I start shouting downstairs for Monica to come up.'

'You think my wife will believe your ludicrous story? I'm in here interviewing a lady for a position in my firm, and you burst in here in a jealous rage and start throwing accusations. You think she'll believe you over me?'

'I do actually. When she finds out what Zoe is.'

Campbell stood, looking confused. 'What do you mean?'

'Tell him.'

Zoe smiled and stood up. 'I'm not a lawyer. I'm a high-priced hooker. I was with him at that social evening when we first met.'

'So, you want me to call Monica up now? Test out your little theory?' Sullivan put the bottle down and walked towards the door.

'Wait!'

Sullivan stopped, and turned, and knew in that instant he'd just accelerated himself up the ladder.

'Let's talk,' Campbell said, sitting down in a chair.

Sullivan stood, looking at him. 'You're going to cite ill health as the reason for handing over the company to me.'

'What?' Campbell said.

'I know it was Monica's father who bankrolled you. She's the real power in the family. It would be such a shame if he found out not only were you shagging around behind his daughter's back, but with a prostitute to boot.' He looked at Zoe. 'No offence.'

'None taken,' she said.

'Well, I've taken offence, you bastard!' Campbell said.

Zoe stood up. 'I'll go downstairs and introduce myself to Monica.'

'Good idea.'

'Stop!' Campbell said. He looked at Sullivan. 'You're a bastard, you know that?'

'I know. And you'll find out what a real bastard I am if you don't

103

sign the papers I have here.' He pulled out an envelope from his inside pocket. 'They'll be witnessed by Miss Alexander. Don't worry, she's a lawyer, remember?' He winked at Campbell.

'You can't do this to me.'

'I can. I'll be senior partner at your firm. Your father-in-law will be told you have heart problems. That you've been seeing a specialist in London about it, and if you drop down dead at any minute, the firm will go belly up. Don't worry, Zoe's been entertaining a cardiologist in Harley Street whose wife would be devastated if she found out. All he has to do is confirm he's been seeing you if anybody asks, which I'm sure they won't, as you'll be convincing. Your father-in-law will ask why you don't sell to one of the more senior partners. You'll tell him there have been some underhand deals going on, and I was the one who discovered it. There's nothing concrete, but you can't trust any of them. The only man you trust is me.'

'He'll expect me to sell my partnership.'

'You tell him I have indeed bought your firm.'

Campbell laughed. 'And where would you get the money to buy me out?'

'Simple; you're going to give it to me.'

Campbell shook his head. 'You think I'd give you that kind of money because you caught me shagging a whore.'

'Offence taken,' Zoe said.

'No, I expect you to give me that kind of money, or I'll make a call to the fraud squad and give them the details of how you've been ripping off people for quite a while now. I'm sure you know what a Ponzi scheme is. I'll also call a man I know called Michael Molloy and tell him you raped a good friend of his.

'He won't need proof; Zoe will be totally convincing, and then Molloy will send some men round to your house to cut your dick off.

'So you have a choice: I can leave now and you can deal with the fallout, or you can give me some of that money from the Caymans, and I'll pay you for your firm. The figures are in the paperwork.' He took the papers from the envelope and handed them over.

Campbell snatched them. 'I'll have them signed at my own lawyer's in the morning. You'll have them back by midday and then I'll talk about me wiring money into an account of your choice. Satisfied?'

Sullivan smiled. 'Good choice. And you'll still get to keep the money from your little Ponzi scheme. If you're going to retire, I'd do it soon. Disappear down to the Caribbean or something. These schemes fall apart sooner or later.'

'Business advice from a crook. How ironic.'

'Well, I'll be off now, Farquhar. Nice doing business with you. Come on, Zoe.' He and Zoe walked to the door and were stopped by Campbell asking a question.

'Your name's not Zoe Alexander, is it?' he asked.

'No, it's not,' Moira Kennedy answered, as Sullivan opened the door.

Outside in the cold, Moira laughed. 'High-class prostitute, indeed. I'm sure the boss would be happy about that.'

'Talking of which, when are you going to tell him?' Sullivan held onto her.

'That's something I wanted to talk to you about; I have a big job coming up, just a quick thing, then I'll be finished with this line of work. First though, he wanted me to ask you something.'

'Go ahead.'

'He wants us to work together again.'

'What? No way. I left that crap behind a long time ago. I've got Campbell's practice now and I'm going to make a success of it.'

'Oh please, Richard. Just this one job. You saw how good we are tonight. We can pull this off.'

Sullivan knew he owed her big time. 'Okay. Tell me what it is.'

So she did. 'One more thing; you'll have to use your undercover name.'

Sullivan rolled his eyes. 'I thought he'd be dead and buried by now.'

'He will be soon. Then we can start our new life.'

Except life for Richard Sullivan was never going to be the same again.

TWENTY-EIGHT

'How did you know what car she was in?' Kim asked. She was standing near the window, looking out through the gap in the curtains at the North Bridge below.

'She called me again when she got to the last pub.'

She turned back and looked at Miller. 'Which was?'

'The Admiral's Rest. Down Constitution Street.'

'I don't know that one either. I think I was in London too long. Sorry.'

'Nothing to be sorry about. It's near Lamb's House, where Carol's wallet was found tonight.'

Charlie was sleeping on the settee now, bored with being petted. Miller was glad he felt comfortable round Kim. For some strange reason, it made him feel less stressed inside.

'It's near where she was killed, isn't it?'

Miller nodded. 'She was told to leave the Nova outside. She went in and called me again from her own phone after she went into the bathroom. She updated me about what happened at Broomhouse. Then the payphone in there rang.' He looked at Kim. 'She was to dump the money in an industrial bin near an office block up the road from the pub and jump in a taxi. He'd be around, watching.'

'Why don't your bosses think it was the kidnapper who killed her?' Kim asked. She wrapped her arms around herself then wandered back to her chair and sat down again.

'Gary Davidson, one of my team, saw the Jag scream past. Nobody else got to Carol before Gary. In all the commotion, the kidnapper must have walked up to the bin, and taken the money. Gary was so distraught, he didn't see anybody. By the time I got there, I wasn't even thinking about the money.'

'Did they ever find the Nova?'

'It was still at the pub. The only prints were Carol's, like he'd wiped it before he parked it at Broomhouse. Sullivan's Jag was found in Kelty, a couple of days later. Wiped clean. And once again, the brass said it was probably somebody living in Fife who didn't want to spring for a fast-black home. Sullivan originally comes from Kelty. Sullivan said he reported the car stolen earlier. Maybe somebody took it to go from pub to pub. Who knows? There's a lot of "ifs" and "buts".'

Kim shook her head. 'What about the little boy? The victim?'

'We never found him. We never heard from the kidnapper again. We assumed he got his money but he didn't keep up his end of the bargain. We don't know what happened to little Terry.'

TWENTY-NINE

Tuesday

Kim was waiting for Miller in the kitchen as if she'd never gone home.

'Morning,' he said to her, giving her what he hoped would pass for a smile. He didn't usually do smiling in the morning.

'Morning, Frank.'

'Hey, son. Want some bacon and eggs?'

Miller made a face. 'You'll clog your arteries with that stuff.'

'Nonsense. I've been eating this all my life.' He turned back to the frying pan.

Miller poured himself a coffee from the pot and topped up Kim's. 'I didn't hear you come in.'

She added some milk from a little jug that sat on the table. 'I was here around eight.'

Miller looked puzzled for a moment. 'Eight? It's only seven.' He looked at the clock on the wall: eight fifteen. 'Oh.'

'Nice to be able to lie in,' Jack said, dishing up the bacon and eggs.

Miller drank some coffee. 'So what brings you round at this ungodly hour?' Miller said.

'Hey, leave the lassie in peace. It's nice to have somebody pleasant to talk to in the morning.'

Kim smiled. 'I'm an early riser and I was on my way to the station.'

'I called her and asked her round for breakfast,' Jack said, looking at his son, as if daring him to argue.

Miller shrugged. Drank more coffee.

Kim nodded and finished a mouthful of bacon and eggs before saying, 'I was thinking about Richard Sullivan and him buying Lamb's House.'

'It was for sale for a long time.'

'It's not a coincidence that he bought it and Carol's wallet was found there. Do you think somebody's trying to set him up?'

Miller looked at her. 'I think he's a very clever man, and I wouldn't put it past him to try and make it look like somebody was framing him.'

'I don't think he'd dirty his own hands,' Jack said.

'Someone went to a lot of trouble to plant the wallet there last night and lure me there with the intention of killing me. That place is a maze inside, but he knew his way around. Like it was familiar to him.'

'We should look at who knew Sullivan had bought the property, and see how many enemies he has,' Kim said.

'Robert Molloy would be nasty enough to set up Sullivan, but I can't see him having my wife killed.'

'It's something we should be looking at, Frank,' Jack said.

Miller knew they were both right. 'When you're ready, we'll head to the office,' he said, adjusting his tie in the mirror on the living room wall. 'What you doing today, Jack?'

'Just out and about.'

'Just watch yourself.'

'You too, son.'

Outside, Miller and Kim walked carefully up High Street to the station. The pavements had been given another coating of snow, making them like an ice rink. The rush hour traffic moved slowly. Commuters who lived out of town and arrived every morning like a marauding army. Gloomy faces looked out through windscreens, like automatons.

'Your dad seems like a good guy.'

'He is. My mum died a couple of years ago, so he moved in for a little while, just 'til he got used to the idea of living on his own. And he's been with me ever since.'

'I miss my dad so much.'

Miller looked at her for a moment. 'Where's your dad buried?' He'd been doing a lot of thinking about Neil McGovern's death and now it was preying on his mind.

She looked at his face. 'Dad hasn't been released by the PF in Lanark yet. When he does release him, we'll have the funeral then. It's all to do with him dying in the State Hospital.'

'Have you seen him?' Miller looked down at the pavement, watching where he was placing his feet.

'No. Mum said we can't go and see him. Not yet. They can't know I was related to him. He'll be processed first, then when they release him, he'll be brought back to Edinburgh. A fake, distant relative will claim him. Then we'll get to see him. Why?'

He smiled at her. 'No reason. Just asking.' St. Giles' Cathedral sat on their left, just past the station. It was the burial place of John Knox, a man who still brought visitors to the city, over four hundred years after his death. Miller liked the little café below, where he'd spent many an hour, seeking solace and thinking time. It was a pleasant place to spend a while, unlike hundreds of years ago when one corner of the church was a prison for harlots and whores. Miller imagined what it would be like now if they emptied the massage parlours. It would be full to overflowing.

'Were you there the day your dad died?' Miller asked.

Kim looked puzzled. 'Why are you asking these questions, Frank?'

'As I said, I'm just curious.' A bus passed by, its wheels sizzling through the slush at the side of the road.

'No, I wasn't there. I'd been given the job of relief doctor, so I could be near him, but I was sent to check up on a patient who'd been taken to the Royal Infirmary in Glasgow. I just wish I'd been there. Maybe I could have saved him.'

'You can't blame yourself for that.' Miller didn't ask her any more questions.

They went in through the front entrance of the station. The investigation suite was coming to life. The others were gathering for the morning briefing, and the room was filled with the white noise of general chit-chat. Scott came over to Miller.

'How are you this morning, boss?'

'Not as bad as I look, I'm sure.'

'Hi, Kim.'

'Hi, Tam.'

Detective Superintendent Paddy Gibb came in, looking more tired than Miller. 'Right, people, listen up. Now we have to work on a case from twenty-five years ago. The Moira Kennedy murder. Raymond Cross was charged, but he disappeared with a detective who'd come up from London. Who was that guy? We didn't find out back then, but it's worth going over again. We might have missed something. Where did they go? That's a question we asked back then and didn't find the answer. So why did Colin Fleming have that name in his diary? We're going to go back and take apart that murder enquiry. We need to know what triggered him to come back now. I've asked DI Shaw to dish out the areas we need covered. We all know somebody tried to kill DI Miller and our colleague Dr Smith in the fire last night, so be careful. If this guy we're chasing thinks you're getting in the way, he'll take you out of the picture.

'I want CCTV from any shop in the area round Lamb's House.

See how he left the scene. Maybe we'll get a description. I want uniforms flooding that place. Don't take shite off anybody. I've already been on the phone to the PF who'll make a call of her own. Just to smooth the path for any warrant we might need. Let's get to it.'

With that, he walked to the back of the room.

Miller turned to Kim. 'You staying?'

'No, I was just here to get an update. I have to go to the PF's office. I'll catch up with you later.' She put a hand on his arm.

Miller liked her touch. He knew one day he'd have to move on. Feeling a woman put a hand on his arm was a wake-up call for him and he'd have to carry on with his life. Carol wouldn't mind. It didn't mean he'd ever give up looking for her killer.

Kim took him aside for a moment. 'I know that was a battery powered candle he put there on the fireplace in Lamb's House last night, he wouldn't risk one of the contractors coming in and finding it.'

'I know. That's why he sent me there.'

'My point is, Frank, how did he know you'd go there last night? What if you decided to pick up the letter today instead of last night? What if you couldn't figure out the puzzle and decided to throw the letter away?'

Miller could see what she was getting at but didn't put it into words. So she finished it for him.

'He was watching you, Frank. He was watching you and me, and we didn't even see him. I think you inadvertently know who Raymond Cross is. You just don't recognise him.'

THIRTY

Miller went into his office to catch up on some paperwork. Dozens of other officers were down in the secondary suite, collating information and running it through the HOLMES system. The door to Miller's office opened. Paddy Gibb himself. He came in and sat down. Handed Miller a piece of paper.

'You okay after last night, Frank?' he said, lighting up a cigarette. Smoking hadn't been banned in the old days and some habits die hard.

'I'm fine, and so is Kim, from what I can see. Maybe delayed shock will set in with her later.'

'Maybe you too. I know I'd feel like shit if somebody tried to burn me arse to ashes.'

'I've got Jack to yell at if I feel stressed.'

'Don't forget he's bigger than you.' More smoke. 'So, how are we on Fleming's case?'

'We're going through all the paperwork: statements, witness reports. Forensics sent through copies of every fingerprint they found in that room. We're checking them with the builders who're working on the renovation, then checking their alibis, but I'm willing to bet we'll come up with nothing significant. We're also checking CCTV from sources around Haymarket, but there are still a lot of places to check. Nothing so far. Nothing much else to go on, at the moment. Raymond Cross coming back after twenty-five years is our best bet.'

Gibb was one of the better bosses, as bosses go, but at the end of the day, when the shit fell down, it would inevitably reach Miller's desk.

'I've got a meeting with the chief and Elliot.' DCS David Elliot, head of Serious Crimes and CID. 'We're getting all the manpower we need, so I'll leave you to it. As you saw, one of them is Gary Davidson. Just keep an eye on him, Frank. His father was murdered only a couple of months ago, and I don't want him going postal.'

'He'll be fine.'

'It's been a while since the incident, but mud sticks.'

The *Incident*. Nobody wanted to come right out and say, *the time when Gary was accused of taking a backhander from one of Edinburgh's unsavoury characters*. The man in question was a high-powered drug dealer, and despite a microscope being shoved up his arse, Gary came away with an unblemished character. Everybody wondered, but nobody could prove anything.

'I'll make sure he's alright.'

'And when I say, keep an eye on him, I don't mean go around teaching him all your fucking bad habits.'

'I'm the one who keeps this department ticking like clockwork.'

'Sure you do. You keep telling yourself that, son.' Gibb stretched. Took another long drag on the cigarette and blew the smoke out slowly. 'You need to start smoking, Frank. You don't know what you're missing.'

'Lung cancer. Emphysema. Bad breath.'

Gibb blew his breath into his hand and sniffed it. Shrugged. Nothing a packet of Polos wouldn't take care of. 'My wife hated the smell of smoke.'

'Didn't stop you though.'

'God bless your heart, Frank. Trying to make an old man feel better.'

'It's what I was put here for, Paddy.'

Another draw. More smoke in the room. 'We need to find this fucker Cross,' he said, almost to himself. 'I can feel me pension slip away as we speak. I don't want to be a lollipop man when I'm finished here.' He stood up, stretched his arms and ground out his cigarette on the edge of the old, worn desk. Flicked the butt into the waste basket.

Tam Scott knocked and came in. 'Sorry. I didn't know you were busy,' he said, and made to leave.

'No, no, Tam come right in,' Gibb said. He turned to Miller. 'And if I catch you smoking in here again, you'll be out on your arse.' He winked.

'He was smoking again, wasn't he?' Scott said, closing the door.

'See nothing, hear nothing, Tam.'

'I'll remember that next time you ask for a report.'

Miller shook his head, wishing it were time to take more painkillers. Jack had supplied him with a couple of Paracetamol at breakfast. He stood up and put his jacket on. Looked out the grimy window. The sky was a dull grey as it emptied its load of snow 'You feeling okay, boss?'

'I'm fine now, Tam. I was just tired last night. It was a long day, what with us being on call.'

'Then some bastard tried to kill you and Kim. Just wait 'til we get hold of the fucker, I tell you.'

Miller yawned. 'I need to get some fresh air, Tam. Come on. Let's go for a drive.'

They left his office, and signed out a pool car. It was so cold, they could have been in Siberia.

'Where are we going?' Scott asked.

'The State Hospital.'

THIRTY-ONE

Richard Sullivan finished off some paperwork and got up to use the private bathroom in his office.

He looked at his reflection in the bathroom mirror and brushed his hair. He thought he didn't look anything like his fifty years. His hair hadn't turned grey, he was fit and had money. Life was good.

Lunchtime, he decided, although it was a bit early. He pulled on his suit jacket and woollen overcoat. Walked downstairs into the cold. The pavements were still slick, becoming slicker as each hour passed, so he watched where he was walking. Dr Martens today, instead of his usual black brogues.

A year after taking over the firm, Sullivan had downsized and moved the business down to Leith Docks, into a Victorian building, which had character and charm. He still had plenty of business though, back in the day, thanks to a man called Robert Molloy.

'Well, well, look who it is,' a voice said, from behind him.

He turned, and saw a man standing next to a black car. *Talk of the Devil.*

'Molloy. I thought the air smelled a bit iffy this morning. What brings you down here? I don't think the neighbours would appreciate your sort here.'

Robert Molloy looked at him. 'You finished? Good. I want a word. Get in the car.'

Sullivan looked across the road to where Geddes Fyfe was standing outside the front door of the office, smoking a cigarette. Fyfe saw Molloy and stamped the cigarette into the snow before starting to cross the road. A Transit van sped round the corner and stopped in front of him, blocking his view of Sullivan.

'I wouldn't do anything stupid, mate,' the passenger said, jumping out of the van. The back doors opened and six men dressed in black jumped out and walked up to Fyfe.

'I'm just going over to talk to my boss,' Fyfe said, standing his ground. He had a grin on his face, showing defiance.

'Go ahead. Then the next time you talk to him will be through a medium.'

Fyfe stopped. Outnumbered, he stepped back onto the pavement.

'Wise choice. They're going for a ride. He'll be brought back in one piece, or he can be brought back in a body bag. Depends on whether you follow us or not.'

'I'll wait inside,' Fyfe said, going into the office.

Sullivan turned back to Molloy when he saw the men standing in front of Fyfe. Watched Fyfe walk back inside. Nice to see he was ready and willing to put his life on the line for him.

'Come on, Richard. Let's get some lunch. I know a nice wee café down the road. I won't take up much of your time, I promise.' Molloy was smiling at him, and Sullivan guessed he didn't have much choice. He got in the back of the BMW with Molloy. The heated seats were already on.

The driver pulled away, and the Transit van followed.

'I've always liked it down here,' Molloy said.

'No, you haven't. You weren't interested in helping me get that casino off the ground.'

Molloy looked at him. 'You're right of course. I lied to make you feel good.'

'Fucking off and letting me go have lunch on my own would make me feel good. This kidnapping gig makes me wonder what your intentions are.'

Molloy laughed. 'Kidnap? Jeez, Dickie, you make me sound like a monster.'

Sullivan watched the Ocean Terminal shopping centre slip by as they headed for Newhaven.

'How's business, Richard?'

'Can't complain.'

'I hear things about you. Through the grapevine.'

'All good, I hope.'

Molloy smiled, and looked at him. 'You wish.'

Sullivan shrugged, and they sat in silence until the car and van pulled up outside a small café on Newhaven Road. He turned to Molloy.

'The Balmoral not open this early?'

'You'll love this place. I own it. Reminds me of my roots.'

Outside, the wind whipped across from the sea. Inside, the smell of hot food hit Sullivan's nostrils. They ordered from the blackboard, which hung on the wall behind the counter. He and Molloy sat at a small table near the back, while two of Molloy's men sat at another table and drank coffee. Three workmen sat at another table, eating and reading their tabloids. The rest of Molloy's men were visible outside.

'What's with the posse, Molloy?'

Their lunches arrived.

'There are so many nutters around, don't you think?' Molloy forked some bacon into his mouth and washed it down with coffee. 'Take that lowlife you bum around with. What's his name again?'

'You know his fucking name.' Sullivan began to eat.

'Ah, yes; Geddes Fyfe. Likes to think he's a lawyer, but he's

118

nothing more than your lackey. He's a bit of a nutter. Not in a scary way, mind, but more in a loose cannon way. Don't you agree?'

Sullivan tucked into the pie and chips. 'Just get on with what you want to talk to me about.'

Molloy nodded. 'How did that copper's wallet end up in Lamb's House?'

Sullivan put his knife and fork down. He was impressed by how tasty the food was. 'I don't know how it got there. I only bought the place. I had a quick tour before signing on the dotted, then it's all been down to the contractor after that.'

'Seems a bit suspicious if you ask me.'

'Well I didn't.'

Molloy pointed his fork at Sullivan. 'No, you didn't. Doesn't make it any less suspicious. She arrests you a while back, then she's killed by your car and her wallet's found in your place. I would say that's mighty fucking suspicious.'

'What can I say, Molloy? Somebody took her stuff and left it on a fireplace. Besides, she was the one who was the monkey on *my* back. I did nothing to her.'

Molloy was silent for a moment. 'I never said exactly where it was found.'

Sullivan maintained eye contact. 'I got a visit last night. As the owner, that's hardly surprising. The copper told me all about it.' He looked at his watch. 'Why are you so interested?'

'As you know, I'm a businessman in Leith. The Blue Martini's my pride and joy. I love being on her. She makes me feel good.'

'We're still talking about the boat, right?'

'Your crudeness doesn't surprise me, Richard. That's why you're still alone. You don't have a girlfriend right now, do you?'

Sullivan kept a poker face, half expecting the question to pop up. 'Not at the moment. I do enjoy the company of a woman, if that's what you're insinuating.'

'I'm insinuating nothing of the sort. I do, however, have another question.' Molloy stopped eating for a moment. 'Did you have any contact with Colin Fleming recently?'

It was said in a casual tone.

'No. Why would Fleming contact me?' Sullivan hoped Molloy didn't see through the lie.

'He hated you. He thought you killed Carol Davidson. Maybe not by your own hands, but he thought you had her topped. Paid some arsehole to knock her down. Did you?'

'What? Not you as well. Everybody knows Carol Miller and I didn't send each other a birthday card, but I wouldn't kill anybody. Especially a cop. I hope you made that clear to Fleming.'

'Colin was a bit fiery tempered. When he got an idea in his head, he was like a pit bull who'd clamped itself onto your private bits.'

'He was a nutter you mean.'

'Whatever. So here's what I think might have happened to him on Sunday night: he goes to that hotel for some reason, and you knew where he was going. You followed him, saw he was carrying something, and decided to rip him apart, and steal whatever he was carrying. Something that belonged to me.' He put more bacon in his mouth and pointed the fork at Sullivan, waiting until he'd swallowed before speaking again. 'Is that about right?'

Sullivan casually forked some pie into his mouth. 'You're right.'

Molloy kept the fork where it was. 'You what?'

'I said you're right; this pie's fantastic.'

'Stop being so fucking flippant. He was carrying something belonging to me and I want it back.'

'Sorry to disappoint you, Bobby Boy, but I don't know what the hell you're talking about.'

Molloy carried on eating. 'To be honest, I didn't think you did, but I wanted to make sure. If I thought you'd taken my stuff, I'd have somebody blow your legs off.'

'As usual, you don't mince your words.'

'I can't afford to. Some of these little scum buckets who're operating now would love to eat me up, but there's life in the old dog yet.

Plus, my nephew still operates down south, and he has a veritable army. And he loves his uncle Robert.' A smile like a shark now.

'Well, as much as I'm having lots of fun, I still have to get back to my office. Oh, and if that psycho can burn down Lamb's House with a cop in it, I'm assuming he won't have a problem burning an old boat with you in it.'

'He wouldn't dare.'

'I wonder if that was Colin Fleming's philosophy?'

Molloy finished his lunch. Finished his coffee. 'That was brilliant.' He looked at Sullivan. 'Let me also be clear on one more thing; if I ever find out you had anything to do with Carol Miller's death, you'll wish you'd never clocked eyes on her.'

'Again, nothing to do with me. Now, is there anything else?'

'I wanted to give you a friendly warning, that's all. Now, my man will give you a lift back along the road. In the van.'

'Take care now, Molloy,' Sullivan said, as he got up. Outside, one of the gorillas had the engine running. 'Back to where we came from. Apparently the Beemer's broken down or something.'

'Think yourself lucky you're not riding in the back,' the driver said, doing a U-turn.

THIRTY-TWO

Heavy snow was falling, causing snarl-ups. There were several accidents on the A70 as they made their way southwest out of the city.

'Are we there yet?' Scott said, looking out the window. This was unfamiliar territory for him.

'You're worse than a kid, Tam. We'll be there in a minute.'

Miller slowed down and turned left into a side road that was hidden by a high wall. It could have been a country estate they were turning into, but the sign told them they'd arrived at the State Hospital.

'This is the old one,' Miller said. 'You ever been here?'

Scott shook his head. 'No, just the new one in Carstairs.'

Miller peered out through the window, seeing only snow-covered trees but he knew the place was crawling with cameras and pressure sensors. The last line of defence before a patient made it to the road and freedom. 'They opened this place for the real bad guys. Men they know aren't going to leave except in a box.'

'I read in the papers they'd closed it.'

Miller looked at him as he drove slowly along the driveway. It had been gritted, but the snow was piled at the kerb, blending with the snow on the ground. 'They had. Then the new one was getting full, especially after they closed Gogarburn years ago. So they re-opened this one.'

Gogarburn had been the name of the psychiatric hospital on the outskirts of Edinburgh. It had been replaced by a bank HQ, a brand new building thrown up on the footprint of the old hospital.

They came up to a gatehouse. It was attached to a twelve-foot-high wall, which itself had razor wire on top.

A guard came out to meet the car, while another one watched from the warmth inside.

'DI Miller to see Dr Harvey Baker,' Miller said, after rolling the window down. The wind blasted into the car as the guard checked their warrant cards. 'Follow the driveway right up, sir. You'll come into the car park for the admin block.'

Miller wound the window up as the guard waved to his partner. The gate in front of them rolled to one side to let them through. It looked like it was strong enough to stop a tank.

More snow-covered trees, another long driveway. Then the trees thinned out and they came into a clearing. Before them was a tall, red brick Victorian building. Wide steps led up to the door. In front of the building was the car park, looking totally out of place. Staff cars were scattered around the parking spaces and Miller pulled in beside a Mercedes ML-Class, the insignia slipping sideways as they stopped.

'I wonder what this place was?' Scott said, as Miller turned the engine off.

'Some Hooray Henry's country estate, probably.'

They hurried through the snow to the steps and up into the reception area. It was warm inside, and they found themselves in a reception area no bigger than a small shop. On the left was a desk with a guard sitting at it. Doorways were in the left and right-hand corners, in front of them.

'DI Miller,' Frank said. He looked up at the CCTV camera pointed at him, thinking it wouldn't do the guard much good if somebody was trying to take his head off with an axe.

'The gatehouse called ahead. Somebody will be along shortly. Please have a seat.'

They sat on the modern office chairs, opposite the guard. A table was covered in old, out-of-date magazines. The same kind that were found in doctor's surgeries.

'I heard there was a series of escapes from here,' Scott said to Miller, as he looked at a cheap print on the wall.

'A long time ago,' a voice said, from behind them. 'Before it was opened up again.'

They turned, and saw a young woman standing at an open door. She was dressed in a knee-length skirt and a white cotton blouse. She had black hair and wore fashionable frameless glasses. Neither of them had heard her approach.

'DI Frank Miller. This is DS Scott.'

'Please, come this way.' She turned round and started walking away. The two policemen followed.

THIRTY-THREE

The office was basic, and Miller wondered what part of the house this would have been, a long time ago when it had been a private dwelling.

'Please, sit down, gentlemen,' the woman said. 'My name's Dr Catherine Armstrong. I'm head co-ordinator here at the hospital.'

The two detectives stayed standing. Better way to defend themselves if a nutcase came into the room with a hammer, which had happened to Miller one time. So now they stood, and never had their backs to the door.

'I called ahead and asked to speak with the director, Harvey Baker,' Miller said.

'Somebody will be here to speak to you shortly.' She left the room.

Miller looked out the window and saw the massive hospital set out in the distance. It was a huge, red brick building, just like the admin block they were in, built at the foot of surrounding hills, in a large valley. It was surrounded by a high-security wall and two razor-topped wire fences.

'Looks like the set for a movie,' Scott said, having a quick look out the window.

'So there's quite a few hurdles they'd have to get over in order to get out,' Miller said.

The whole scene was covered in deep snow, looking like a painting, rather than a structure through a window. The sky was still heavy with snow and it came down with a vengeance.

Just then, the door opened again. A man, dressed in a suit, walked in and closed the door behind him. He was balding and in his late fifties. Glasses that might have been fashionable twenty years ago, sat on top of a beaked nose.

'I'm Humphrey Dugan, the director,' he said, making no effort to shake hands. Instead he sat behind his desk. 'Detectives...?'

'I'm DI Miller. DS Scott.'

Dugan let out a sigh. He didn't try to conceal his boredom. 'What can I do for you, gentlemen?' He looked at them as if they were pupils brought before the headmaster for punishment.

'I was expecting Harvey Baker,' Miller said.

'He's off sick right now,' Dugan said. 'I'm filling in for him. He's ill and won't be back for a while.'

'I wanted to ask you about Neil McGovern, a patient who was here a couple of months ago.'

'Yes. Dr Armstrong said you called ahead.' He pulled open a drawer and brought out a folder. Passed it over to Miller. 'That's a copy of all his files, medical files included. You can keep that. If there's anything I can help you with right now, fire away.'

'How well do you know the case?'

'I wasn't here at the time, but I was briefed on his death.'

'What was the cause of death?' Scott asked.

The deep-thinking frown again. 'I think it says McGovern died from a brain haemorrhage. He just collapsed and died.'

Miller looked at him. 'So you know the results of the post-mortem, then. Where was this done?'

'I can't recall. It's in the file. Probably Airdrie. Edinburgh's not in the jurisdiction, as you may well be aware.'

Miller nodded. Not quite true, he thought. If the person comes from Edinburgh, then they have the right to have the PM done there. Dugan's accent was south coast of England, so he might not have known that, but considering he was the director of the place, he should have.

'Who did the post-mortem?' Scott asked.

'Home Office pathologists. Which is normal when a patient dies here.'

'Where's he buried?' Miller asked.

'I'm quite sure he was cremated.'

'What would have happened to the ashes?'

Dugan held out his hands. 'I'm led to believe, if a deceased person doesn't have any family, the ashes are scattered in a garden of remembrance. It's good for the roses, apparently, but I wouldn't know. I use regular compost, myself.' He smiled at his own humour, but was the only one.

Miller knew the hospital wouldn't know Kim was McGovern's daughter. His fake bio said he had no family.

'Thanks for your time,' Miller said, taking the file, but knowing it wouldn't hold anything he didn't know already.

Dugan stood up, and shook their hands. 'Only too happy to help the police.'

Outside, Miller held on tightly to the file as a strong wind blew through the car park. Dugan was lying through his teeth, and Miller wanted to know why.

'Back to the office?' Scott asked.

'No. Fountainbridge. There's a woman I need to talk to. Call Kim and we'll pick her up first.' Five minutes later, they were on the main road, heading for Edinburgh.

THIRTY-FOUR

The office block was a modern affair, standing on the footprint of what was once a car dealership in Fountainbridge. It belonged to a major bank now. The area had a history with brewing, but that industry had taken a hit and factories were sold off to developers. It didn't stop them making the booze, they just changed their location.

They'd picked up Kim at the station and headed straight back out.

The security guard was waiting for them at the back door. 'DI Miller. I need to speak to Andrea Kennedy.'

Moira's sister had been easy to find; her place of employment hadn't changed in twenty-five years. Location of the building, yes, but a quick call to head office had given them her new location and job title.

'Is she expecting you?' the guard said.

'Yes.' The heat was getting to Miller, sapping his energy. He needed to be back in his bed. His whole body was stretched taut, like piano wire.

'She's on the fifth floor. You can use the lifts back there.'

The fifth floor gave a spectacular view of New Town and towards the west. Miller saw the spires of St Mary's Cathedral in Manor Place. He wondered what the designer of that place would have thought about this building. The phrase, *turning in his grave,* came to mind.

Miller asked where he could find Andrea Kennedy and was directed to her office.

'Ms Kennedy? I'm Detective Inspector Miller.' He introduced Scott and Kim.

A woman dressed in a black skirt suit stood up from behind her desk, 'I'm Andrea Kennedy.'

Knowing she was Moira's older sister, Miller guessed Andrea was in her mid to late forties.

'How can I help you today?' she asked, sitting back behind her desk. Miller and Kim sat, while Scott stood near the door.

'I want to ask you what you know about Raymond Cross.'

The smile faded slightly. 'What do you want to know?'

'We're just doing some background on him. I believe he was your sister's boyfriend at the time she was murdered.'

Andrea nodded slowly, as if thinking about that night made her feel ill. 'He was.'

'How did he seem to you when you first met him?' Scott asked.

Andrea looked at him. 'He seemed normal. She'd been out with worse.'

'Did he ever show any sign that he could be violent?' Kim asked.

Andrea took in a breath and let it out slowly. 'I only met him the once. Moira and I had a very strained relationship. We didn't see each other very much.'

'Your boyfriend was Michael Molloy, wasn't it?' Miller said.

Andrea nodded. 'Yes. I know he had a reputation back then.'

'Still does.'

'Nobody understood him like I did.'

'So Cross hung out with a psycho, and none of it rubbed off, is that what you're saying?' Miller looked at her.

129

'What do you think made Raymond go off his head that night at the hotel?' Kim asked her.

'I don't think he did. Michael was convinced somebody else did it, but he knew the police might want to fit him up for the murder. Him or his father. Whoever it was, nobody ever served time for my sister's murder.' She looked at Miller. 'Have you spoken to Harry Davidson's daughter yet?'

'Julie? What about?'

'That night, of course. She was there with her father.'

'She was at the hotel?'

'Yes. I'm certain. I asked Michael about her, and he said, "It's that copper's daughter."'

He looked at her. 'I have to ask this, so please don't be offended; where were you between ten o'clock Sunday night and two o'clock Monday morning?'

'With Michael.'

'Molloy?'

'Yes, Michael Molloy.'

'You kept in touch with him?'

She smiled at him. 'He wasn't just my boyfriend; he was my husband.'

THIRTY-FIVE

Sometimes the bar looked like there'd been a fight the night before, Jennifer Wilson thought, as she shut the door behind her. The lights flickered as they came on, and the place didn't have the same ambience without the mood lighting. She locked the door behind her.

She made her way through to the back, stepping over the detritus of the night before.

Jennifer let herself into her office and switched the lights on. There was a window overlooking Rose Street Lane, a grubby little back street drunks used for a toilet.

She opened up the blinds and the light rushed in. The sky was grey as if it was in a bad mood, and snow was still piled on the window sill. She looked out at her car. Did a double-take. Some bastard was scratching it!

'Fuck me,' she whispered. The guy was standing with his back to her. He was wearing a woollen hat and thermal gloves, and was holding something long, about the size of a screwdriver, turning it round and round on the bonnet.

She hadn't even had a chance to take her jacket off and some wanker was vandalising her car. Had she thrown anybody out of the bar last night? She didn't think so. Then she saw red. Her car. The one thing she loved in life.

'Hey!' she shouted, rapping her knuckles on the glass. He stopped, his back still to her. Then he carried on again as if nothing had happened. She knocked again, harder this time. He stopped once more, then turned round slightly. She saw the long, unkempt dark hair sticking out from the woollen hat, but couldn't make out his face.

He turned back to her car and started the scratching again.

Jennifer walked round her desk and opened the alarm box that would deactivate the alarm on the fire door, then went out into the corridor. Pushed the bar and the door swung out, cold air rushing in at her.

He was standing right there at the door. Grinning at her. He'd pulled a balaclava down over his face.

'Hello, Jennifer. Remember me?' Before she could answer, he pushed her inside, taking a step and pushing her again, harder this time.

Jennifer sucked in her breath, wanting to scream, but couldn't. He stepped inside and closed the door behind him, pushing it with his back, keeping his eyes on her.

'Take what you want, but I don't have last night's takings. I banked them. Take anything else you want.'

'I don't want anything you have,' he said, then she turned, running into her office, thinking if she could just lock herself in there, she could call for help.

He was right behind her.

She wanted to fight, but couldn't even turn round before the cold steel of the knife slid across her throat.

He pulled the knife away from her.

A hand went to her throat, as she felt panic grip her. Then she turned round. Her eyes wide, brow furrowed in confusion. Why didn't he just rob her?

Then, in the fleeting moments before her brain shut down, she realised this wasn't about money. It was connected to the text Colin Fleming had sent her.

Be careful. He's back.

THIRTY-SIX

Scott fought his way through the heavy traffic, coming out of the Western Approach Road into Lothian Road, the siren blaring.

The snow was falling harder and covering the road quicker than it could be salted.

They slid down Cockburn Street, up Waverley Bridge and along Princes Street. The Castle sat and looked down at them like a disapproving matriarch.

Hazel Carter was in the pub, along with Andy Watt.

'She's through the back, sir,' Hazel said.

'Is it like the last one?'

'Worse. He made a real mess of her.'

They walked along the rear corridor, Miller, Scott and Kim following. Paddy Gibb was standing, talking to two uniforms.

'You sure you want to be here?' Watt asked Kim.

'I'm a doctor. I've seen worse.' You sure you want to be here, Grandpa?

Miller looked round. Jennifer Wilson was lying on her desk, half naked. She'd been opened up from the neck to below her waistline. Her intestines were scattered on the floor. Blood was splattered on

134

almost every surface. It was almost the same as the tableau in Colin Fleming's office.

'Do we know who she is?'

'Jennifer Wilson,' Gibb said, 'the manager.'

'Whoever it was must have been covered in blood. Surely somebody saw something,' Miller said. 'Unless he cleaned himself off before he left. Anybody check the toilets?'

'A SOCO said they had. They're clean.'

Scott looked at Gibb. 'There are a lot of weirdos going about Edinburgh nowadays, so don't count on anybody making a phone call.'

'How true, sergeant,' Gibb said, 'and most of them are in uniform branch.'

'Where's Hazel?' Miller asked.

'In the ambulance with the old women who found her. They don't look like the type to do this sort of thing, but then Fred West was a doctor. One of them was passed out when the woolly suits got here.'

'How did the killer get in?' Scott asked.

'The front door was locked when the cleaners got here, and Miss Wilson here still had her keys in her handbag, but there are footsteps from her car to the emergency exit. We found the keys so the Beemer's definitely hers.'

'She must have let him in, then,' Miller said.

'The question is, why?' Andy Watt said, coming in.

Miller had on latex gloves and pushed the bar. The door opened wide. No alarm came on, despite a warning saying one would if the door was pushed. 'Did a SOCO switch the alarm off?'

Nobody had.

'I've been along here before, and I've seen the draymen loading the drink through the cellar doors that open up in Rose Street, so she wouldn't have opened it round here for a delivery. So why would she open it?' He looked in the office and saw her handbag lying on her chair. Picked it up and rummaged around inside. Picked out her

BMW car keys and went back to the door. There was only one car in the lane and it was a 3-series. He hit the remote and the doors unlocked. He saw the footprints in the snow, leading from the car to the back door. He walked over to it, careful not to mess up the footprints that were already there and saw the damage on the bonnet right away. Although it had been snowing, the woman's commute had cleared the snow off the bonnet. He started to walk back inside when the mortuary van turned into the lane, skidding a little on the snow. Gus Weaver was driving. The older technician jumped out as Adam Dagger pulled up behind in his beat-up Volkswagen.

'Where's Julie?' Miller asked Weaver, as he jumped out of the van.

Weaver smiled at him. 'Late shift.'

Dagger yawned as he slammed the driver's door. 'I was hoping for an easy day,' he said, walking up to Miller.

'Somebody has other ideas, doc.' Miller led them into the office, then spoke to Gibb.

'The bonnet's all scratched to hell. Maybe she saw him doing it and confronted him. That was his way of getting in.'

'That makes sense,' Kim said.

'Look at this.' Scott had opened the door to what they'd thought was a closet. It wasn't; it was a bathroom. With a shower. The cubicle was wet as if somebody had used the shower not long ago.

'So he cleaned up in here before he left. No wonder no one saw anybody covered in blood,' Miller said.

'I think we can rule out robbery,' Gibb said. 'The safe's been opened and there's still money there. It doesn't look like a night's takings, but surely she would have given up the cash rather than risk dying.'

'I'll find out what bank they use and check it out,' Watt said, leaving.

'Now all we have to do is find a motive. Run this woman through everything we've got,' Gibb said.

'She's a friend of Robert Molloy. He owns this place.'

'Get onto that, Frank.'

Adam Dagger came over to look at the body before putting his case down. 'Just like Colin Fleming, eh?' he said, looking at Gibb. 'A serial or a copycat?'

'Serial,' Gibb answered. 'We didn't release any details to the press, did we, Frank?'

'Not that I know of.'

'And it had better stay that way. You heard Norma Banks.'

Dagger started by looking at the corpse without touching it, examining from different angles. Then he stood up straight. 'I don't suppose you have leads?'

'A name from the past. Nothing concrete.' Miller looked at the corpse. 'Do you think this could be the work of a doctor, or maybe somebody with medical training?'

'It's hard to say. Maybe if he'd cut her heart out or something, we could tell, but not just by opening her up. A doctor, or a bricklayer could have done this. Anybody with a large knife and a screw loose. Maybe somebody with no previous, if we're unlucky.'

'Or maybe somebody like Jack the fucking Ripper, given my luck,' Miller said.

THIRTY-SEVEN

Miller left Watt to check with the bank to see if the takings had been deposited, and accompanied by Kim left the pub, leaving Scott as his eyes and ears.

'Where we going, Frank?' Kim asked.

'Not far. Just somebody I need to go and see.'

They stopped outside a nightclub at the east end of George Street, called simply, *The Club*. The wind was biting now, lifting some of the snow that had fallen and throwing it across the road.

The building itself had been a bank at one time, with large stone columns supporting a portico. They climbed the wide front steps and went into the lobby area, where they were met by two bouncers. Even during the day, Molloy wanted somebody guarding the entrance to his fort.

'DI Miller. We'd like to speak to Robert Molloy.'

'I'll see if he can fit you in,' the larger one said. Miller knew him well. Greg Sampson. He was an ape who would have been digging ditches if he hadn't worked for Molloy.

'That's okay. I know where his office is,' Miller said, and they walked past the men.

138

Sampson was speaking into a cuff microphone, then hurried past them. He walked in front of them up the stairs to Molloy's office. Sampson knocked and they heard somebody shout, "Enter".

'Mr Miller!' Robert Molloy said, smiling at them. Sampson backed out of the room.

'I need to have a word with you, Molloy.'

Robert's smile didn't falter. He was sitting on a leather sofa on one side of the room.

'Who's your new acquaintance?'

'Investigator Smith. She's with the PF's office.'

'I've heard a lot about you, Mr Molloy,' Kim said.

The room was huge, with a fireplace against one wall, the fake logs surrounded by gas flames. Paintings hung on the wall, by artists Miller didn't know and didn't want to. He was sure they were worth a fortune, but he wouldn't have given them house room.

A huge desk was near the window. 'Don't believe everything you hear about us, Miss Smith.' Sitting in a chair behind it, was Robert's son, Michael. 'What now, Miller?' He didn't smile.

'You own the Fiddler's Elbow in Rose Street.'

'You asking, or telling?' Michael said.

'Where were you this morning?'

'Why the sudden interest in my whereabouts? Was a bank turned over or something?' He laughed, and smiled at his father. 'And what's it got to do with my pub?'

'Your manageress was murdered in there this morning.'

Both Molloys stopped smiling. 'Jennifer?' Robert said.

Miller nodded. 'We're trying to find the next of kin for an ID, but we believe it's her.'

'What the hell happened to her, Miller?' Michael said.

'Again, where were you this morning?'

'Oh fuck off. I can get thirty witnesses to swear I was here in my club if I want.' He suddenly stood up. 'You know I wouldn't murder anybody, especially one of my staff.'

'Just answer the question, Michael,' Robert said.

Michael took a deep breath and sat back down. 'We were here all morning. Me and him.' He nodded towards his father. 'Going over accounts, if you can believe that.' He left out the part where his father left to have lunch with Sullivan.

'When's the last time you saw Jennifer?' Scott asked.

Michael rocked in his chair. Looked at Miller as if he'd asked him to summarise all of Shakespeare's works in one sentence.

He shrugged his shoulders. 'Last week sometime. She pretty much runs the bar herself, with minimal supervision.'

'Molloy?' Miller prompted.

Robert held out his hands. 'Not for a while. As Michael said, she was a good worker who needed little supervision. I wish all my staff were like her.'

'Were you two good friends, Michael?' asked Miller.

'Was I shagging her you mean?'

'Yes, that's what we mean,' Kim said. She looked over at Michael as if she wanted to slap him, a thought that went through a lot of people's minds when they met him.

'We were good friends, and she worked for me. I trusted her.'

'Do you know anybody who might be pissed off at her enough to slice her open?' Kim said.

The colour drained from Michael's face. 'What do you mean, slice her open?'

'She was disembowelled.'

'Fuck me,' Michael said, his voice now barely a whisper.

'Somebody obviously doesn't know who they're fucking with,' Robert said. 'Was it a robbery?'

Miller shook his head. 'One of the Crime Scene technicians opened the safe and there was money still there. We're going to check with the bank to see if she made a deposit with any takings. It looked like she was the target.'

There was silence in the room for a moment.

'She did make the deposit. The takings are deposited every night by a member of my staff. I checked the balance this morning. The only money that should be there is money for the floats.'

'There wasn't a lot of money in the safe,' Miller confirmed.

'You got any idea who could be doing this, Mr Miller?' Robert said.

'I was hoping you could tell me.'

'That doesn't inspire much confidence in the police force, I must say.'

'I only know three people have been murdered in as many days, and they all have connections to you. Did they piss you off or something?'

Michael glared at Miller. 'Once again, we had nothing to do with those murders.'

Robert opened his hands, as if in prayer. 'What you believe, Inspector Miller, is nothing to do with me. I'm not going to be able to change your mind, but all I will say is, we know nothing about the Flemings or Jennifer's deaths. And the more time you spend in here with us, the more time the real murderer has to escape.'

'I don't think he's going anywhere,' Kim said.

'I'm assuming you two will have an alibi for Sunday night,' Miller said.

Robert looked at his son then back at Miller. 'The same thirty witnesses, Mr Miller. Besides, Sunday night's party night in the club and we were both there, with plenty of people to verify it. I told you that already when you came to my house yesterday.'

'What was Fleming doing in that hotel?' The heat in the room was starting to make Kim sweat, but she didn't undo her overcoat.

'You tell us,' Michael replied, 'you're the fucking detectives.'

'What my son means is, we don't know what he was doing there.' Robert looked at Michael with a warning. 'As I told you yesterday.'

'Can you give us some background on Jennifer Wilson?' Kim asked.

'Sure. She lived alone, wasn't seeing anybody. A hard worker.

Trustworthy. She was a nice woman. I can't believe somebody would do that.'

'If you can think of something that might help catch her killer, be sure to give us a call,' Miller said, knowing there was more chance of Molloy tying a length of chain round the killer and dumping him out at sea than contacting the police.

'I have your number on speed dial.'

'That'll be all for now,' Miller said. 'If we need to ask you any more questions, we know where to find you.'

'I'm always at your service, detective.'

'One more thing before we go; do either of you know Raymond Cross?'

There was the briefest glance between Michael and his father, but they said nothing.

'I'm not familiar with that name,' Robert answered. 'Are you, Michael?'

'I think he plays for Aston Villa.'

'Excuse my son being a smartarse. Just answer the question.'

'Nope.'

'Nope, you won't answer the question?' Miller said, 'or nope, you don't know him.'

'I don't know him, fuck.'

At that moment, there was a knock on the door. Robert shouted for the person to come in. A young woman walked in, looked at the two detectives, and then at her boss.

'Sorry to disturb you, sir, but there's a gentleman here to see you. He says he has an appointment.'

Robert looked at his watch. 'Oh yes.' He looked at Miller. 'Mr Miller, this is Sienna Craig, one of my security staff. She made you coffee yesterday morning when you came to my home.' Then to Sienna. 'This is one of Police Scotland's finest.'

'I remember,' Miller said, to Sienna. 'You make good coffee.'

'Do you know where we can find any of Jennifer's relatives to inform them of her death?' Miller asked.

Robert Molloy shook his head. 'I don't know if she had any immediate family. I'm not sure about distant family.' He looked like he couldn't care less. 'If you'll excuse me, I have to meet with a supplier. Alcohol, not heroin.' He laughed at his own joke.

'We'll see ourselves out,' Miller said, and stopped before they left the office. 'Oh, by the way, Michael, we had a nice chat with somebody you know well.'

'Really? Do tell.'

'Andrea. Your ex-wife.' Miller smiled. 'Take care now.'

THIRTY-EIGHT

The station was jumping when they got back. The old building heaved and creaked as the heat from inside met the biting cold outside.

Kim said she wanted to have a look at some old records in the basement so headed downstairs as Miller walked upstairs. DI Gary Davidson was in the investigation room, laughing with a young female uniform. He smiled when he saw Miller. He'd been sitting on the edge of a desk, but got up and walked over to his brother-in-law.

'Hey, Frank, how's things going?'

'Slow, Gary.'

'Rosie's always asking when you're coming round. She doesn't want you to stay away because you think you did something wrong the night my dad died.' His face turned sombre. 'We're family and family's what counts. Am I right?'

Miller nodded. 'You're right, Gary. Tell Rosie I'll come round for dinner one night. You know once I get my boots off and my feet up in front of the fire, you might not get rid of me.'

Davidson laughed again. 'Good man.'

They walked towards Miller's office. 'I went to the crime scene yesterday, Frank. I hope you don't mind. I ran it by Gibb and he said it was okay. I have to admit I'm worried, mate. Colin Fleming was a friend of my dad's, and now he's died the same way. And at the hand of some psycho my dad caught all those years ago. Any idea why he's come back now?'

Miller stopped before they got to his office. 'No idea, Gary. That's what we're asking ourselves now; what's made him kill again after all these years?'

'You know, sometimes men go crazy when they learn they have a terminal illness. Maybe Cross found out he's dying. Taking out people who pissed him off back then.'

'It's worth thinking about, but the problem is, we don't know what name he was using. He could have been using his real name, but it's doubtful.'

Davidson slapped his right arm again. 'You're right. But we can keep an open mind about it.'

'We will, Gary. And thanks again for the invite.'

Davidson winked at him, and walked away.

THIRTY-NINE

'Kim, it's me. How are you doing?' Miller said into the phone, rubbing one eye. His office felt stuffy. He hated staring at the computer for hours, especially when it was futile; his Internet search had proved fruitless.

'I'm not having much luck. A lot of this stuff's just basic reports and files we've already looked at online.'

'I need to stretch my legs. I'll be right down.'

He hung up, and left his office. Started thinking about Carol again. He wished, more than anything, he could turn the clock back and take Carol's place.

He rode the lift down into the basement where the records were kept, those old enough not to be on computer. One day, they'd all be transcribed onto hard drives, but for now, it was all boxes full of papers. He stepped into a long corridor wondering, not for the first time, what this place would have been hundreds of years ago.

A camera tracked his every move down to the evidence locker room. Two uniforms sat in there, older blokes who'd once stamped the beat in Edinburgh, and were now waiting to stamp their pension books. One of them made him sign the log book and then buzzed him through.

The records room was long, with hallways running off it. Just like the crypts, Miller reminded himself. They had been vaults of some kind many years ago. There were racks on either side, all of them holding boxes. They were starting to smell musty, and he wondered if somebody was actively archiving all the information. He heard the sound of paper rustling up ahead. Turned the corner, making sure he scraped his shoe on the concrete floor before he turned, so Kim heard him coming.

'Hi, Frank,' she said, smiling.

'How you doing?' It was much colder down here, in direct contrast to his office. She was in an area with two desks and two chairs, where somebody searching for stuff could sit and browse.

'I've been going through this stuff from the murder back in the nineties.' She waved a sheaf of papers at him.

'Find anything?'

'Nothing jumps out at me.' She put the papers on the table.

'There has to be some kind of connection to the Moira Kennedy case.'

'Where does Jennifer Wilson fit into all of this?'

'The only connection is, she works in one of Robert Molloy's bars, but of course, his alibi is tighter than a Scotsman's sporran. We're trying to track down the next of kin now but we don't think there is any.'

'So Colin Fleming did a lot of work for Molloy, in whatever capacity, and now this woman was murdered. We know Fleming was one of the arresting officers back then, when Cross was arrested. So was Harry Davidson. Those two we can connect to the Moira Kennedy murder. So where does Jennifer Wilson fit into that murder? So far, the only connection to them all is Molloy.' She looked at Miller, stood up and stretched her back. 'I need a drink.'

'You okay after last night?'

'I'm fine. I've been in worse situations.' She didn't elaborate and Miller didn't ask.

'I'm finished for the day,' he said,' but I need to do one more thing. You and Tam can come along if you like.'

'Okay. I'm finished with this stuff anyway.' She smiled, and he watched as she picked up the box, not knowing if he should be offering to help, but deciding if she was capable of blowing a man's head off, she could lift a small box onto a shelf.

They rode the lift up together and he fetched Tam Scott from the office.

They signed a pool car out. Ten minutes later, it was rattling its way up through the pen onto High Street.

Darkness was coming down faster than a runaway train. The snow was relentless, catching out pedestrians and motorists alike. Kim had good control of the car as it slid on the mushy snow.

'Which way?' she asked.

'Left. We're going back to the hotel. I want a word with the manager.'

FORTY

The hotel was still under police jurisdiction and a uniform was at the door. He nodded when he recognised Miller. The light in the sky had died now, and in its place was a biting wind. Little pockets of snow were thrown up from the ground, but at least the main barrage had stopped for the time being.

Inside, another uniform was standing at the bottom of the stairs. 'Forensics still upstairs?' Miller asked.

'Yes, sir. They're taking the room apart.'

They walked across to the reception desk. Miller hit the little service bell on the counter, and a woman entered from a back room. Her name badge said she was Melinda.

'Sorry to keep you, sir,' she said, trying for a smile but failing miserably. Miller supposed having the police crawling all over the hotel wasn't good for business.

'I'm looking for Donald Goram. Is he in?'

'Yes. Shall I tell him you're here?'

'That won't be necessary,' Scott said.

'He's through in the bar.'

'We'll find him,' Miller said.

149

Donald Goram, was sitting at the bar, drinking alone.

'Mr Goram?' Miller asked

Goram finished his drink, the ice cubes rattling around in the bottom of the glass. He looked at the barman. 'Another one of those, Vince.' He turned to look at the two detectives.

'Right first time, officers. You have the advantage.'

'DI Miller. This is DS Scott. Special Investigator Smith. We'd like to ask you a few questions about the occupant of room five oh two.'

Goram was slightly built, but looked like he could look after himself in a fight.

'Can I offer you a drink?'

'No. I'd like you to tell me what you know about Sunday night,' Miller said.

'What a nightmare. I don't know who he was.'

Miller wondered if he was lying, or whether he wasn't in on whatever went down.

'Why was he in one of the rooms on the floor that was being refurbished?' Scott asked.

Goram shrugged. 'I don't know. I've never seen him before.'

'How well do you know your staff?'

Goram took another drink. 'We don't hang out socially, if that's what you mean.'

'How long have the workmen been here doing the refurbishment?'

'A few weeks. The speed they work at, Scotland will have won the next World Cup the time they're finished.'

'One more thing; I don't want anybody coming into this hotel until we give the all clear. We'll have uniformed officers posted at the front door.'

Goram groaned. 'This isn't exactly going to drum up business.'

They left the bar, and caught up with Kim. 'Did you get anything from Melinda?'

Kim shook her head. 'Nothing more than her original statement. It would seem the only dodgy one here is Goram.'

'Do you think he could have done it?' Miller asked Scott.

'Fleming was quite a big guy, and I think he would have knocked Goram out.'

'I wonder if he went there to hook up with a woman,' Kim said.

'I get the feeling it's a little bit more complicated than that,' Miller said.

'If he was lying on the bed and promised sex, it wouldn't be hard to slit his throat,' Kim said. 'Especially if he was handcuffed.'

'They didn't find handcuffs, though,' Scott said.

'That's how I would have done it.'

Scott looked at her. 'I wouldn't be taken in like that.'

'Everybody's got to sleep, Tam,' Miller said.

FORTY-ONE

Miller was feeling hungry, but food was the least of his worries. 'What did you think of Goram?' he asked, as they got back in the car.

'I've seen his type plenty of times,' Scott said.

'Bloody weasel,' Kim agreed.

Miller cranked the engine over. It seemed colder in the car than it did outside.

Kim was sitting in the front, pulling her collar together to try and keep some heat in.

Miller was about to put the car into gear when his mobile phone rang. 'Hello?'

'Detective Miller?'

'That's me.'

'This is control, sir. I thought you'd like to know about a call we just received. The city pathologist, Julie Davidson, was attacked on her doorstep.'

Miller's heart froze solid. He couldn't breathe for a second. Couldn't find the right words to say. Like trying to run in waist-deep water. 'Where's she now?'

'At home. A taxi was coming past her house, so her attacker ran off. She got back in her house and locked the door. Then she called us.'

'Get more than one patrol car down there. Give it everything you've got. ARU if there's one in the area. If that guy comes back, he might kill her. I'm on my way.'

'I'll get onto that right now, sir.'

Miller hung up. Looked round at Scott. 'Julie's been attacked. In her house.' His face was deathly pale.

Scott opened the door. 'Get out, Frank. Let me drive.'

'I'm fine.'

'Let him drive, Frank,' Kim said.

Scott had the front door open. 'Out. Let me in.'

Miller got in the back.

'Where does she live?'

'Literally round the corner. Orchard Brae Avenue.'

The car slid, as Scott gunned the engine. Took a right at the end of the street. Right onto Queensferry Road. Right at the lights then first left, behind an office block. The roads were slick with snow, but Scott kept control of the car. He raced down the road. 'Which house?'

Miller pointed to a townhouse on their left, with a light on above the door. They heard the sirens coming in fast.

Miller got to the door. An ARU pulled into the street, and shot down to them, its blues and twos going.

Julie opened the door. 'Oh, Frank. Thank God you're here.' She had blood running down her face from her nose, and her hair looked like it hadn't been brushed for a week.

'What happened, Julie?' He put his hands on her shoulders as the two ARU officers climbed out of the car. Locked and loaded. They weren't fucking about. Miller recognised one. They all went inside and closed the door behind them. The laundry room and the garage door were off the hallway. Upstairs was the living room. They walked up.

'Did you see which way your attacker went, ma'am?' one of the armed officers asked.

153

She shook her head. 'No. A taxi came into the street and he ran away.'

'What was he wearing?'

'Dark jeans. A dark hoodie, and a black ski mask. He was carrying a knife.'

The man got on his radio to his partner who was still outside the car and relayed the description. Then to control. Another patrol car came racing down the road. He looked out the window.

'My partner's going to have a quick look round,' he said, as the other two officers got out of the car. Still another siren split the air. 'That'll be the ambulance,' Miller said. Two uniforms came upstairs as another patrol car entered the street.

Julie said she felt dizzy and sat down on the settee. Kim went through to the kitchen and soaked a tea towel and brought it through. Applied it to Julie's nose.

The paramedics came in. A man and a woman. Started attending to her, asking the usual questions to see if she showed any signs of concussion.

Miller stood back, to let them work, and turned to Kim. 'Make a call for me, Kim, please. More uniforms for a door-to-door, then have the team track down the taxi driver. He or she might have seen something.'

'I'll get on it.' She left the living room, and went through to the kitchen.

'You're safe now, Julie,' Miller said.

'I know,' she said, her voice thick as if she had a head cold.

'Did he say anything to you?' Scott said.

'No, but I'm worried. My sister was killed, my dad was murdered, and now Colin Fleming and his wife were murdered too. Maybe this guy wanted to murder me. I'm not sure of anything anymore.'

Her nose was badly swollen.

'Don't worry, we're here now. You're going to the hospital. You need to get your face looked at.'

'You have a way with the women, Frank, did anybody ever tell you that?' Then she passed out.

The paramedics worked on her, bringing her back round.

'Gilmour, Watt and Hazel are on their way, Frank,' Kim said. 'Half the station too.'

Miller nodded, stepping out of the way of the second paramedic as they brought Julie back round.

Miller turned, as the room was filled with more radio chatter. A uniformed sergeant came in with two constables. 'Good to see you, Eric. I need your boys to do a door-to-door, see if anybody saw the guy who attacked Julie on her doorstep.'

'I'll get onto it right away, sir,' the sergeant said. 'I'll get more bodies down here. We've got patrol cars blocking the exits round here, but to be honest, if he was driving he's probably well away by now, but we'll do what we can.'

'Thanks.' He watched as the sergeant took the uniforms back outside.

The second paramedic came over to Miller 'We're taking her to the ERI. I don't think her nose is broken, but the doctor will determine that. Looks like a nasty hit though.'

'Thanks. I'll ride with you. Tam, could you bring the car up to the Royal? I need Gilmour and Watt to help with the canvassing and to get onto the cab companies.'

'Sure, I'll help out, then I'll meet you at the hospital.'

'I'll stay here as well,' Kim said. 'I'll catch up with you later.'

Miller thought she might be packing her gun. Just the way her hand went to her side in a reflex movement. He nodded and left.

FORTY-TWO

Michael Molloy jumped up from the big leather chair in his office and pointed at the monitor over to his left. One of his men stood in front of his desk.

'What's Goram doing sitting down there? I told him to sit tight until I called for him.' He gritted his teeth

The big man looking at him was an ex-heavyweight boxer called Greg Sampson. The man couldn't spell his own name, but he could put somebody's lights out without breaking sweat.

Michael waited for an answer.

'What's Donald Goram doing in my club, Greg?' he shouted.

Sampson looked confused. 'I'm sorry, sir. I *thought* he wasn't supposed to come here tonight. He said he wanted to speak to you. He told me he always had free drink when he came here.'

'Did he now? My father would be extremely pissed off to hear you let Goram in here. Goram was to come round here and come in the back door. This is the kind of shite that will put us all in prison, and when I say us, I mean you. It won't be me getting fucked in the showers, Greg. Now get downstairs and get him down to the basement before anybody sees him. Do I need to do everything around here?'

Sampson was already picturing pulling Goram's arms out of their sockets. 'Apologise to your father for me, sir.'

'There'll be no need to involve my father in this,' Michael said. He was more worried about what his father would think of *him*, rather than what he would think of Sampson. Besides, his father was fannying about on that boat of his. *An oasis of calm in a sea of stress*, he'd said. Load of pish. He wouldn't have to know about this.

'Move man! All we need is the filth coming in and seeing that dozy bastard sitting there drinking and we'll all look like a bunch of arses. Now move!'

Sampson turned and ran from the room. For a big man, he moved deftly on his feet. Michael could almost hear Goram's fingers snapping. He unlocked a desk drawer and took out the Glock 24 that sat in there.

Things were getting out of control now and Raymond Cross was slowly getting the upper hand. He'd never trusted Cross in the first place, but all those years ago, his father had said he was a good man. Useful. His father had been wrong, and now they were paying the price.

Michael Molloy left his office and walked quickly down the stairs. Two of the coppers who'd arrested Cross – Colin Fleming and Harry Davidson – were now dead, murdered in the same way Cross's girlfriend had been. And now one of Molloy's staff had also been killed the same way. He wasn't going to take the risk anymore.

He carried on down to the private suite.

The place where nobody would hear a gunshot.

FORTY-THREE

The new Royal Infirmary was based at Little France on the south side of Edinburgh. A brand new building had replaced the old, out of date hospital, which had been converted into flats. Julie had been taken right through to the receiving area where doctors and nurses attended to her. He'd been asked to leave and had gone into the waiting area where he walked over to the vending machine.

Scott turned up a little while later. 'The house is secure,' he said. 'I've got a patrol car going by at intervals, but I'm sure whoever was behind it's long gone by now. I don't think he'll be back. Kim's there waiting anyway, and I think she has her nine mil friend with her.'

'She can certainly look after herself,' Miller said, feeding some coins into the coffee machine. He paid for two cups of coffee. 'Don't say I never put my hand in my pocket,' he said, handing one to Scott.

'Are you having the same feeling I'm having about this attack, boss?' Scott asked.

Miller nodded. 'Yeah. It's too much of a coincidence to be anything else. Just don't voice that opinion to Julie.'

A nurse came over to them. 'Miss Davidson would like to see you now.' She led them through to the treatment area, pulled a curtain back, and Miller saw Julie sitting up on the examination bed. She had a bandage over her nose, and was wearing a hospital gown.

'Why I needed to strip for a bruised nose is beyond me,' she said, trying to laugh but only groaning in pain instead.

The doctor appeared, a young man who looked like he'd just left school. 'Are you family?' he asked.

'I'm DI Miller. DS Scott. We're investigating this assault. We're also friends of Miss Davidson.'

The doctor all but shrugged. 'Miss Davidson's nose isn't broken. We've cleaned it up, but it's going to hurt in the morning.' He looked at Julie. 'Take some time off work, doctor. You might get dizzy spells, but take the painkillers and follow up with your own GP.' He addressed Miller. 'She can go after they bring her the painkillers from the pharmacy.' He turned and walked away.

'Let me get dressed and you can take me home, Frank.' Julie pulled the gown tighter round her as Scott passed her clothes to her.

'You can stay with me, Julie,' Miller said. 'I don't want you staying on your own.'

'Thanks, Frank, but I wouldn't hear of it.'

'How about if I stay with you, instead? Just for tonight. Make sure you're okay.'

'I'm fine, Frank, honestly. I just got a fright, that's all,' Julie replied, but there was relief in her voice.

'You know we're here for you, Julie.'

Julie smiled. 'Thank you.' Tears filled her eyes. 'Look at all the trouble I'm causing. I'm so sorry.'

Miller walked over to her. Put his arm round her shoulder. Scott left, and pulled the curtain closed behind him. Waited outside.

'You've nothing to be sorry for, Julie. You're family, and you know I'd do anything for you.' He wiped a tear from her cheek. Kissed her on the forehead. 'I nearly crapped myself when control called me.'

She sniffed, and looked at him. 'Really?' A weak smile now.

'Really. What with everything that's going on.'

'Did you think Raymond Cross would come after *me*?'

'I don't think this was Cross. I think it was a random attack. Probably somebody trying to get into a house to rob it. Don't worry, he won't be back. He'll move on to an easier target.'

The nurse came in with a plastic bottle containing painkillers. 'If you want to wait in the waiting room, I'll come and get you when she's ready to leave,' she said, to Miller.

'We won't be far away, Julie.'

'We need to find this bastard, Frank,' Scott said, as Frank joined him.

'I know. I think Julie's on his hit list. The question is, will he try to kill her again?'

'We also have something else to think about,' Scott said. 'Will he try and kill *you* again?'

FORTY-FOUR

The private suite in the basement was exclusive. Nothing more than a large room that was once a coin sorting room back when the building was a bank, it had been converted to entertain special guests. A few couches were scattered around, just the right size for a man to get cosy with one of the girls Michael employed. It was painted in dark shades, with mirrors on the walls, and coloured lights ready to set the mood. They weren't on right now, just some subdued lighting.

'It's a bit quiet, isn't it?' Donald Goram said to Sampson.

'Not for long. Please sit down, sir.' Goram sat down on a couch.

'Now, why have I been invited down here again? Employee of the month, was it?'

Sampson stood and watched him, not answering the question. Walked round the back of the couch. Goram's smile disappeared as he felt the rope going round his neck. He tried to grab it, and thrashed on the couch as the rope was pulled tighter. Michael Molloy came in, and strode over to Goram and pointed the gun at his face.

'You stupid bastard! I told you not to come here until you were called for. What are you playing at?' He was screaming now, feeling himself lose control, but unable to do anything about it.

'The cops came round asking questions. I thought you should know.'

Sampson had a tight grip on the rope and pulled Goram down to the floor. He was feeling revved up, and the chance to get back at Goram made him happy. 'You should've listened to Mr Molloy more closely, Donald,' he said.

Goram looked at him. 'You're dead, you know that? I'll see you get what's coming to you.'

Both men ignored him. 'Where's my money?' Michael said. 'You and that useless fucker Fleming said you'd get Cross no problem, yet he gets himself topped, and you're running about with your finger up your arse while Raymond Cross walked out of there unnoticed, with a bagful of our hard-earned.'

'I told you what happened. The room was being watched, Fleming had the money, and everything was going according to plan. Except Cross didn't show.'

'Well I think he did! He cut Fleming wide open, didn't he? Or did you do the job and stash the money for yourself?'

'You know I wouldn't do that.' Sweat was rolling off Goram's head, but his hands were too busy holding onto the rope round his neck to worry about wiping it away.

Michael looked at him. 'Let him go, Greg.'

Goram rubbed his neck. 'That's better. Now we can talk about this like real men.'

Michael shot him in the head. Tried to slow his own breathing. 'Make the phone call, Greg. Have him disposed of and get this place cleaned up.'

He walked out of the basement feeling better than he had in days.

FORTY-FIVE

Julie walked into her living room, feeling the pain starting to come back. She'd changed into pyjamas and a dressing gown. 'Thanks for coming in with me, but there was no need.'

'Don't be daft. Just make sure your alarm's on,' Miller said.

'I will.'

Scott was in the kitchen making tea, while Kim was going around the house, checking it one last time.

Miller looked out the living room window at the snow, which was starting to fall heavily again. There were still patrol cars in the street, and he could see uniforms walking about, finishing the door-to-door.

He called Jimmy Gilmour for an update. 'How are things looking, Jimmy?'

'I got hold of the cab company whose driver was down here. He doesn't remember seeing anybody, but his fare was drunk and he was trying to get the address out of him, so he wasn't paying attention.'

Miller could hear the noise from the traffic outside. The escape of compressed air as a bus driver applied his parking brake. A car driving by on the slushy road. A mini ice-age they were calling it, wintertime bringing a ton of snow with it every year.

'Anything from the door-to-door?'

'Nothing.'

'Okay, keep at it, Jimmy. I want that bastard nailed.'

'We're on it, boss.'

He hung up, and then the phone rang. 'Miller.'

'Frank! It's Jack.'

'What's up, Jack?'

'I heard about Julie,' Jack said. 'Any news about catching the bastard yet?'

'Nothing yet. She's pretty shaken up and she's got a sore nose and cheek, but nothing broken.'

'You know Julie can stay with us anytime.'

'I told her that, but she won't hear of it.'

'Hopefully it was a random attack.'

'You and I both know this wasn't random.' Miller lowered his voice. 'Raymond Cross is going to come back.'

'Raymond Cross? Why would he attack Julie?'

'We don't know. Maybe because she's Harry's daughter? Maybe because he's not right in the head.'

'Stay alert.'

'I will. You too.'

'Don't worry about me, son. If Cross comes here, he'll get his balls booted over the back of his fucking head.' He hung up.

'I'm going to bed. I feel tired. It's the effect of those co-dydramol pills.' She looked at him. 'Thanks for being here for me, Frank.'

'You don't have to thank me, Julie. You were there for me when Carol died.'

'That's what family's for.' She took the bottle of painkillers out of the gown pocket and popped two of them. 'You know, I bought this townhouse thinking I'd be safe. A neighbour on either side. It made me feel... cosy. You know what I mean? Now I don't feel safe at all.'

'I know what you mean. If you don't feel safe in your own home, where can you feel safe?' Miller hated the sound of those words. Regretted saying them.

'Julie, I have a quick question before you go to bed.'

'Sure. Ask me anything.'

'Why were you at the hotel with Harry the night Moira Kennedy died?'

Julie looked at him. 'I was there with a bunch of other students. One of them knew Moira Kennedy and we got an invite. I was so scared when Moira was murdered. My dad turned up and I thought he'd go mental. He was horrified, but told me to give a statement and then leave. Not to talk to anyone about it. He was one of the lead detectives, and it mightn't go well for his career if his daughter was there, so I didn't speak about it after that.'

'Did anybody see you?'

'Colin Fleming let on. He knew I was a student. And your father of course, but to be honest, when I saw Moira, I was sick in my dad's car. I almost gave up medicine after that.'

Miller nodded. 'Okay. I just wondered why you never mentioned it before, that's all.'

'Who told you I was there?'

'Andrea Kennedy. I was talking to her and she happened to mention it. I was just curious about it, but I can see why you didn't say anything.'

She smiled at him. 'Thanks for caring, Frank.'

'We'll be off. Call me if you need me.'

'I'll see you in the morning.' She kissed Miller on the cheek.

He, Scott and Kim left, and Miller dropped Kim off first, since she lived closest in Stockbridge, then Tam, who lived over on Southside.

Back at his own place, Miller was dismayed to find once again, Jack had gone out gallivanting. Charlie, his cat, came up and sat on his lap, shedding hair onto his trousers. He put the TV on, but couldn't concentrate. Then his mobile phone rang. It was Ian Powers.

'I've got that information you asked for,' he said, sounding pleased with himself.

'Thanks, Ian. I appreciate you getting back to me so quickly.'

'Not a problem. Let me see now...' He heard Powers rustling some papers. 'Lamb's House. It was built in the fifteen century.'

'Ian, let me stop you there, my friend. I've had a hoor of a night, and I'm kind of feeling knackered.'

Powers stopped himself. 'Okay, okay. Lamb's House. Owned by the National Trust for Scotland, they leased it out to Leith Old People's Society, who used it as a home for the elderly. Then the National Trust sold it. It had been sitting empty for a few years. The National Trust sold it to Richard Sullivan.'

'I know all this, Ian.'

'I thought you might, but you know what a nosy bastard I am when I get going. So I played around with the council's servers a bit, and was looking at people who'd worked there when it was an old folks' home. Nothing jumped out at me, but a patient's name did; Harry Davidson's mother was a patient there. She died in eighty-four. Probably doesn't mean anything, but it was the connection that got me.'

'Thanks, Ian.'

Miller hung up, the tiredness hitting him. He was getting old before his time.

Harry Davidson's mother was a patient in Lamb's House thirty years ago. His daughter's wallet is found there after she's murdered. She was killed by the car belonging to the new owner of Lamb's House. Doreen Myers, one of the victims from two years ago, found dead on the construction site of a new casino Sullivan was a partner in.

Once again, Richard Sullivan's name had popped up.

He grabbed a sandwich, and watched some meaningless TV. The cat lay beside him on the couch, purring as Miller petted him. He thought of Charlie as being a part of Carol as she'd picked him out, and he prayed the little animal had a long life still. He showered and went to bed.

Thought about Carol, and slipped into the abyss.

FORTY-SIX

Wednesday

Andrea Kennedy couldn't believe how cold it was. What the hell was going on? It was dark in here, and colder than any place she had ever been in.

And darker.

She couldn't see a thing in front of her, and for a moment, she thought she had gone blind. Where the hell was she? And how had she gotten here?

Her head felt like it had exploded.

She heard a click, and then blinding light from a flashlight hit her eyes. She tried to lift a hand to shield her eyes but couldn't move her arms.

'Who... who's there?' she asked.

No answer at first, then she heard what sounded like feet on the ground, a low shuffling sound, barely perceptible.

'Hello, Andrea,' a voice answered. It was muffled.

'Who are you? What am I doing here?' Fear shot through her,

freezing her bones. She couldn't think what had happened to her. Snippets of her evening flashed in her mind; she'd gone to a bar with some of her friends. The usual happy hour brigade were there, office workers grabbing a couple before heading home. She didn't remember the name of the pub, but she thought it was their usual one. Near the office. More and more people had come in, and they were packed in like sardines. She was having a laugh with her friends, then... nothing. She couldn't remember going home. *That's because you didn't make it that far.*

She was lying on a table, but it felt cold. It was high up because her arms were hanging over each side, but something was tied to each one, weighing them down. Her legs were straight out, and they were tied together. Something pulled at them, like they too were tied to something heavy.

'You don't know me, but I know you.'

Her mind was becoming clearer. She guessed she'd been drugged. She didn't know what time it was, but it wouldn't matter; this room was pitch black, the flashlight helping to blind her. Had she been raped? She didn't think so. She would have known if she had. So what did this guy want? Maybe he was going to wake her up first before touching her. Watch the terror in her eyes as he defiled her.

'My husband will kill you, whoever you are,' she said, her voice sounding thick, as if she had a cold. She began shivering even more, seeing her breath mist in the light.

Laughter. 'Oh yes, Michael. He's not your husband now though, is he?'

Maybe this was somebody getting back at Michael, teaching him a lesson through her. 'If it's money you want, I'm sure that can be arranged. How much do you want?'

A gloved hand grabbed her face and squeezed. 'It's not about money.' The hand retreated as quickly as it had appeared.

'Then what's all this about?' It suddenly hit her. She knew what this man wanted: death. Was this the same man who'd killed Jennifer Wilson? The thought made her shake even more.

Silence. Just the sound of her rapid breathing. Then the light died, leaving stars flashing in front of her. She closed her eyes, and the afterburn glowed brightly.

'Did you kill Jen and the others? Is this about Moira's death?' *Are you the man they caught? Didn't you fucking die?*

'Enough with the questions.'

'You can't bring me here and not talk to me. Is that you, Raymond? You know we can talk. You know I'm your friend. Michael told me they're looking for you, but I don't believe you came back after all these years to harm us.' That was *exactly* what she believed. Maybe he'd been put in a mental hospital somewhere far away and managed to get out somehow.

'It's time for us to go.'

'Go where?'

'You'll see.'

'What time is it?'

'Never mind what the time is.'

'Is it morning? Have I been here all night?'

'Of course you have. Now get up.'

'I can't. You've tied me up.'

'Your muscles are just stiff with the cold, that's all.'

Andrea heard his feet scrabble about on the ground. She tried to move her arms, found she could. Slowly, so very slowly. Her right shoulder felt as if it was tearing in two, and she let it flop back. She realised she was still wearing her overcoat, but it was open and hanging down the sides, adding weight to her arms.

Make small movements, Andrea. Get the blood into the arms, then you'll be able to get up. Small movements, starting off by flexing her fingers, then moving her wrists round in small circles, then gradually bending her arm.

'You didn't answer my question,' she said into the darkness, feeling she was getting somewhere with Cross. Finally, she was able to bend her arms and she started on her legs. Flexing slowly, then bending each one in turn. Cross didn't answer her question.

'You can talk to me, Raymond. You know that, don't you?' Maybe if she could connect to him on a different level, she could persuade him to let her go. She sat up, taking her time, every muscle in her body on fire.

There was a dull glow coming from somewhere else in the room. She blinked her eyes a few times, trying to adjust to the dark. Finally, the pitch black became darkness, like a bedroom might look in the middle of the night. She looked down at the ground; it was only a few feet away. She slipped off the table and turned to look at it; it was a sarcophagus. Ornately carved round the side, it looked like it was made of marble.

The walls were made up of crypts where people had been interred in their coffins, but by the musty smell, a long time ago. It wasn't the cold making Andrea shiver now; it was the thought of being in this place.

Raymond Cross wasn't in the room anymore. He'd shone the flashlight into her eyes to blind her momentarily, and now her eyes were adjusting to the dark by the second. She realised it wasn't pitch black.

She walked towards the glow, which seemed to be round a corner. She crept slowly towards it, and carefully looked round. It was a short hallway leading up to an iron gate. A flaming torch burned in a holder on one wall.

Andrea walked towards the gate, careful not to make too much noise. She was glad she was wearing the sensible flats she wore to work rather than high heels. She pulled her overcoat tighter as she walked through the entryway. More oil torches lit the corridor outside. She looked from left to right. Realised she was at the end of the passageway, this gate being next to a stone wall. She turned left. More gates lined the walls on either side.

What was this place? *Where* was this place? Only a few torches illuminated the corridor, and after that, it was complete darkness. She didn't know which way to turn to get out of here. Why was he doing this? And where did he go? Over to the right, another gate was open.

She could see another light on in there. Is the exit through here? Should she go in? *What choice do you have?*

Andrea walked past the other gate, careful not to let the rust get on her coat. It wasn't an exit. This place was like the other one she'd just left. She knew what these places were called, but the word just wouldn't come to her. Some burial place. *Crypt.* Yes, that was it.

'Raymond? Can we talk?' Her voice sounded tinny. No answer. She walked into the other room, expecting him to be there, to want to talk to her, to tell her this was all a mistake. They could go home now.

Raymond wasn't in the room. She wanted to turn and run, but her legs were like lead.

'This is what it's all about,' she heard Raymond say, behind her.

She turned round to look at him, just as the axe swung down and hit her in the neck, severing her carotid.

FORTY-SEVEN

Miller woke up feeling tired. He'd tossed and turned all night thinking of Carol. It would have been his wife's birthday today. Twenty-eight, if she'd lived.

After showering and dressing, he called Julie.

'I'm fine, Frank. Thanks for calling. Those painkillers knocked me out. I'm standing at the living room window right now and there's a police car sitting downstairs. Oh, one of them's looking up. Hold on while I wave.' Silence for a few seconds. 'I'm just out of the shower, but I'm going to put the kettle on for those two guys down there. I know they haven't been there all night but I appreciate them coming round anyway.'

'Okay, call me if you need me.'

'Will do. Bye.'

Miller hung up, and fixed his own breakfast. Coffee and cereal. Jack was still out, and Miller pondered on how the power struggle he'd had with his father as a teenager had shifted, with Miller being the one who worried now. Wasn't that the way, though? The elderly became as dependent as small children, relying on their own family to look after them.

He made his way up to the station via Starbucks, walking through the accumulated snow, thinking how nice it would be to be in Tenerife right now.

Hazel Carter sat at her desk, her fingers hammering over her keyboard. Andy Watt was looking at the drinks machine, as if willing decent coffee to magically appear.

'Not going to happen,' Miller said. He saw Kim sitting at a computer and handed her a cup of coffee from Starbucks.

'Thanks, Frank.' She took a sip of the coffee.

'Aw here, where's our freshly brewed coffee?' Watt said.

'I need you focused, today, Andy. Caffeine always seems to make you mental.'

'I'm sure you just broke some employment rules there.' He popped some coins into the machine. 'I'll make this decaf then, boss. Decaf always makes me work harder. Said nobody, ever.'

Gary Davidson was sitting in a chair on the other side of the room, gently swinging it from side to side, holding a pencil between both hands, twirling it with his fingers. He got up when he saw Miller come in.

'Hi, Frank. Can I have a word?'

'Sure, Gary. I want to talk to you too. Want to go into my office?'

Davidson nodded. Miller closed the door behind them and sat behind his desk. Davidson remained standing.

'What's up, Gary?'

'I wish you'd told me about finding Carol's wallet.' He looked at his brother-in-law.

'Sorry, mate, I was going to but the way things went down, it slipped my mind.'

Davidson was agitated. 'I also heard Richard Sullivan's bought Lamb's House and that's where her wallet was found.' He pointed a finger at Miller. 'If I find out he touched my sister, I'll kill the bastard, Frank, you know that.'

'Gary, take it easy. We don't know anything about it. Nobody's

173

accusing Sullivan. Yes, it's a coincidence, but there's no proof. He bought Lamb's House a long time ago.'

Not for the first time, Miller wondered if Davidson was on something. Maybe hungover, or maybe he'd drunk too much coffee, whatever it was, he was like a caged tiger.

'Don't do anything stupid, Gary.'

'There's nothing stupid about protecting my sister.' He looked at Miller. 'So what did you want to say to me?'

'Did Julie call you?'

'No. Why?'

'She was attacked at home last night.'

'What? Is she alright?'

'Yes, she is. She's got a sore face, but she'll be okay.'

'Why didn't anybody tell me? Once again, I'm kept out of the loop. Julie's my sister.'

Miller took a deep breath. 'We think she was targeted, Gary. She's wondering if it might be Cross, but I don't want to upset her. We think it could be, but we're not sure.'

'Is somebody with her?'

'Yes, there's a patrol car outside her door.'

Davidson shook his head. Ran a hand through his hair. 'No, he'll just try when she's at work one day. Or at the supermarket, or any other place she goes.'

'She's safe, Gary. We've got her back.'

'Just like we had Carol's back?' Davidson walked out.

FORTY-EIGHT

Miller put his coat on, and made his way down to the car park at the rear. The sky was dark grey, and a chill wind was blowing. The snow was forecast to come back with a vengeance later in the day.

He stopped at a florist, buying a bunch of flowers, before carrying on to Warriston cemetery. Miller turned the car left. There was an extension off the newer part of the graveyard. It was like they were running out of space and had decided to just clear some weeds away and stick a fence round it. At one time, it had only been waste ground that bordered this part of the cemetery, but now in the distance, he could see detached houses. He wondered how the selling agents had described the view to prospective buyers; *quiet neighbours,* maybe.

He left the car on the track, leaving the warmth of the interior for the freezing cold wind. The sun was out, but was obviously there for illustration purposes only.

He walked down the path to his friend's gravestone. A black marble affair with gold lettering. He was getting closer. A large monolith was in front of it. He read the inscription, wondering about the people who were buried there.

He stepped off the path, past the monolith, and approached Carol's gravestone. It wasn't far from Harry's.

Something was wrong. Footprints were in the snow in front of the grave. He looked at the inscription on the stone: the name, the date of her birth, the date of her death. This was the only thing that marked her existence. He felt a deep longing inside; words left unsaid, and good times remembered, never to be recreated.

He laid the flowers down at the headstone. 'Happy Birthday, my darling. I miss you every day. We had some good times though, didn't we? More than some people get to have in a lifetime.'

He looked at his wife's name again, then walked over to Harry's gravestone. The footprints were here too. All the snow around was untouched, except a trail led between the two gravestones.

Somebody had been here already.

As he reached into his pocket for his mobile phone, he sensed rather than heard the presence behind him. Then the gun touched the back of his head.

'Hello, Frank,' the voice said. 'I'm back.'

FORTY-NINE

Miller felt the gun barrel move away from his head.

'Turn around,' the voice commanded.

Miller turned round slowly, expecting to be shot in the head.

'What's wrong, Frank? You look like you've seen a ghost.'

Miller glared when he saw who it was.

Neil McGovern.

The gun he was holding was a Sig Sauer 9mm automatic. Pointed right at Miller's heart.

McGovern smiled. 'Aren't you going to ask how, Frank?'

Miller looked at McGovern; the man looked different from when he'd last seen him nine weeks ago. Just after he'd killed Harry David-son. Now he had blond hair, sticking out of the black woollen hat, and he was wearing fashionable, black-rimmed glasses

'So, your department faked your death for you after all. Kim told me that had been the plan, but then you "died".' His mind was spinning, and he kept asking the same question over and over; was this Neil McGovern? Yes it was. His instinct had been right all along; McGovern didn't die in that hospital. 'It's the small details that get you in the end, McGovern.'

'Care to elaborate?'

'Your daughter was put into the hospital as the duty doctor, but she wasn't on duty when you supposedly died. Your body's away in some funeral parlour in Airdrie, or wherever. Kim hasn't even seen your body yet. I'm a detective. I get suspicious about things, and after a while, you get a feel for things. This didn't add up. The warden at the hospital told me you'd been cremated. I had a feeling he was lying to me, and now you've proved me right.'

'I knew you'd work it out, Frank. That's why I was pleased when you went to the hospital asking questions.'

'Your daughter's working with me.' Miller was still shivering. It's just the adrenaline rush, he told himself.

'I know she is. And you'd better be keeping an eye on her. Although I have a couple of my men watching her round the clock.'

'Why don't you tell Kim you're still alive?'

'She has to believe I'm dead. Everybody has to believe I'm dead. That way, that fucker Cross will keep away from my family, and maybe we can catch him.'

'Do you know where he is?'

McGovern shook his head. 'Do you think I'd be standing here talking to you if I did?'

Miller looked around him, at the snow-covered gravestones, and wondered if McGovern's associates were watching him now. 'How did you know I'd be here?'

'It's Carol's birthday. I figured you'd come here so we followed you. I wanted somewhere quiet where we could talk.' He put the gun away.

Miller relaxed a little now the immediate threat was removed. 'Kim told me what happened that night with Harry. How Cross came into the crypts when she was with you.'

McGovern looked at him. 'I thought he was going to kill me that night. By the time I get him, he'll wish he had.'

'It would have made the perfect cover for him, apart from the fact we would have known it wasn't you if you'd died and the killings kept on going. Not bright, is he?'

'No, he's not. But I believe killing me would have bought him some time and that's all he wanted.'

'What was it Harry wanted to tell you that night?'

'He was going to tell me who'd killed the three women two years ago. He found out, but he didn't tell me before we were attacked.'

'That doesn't make sense. How would he suddenly find out?'

'I didn't find that out.'

'What did Harry actually say to you the night he died?' Miller asked.

'He was dying when I got into the crypt. He managed to whisper *Raymond Cross*. He also said you were in danger. That's all he managed to say before I was attacked.'

Miller looked around him. 'What if Cross is here now? Can you be sure you could shoot him?'

'No need. Show him.'

Miller heard a twang, like a large elastic band snapping, and a little puff of snow exploded to his right.

'I have one of my men behind you. They're used to creeping up behind people with silenced guns. They'd take Cross out with a head shot before he even got near me.'

'Unless he's got your face in the crosshairs.'

'Not his style, Frank.'

'How do you know?' he asked, but then he heard the roaring of a V8 and a black Range Rover came storming over the snowy road as if it was floating, before coming to a halt. The windows were blacked out.

'I'll be in touch,' McGovern said. 'Let me tell you though; this meeting has to be kept from Kim. I don't want her in the firing line. It's bad enough she's working for Norma.' He turned and walked to the car. Turned round. 'Concentrate on why Harry thought Raymond Cross is the killer you were hunting. Why he killed those three women two years ago. Now you know I'm still alive, don't go

179

wasting your time looking for me.' He climbed in and Miller watched as the window slid down. 'Between the two of us, we'll take the bastard down.'

Miller watched the car turn on the snow-covered grass, disturbing the dead below, and then it was roaring out of the cemetery. He turned to where the gunman would have been. There was nobody there. A few seconds later, he heard another of the car's doors slam, and then the Range Rover was gone. *The sniper getting in.* These guys were good.

Miller walked back to his car, his boots crunching the snow. Wondered what Kim would say if she knew her father was alive after all.

Then his phone rang.

FIFTY

Tam Scott was waiting for Miller in reception. His call had been short and to the point. *There's been another one boss. The office in Fountainbridge.*

'This is getting worse,' Scott said, when Miller came in.

'Do we know who it is?'

'Andrea Kennedy.'

'What?' Miller was surprised. He rubbed a hand over his face. 'Is this connected with the others?' They stepped into a lift being held open by a uniform.

'There's no doubt. See for yourself.'

They made their way up to the third level where it had been cordoned off.

'Who found her?' Miller asked.

'Older guy from the mailroom. She's in a huge walk-in stationery closet.'

'Does he look good for it?'

'I wouldn't think so. He's an old bloke who works in the first-floor mailroom.'

'Run him through everything we've got,' Miller said.

'We started already. Nothing so far. He's as clean as a whistle. Not even a parking ticket.'

'Where's Kim?'

'She's interviewing the security guard with Watt.'

Miller walked over to the closet door where more uniforms and the duty doctor, Malcolm Shields, were congregated. Jimmy Gilmour was standing with Hazel Carter.

'Morning, everybody,' Shields said.

'Morning, doc. Where is she?'

'In here, Frank.' The older man looked at Miller. 'I can't wait to retire now, believe me.'

'You okay?'

'It never fails to amaze me what some people can do to others.' The old doctor led them into the room, muttering away to himself.

They walked into the closet, which was huge. His eyes were drawn to the female sitting slumped back in an office chair, her front opened up, just like Colin Fleming had been.

'I pronounce her life extinct,' the doctor said. 'Dagger's on his way over from the mortuary, and I'm on the way to the golf club. I need a stiff gin.' With that, he promptly picked up his black bag and left.

'Thanks, doc.' Miller looked closer at the dead woman's face. 'Why would he have picked her out?' Yet, he knew the answer; Andrea had been there that night, twenty-five years ago.

Just then, Jake Dagger walked in. 'This is getting like a boys' club. How's things, Frank?'

'Not happy about this, that's for sure.'

Dagger did a prelim exam. Stood up, after looking at the head. 'She wasn't killed here. It looks like the neck wound killed her and she bled out before being brought here. You should check the security tapes.'

'We did, and they've been destroyed,' said Hazel.

'I wonder if she has any connection to the Flemings?' Dagger said.

'Andrea Kennedy was married to Michael Molloy. Jennifer worked for them and so did Fleming. Whichever way we look at it, this has something to do with the Molloys. Cross hates them so much, he's prepared to kill them all,' Miller said.

'What's the purpose of it all? Revenge? It's unusual for somebody to wait this length of time.'

'I've never heard of somebody waiting this long. Unless he was in prison,' Scott said.

'I don't think so, Tam. He was still a wanted man. That never went away. They would have run his fingerprints and we'd have found out.'

'True. So what made him crack, then?'

'That, my friend, is what I'm going to ask him when I get hold of him.'

FIFTY-ONE

Robert Molloy sat at his desk on the Blue Martini going through paperwork. Sean would have taken to this stuff like a duck to water. His dead son was always a dab hand at being a businessman. They probably would have had a lot more legit businesses by now, but with Michael as his partner, it was lucky they weren't down the toilet.

Tai Lopez came in with a coffee. 'Can I get you anything to go with that, Mr Molloy?' she said, smiling at him.

Molloy felt the hairs on the back of his neck stand on end for just a moment. He smiled back at her. 'I'm fine, Tai. Thank you.'

She kept her smile in place as she left the room. Molloy looked at the door as if expecting the young woman to come running back in with a knife, but it stayed closed. He shook his head, and looked at the paperwork again, but it was all a mess. He'd have his accountant or somebody look at it. It was all bills, not something he'd normally deal with but today was always a bad day for him.

Thinking about Sean made him think about Carol Miller. It would have been her birthday, and instead of celebrating it, she was lying in the ground. He felt frustrated and angry, knowing whoever was responsible for her death was still out there.

Molloy felt himself getting emotional and swept the papers off the desk. The coffee cup went crashing onto the wooden floor and the door burst open. Tai rushed in. She looked around and only saw Molloy sitting at his desk, no threat anywhere to be seen.

'Are you okay, sir?' she asked.

'I'm fine, Tai. Just frustrated, that's all. Go back to your office.'

'I can have somebody clean that up.'

'Leave it. I'm not in the mood. Just leave.'

She left and closed the door behind her.

Molloy wondered how long Sienna was going to be. One of Molloy's men had been working on updating their database when he noticed somebody had hacked into their system. Fortunately, Molloy could afford the best protection, not only for himself, but for his computer system. The last thing he needed was somebody finding something they shouldn't and holding a gun to his head.

Molloy's mobile rang, the vibration mode making it dance round on his desk as if it was alive. He snatched it up. 'What?'

'We have him. You need to come now.'

'Don't do anything 'til I get there.'

Molloy picked up his desk phone. 'Tai, I need to see you again.' He hung up and watched the snow gently falling outside, landing on the dark river, where each flake died a sudden death. The Water of Leith sounded romantic until you looked at it, and when you saw the detritus floating by, it no longer looked or sounded romantic.

A few minutes later, Tai came back into the office.

'Is Sienna back yet?'

'No, sir.'

'Get the car. We're going to George Street. You're driving.'

Tai Lopez smiled at him, and Molloy had a brief *You're no longer in Kansas, Dorothy* feeling. Maybe he'd get Sienna to have a private word with her, but then again, which one of them did he trust the most?

FIFTY-TWO

Andy Watt was sitting on one of the chairs opposite the security guard. Kim was in the other chair, talking to the man.

'What's your name again?' she asked, as Miller and Scott came into the room.

'Clark Paterson,' the guard replied. He was a rotund man, who looked like he took an extra big breath when he was getting his uniform on, to suck his gut in. His hair had receded a long time ago. There was a thin sheen of sweat above his lip and he smelled of cheap Christmas cologne. 'I didn't do anything. I didn't touch her.'

'I'm DI Miller. This is DS Scott.' Watt stood up and gave Miller a seat.

'What's this? Good cop, bad cop? I get drilled by that old bastard and then you come riding into town to save the day?'

'Old bastard?' Watt said, gritting his teeth, but Miller held up a hand.

'You have to realise you're the number one suspect at the moment,' Miller said. 'You're the only one who was here.'

'I didn't kill Andrea,' Paterson said.

'It's Andrea, is it? That's cosy. Did you try it on with her and it got

186

out of hand, so you thought you'd give her a right old seeing to?' Scott said, sipping his coffee.

'Why don't you tell us what happened, Mr Paterson,' Kim said, putting her coffee on the table.

'I've already told you.'

'From the beginning. So the others can hear for themselves.'

Paterson took a deep "For fuck's sake" breath, and Miller could see the mental wheels turning. Trying to keep his story straight?

'It was about five thirty and I was doing my rounds. I was walking back towards the room here when I got hit on the head and bundled into the cleaning cupboard.'

'Did you get a look at him?'

'No. He hit me from behind and when I was pushed into the cupboard, I was pushed face down.'

'And you managed to free yourself,' Scott said.

'The ropes weren't that tight. I just worked at them and I finally got free.'

'How would he have gotten in?'

'The front doors are left open from around five so the paper delivery guy can drop off the papers that get put on the senior management's desks.'

Miller continued, 'Was there anything missing?'

'Not that I could see.'

'Nothing from the front desk? Keys? Visitor's badges?'

Paterson shook his head.

'What did you do when you got out of the cupboard?' Scott asked.

'I checked the building.'

'Did you call the police?' Miller knew the answer to this too. He took a sip of coffee again, hoping the caffeine would start to rush into his blood like it had earlier.

'No, I didn't.'

'Because you were upstairs murdering Andrea Kennedy,' Watt said.

'I didn't touch her!' Paterson said. 'I liked her a lot, but we only worked in the same building, that's as far as it went.'

'Why didn't you call us?' Miller asked.

'Because I thought I'd get fired. For letting somebody get the better of me. They could have stolen anything. I thought it was weird they didn't take anything, but I figured they might have thought it was a bank branch or something, then when they realised it wasn't, they scarpered.'

Kim intervened. 'We're suspicious, Mr Paterson because somebody smashed the CCTV. Even the server where the footage is stored.'

'It wasn't me.'

Miller believed him. Their murderer had slipped in with Andrea, belted the security guard, and then disabled the security footage before leaving. 'Don't go anywhere, Mr Paterson. A patrol car will take you to High Street station where you'll be interviewed again.'

'Do I need a lawyer?'

No, but you'll need a priest to read you the Last Rites if Michael Molloy thinks you killed his ex-wife, *Miller thought.* 'Only if you think you'll need one. Guilty men usually do.'

Outside in the hallway, Gibb had taken his cigarettes out and popped one out of the packet. Just holding it made him feel better. 'There's no sign of Andrea's body in the building. I want you to tell Michael Molloy his ex is dead.'

'It would be better coming from a senior officer.'

'You were a friend of his brother, it'll be better coming from you. Wait until she's at the mortuary though; I don't want that rambling idiot coming up here.'

'I want to go and check on Julie so we'll do that and I'll get Dagger to give me a call when Andrea's taken down to Cowgate.'

FIFTY-THREE

He could hear their feet hitting the stone floor as he ran to the end of the hallway. One corridor looked much the same as the other, and he was lost. Who knew what these places were like? Deep under the streets of Edinburgh, a whole world existed, one from the past.

Some of these places had been turned into tourist attractions, like Mary King's Close just off High Street. He'd taken his daughter there once, telling her it was haunted.

He wondered if his own ghost was going to come back and haunt this place after they killed him.

Sweat was lashing off him, running down his torso, soaking into his shirt, glistening on his forehead.

It was dark down here, the only light coming from the flashlight on his phone.

He came to a junction; left or right? He shone the light both ways, but they looked the same. He was lost, and didn't know which way to go. Left seemed the better choice, so he took that. Started running again, then stopped. The corridor turned right at ninety degrees.

He couldn't hear the footsteps anymore. Had he come the right way? *No good second-guessing yourself now.*

He walked round the corner and shone his light ahead. Stopped dead.

There were two men standing in the corridor, waiting for him.

He turned back. Two men were walking slowly towards him.

He took out his baton. 'Which of you bastards is going to get it first,' he said, to the approaching men.

Too late, he heard the soft-soled shoes on the stone floor behind him just before the black bag was put over his head and the fists rained down on him. Then something hard hit him on the head and he felt his knees buckling.

Then it was all over.

The water hit the man in the face and he woke up, shaking his head and gasping.

'About fucking time,' Michael Molloy said, slapping the man hard. The prisoner was tied to a chair, his hands behind his back.

'You're fucking with the law, just remember that,' Gary Davidson said, shaking his head again, trying to get the water out of his eyes, his left cheek stinging.

Robert Molloy smiled at him. 'Oh, I think you lost the right to play that card a long time ago, don't you?' He nodded to Greg Sampson who was standing close by. 'Untie Detective Davidson. He's not going anywhere.'

Sampson did as he was told.

Davidson rubbed his wrists. 'I'm up to date with everything. There's no need for this.'

'Yes, I know you are, but all I wanted to do was ask you if you'd heard anything about the man we're looking for.'

'This is inappropriate. Abducting a police officer. I could fuck you over for this.'

Robert laughed. 'But you won't. We have audio and visual

evidence of your habits. The gambling, the whores. Imagine Standards getting a hold of that?'

'I don't know any more than you do.'

'Why don't I believe you?' Michael said.

'The whole department's running around like headless chickens.' He looked at his watch. 'I'm supposed to be working.'

'Tell them you were following up on a lead. Tell them whatever you like, but you'll leave when we're done having our conversation.'

'Okay, have it your way.'

Robert paced around the room. 'Do you know what this room was? It was one of several high-security vaults. That was one of the reasons the bank had this building to begin with. We're deep underground, under George Street. In what was once gold storage. Now it's a place where I can talk to somebody without being disturbed.' He stopped and looked Davidson in the eyes. 'Space is not the only place nobody can hear you scream.'

'I'm not about to scream.'

'That's right, you're not. However, if you don't start doing some work for me, your wife and daughter will be brought down here and I'll make you listen to *them* scream.'

'You wouldn't fucking dare.'

'Call your wife, Gary,' Michael said.

'What?'

'Do it.'

Davidson took his phone out and called his wife. 'Rosie? No, nothing's wrong, I just wanted to call you.'

'What's the emergency, Gary? Is everything okay? I got really scared when that other detective called and said he'd been sent to pick up Claire.'

Davidson suddenly felt his legs begin to tremble and his whole body starting to shake. 'What did he say to you?'

'The school called first to say one of your team was there. He needed to take Claire to safety. I spoke to him but he wouldn't reveal any details. Claire would be fine, but she was going to be taken to the station where she'd wait for you to pick her up. The school confirmed he'd shown his warrant card. Everything's okay, isn't it, Gary?'

Davidson cleared his throat, his mouth dry. 'Yes, of course it is. Just some big mouth making threats. He knew Claire's name, so we erred on the side of caution and sent somebody to pick her up, that's all. I'll pick her up at the station later. She's fine, and the threat was taken care of.'

'Oh, that's good. I was worried there for a bit.'

'Well, don't worry, Rosie. Everything's fine. It was just protocol. I'll talk to you later.' He hung up, shaking uncontrollably. Sampson appeared with a glass of brandy. Handed it to Davidson.

'Calm yourself,' Robert said. The room was large and had no windows. The huge steel door was inches thick and looked like a giant safe door. It made the place feel cold.

Davidson drank some of the amber liquid. 'One of my team?'

'It would surprise you what money can buy,' Michael said. 'Like, official-looking warrant cards. My man has your daughter right now, and she's perfectly safe. In fact, she's safer than if she was going to walk home alone. There's a backup team watching them. If you agree to my terms, she'll be dropped off back at school, with the story that the threat was neutralised. No harm, no foul. Nobody will be any the wiser.'

'*I'll* be the one who knows.'

'You have a choice here, Gary. You keep your eyes and ears open for us in regard to the Cross case, or the next time I send somebody to her school, there'll be a different outcome.'

Gary finished the brandy. 'I guess I have no choice.'

FIFTY-FOUR

Ian Powers flicked the kettle on and looked at the clock on the cooker; nearly midday and no work done. *No problem, my fine friend, you'll get going soon.*

Powers' official job was a freelance computer programmer, but he made more money from hacking than he did by playing games.

He'd been quite happy to do a favour for Miller; after all, he was the man who'd kept him out of prison. So he'd been willing to find the information he'd wanted, but then Powers' curiosity had got the better of him and he'd dug further. And then he'd backed out immediately. He'd closed his computer down at that point, of course. It was one thing sticking it to somebody, and another thing fucking with Robert Molloy. He'd read about the psycho, and vowed never to get involved there. He didn't want to spend the rest of his life eating sirloin steak through a straw.

The kettle clicked off and he poured the hot water onto the brown granules. He was about to get the milk from the fridge when there was a knock at the door. Nobody had pressed the buzzer downstairs, so it must be a neighbour. Or maybe Linda, his girlfriend, had conned her way in by buzzing another neighbour, to surprise him.

He walked to the front door. Looked through the peephole. A young, blonde woman was standing looking at the door, smiling. She was wearing a black polo neck under a black leather jacket. Her hair was short, and she was holding a hat.

Who is this? What does she want? Why don't you just open the door?

He opened the door.

'Hello,' he said, glad he hadn't decided to stay in his pyjamas all day. 'Can I help you?' He smiled what he thought was his winning smile.

'Hi, my name's Carrie and I'm staying with a friend downstairs, but I've lost my key. I've tried the other neighbours, but nobody's answering. Could I use your phone? My mobile's in the house too.'

'Oh, sure.' He looked her up and down; nice figure, he thought. 'The kettle's just boiled. Would you like a coffee?' He stepped back and she took a step forward.

'That won't be necessary, Ian. I won't be staying long.' Her smile dropped, and fear shot through him, and he knew. Just knew deep down, why she was there without her actually saying so.

He made to push her out of his flat, but she was far too quick for him. She grabbed his hand, twisted it and bent it back, forcing him down onto his knees.

'Who are you?' he asked. A large man stepped into view and watched them.

'Somebody you'll never get into bed with. That *is* what you were thinking, isn't it? I'll get this blonde bimbo into my flat, give her a coffee, and then shag the arse off her.'

'Did you get fired from Avon or something?' he said, but blondie just bent his arm even more. He let out a yell.

'What do you want? Money? I don't have much but you can take my watch. It's only a Timex, but it's all yours.'

'I don't want your watch, and I don't want your fucking money.' She threw him down to the ground. He rolled onto his back, and she stepped forward, straddling him. He noticed the black boots, with little bits of snow round the stitching at the front. They were tucked under her black jeans and they weren't fashion items.

Powers pushed himself up. He was going to get up and give her a slap. His mother had told him to never hit a woman, but fair's fair. She'd nearly broken his arm. Okay, maybe not slap her, but at least tell her to fuck off, or he'd call the police. Somehow he didn't think she'd listen though. She was standing watching, smiling at Powers discomfort. She reached down and grabbed his hair, half pulling him up, wrenched his head back, bent down and looked him in the eyes.

'If you ever hack into Alamo Lettings again, I'll come back and slit your fucking throat. Please believe me when I say this.' She ran a finger across his neck, simulating a knife. 'And don't even think about going to the police with this, or we will meet again, and I promise you one thing; next time you *will* be fucked.'

She threw his head back, and it bumped off the floor. The man was smiling. Greg Sampson and Sienna Craig turned round and left, gently closing the door behind them.

FIFTY-FIVE

Miller asked Kim to drive. Julie was safely locked in her house and Kim had told her they'd all be down shortly. There had to have been a trigger point, something that set Cross off. Miller had a feeling it started with Harry Davidson. He'd been there at the hotel twenty-five years ago, along with Miller's father. And Colin Fleming. Now, out of the lot of them, only Jack Miller was still alive.

The snow had turned to sleet when they got out of the car. There was a patrol car outside Julie's house. Miller walked up to the car door, pleased to see the uniform get out before he got there or saw who it was.

'You guys can go have a break now. We're going inside.'

'Thanks, sir. The relief car will be here in half an hour.'

'Good job. Now off you go and get some lunch.'

Scott was on his phone at the door. 'I didn't want to spook her,' he said, cutting the call.

A minute later, Julie came down and opened the door. 'Hi. What's happening?' She smiled at them.

They all stepped inside. 'There's been another murder, Julie.'

She was silent for a moment. 'Just like the others?'

196

Miller nodded.

'Who is it?'

Miller looked at Scott, as if he was asking for permission before telling her. 'It was Michael Molloy's ex-wife.'

She looked shocked. 'Well, we know what the connection is, that's for sure.' They went upstairs.

'Hey, how are you doing?' Kim said.

'Bored out of my skull. I should get back to the mortuary. They'll be needing me.'

'Take it easy,' Kim said. 'The doc said rest.'

'I've rested enough.'

Miller looked at her. 'Kim's right. They're still processing the scene. She won't be taken to the mortuary until later on, then I'll have the thankless job of telling Michael Molloy. Not yet though.'

Julie relaxed a bit. 'I have to go back to work tomorrow though.'

Kim looked at Miller. 'I can take Julie to work. She won't be alone. Then I'll pick her up again and won't leave her side.'

'I'd feel safer there. I know he won't be coming back here, but at least it would get me out for a bit.'

Miller looked at Scott. *This wasn't a random attack. How do we tell her we know for sure?* 'Just think about it for the rest of the day. See how you feel later.'

'I need to talk to you about something, Frank. In private.'

Miller looked at the other two.

'I'll start making the soup,' Scott said.

'I'll help.' Kim followed Scott through to the kitchen.

'I wanted you to hear it from me first,' Julie started saying, 'before you heard it second-hand. This is my last week at the mortuary. I'm leaving, Frank.'

Miller looked shocked. 'Leaving? Where are you going?'

'I applied for a job in London and I got it. I gave my notice at the end of the month.'

'And I'm just hearing about it now?'

She put a hand on his arm. 'I didn't want you to try and talk me out of it. I need to do this. There are so many bad memories for me here in Edinburgh. I hope you understand.'

'Where are you going to live? Do you have a job?'

'Yes, I'm going to be working in St Luke's Hospital mortuary. I already have a flat lined up, somewhere to live until I sell this place.'

'When are you leaving?'

'Saturday. The removal men are coming next Monday for my stuff and an estate agent's going to start the selling process.'

'That's only a few days away.'

'I know, Frank, but I thought it was for the best.'

Miller stood silently for a moment, taking it all in. 'You're going to be all on your own down there.'

'I'll make new friends. You can come down and visit me, if you like.'

He gave her a hug. 'Of course I'll come.'

Miller couldn't help feeling he'd just lost another member of his family.

FIFTY-SIX

DCS Elliot stood at the front of the room, foaming at the mouth. Miller knew the shit would soon trickle down to his level, and then he'd have to kick some arse. Elliot was bleating on about clear-up rates, and how these murders were going to fuck up everything for the next fiscal year, and it was only February.

'I'm going to hand you over to Harvey Levitt.' He indicated for the psychologist to step up.

Levitt held up his hands as the voices started to chatter. 'Thank you, ladies and gentlemen. I was asked to give my input. Let me tell you, we have an angry person out there.

'Killing somebody's bad enough, but to then disembowel them takes a lot of rage. Be warned: when we get near this guy, be careful. He won't hesitate to kill any one of you.' He took a deep breath, and let it out slowly. 'Today, we found Andrea. The speed with which Cross is killing is phenomenal. He's certainly heading for his Crash Point. I've a feeling he's going to be like a Special Ops team; in, out and away before anybody knows what's going on. It seems he's on a mission, killing people who were associated with Michael Molloy at some point. We don't know who – if anybody – is next on his list, but if he's working to an agenda, then he's about to run out of steam very fast.'

A hand went up from Hazel Carter. 'Why the difference now? Why doesn't he take his time like two years ago?'

'Good question, sergeant. It's not an exact science, but we can learn from the past. Let me answer your question with a question; you wake up in the middle of the night and you smell smoke. You realise the house is on fire. You have to get out. You have time to maybe pull on a pair of jeans, maybe grab your laptop. You don't go around the house grabbing other things. Why not?'

Hazel thought about it for a second. 'You need to get out or you're going to die.'

Levitt pointed at her. 'Correct. You don't have the luxury of time. You're not just in a hurry, you're desperate. Time's not on your side. You know you don't want to run outside naked. Your laptop has important information on it, and it's right there in its bag next to your bed. So you grab it on the way out. What you don't do is go around the house looking for stuff. You don't have time.

'Our killer doesn't have time. Before, he was controlling the time-frame. Now he knows he doesn't have the luxury of time, for some reason.' He paused for breath. 'I helped track down a killer who was dying of cancer. He only had weeks left to live, and was angry at the world, so he wanted to take out his revenge on it before he died. Maybe you could check terminally ill patients who had a connection to Molloy. Maybe it's somebody with a court appearance due and he knows he's going away for a long time.'

Detectives started scribbling in their notebooks.

'Whatever it is, ladies and gentlemen, I think our friend will be done shortly. Nobody can keep up this pace. If I was a betting man, I'd say by this time next week, it'll all be done and dusted. We'll either have him in custody or we'll not see him again for a very long time, if at all.'

He stepped away, and the chatter began. Elliot indicated to

Miller he wanted a word in Miller's office. 'You can come too, Harvey.'

'What's going on, Frank?' he said, closing the door behind him. He sat down across from Miller and let out a sigh while Levitt stood.

Elliot was in his late fifties, a career copper who'd risen through the ranks before politics had taken over.

'Raymond Cross is out of control. We're trying everything to nail him, but it's not easy,' Miller said.

'This is getting out of hand. The penguins sitting down in Holyrood are flapping their wings. We've had nearly the whole annual murder rate in the space of three days. What the fuck's going on?'

'If I may, chief superintendent,' Levitt said, with a smile. 'This is one of the hardest cases I've ever worked on, either here or back in the States. The team are working hard, but this guy's very clever.'

'I know that, Dr Levitt; we haven't caught the fucker yet.'

Levitt kept smiling. 'Raymond Cross is very clever. Smart enough to make up an elaborate clue to leave for Frank to lead him into a trap in Lamb's House. Even though he must be exhausted, he's driven by pure hatred, and that's some motivation. That, combined with his cunning, means he's already planned all his moves and the only way we're going to get him is if he slips up.'

'Do we have a list of the people who were at the hotel the night Moira Kennedy was murdered?'

'We're tracking them down, but a lot of them aren't around.'

'What about where Cross lived when he was arrested?' Elliot asked.

'Hermiston Court,' Miller answered.' It was one of the four tower blocks that were demolished up at Sighthill a few years ago.'

Elliott shook his head. 'How's Julie Davidson?'

'She's scared. She wants to go back to work tomorrow, so we're going to let her. She'll have her colleagues there, and she'll be taken to work and picked up again, so she won't be alone. I don't think it's a good idea, but she insists.'

'There's nothing we can do to stop her. We can only advise her.

I'll get the patrols increased round there.' He paused. 'Do you think this is connected with what's going on, or a random attack?'

'I think you know the answer to that already, sir.'

'I was worried you'd say that.' Elliot left the office.

'Thanks for having my back, Harvey.'

'No problem. I thought Elliot needed it spelling out that we're not dealing with an ordinary killer here.'

Miller's mobile phone rang.

'Hello?'

'Hello, Frank. I heard our friend's been at his capers again.'

It was Neil McGovern.

FIFTY-SEVEN

Miller thought about Neil McGovern's words, as he and Tam drove up High Street. He'd told Kim they'd pick her up later. The afternoon was dull and freezing cold, and his face felt numb. He'd received the call from the mortuary as they left the office; Andrea Kennedy was with the pathologists.

'I want a quick word with Norma Banks, Tam.'

'Anything I should know about?'

Miller thought about it for a moment. He trusted Tam more than he'd ever trusted anybody in his life. 'Listen, mate, I'm going to tell you something, and it needs to stay in this car.'

'That goes without saying.'

Miller turned into Chambers Street. Pulled onto the single yellow. Stopped the car and looked at Scott. 'Neil McGovern's still alive.' He turned the engine off and popped the police sign on the dash.

'Is this a wind-up?'

'I wish it was, Tam.'

Scott looked out the window, and then back at Miller. 'How do you know?'

'I spoke to him.' Miller filled him in on Kim being McGovern's daughter and how she thought he was dead. 'I didn't want to say anything at the hospital, but I didn't think McGovern was dead.'

'This is getting complicated, Frank. What are we doing here?'

'I want to see if Banks knows.'

Scott opened the door. 'Okay, let's go and see what she has to say for herself.'

Just thinking about McGovern made Miller question his own sanity.

The procurator fiscal's office was located within the new court complex. Miller and Scott showed their warrant cards to the security men at the front entrance and made their way up the stairs. Miller felt cold, not just on the outside.

They passed through the security scanner before being allowed into the office reception, where more security men were waiting.

'I'd like a minute with Norma Banks, please,' he said, to the receptionist.

'I'll see if she's available.' A phone call later, and the two detectives were being led through to one of the offices in the back.

'Frank. Good to see you again. Detective Scott. Have a seat.'

Miller and Scott sat down opposite the woman, and looked around the room. It was large, with files piled up on the floor in a corner.

'What brings you here, Frank?'

'I wanted to ask you a few questions about your husband, that's all.'

'Ask away.'

'I was wondering why the Home Office sent two pathologists to Airdrie to perform the autopsy on McGovern.'

Norma rocked back in her chair. 'How did you find that out?'

'I went to the State Hospital and spoke to somebody.'

'It's protocol. Is there a problem?'

'I just wondered why, that's all.' He looked at her. 'Have you seen a copy of the post-mortem?' Miller asked.

'No I haven't. I don't need to; the hospital's not in my jurisdiction.'

'Have you seen your husband's body?'

'What's this about, Frank?'

'I was wondering if you'd actually seen him.'

'No, I haven't.'

'Where is he now?'

'Frank, I shouldn't be discussing this with you, you know that.'

'This doesn't make sense.'

'It does make sense.' She took a drink of her coffee and looked at him over the rim of her cup. 'I know it must be hard, Frank, but McGovern's dead and gone.'

Except Miller knew he wasn't. 'You came to me, remember? You sent your daughter to work with me, and now you're keeping things from me.' He could see her cheeks turn red, as if he'd touched a nerve.

Scott shuffled uncomfortably.

'Maybe we should be having this chat in private,' Norma said.

'Why? We already told Tam, McGovern wasn't responsible for killing Harry. I trust him with my life.'

'Praise indeed,' she said.

'So why don't we cut to the chase and you tell me you know your husband isn't dead.'

Norma's eyes were as hard as ice. She put her cup down on the desk. 'I love my daughter more than anything. Cross thinks Neil's dead, and that way, he'll stay away from my family. It has to stay that way. Neil's been working in the background, conducting a parallel investigation. We can't let anybody know he's still alive.'

'I've spoken to him. We met in Warriston cemetery when I was visiting my wife's grave.'

'He's not getting very far, Frank. I'm sorry for the deception, but we need your help. You were close to Harry. The killer's coming after you. Maybe we'll get him.'

'Or maybe he'll kill Frank and we'll still be running round in circles,' Scott said.

'People are still dying. Cross has to be stopped any way we can.'

Miller stood up, and Scott followed his lead. 'Anything else you're keeping from me?'

Norma shook her head. 'Nothing. You know it all now. Well, everything I can discuss with you.'

Miller didn't like the sound of that, but said nothing.

Outside, the wind was sinking its teeth in.

'Come on, let's go and get Kim and I'll tell Michael Molloy his ex-wife's dead.'

'Talk about lighting the blue touch paper.'

'If Molloy gets to Cross first, the Edinburgh tax payers won't have to worry about footing the bill for a trial.'

FIFTY-EIGHT

Miller pulled up in front of Molloy's club in George Street. He and Scott had picked up Kim on the way. He thought about his friend again. Sean Molloy, youngest son of one of Edinburgh's biggest gangsters. And they were friends. Who'd have thought it? Professional Standards had gone apeshit, telling Miller he'd be booted out of the force, but Sean had no connections to his father, and they'd grown up together. Miller's saving grace had been him agreeing to keep his ears open, and report back to his station commander if he heard anything about Robert Molloy. The brass had turned the situation from being an embarrassment to a potential goldmine. Miller had agreed, but privately, he'd thought they could all go and fuck themselves.

He'd told Sean.

'They want me to spy on you, Sean,' he'd said one night in the pub.

'What? They'd stoop that low?' Sean was easy-going, far different from his older psycho brother, Michael.

'Believe it, my friend.'

This was back in the day when Miller felt relaxed going out to the pub. His wife was back home doing her own thing, work was good and Carol knew all about Sean. Had met him many times and they liked each other. That night though, there'd been a dark cloud hanging over them.

'What did you tell them, Frank?'

Miller looked his friend in the eyes. 'I told them I would, of course.'

Sean had laughed and clapped his friend on the shoulder. 'And of course you aren't. Why else would you be telling me?'

Miller had smiled. 'I'll tell them what they want to hear. Or rather, what they don't want to hear.'

Their bond had just got tighter. Thanks to the brass at Lothian and Borders.

Sean Molloy and Frank Miller had known each other since high school, and he still missed his friend. He remembered the laughs, backing each other up when a fight went down and double-dating a couple of girls in fourth year.

He closed his eyes for a moment, feeling himself being over-whelmed. First Carol dying, then Sean. If there was one time in his life he'd needed Carol by his side, it was at Sean Molloy's funeral. But he'd been there on his own. Standing in the cold, watery sun, letting the wind blow through his jacket as if it was Sean himself saying goodbye.

He brought himself back to the present. 'Come on, Tam, let's get this over with,' Miller said, getting out of the car.

Glen Sampson wasn't in the club this time. It was another suit. Shaved head, just like Sampson. Miller wondered if they went to the same barber and got a group discount.

This time, Miller walked past with Scott and Kim without a fuss.

'So much for their security,' Scott said.

'I'm sure the doorman will be mopping out toilets tonight, for not paying attention.'

They stopped at the foot of the stairs. 'Listen, if Molloy's in here, it might be better if I tell him alone. That way he can be a buffer when we talk to his son. If either of them are here.'

'And if he's not alone and Michael goes mental?'

'Wait in the bar and give me a heads-up if any of those wankers come up here in force. And *"keep your eyes peeled"* doesn't mean start getting blootered. Keep your eyes on him, Kim.'

'I'm sure they're watching us on CCTV,' she said.

'You'd think.' Miller watched as Scott and Kim walked away. Then he walked upstairs to Robert Molloy's office.

'You took your time,' Molloy said, from behind his desk. 'I was watching you on the camera. Where are your two buddies?'

'I sent them to the bar.' Miller headed over to Molloy's drinks cabinet. Held up the decanter. Molloy shook his head. Miller poured himself a small measure then sat opposite Molloy.

'Is that what you came here for? To offer me my own whisky?'

Miller smiled. 'No. I'm the bearer of bad news.'

'Don't tell me they've caught you dipping your hand in the evidence locker?'

'Fuck you.'

'Well, what have you come to accuse me of doing now?'

'I've known you a long time. Just like my old man has. Sean and I grew up together. He was the best friend I ever had. Despite his name being Molloy, he didn't let that stop him in life.'

Molloy looked at Miller. 'He always thought highly of you, Frank. He thought more of you than his own brother.'

'Sometimes that's the way.' Miller sat and thought about the man he'd regarded as the brother he'd never had.

FIFTY-NINE

Sean Molloy grew up with Frank Miller after they became friends at high school. As an adult, Sean was well aware of what his family was like, and managed to stay away from them, from their influences. He always had time for his father, however, showing the old man respect. They had lunch once a month and that seemed to be enough for Robert.

Sean started his own corporate security and limo company with a bank loan. He didn't want help from his father. He wanted to stand on his own two feet. What he didn't know about was the attempt to scupper his business before it had a chance to gain a foothold in the community. Some wannabe from West Lothian had a similar business, and thought Sean Molloy was stepping on his toes.

Most nights, Sean would work late. The drivers could be trusted to bring the limos back in one piece and lock up, but it was always late evening when Sean was alone.

Miller didn't know if it was fate or what, but he'd asked Sean if he felt like going for a pint one night. He'd pick him up, and then he'd drop his car off and they could catch up. He hadn't seen his friend in a while, and Sean had readily agreed.

Miller could see the smoke before he got to the industrial site. As he drew closer, he could see the flames licking out of the roof of Sean's warehouse. After calling treble nine, Miller tried to enter the building, but was beaten back by the heat. He looked in through the office window on the ground floor and saw Sean tied to a chair, rocking back and forth, trying to free himself.

Miller drove his car through the far side of the office wall, jumped out and cut Sean free. His friend was injured after being beaten, so Miller threw him onto the back seat of his car and reversed out just before an explosion took out half the warehouse and all the office area.

'Bloody hell, Sean. Who did you upset?' Miller said, watching as the Newcraighall fire crews arrived. It would be ten more minutes before backup from other stations arrived.

Miller's car was a write-off, but Sean was alive.

The ambulance took him to the Royal, where they treated him for smoke inhalation, broken ribs and various cuts and bruises.

Robert Molloy arrived as Miller was leaving the hospital. Sean had been admitted. Molloy stopped Miller in the corridor, speaking quietly with him when nobody was about.

'I heard what you did for my boy. I won't forget this, Frank. A friend of mine owns a dealership. He'll set you up with a new motor.'

'Yeah, and Standards would be breathing down my neck. Don't worry, it was insured.'

'Anyway, as I said, I won't forget it.'

Two weeks later, a businessman from West Lothian was found dead in the remains of his mansion after an electrical fire burned it to the ground. It was ruled an accident.

After that night, Molloy Limos and Security flourished. Nobody ever tried to burn down the premises again.

Sean Molloy started making decent money. Wanted Miller to join him. Frank thanked him, but turned him down. Miller used the limos a couple of times, once when he'd taken Carol out for her birthday. Sean celebrated with them later. Miller wanted him to be the godfather now he and Carol were trying to have kids; Sean agreed. Miller told him it wouldn't be long, hopefully. Sean laughed and told him he'd be there.

He wasn't.

A year later, Sean Molloy was dead.

The cancer wasn't detected at first. It started with a cough. Just a tickle that got worse. Sean hated doctors, and wouldn't go and see about it. He had a live-in girlfriend by this time – Liz – and she pestered him to go and get checked out. He didn't. The cough stopped. Sean told her she'd worried about nothing.

Then the tiredness hit him. He couldn't get out of bed at first, then it was a struggle. Miller came round to see him one day and couldn't believe Sean had lost so much weight. Sean struggled to get out of bed, and when Miller helped him, Sean collapsed. Miller called for an ambulance. Went with Sean to the Royal. The new one this time. Sean told the doctor on duty he had some back pain. They took an X-ray of his chest. Meanwhile, Miller called Robert Molloy.

When Miller went to see him the next day, Robert Molloy was there. For the first time ever, Miller saw Molloy as an old man. His eyes were red. He'd been crying. He was waiting outside in the corridor, looking out the windows that looked down onto a courtyard.

'How's Sean?' Miller had asked quietly.

Robert Molloy looked at Miller. 'Dying,' he said, simply, and held onto Miller. Cried his heart out without shame. Miller held him.

Then the crying stopped and Molloy wiped his eyes. 'If it was Michael in there, I'd be sad, but it wouldn't hurt as much.' He looked Miller in the eyes. 'Sean was the good son. I loved him more than I love life. If I could trade places, I would, in a fucking heartbeat.'

'What's the diagnosis?' Miller asked as rain pattered against the glass, gently at first, then a downpour. Driven by a wind. It was an image he'd never gotten out of his mind.

'Stage four lung cancer. It's spread to his liver and his bones.'

'Fuck me,' Miller said, quietly. 'Sean never smoked in his life.'

Molloy shook his head. 'It's genetic, apparently. I might have it and not know. Michael might have it. Their mother died of a brain aneurysm but as far as we could tell, she didn't have cancer.'

'I'm so sorry, Molloy.' Miller stood awkwardly for a moment. 'I'd like to see him, if that's okay with you.'

Molloy looked at him again. 'You saved my little boy's life. You're the one who went into a burning building and saved him, nobody else. He said you were like a brother to him, the brother he never had. Not like the one he's got. Of course you can go and see him.'

They went into the room. Sean was on morphine. A tube came out the side of his chest, and a urine-coloured liquid ran down a clear hose to a plastic container with measurements marked on the side.

Sean was awake, but Miller didn't know if his friend recognised him at first.

'Frank,' he said, his voice low. 'Thanks for coming.'

'Good to see you, buddy.' He sat at the side of the bed. Miller had a "Get Well Soon" card in his inside pocket, but kept it there. He'd kept it with private papers ever since and never opened it.

'Here's me lying in bed when there's so much to do.' He tried to laugh and coughed.

The room was quite big, with its own toilet, and a small wash-basin outside the door to the toilet. Miller noticed a vase of flowers, and wished he'd brought some. He'd bring some next time.

'I always said you were a lazy bastard,' Miller said, and smiled. He held his friend's hand. Sean smiled and gave a brief laugh.

Miller turned to look at Molloy. 'Where's Liz?' he asked, quietly.

'I sent her home. She's a basket case. I have somebody looking after her. I told her she could come back when she gets some rest.'

Miller looked back at his friend. 'Don't worry, buddy, you'll soon be up and about.'

Sean smiled weakly. 'It doesn't feel like it. I think I have some kind of chest infection. That drain thing is a pain.'

Miller stood up. 'You get some rest now. I'll come back later, Sean. See how you're doing.'

'Okay, buddy. We'll get a pint as soon as I get out of here.' Sean's voice was hoarse, as if he had a cold and not lung cancer. Miller walked out of the ward, the last time he'd ever see his friend alive.

Back out in the corridor, Robert Molloy shook Miller's hand. 'Thanks for coming, Frank.'

'You don't have to thank me. Sean's my friend.'

He turned and walked away, halted by Molloy calling to him. There was nobody else within earshot. 'One more thing; if you ever tell anybody we hugged in the Royal Infirmary, I'll have your legs broken.' He smiled at Miller.

'Fuck off, Molloy,' Miller said, smiling and shaking his head. He walked out into the pouring rain.

SIXTY

'So, are you going to tell me what's up?' Robert Molloy said.

Miller could feel the heat building up in Molloy's office. Wished he had time for a beer. 'I have some bad news.'

Molloy looked at him. 'So you said. Go on.'

'Andrea was murdered this morning.'

'What?'

'She was found murdered in her office.' He didn't elaborate on the state she was found in.

Molloy looked at him. 'Is it linked to the others?'

Miller nodded. 'She's been taken to the mortuary. We'll have to get Michael down there to make a formal ID as she doesn't have any other next-of-kin. So I've been told. Where is he?'

Molloy shrugged. 'Out fucking about somewhere.'

'How well did Michael get on with her?'

'He still loved her. He let her live rent free in one of the properties at South Gyle. They were always going out together. They got on better than they did when they were married.'

'Do you know if she had any problems with anybody?'

Molloy shook his head. 'Are you kidding me? If anybody gave her a problem, Michael would've stopped that in a second.'

'You know I have to ask this, but do you know where Michael was around six this morning?'

'Yes. Here with me. We had a late night last night. With a group of people. He didn't leave to go home until around eight. A driver took him home.'

'Can't keep up with you, Molloy?'

'You know what youngsters are like nowadays.'

'I'll have to get some people round to talk to the witnesses.'

'I'll arrange to have them available.'

'They're not going to be the real witnesses, are they?' Miller looked at the older man.

'Of course not. But believe me, if I thought the little bastard had killed Andrea, I'd have his balls cut off and have him thrown in Leith Docks. Tell you some guff about a rival doing it. I loved Andrea too. She was a sweet woman.'

Miller knew if Molloy found Cross first, he too would be found in Leith Docks with his balls cut off. Which would cause him no end of problems. 'Maybe you could have a word with him. Break the bad news.'

'I'll do that.'

'Now that it's just you and me, and nobody else listening, why don't you just tell me what the hell Fleming was doing in your hotel? Maybe it'll help us catch whoever killed Andrea.'

'If I do and I ever find out you were wired...' The threat was implied if not quite spoken.

'Piss off, Molloy. I could've got to you through Sean, but I told him about their plan upstairs, and we had a laugh about it. There was no way I was doing that. And I give you my word, I'm not wired. I'm not asking you to incriminate yourself, just help me out here.'

'I was being blackmailed by Cross. He said he had some proof Michael killed Moira Kennedy. It was pish because Michael didn't kill her. He wanted a hundred thousand, or the proof would get mailed to the press and anybody else he could think of. So we sent Fleming along to deal with him, and a bag of money to lure him. Seems Fleming couldn't handle himself like we thought he could. He died, and the money was taken.'

'He knew you'd send Fleming along to do your dirty work. He set a trap for him and stole your money.'

'I don't suppose I'll ever see it again.'

'I wouldn't bet on it.' He'd placed his hand on the door handle when Molloy spoke.

'Do you think you'll catch this guy, Miller?'

Miller turned round. 'Either that, or he'll catch us.'

SIXTY-ONE

Outside, the temperature had dropped, and a snow flurry had kicked in. Dusk had descended. Miller called Julie once they'd got in the car.

'How are you doing?' he asked her.

'I'm okay. Nothing eventful happened. Don't get upset, but I popped into work to let them know I'm coming back tomorrow.'

Miller felt his heart beating faster. 'You need to be careful, Julie.' He heard her give a short laugh.

'I know, Frank. I'm being careful. I just needed to get out of the house for a little while.'

'You're still at the mortuary?'

'Yes. I hate being off work.' He heard the rustle of her jacket. 'What have you been up to?'

'Talking to Robert Molloy. He's going to break the news to his son about Andrea Kennedy.'

'You need to be careful as well.'

'I know.' They were stopped at a traffic light. 'Well, why don't I order some Chinese in? I have Tam and Kim with me.'

'Sounds good.'

He looked at Scott and Kim and they both nodded.

'We'll order Chinese from a carry out place I know down in Stockbridge.'

'I'm almost done here. I'll see you in a wee while.' Julie hung up.

Miller dialled Jack's number.

When McGovern had called him earlier, he'd told Miller he had to look deeper into the Cross case. Had they missed something? Miller wanted to go through his father's old notes. Jack kept papers at home, some of his old case files, or copies of them at least. He wondered if Jack would mind if he had a look at them.

His call to Jack went to voicemail. He called the house phone, but it went to the answer machine. 'Jack's not answering his phone.'

Scott turned into North Bridge. The Balmoral Hotel on their right was lit up. Scott took the next right into High Street. Parked round in Cockburn Street.

'Why don't I drive down to Stockbridge now and pick it up?' Scott said.

'The traffic's heavy.'

'So? By the time we phone it in and the driver delivers it, we could be finished and you could be doing the dishes.'

Miller smiled. 'Fucking dishes. Paper plates in my place, Tam. Good idea, though. Tell me what you want, I'll call it in and it'll be waiting for you. Although, since we're up here, go to the one in Dundas Street, it's quicker.' He gave Scott money for the food. 'I'll see if Jack's in, and if he is and wants something, I'll text you.'

'Okay, boss. Kim can come and give me a hand to carry the stuff.'

'Sure, I'll come with you,' she agreed.

The flat was in darkness and Charlie came running along the hall to meet him. Miller put a light on and petted him. The cat followed him into the kitchen, and walked round Miller's legs, rubbing his head on his trousers. His bowl was empty.

Miller fed him and changed the water bowl then went back down the hall to pick up the mail. No answer from Jack's mobile. Where the hell was he? It wasn't like his old man to forget about the cat. One of them was always coming home to feed him.

He went into the living room, followed by Charlie. The cat sat and licked a paw then used it to wash his face. If only life was that simple for Miller. He switched a lamp on and called his father again. It went to voicemail once more.

'Jack, you forgot to feed Charlie. Are you coming back tonight? Call me.'

He told himself he was annoyed with his father for not feeding the cat, but deep down, he was starting to get worried about him.

He went over to Jack's filing cabinet. It was unlocked, and Miller opened it. He crouched down, going through the files in the bottom drawer, pulling the yellow files towards him, trying to read Jack's scrawl on the little labels.

He sensed somebody behind him before he heard him. Jack had been in the bathroom and hadn't heard his phone, he thought.

It wasn't Jack.

SIXTY-TWO

Michael Molloy paced around his office like he was trying to wear out the carpet. 'Andrea's dead? How could this happen?' he shouted. Tears were streaming down his face. 'Oh, this is not fucking happening. It can't be.' He clenched his fists, his body taut, as a sense of panic rose inside.

His father was sitting on the leather settee on the far side of the office, holding a glass of whisky in one hand. Now was the time for the twelve-year-old malt. 'He's obviously out to get us.'

'You brought Cross on board. You said he was sound. Yet he killed Moira. Now he's killed Andrea, the one woman in my life I cared about.'

'And who's the one who always said he was innocent? I believe that was you, Michael.'

'I thought he was. I thought he was in the room with us when we were partying. Now I'm not so sure. If he was innocent, why's he killing people we know?'

'I wish I knew.'

Michael held his hands out. 'The cops know nothing. They don't know where Cross is. They don't have a clue. So Cross is walking

221

about, killing anybody who takes his fancy. And what about Miller? He might look like a dumbo, but he's got more than two brain cells. He's going to figure things out. He already knows Fleming was at the hotel to meet Cross. He'll connect us to it.'

'He knows it's my hotel, so he already knows we're connected.' He didn't want to tell his son he'd already told Miller why Fleming was there.

'He doesn't know we sent Fleming there that night,' Michael said, sitting down.

Robert got up and poured himself more whisky. 'Sunday night was a mistake. We all know that. We won't make that mistake again.'

'Are you sure you didn't send somebody round to smack that pathologist woman?' Michael asked.

'Of course I'm sure! You think I pick people at random and send somebody to their house? Are you daft or something?'

He looked at his father. 'I need to break somebody's kneecaps right now. Who do we know who's been pissing us off lately?'

Robert Molloy shook his head. 'Forget about it. I know we're all feeling it just now, but you need to focus. Right now, I'm preparing a nice, long session with Raymond Cross when we get hold of him. I'm going to have somebody rip him apart.'

Michael wiped at the tears on his cheeks. 'I want to watch.'

'You'll get your chance, son. Don't worry.'

SIXTY-THREE

The lamp smashed into the side of Miller's head, knocking him off his feet. The room went dark as he landed on his side. Instinct told him to roll, like he would if he were caught in a fight outside. His living room had more obstacles than a bar, namely the couch. He rolled sideways into it. The person who'd hit him with the lamp was silhouetted against the light in the hall. Miller saw movement, saw the glint of the knife as it came down towards him. He jerked his head as the blade neared his face. The knife sliced into the side of the couch.

Charlie jumped onto the TV stand and ran behind the TV.

Raymond fucking Cross is in your flat! his mind screamed. *Knife. Control it. Keep it away from your body.* All the commands he'd learnt in training were coming back to him. He was at a distinct disadvantage, lying down while this guy was on his feet, trying to stick him.

Well, get him off his fucking feet! Miller kicked out, hard, catching Cross on the side of the leg. Then the rules changed.

Cross brought out a gun. Pointed it right at Miller's face. A Sig Sauer 9mm. Miller stared at where the face should be and saw only a black mask with eye holes. There was nothing that stuck out.

223

'Go ahead.' Miller heard his own voice, but it sounded strange to him.

Cross merely walked over to the file Miller had taken out, took the papers from it and shoved them into an inside pocket of the short jacket. All the time keeping the gun steady.

He backed towards the living room door. Held up the fingers of his left hand. Put his index finger to his lips. *Shhhh.*

Then he left.

The message was clear: keep quiet for five minutes or I'll shoot you.

Where the hell did he get the gun? How did he get in here? Had he been waiting and then jumped out?

All those questions were going through his mind as he picked up his mobile phone. 'Tam? Raymond Cross was in here. Attacked me! If you're still nearby, can you swing back, but don't approach! He's armed. Just see if you can spot him.' Miller was on his feet now. Looking out the living room window just in case. 'He's wearing a short, black jacket. He had a ski mask on but that will be off now. Just have a look, but be careful. I'm going to call control.'

'Okay, mate, but *you* be fucking careful. We'll be back in a minute.'

Miller hung up. Called control. Requested ARU backup but knew Cross would be away before the 4x4 got here. Unless it happened to be around the corner, which it probably wasn't.

He put his hand to the side of his head. It felt warm and wet. Blood. Tried calling Jack again. This time the call was answered.

'Dad, don't worry but Cross attacked me in the flat.'

'Are you alright? Where are you now?'

'I'm still here. Help's on its way. Where are you?'

'At a friend's house. I'll be right there.'

'No. Stay where you are. I don't want you near here just now. Can you stay overnight?'

'Frank, I'm not ten. I'm not hiding from that bastard. I'm fifty-five years old, not seventy-five. I'll be home later. Just watch your back.'

'I'll be fine. Tam's coming.'

'That bastard. If I get my hands on him, I'll wring his fucking neck. Me and the boys have a nice wee plan lined up for the bastard if we get to him first.'

Which probably included smashing beer bottles over his head, *Miller thought, but kept it to himself.*

'Don't put yourself in danger, Jack.'

'Okay, son. Call me if you need me. Otherwise, I'll see you later.'

A few minutes later, Scott and Kim came bursting into the flat. 'Fucking hell, what happened, Frank?' Scott said.

Miller told them.

'Let's get that looked at,' Kim said.

'Did you see the bastard, Tam?'

Scott shook his head. 'Sorry, there were so many people with dark jackets on.' Kim went through to the kitchen and soaked a towel. Pressed it to Miller's head.

'Hold that there and I'll call for an ambulance.'

'I'm fine, Kim. Control are sending one with the ARU.'

Miller sat on the settee and took hold of the towel. Six minutes later, sirens filled the street. The ARU officers came in, locked and loaded. Followed by two ambulance paramedics, after the flat was declared clear. 'It's just superficial,' one of the ambulance crew said. 'Maybe best to have it seen to.'

'If it's just a small cut, I'll be okay,' Miller said.

'It won't even need stitches, but if you start to feel dizzy or sick, you need to have it checked out right away. It could be concussion.'

'I don't think that'll be necessary. It was a cheap lamp.'

'This is one of the times when being cheap paid off,' Scott said.

Just then, Paddy Gibb came in, after clearing it with the ARU guys.

'God help us all, Frank, what the hell's been going on?' He looked at the broken lamp.

'Raymond Cross was here. He attacked me.'

'Fuck me,' he said.

225

'He had a gun pointed right at me, and he took some of my dad's old files. I think that's what he was after.'

The paramedic stood up. 'We'll get going. Remember, dizzy or sick, go to the A&E.'

'I will, thanks.'

'What was in the files?' Gibb asked.

'My dad had some old files on Cross from way back. That's what I had out to look at, and that's what he took.'

'I wonder why he didn't shoot you?' Scott asked.

'He tried to stab me, but I fought back. That's when he brought out the gun. Maybe he figured he wouldn't be able to stab me, and firing the gun would bring him a lot of attention.'

'That makes sense,' Gibb said. 'You need to have a talk with Jack about those files. Did you see what was in them?'

'No. I'll ask him later. He's with his pals just now.' Miller had a strange feeling in his gut.

Charlie still cowered behind the TV. 'The cat's scared,' he said. 'He doesn't like strangers too much.' *Yet he took to Kim right away.*

Kim walked over to the TV and talked to the cat like somebody might talk to a baby. He came round to see her, rubbing his head on her hand. She scratched his chin and he started purring.

'He likes you,' Miller said, wondering if Charlie missed Carol.

'He was scared, that's all.'

He needed to ask McGovern if he'd been armed the night Harry died, and whether he still had the gun if he had been. He had a feeling he knew what McGovern was going to tell him. *That Raymond Cross took it off him and was running about with the fucking thing now.*

Gibb left the flat. The ARU guys stayed and a short while later, Maggie Parks came in with some team members. 'We're going to dust for prints and have a scout around, if that's okay, Frank.'

'Yeah, that's fine.'

Kim put Charlie onto the back of the couch where he settled down. His big scratching post, Jack called it.

'I wonder what was so important in those files Cross took?' Scott asked.

'I don't know, but Jack was always fannying about with them.'

There was something niggling away at the back of Miller's mind, something he was trying to grab hold of, but it kept slipping away. They heard a commotion outside in the hall, and one of the ARU guys arguing with somebody.

'I'm family!' they heard a woman scream. Next thing, Julie Davidson came rushing into the living room, closely followed by the armed officer, who looked like he only needed the slightest excuse.

'She's okay,' Miller told the officer, who looked disappointed he hadn't opened fire.

'Are you alright?' She took her red jacket off, the melting snow running off onto his carpet. Charlie jumped off the couch and went running across to her. 'Hey, baby!' she said, picking the cat up. Charlie rubbed his face on her chin and Julie forgot about Miller for a moment.

'I'm fine, Julie,' Miller answered, though he wasn't sure she'd heard him.

She looked at him, still holding the cat, who seemed perfectly comfortable in her arms. 'You look awful. What happened?'

He gave her a brief rundown. Emphasising Cross had only got away because he had a gun.

'You poor thing.' She put the cat down. Her composure started to crumble. 'When I heard, it brought back memories of my dad.' She sat down in a chair. 'Do you really think it was Cross?'

Miller nodded. The cat came over to him and rubbed his legs before going back to Julie. 'Yes, I think it was the guy who killed Harry.'

'What does he want? To kill us all? First my dad, now you. Is he going to go through my whole family?' Full on tears now. Miller went over and sat on the arm of the chair and put his arm around her.

'It'll be fine, Julie. I think he wanted something my dad had, and now he's got it. He won't be back to bother us.'

He looked at Scott, who raised his eyebrows in a *you better fucking hope not* look.

SIXTY-FOUR

Everybody left Miller's flat except Kim.

'I'll make sure a patrol swings by your place,' Miller said.

'There's no need.'

'Unless you want to stop here?' The words were out before Miller had put any thought into them. He closed his eyes and shook his head. 'Jeez, listen to me. I meant you could have the spare room.'

She laughed. 'Don't worry, I know what you meant.'

'Jack will be home soon. I was worried Cross might come looking for you.' I'm taking a fucking beamer now, he thought, feeling his cheeks go red.

'How about if I stay, and we all look after each other?'

'That's good.' Miller added, 'I can't help worrying, especially after... well, you know.'

'I'm glad you worry, Frank.' She walked over to him and smiled. 'That bang on your head's obviously affecting you.'

'It is?'

'Yes, your face is all red.' She laughed. Which made his face go even redder. 'Would you like a coffee?'

'I'm okay thanks, but you help yourself. I want to look at some of Jack's files, see if I can find anything.'

He sat on the settee, and switched on his laptop as Kim went through to the kitchen. He was glad she felt at home in his place. Charlie looked up at him, decided this was nothing that was going to entertain him, and put his head back down. It felt good to have a woman in his home again, even if it was just a colleague. His father had told him he needed to get out and about again, that he was too young to be considered a widower, even if that's exactly what he was.

'It would be like I was cheating on Carol,' he'd told Jack, one night.

'I know you might feel like that, but you can't keep carrying the guilt around with you. You've nothing to feel guilty about. Harvey Levitt told you that. Going out socialising is normal.'

What Jack had said made perfect sense, but still Miller held back, throwing himself into his work. Even when he had a holiday, he hadn't gone anywhere. Instead, he went to the pub, but luckily he'd reined it in, knowing he was on a slippery slope.

He took his flash drive out and plugged it in, then opened the file he'd copied from Jack's computer: *Raymond Cross*.

'Mind if I sit beside you?' Kim asked.

'No, not at all.'

Miller read through the file, not noticing anything he hadn't read before. Until a name jumped out at him.

Jennifer Wilson.

'Isn't that the woman who died in the bar?'

'It has to be the same one.' There wasn't a photo, and he was surprised she hadn't changed her name, or maybe she'd gotten married, divorced and went back to using her maiden name. Then he remembered Molloy had said she'd never been married. He was sure she was the pub manager who was now lying in one of the coolers in the mortuary.

He looked at the names of the women who'd given Molloy an alibi back then: Andrea Kennedy, Jennifer Wilson and Toni Cooper.

He wondered if Toni Cooper became Toni Fleming.

Cross had gone to the party twenty-five years ago with Moira Kennedy. Maybe he thought one of the Molloys killed her and covered it up. Hence the blackmail.

Cross now had Molloy's money. Miller wondered if Harvey Levitt had been right and Cross would soon be finished with his killing spree.

He also wondered why Cross would try and kill him in Lamb's House, but not shoot him when he was a sitting duck.

SIXTY-FIVE

'I won't be long,' Kim said to him, pulling her jacket on. 'It won't take me five minutes to throw some stuff into a holdall. My rental car's downstairs so I won't have to walk far.'

'I can walk you to your car. I'm not saying you can't look after yourself or anything, far from it, but Cross is mental, and—'

Kim smiled, and put a hand on his arm.

Miller's phone rang. A number showed up on the screen. McGovern.

'Sorry, I have to take this.' He went into his room. 'Miller.'

'I heard what happened,' McGovern said.

How? Miller wondered. 'Everything's fine but he got away.'

'You were lucky.'

'We need to talk,' Miller said.

'I'll give you a call tomorrow. See if I can fit you in.'

'You'll fucking meet me now. Cross tried to kill me and I need to talk to you.'

'Now, now, Frank, let's not get upset. I'll meet you.'

'Stop being so fucking flippant.'

A pause. 'So where?'

'At the station. I'll head there now.'

McGovern laughed. 'I'll be there before you, Frank.'

The line went dead.

Miller was pissed off with himself for letting Cross get so close. How did he get in without Miller hearing? He'd already thought he must have been inside the flat, waiting. He'd obviously picked the lock.

Just like Kim had.

Now McGovern was being an arse. He went back to the living room, where Kim was petting the cat.

'I have to go out and meet somebody, but hopefully I won't be long. You can take these.' He went into the kitchen and took a set of keys off a hook. 'That'll save you using your lock picks.' He smiled at her.

'Are you never going to let me forget that, Frank Miller?'

'One day.'

'I'll go and get my things and come right back. Won't be long.'

It took Miller ten minutes to get to the station. McGovern couldn't possibly have got there before him. Snow was coming down, making the already slippery setts even more dangerous. Still, as long as they looked good for the tourists that was the main thing. He walked through the front door in Parliament Square. 'Anybody ask for me?' he asked the desk sergeant.

'No, sir. Nobody's been through the doors for a while.'

Miller nodded and headed upstairs. The squad room was quiet, with only a few lights on. Some of the night shift guys were in. The Skeleton Crew they were called. He heard laughter coming from the back of the room.

'So there I was, me trousers round me fucking ankles, and in she walks!' he heard an English cockney voice say. *Please God, no.* Miller's heart thumped in his chest. Walked round the corner to where the vending machine was. Two of the new guys were sitting on chairs, being entertained by somebody sitting on a desk.

Neil McGovern.

They looked at him as he walked round the corner. Just as well I don't have a fucking Uzi with me, *he thought.* So much for staying alert!

'There he is!' McGovern said, jumping off the desk. 'I got your message. You wanted to see me?'

Oh, here we fucking go. Miller could feel the anger rising inside him, but he forced a smile. What name would he have given himself? It wouldn't be McGovern. Bloody hell.

'Good to see you again, DI Smith,' Miller said. 'Thanks for coming so quickly.'

McGovern smiled even more. *You got that right, Frank,* he seemed to be saying. He'd hoped McGovern would use his daughter's name. If he hadn't then they were both fucked.

'No problem. You needed to speak to me about a witness in your enquiry?'

Miller kept smiling, imagining putting a gun to McGovern's head and pulling the trigger. He could maybe get the other two guys to help him hide the body. They could bury him in the woods. *Nobody would ever know...*

'Let's grab a coffee and use the conference room,' he said.

'Sure, Frank. The lads here were keeping me amused until you arrived. In fact, I think I'd like to work here. Maybe I'll put in for a transfer.' He looked at Miller again, challenging him. He rummaged about in his pocket for change for the machine. *Where do I work?*

'Wouldn't the Met miss you?'

'You kidding me? I'm up here doing some work just now and nobody even knows I'm gone! Gives me a chance to catch up on some Scottish hospitality.' He winked at the two sergeants and they laughed.

They got coffee from the machine and walked out into the corridor. They could have been in any anonymous office building in the city. The cut from the lamp wasn't obvious now, and he wasn't about to tell McGovern about it, especially the bit about Kim coming to spend the night with him. They went along to an interview room, one without a two-way mirror. Just in case Miller felt like hitting McGovern with a chair.

'I don't believe this,' Miller said, closing the door and sitting down at the table. McGovern sat opposite.

'Do you like me new look? I think it's quite dashing meself.' He ran a hand through his black-dyed hair. He was wearing fashionable, black-framed glasses. Nobody would ever suspect this was Neil McGovern, even if they were told to their face it was.

'How the fuck did you get in?' Miller asked. 'The desk sergeant said nobody's been in the front entrance for hours.' He sipped some coffee, trying to calm himself down. *Maybe caffeine isn't the way to go, Frank.*

'Old Eric? He couldn't find his own shoelaces without a map and a compass.' He drank some more coffee and smiled, like a schoolboy who just cheated on an exam and nobody could prove it. 'Meself and a couple of colleagues caused a brief outage in the power. Not long enough for the generator to kick in, but long enough to get the back door open. You might want to mention that to the suits upstairs. There's a ten second delay. Somebody might take advantage of that.'

'Fuck me. You're taking a chance letting yourself in. What if somebody had seen you?'

'Relax, Frank, you're going to give yourself an ulcer.' More coffee. More smiling. He was enjoying this. 'I have me warrant card, and I already have Police Scotland visitors' badges.'

Miller wrapped his hands round the small plastic cup, feeling the heat seep into them. He could imagine two guys dressed in black, pulling automatics on some uniforms. So much shit would hit the fan, he'd have to go and live in the Arctic.

'That's what I want to talk to you about; your gun,' Miller said.

'What about it?'

'Like where the fuck is it?'

'How do you know it's gone?'

'I told you on the phone, Raymond Cross pointed the fucking thing at my head. A Sig Sauer nine mil. Just like the one you pointed at me in the cemetery. Kim carries a Glock. So he either got a gun like yours from somewhere, and had it all along, or he took yours.' He pictured the black Sig pointing right at his face. Expecting to briefly see a muzzle flash, just before a little piece of metal was thrown into his brain at high speed.

McGovern sat back in his chair, the first sign of uncertainty creeping across his face. 'Kim has it.'

'Really? I'm glad you think so. Did she tell you that?'

'Not exactly.' The smile was gone now. McGovern leant forward. 'I asked her when we were in those vaults. I asked her if she had my gun, and she said, yes.'

'Did you confirm it when you were in the hospital?'

'Why is it so important, cock?'

Miller slapped his hand on the table. McGovern didn't flinch. 'I'll fucking tell you why; you lost it and now some nutcase has it and he's going to shoot somebody with it as sure as I'm sitting here.'

McGovern had a bemused look on his face. 'Here's a way to find out; why don't you ask her?'

'Okay, I will, but that might blow the fact you're still alive. How would I know about it being your gun otherwise?'

'You're right there, me old son. 'Tis a pickle we're in.'

'And you can stop talking like you're Oliver Twist, for fuck's sake.'

'I kinda like talking like this. Makes me feel all working class.'

'You and I are both working class. Just because you normally sound like a fucking Hooray Henry doesn't mean you haven't got your hands dirty.'

McGovern laughed. 'You're right, Frank. I'm not quite a toff, but talking like an East Ender was getting tiresome anyhow.'

'So how do we get round this?' Miller asked.

McGovern took a sip of coffee. It was getting cold. 'I don't see a way round this. I *think* Kim *did* tell me she had the gun. Maybe she thought I'd asked her if she had *her* gun.'

Miller looked at him. 'That would make sense. I wonder why he didn't point it at her in the crypts?'

'Maybe he didn't have time. Kim had her gun out after all.'

Miller looked at him, knowing McGovern was an expert liar. 'I think there's something you've not been telling me.'

'Oh? What's that?'

'You see, I started to wonder why you kept telling me to look for Raymond Cross. Why? You have a lot of resources too. Then the answer became obvious; you're supposed to be dead, a supposed deranged killer. So you couldn't go looking. Neither could your friends, or it would raise suspicion. So you get me to start looking into it. And there would only be one reason why you'd want me to do that.'

'Oh yeah? What's that then?'

'He's a friend of yours. You knew him back then, didn't you, McGovern?'

'I don't know what you're talking about, Frank.'

'Yes, you do. I was looking through some of my dad's old files he'd copied from here. It pissed him off that Cross could walk out of the station with the help of somebody else. So I get attacked tonight and files were stolen from me. I wondered what they were all about. Now, I'm no rocket scientist, but I know to back things up. So did Carol. Harry on the other hand, not so much. Carol has a laptop, and I remembered she said she'd backed up files for her dad, in case his machine crashed.

'So I looked at them earlier. And I came across an interesting one. Regarding the surveillance operation from the night Moira Kennedy was murdered. Raymond Cross was a mole for Harry Davidson. He was reporting back to him. So it was obvious Harry had to get him out of the station.'

'You have a vivid imagination, Frank.'

'Yes, I do. So I thought some more about it. That night, how could Harry orchestrate that on his own? Was Colin Fleming in on it? I think he was. Still, it was a lot to organise. Getting a man out of the station? They couldn't do that on their own. So I delved further, and Harry mentions DI Brigham. The detective from the Met who walked out with Cross? I know his identity, McGovern. And I know where he is.'

McGovern laughed out loud. 'And where is he then?'

Miller looked at him. 'I'm sitting talking to him.'

SIXTY-SIX

McGovern smiled. 'See? That's why I contacted you, old cock. Not just a pretty face.' He leaned back in his chair and reached out a hand. Drummed his fingers on the table in front of him, as if he knew he'd reached a fork in the road, and it was time to decide which way to travel.

He sat up straight. 'You've almost got it right, Frank. One thing you didn't find out was Raymond Cross wasn't a mole; he was one of us.'

'That's what Kim said about you.'

'It's true. He was working undercover. I think we trained him a little too well, don't you? Anyway, we got him inside Molloy's little empire, and he was reporting back to me. I was the liaison between Cross and Harry. It wouldn't look too good if he was caught talking to the filth, now would it? So he and I would meet up. He'd give me the skinny on Molloy and I'd meet with Harry. We hadn't gotten anything useful, mind, by the time poor Moira was murdered.'

'So you covered up her murder. Cross got off scot free.'

McGovern held up his hands. 'No, no, nothing like that. That's not how we operate, believe it or not. If he'd sliced her up, he would've been taken care of. No, Cross didn't kill her.'

'That's why you played the role of being DI Bingham from London so you could just walk out with Cross?'

McGovern laughed. 'How did you figure it out?'

'I was thinking about the copies of your ID Kim showed me. I wondered if they were real. Which made me think about fake IDs and that's when I thought maybe you could have faked a Met ID all those years ago. That's why I checked those files tonight.'

'Yes, we did. And pretty good they were too, I must say.'

'Were those department files Kim showed me fake?'

'Of course not. Offence taken, Frank. I wouldn't use my own daughter like that. No, they were real. That's who I am.'

'So what happened to Cross after you got him out of the station?'

'A while before that operation, he'd told me this sort of job wasn't for him. He wanted out. So we let him go. There's no point in having somebody work for the department who isn't giving it their all. A mistake would be made sooner or later, and somebody could lose their life. He left but I asked him to do this one job for me. He came back and did it. Then it went pear-shaped. After I got him out of the station, the department took care of him and he disappeared.

'Then, as I told you in the cemetery, next thing I know, Harry wants to meet me in the crypts. He said he knew who'd murdered those three women two years ago. Not only that, but they were connected to the murder of Moira Kennedy.'

'And he told you it was Cross?'

'Yes. He whispered Raymond's name.'

'I want Cross put away for this. I don't want him disappearing again.'

McGovern smiled, but his eyes were cold. 'You'll get him, Frank.'

'Did Harry mention who killed Moira Kennedy, before the night he died?'

'I'd met Harry a couple of times before. He was reluctant to talk to me, but he wanted to. It just had to be the right time. That night we were in the crypts, he said it was the safest place to be. He was going to tell me who it was.'

'Turns out it was far from safe.' Miller looked at McGovern. 'Do you think you were set up that night?'

McGovern looked puzzled. 'What do you mean?'

'I mean, do you think Harry was luring you there? To set you up as the killer? Maybe he was working with Cross. Have you ever thought of that?'

McGovern shook his head. 'No. I never got that impression. He seemed worried. Why would you ask that? He was your father-in-law. Do you suspect everybody, Frank?'

'You've been in this game a lot longer than me, McGovern. You have those feelings too. Your gut telling you something isn't right.'

'I do, but I trusted Harry.' McGovern's eyes gave the game away; Miller knew the other man was having doubts.

'Let me ask this, Neil; *if* Harry Davidson was going to set you up, what would he have to gain?'

McGovern sat and let the question sink in.

'One more thing,' Miller said. 'Why weren't the two guys in the black Range Rover with you the night you were attacked?'

'Barn doors and horses. I'm thankful they're here now to drive me around.'

'Are they SAS?'

'Dearie me. Look at you. Getting yourself in a right tizzy there, Frank.' McGovern looked at Miller, and the detective could see a hardness there, just like the hardness he'd seen in Kim's eyes the first time he met her. 'I *could* tell you, but I'd have to kill you afterwards.'

McGovern smiled, but Miller got the impression he wasn't kidding. 'Why don't you pull Kim back from the investigation?'

'I think she's in the safest place right now. She works with coppers all day. Besides, I don't think she's a target. I was, but he thinks I'm dead. Which is why we haven't got all the time in the world, cock.'

'Kim's coming back to my place tonight. I can't exactly tell her that two of Her Majesty's finest soldiers would have been protecting her, but I'll be looking after her instead.'

McGovern wasn't smiling now. 'If by "looking after her", you mean—'

Miller held up a hand. 'She'll be in the spare room.'

McGovern nodded. 'It's not me you have to fear, Miller. My wife would rip your balls off and use them for earrings if her little girl was messed about.'

'You have to learn to trust me more.' Miller stood up. 'What's your plan of action now?'

'Just like Cross did all those years ago, I'm going to be escorted out of the station without anybody stopping me.' McGovern got up.

Miller shook his head and walked to the door. 'You just can't fucking help yourself, can you?'

'In my game, you sometimes need to be ballsy, Frank. You need to step out the window and walk along the ledge.'

Miller opened the door and switched off the lights. Looked at the shorter man. 'Is Kim safe when she's not around us? When she's at home at night?'

McGovern smiled. 'She's my little girl. What do you think?'

'I think you might be using her as bait.'

'You don't know me, Frank. That's not something her mother would allow. I don't fear any man alive, but I don't want to get on the wrong side of me missus.'

They walked downstairs.

'Can I say goodbye to me new mates? They might forget me.'

'Can you fuck. I'm sure they'll remember what you look like when the sketch artist comes round.'

'You worry too much, Frank.'

'I don't worry *enough*.'

McGovern laughed. They walked through the pen and out onto High Street.

'You don't have to walk out with me,' McGovern said.

'I want to make sure you leave.' Miller stopped McGovern for a moment. 'I have a favour to ask.'

'Go ahead.'

'Julie, my sister-in-law, is leaving to work in London. She's going to St Luke's. If you know people down there, maybe somebody could check on her, see she's doing okay, without anybody knowing.'

McGovern smiled again. 'Leave it with me. I'll call one of my contacts down there.'

The wind was bringing the temperature down, but the snow had stopped falling. The pavements were slick. Miller pulled the collar on his coat up. Blew his breath into the cold night.

'Remember what I told you, Frank. It's in your hands now. You watch your back with that bastard, Cross. He was a sneaky sod back then, and he obviously hasn't lost the knack. I'll be around though. You just won't see me.'

The black Range Rover pulled into the kerb as if McGovern had used telepathy to call it. McGovern walked over, and Miller saw him listening to the driver. Then he turned to Miller.

'My driver said Kim just left her house. You look after her, Miller.'

'Don't worry, safety in numbers, that's all. Where are you staying?'

'A safe house we have up here. Norma told me you know she's my wife, but I'm not staying at our place. Just in case.'

'Let me ask you something. Norma's been the PF for a couple of years now. How come we never met you?'

'You didn't? I remember meeting you a couple of times. I wasn't introduced as her husband of course, but I was at a few dos she was at.' He winked at Miller. 'Stay alive, Frank.'

McGovern was about to get into the car when he turned back to look at Miller.

'When Harry told me he knew who the killer was, something

occurred to me. I reckon Harry not only knew who Moira's real killer was—'

'But he's been protecting him all these years,' Miller finished for him.

SIXTY-SEVEN

Michael Molloy felt numb as he poured himself another whisky in the darkness of his living room. He looked out through the French doors to his snow-covered back garden. It was dark, but he could see the streetlights in Dalgety Bay across the Forth. He'd been thinking about Andrea, of the good times they'd had. Not just years ago either, but recently. She was a lady, a *real* lady, not like some of the women he knew.

He pictured her face as she lay on the gurney the bloke had wheeled her through on. He'd stood on the other side of the glass partition, looking at the woman he'd fallen in love with all those years ago. Who he still loved. He would never have married any other woman. He'd gone out with plenty, but none he would ever have invited back to his house.

He missed her so much already, and didn't know how he was going to cope without her. He hadn't seen what she was like after Cross had touched her, but he could guess. When he got hold of Cross, he'd make the bastard feel pain. He'd get a team up from London and they'd take Cross apart, bit by bit.

He froze, as he heard his front door open and gently close again.

245

'Hello? Dad, is that you?' There was no answer. Who else would it be if it wasn't his father?

Then he felt a jolt of fear. Something was wrong here. He'd heard about spirits coming back. He didn't want to use the word "ghost", but he'd always been open to such ideas. What if Andrea was pissed with him and came back to haunt him?

He didn't think he could take that.

'Why are you in my house?' he shouted out loud. Then he sensed somebody standing behind him.

'What sort of welcome is that after all this time, Michael?'

Michael Molloy stood transfixed. It wasn't his father and it wasn't Andrea's ghost. He couldn't make out the face for the balaclava, but he knew who it was.

Raymond Cross was in his house. And he was holding an axe.

Miller walked back home where Charlie came running up the hallway to meet him. Jack came out of the living room. 'You okay, son?'

'I'm fine, Dad. You didn't have to come home.'

'I know. I was bored anyway.'

'Kim's spending the night. She wanted to be here in case Cross came back.'

'Good idea.'

His mind still felt like it was in some kind of fugue. He should be having an early night and resting after being attacked, but that wouldn't help catch Cross. Sleep later, he thought. He took a beer from the fridge gave it to Jack.

'You sure you're feeling alright. Son?' Jack looked concerned.

'I'm fine.'

'Well, if you start to feel funny, you let me know. I'll get you right up to the Royal.'

'Any more funny than usual?' He looked at his father. 'How well did you know Harry Davidson?'

'What do you mean?'

'I mean, how well did you *think* you knew him?'

'He was a good friend. I trusted him.'

Miller knew he could trust his father with anything. They'd always had a special bond, and he decided he needed to share this with him now. 'How much did you know about the Moira Kennedy murder?'

'Just as much as you know. Cross murdered her, and then escaped.'

'I want to tell you something before Kim gets here. I need to trust you with this. Nobody hears about it. Okay?'

'Okay, okay. Just get on with it.'

'I'm being serious, Jack.'

'Alright. Tell me.'

'Neil McGovern isn't dead. He works for the government. He was Raymond Cross's handler. He was working with Harry Davidson when Harry was murdered.'

Jack looked stunned. 'This isn't a joke?'

'Do I look like I'm laughing? I spoke to him in the station tonight. And not only that, he was the one who walked out of the station with Cross. With Harry Davidson's help, of course.'

Jack looked furious. 'Are you sure?'

Miller nodded. 'Straight from the horse's mouth, as it were.'

Jack shook his head. 'I don't believe it.' He looked at his son. 'Why would they help a murderer escape?'

'He didn't kill Moira Kennedy.'

'What? Then who did?'

'That's what the meeting was about when Harry was killed. He was going to tell McGovern who the killer was.'

'McGovern's still alive. I don't believe it.'

Miller nodded again. 'His death was faked so he could get out of the hospital. Kim thinks he's dead, and he wants it to stay that way. He wants to know why Cross is murdering people who are connected to Robert Molloy.'

'Why now?'

'That's what we need to find out. Whatever it is, we think Harry was connected. He knew who the original killer was, and he's been covering it up all these years. Now I'm thinking both he and Cross knew who Moira's murderer was and they both covered it up. Cross didn't want Harry to reveal the name, so when he found out, he murdered him and tried to kill McGovern.'

'Harry never mentioned anything to me, son.'

'Of course he wouldn't. It's not something he could drop into the conversation.'

Jack looked at him. 'So Harry was playing everybody along all this time? You don't suppose...?'

'No. Not for a moment.' He didn't think Carol knew Harry's secret.

'I can't believe this.'

'The thing we need to find out is, why?'

'Whatever the reason, now his actions have put Julie in danger.'

Miller needed to make a phone call. With everything else that was going on, he had to know if there was a connection between Richard Sullivan the lawyer, and Harry Davidson the copper.

And whether that had cost Miller's wife her life.

SIXTY-EIGHT

Michael Molloy looked at the axe, his eyes transfixed. Raymond Cross was here, in his own home. But it wasn't Cross, he knew that. The voice was different. *How do you know what Cross's voice sounds like? You haven't heard it for twenty-five years.*

'Why don't you show yourself?' he said, trying to focus his eyes, trying to make out shapes in the dark. He tried flicking the light switch by the French doors but nothing came on. The living room was in darkness, except for the flames licking away in the open fire, throwing dancing shadows around the room.

Silence.

He watched as the figure slowly came into the room.

He focused his anger on the person in front of him. Cross was wearing what looked to be a long, black cloak with a balaclava over his head. 'So you've come back? Or had you never left at all?' Molloy said.

'I left for quite a long time, remember?' The voice was being muffled by the balaclava; only the eyes showed. The orange flames threw shadows around the room like the house was beginning to burn.

He walked closer to Molloy, but Molloy wasn't scared. He'd stood up to mental bastards in pubs before, taking each of them down with a wicked punch, just before he launched in with his feet. So Cross didn't scare him now, rather angered him.

'The money you stole from the hotel room doesn't matter to me,' Molloy said.

'That's good to hear.'

Molloy felt the breath catch in his throat for a moment, before answering. 'You know my father's going to skin you alive, right?'

'I don't think so. You see, he's going to get it tonight after you.'

'You haven't got the balls. The police are all over the place looking for you, but they'll never find you. I'll have you buried alive, and I'll piss on you just before the first shovelful of dirt is thrown on your face.'

Cross held the axe out in front of him, easing ever closer, walking with a slow confidence. Molloy was getting angrier and angrier. *Come on you bastard, just let me smack you, then we'll see who's in fucking charge here.*

'What's this all about? You murdering people who pissed you off? Is that it?'

'It's all about justice at the end of the day. You're just a pawn in the whole picture, Michael. A pawn who got caught up in it all, all those years ago. Now it ends here.'

Cross was fast. Far too fast for Molloy. His hand shot out and hit Molloy on the side of the jaw, knocking him sideways. Molloy fell onto the carpet, his face burning on the rug. Then Cross was on top of him.

Michael Molloy was helpless as the axe came down.

SIXTY-NINE

Sienna Craig left the warmth of her car, and stepped into the freezing cold of the night. She walked up to the back door of the club.

She stopped when she saw Molloy walking along the corridor towards her.

'Sienna, I'd appreciate it if you'd come with me. I'd like to discuss some security issues with you.'

'Yes, of course.'

'Let's take my car.'

Sienna felt an adrenaline rush kick in. Where were they going?' She didn't like surprises.

Back outside, the lane wasn't as darkly disturbing as it usually was, thanks to the snow lighting up the corners and crevices. Robert had his overcoat on, and Sienna watched him as he reached a hand into a pocket. Brought out a pair of gloves and a woollen hat. 'Christ, I hate the winter here. I was talking to Michael about my retirement.'

'You look too young to retire.' She smiled at him.

'Maybe you could come and join me as my PA in Spain. I have a nice house, a big yacht. We could have fun together, you and me.'

You must be fucking joking, she thought, trying not to gag at the idea of this old bastard lying on top of her. That's what he really wanted, wasn't it? 'That sounds like a good idea,' she said, knowing it would never happen.

'Here,' he said, reaching into his trouser pocket. He took out his car keys and tossed them to her. 'You drive.'

She caught them one-handed. Hit the remote and climbed in behind the wheel. Started it up and hit the buttons for the heated steering wheel and the heated seats.

'Where are we going?'

'My place.'

She drove out of Rose Street, the winter tyres cutting through the snow with ease. The street was quiet, which was unusual. Once the service road for the big houses on Princes Street, it had grown over the years, so it was now a haven for boutiques and pubs.

She turned the car into Hanover Street. Molloy lived in New Town, and Heriot Row was one of the most exclusive streets.

There was a space by his front door, a courtesy his neighbours afforded him. Only the foolish and unwary would park their car in front of his house.

'Take off your coat, Sienna. I wanted to talk business with you, but I didn't want to do it in the club. Michael has cameras everywhere as I'm sure you know, and sometimes I think I can't take a breath but he has it filmed.'

She smiled at him, taking off her coat and handing it to him.

Molloy hung it next to his in the hallway. He came back into the living room, picked up a remote control and aimed it at the log fire. It burst into life. An imitation log fire.

'Hundreds of years ago, they would have thought I was practising witchcraft.' Molloy laughed.

'I don't think I could have survived all those years ago, without all the mod cons.'

'That's what people will be saying a couple of hundred years from now, when they're all flying around in spaceships.' He pointed to one of the leather couches. 'Please, sit. Let me fix you a drink. How about wine?'

'Fine. Thanks,' she said, sitting down. The heating had been on before they came in so the living room was already warm.

'I have a nice bottle down in the cellar. I won't be long. Then we can get down to business, and I'll tell you how you can start making serious money with me.'

'Sounds good.'

Robert left the room and she could hear a door opening, then silence.

A pair of large, skinny speakers were hooked up to a cinema surround system, standing sentry at either side of the huge flat-screen TV. She was reaching out for the remote control that sat on the coffee table in front of her when she saw the reflection of the killer on the darkened TV screen.

SEVENTY

Richard Sullivan brought the Audi A5 to a halt outside Lamb's House. Or what was left of it. Now it was a pile of charred rubble.

He turned the engine off and got out of the warmth and walked over to the security fence, once put in place to keep thieves and vandals out, now there to stop somebody from breaking their neck on a piece of blackened timber.

Would he rebuild? It was something he'd have to consider after he got the insurance cheque. Probably not. He'd just walk away from it all.

He shivered in the cold, snow lightly falling down on him.

He wondered what his wife would have thought of it all. She was always full of life and probably would have hated to have been tied down to his business, but he would have lavished everything on her. Given her everything she'd ever wished for.

That was why he sometimes felt like telling Tai he didn't want to get involved. Even after all this time, he still loved his wife. There were times when he'd sit and think about her and take out the photo albums. Look at her smiling face.

The longing would settle over him like a shroud, and he'd put the albums away until the next time.

A dog barked somewhere in the distance and somebody screamed. Leith was going through a transformation, with new flats springing up everywhere, but there were parts that were still danger zones. Where drug dealers and hoors pounded their beat. Yet Leithers were the salt of the earth. It was a working class place, just like Kelty. Work hard, get pished at the weekend. Back to work Monday morning. It had worked for thousands of people over the years. Sometimes money isolated rich people from having fun. *Real* fun. Going out on a Friday night with your mates, meeting some girl at a dance.

He was thinking about the good times he'd had when he was younger when he was suddenly aware of the van pulling up alongside him. The driver had wound the passenger side window down and was leaning over the passenger seat to ask him a question.

'Here, mate, can you help me?'

The accent wasn't from around here. Sullivan stepped through the snow banked up at the side of the road and stood at the passenger window. 'Sure. What's up?'

'I have a question; you seen Raymond Cross recently?'

Sullivan's heart exploded in his chest and he tried to turn and run. His foot slipped on the snow and he fell on one knee. He scrambled up and saw the driver sitting smiling at him.

He didn't see the other man behind him with the black hood.

He felt hands manhandling him into the back of the van.

'Molloy! You're a complete bastard, you know that?' Sullivan said, struggling as the hands pinned him down. 'I told you I don't know what happened to Carol Miller.'

'I'm not Robert Molloy and these aren't his men,' a voice said, close to his ear. He pulled the hood off. The man smiled. 'It's been a while.'

'I was wondering when you'd turn up,' Sullivan said, relaxing.

It had been a very long time since Neil McGovern and Raymond Cross had been in the same place together.

SEVENTY-ONE

Spending so much time with lowlifes had sharpened Sienna's reflexes. Just the slightest touch on her shoulder would have her springing into action. This time, she had more warning, which was just as well, considering the knife her attacker was carrying.

She hadn't heard anything. Wasn't expecting to hear anything except Molloy coming into the living room with a bottle of wine, so seeing this person reflected in the huge TV screen set her heart on fire.

The adrenaline kicked in and she was up from the settee and rolling over the coffee table in one fluid movement. The figure before her was dressed all in black; jacket, trousers, boots. Gloves. Balaclava.

The knife.

Raymond Cross. In the flesh.

A black combat knife. Sienna had seen them before, used by British Special Forces soldiers. Designed to be used clandestinely. One edge was serrated. It was sharp and deadly. Made for killing with extreme prejudice.

Raymond Cross had come here to kill Robert Molloy. Of that

there was no doubt. The only fly in the ointment was her, Sienna Craig.

'Put the knife down and maybe I won't hurt you,' she said, to the figure. She could see around the eyes: Caucasian. Not much help.

No reaction. No backchat. No talking at all. This guy was good. Height? Five ten, maybe.

He started running, as if a starter's gun had gone off in his head. He was running a hurdle race, and this particular hurdle was the settee. Its short height proved no problem; Cross leapt onto it, his right foot landing on the back, immediately pushing off again, the left leg stretching out to land on the coffee table, his right arm back, preparing the knife to strike down.

Sienna had seen it before, many times. Drink made them slow and angry, so you had time to dodge the punch. *Just make sure you take them down before they get a second chance.* Guys like Cross were a bit harder to deal with. You had to adapt in a split second.

In the moment from when Cross started running at the settee, she'd gone into attack mode. She'd told Molloy she wouldn't wear a skirt or dress whilst on duty, and he'd agreed. She needed to be able to fight, she'd told him. Now, she was wearing black jeans and a turtle neck sweater. Just perfect for fighting.

Cross's hand came down with the knife. Aiming at her upper body. It would certainly kill her the first time it connected. Control the knife! she shouted in her head. You control that fucking knife!

The black blade sliced through the air towards her; her eyes locked onto it like a heat-seeking missile. Thoughts weren't tumbling through her mind but were sharply focused, guiding her hand to the knife hand. One chance was all she was going to get. Cross was quick, but Sienna's reflexes were sharper.

As the knife came down, Cross didn't intend to miss, his body following the knife in an arc, putting weight behind it. When it struck flesh and bone, it only had to hit home once, giving him time to drop to the floor, readying himself to strike again, just for fun.

Before he gutted her.

Sienna grabbed his wrist with her left hand, reaching up with her right, grabbing him below the elbow, and using his momentum to throw him into the TV. It crashed over off its stand, taking Cross with it.

Sienna saw the knife. Still in Cross's hand, holding onto the weapon as if his life depended on it, but he was in an awkward position. Hitting the TV hadn't hurt him, but had been enough to delay his next attack.

Sienna wasn't about to let him do that. She saw Cross's gloved hand lying across one of the speakers. Tried to stamp on it. He saw it coming, and moved at the last second. Rolling away quickly, but not quickly enough. Sienna picked up the other speaker, yanking it free from its wires. She knew if she swung it like a baseball bat and missed, she'd leave herself exposed. She used short jabs, looking for a weakness. A whack on the wrist knocked Cross's knife to one side.

She heard a guttural growl coming from Cross's throat, and swung the speaker, mentally tracking the trajectory his head would take if he ducked, which he did. The speaker connected with the side of his head. Instead of falling, he rolled, trying to grab the fallen knife.

Sienna kicked it away, swung again and missed. As she twisted, Cross threw himself at her, taking her down in a rugby tackle. Sienna threw the speaker aside. Feeling herself falling backwards, not wanting to give Cross a weapon.

They tumbled together, Sienna landing on her back. Cross sat up, sitting on her stomach, trying to reach her flailing arms. He grabbed hold of her wrists. She brought her leg up, over Cross's head, and twisted her body, bringing the back of her knee round Cross's throat. He let her wrists go as he fell back. Before his head hit the floor, she released her leg. They scrambled to their feet. Cross launched himself at her.

Sienna grappled with him, her hand scrabbling for his mask. His face was running with sweat. He grabbed her by the throat. Tried punching her in the gut to wind her. She put her chin down, and

258

brought her arm down over his hand, twisting herself down and round. He pushed her away. As she fell over, she rolled.

She looked up, expecting Cross to be picking the knife up, but he wasn't. He was running from the living room. Sienna was on her feet and after him.

He was out the front door, down the outside steps and running along Heriot Row.

Sienna shut the door and locked it, getting her breathing under control. Saw the bag lying in the hall, but ignored it. Instead, she went looking for Robert Molloy. Found him lying on the kitchen floor, unconscious, a line of blood running down the side of his face from his head. A wine bottle sat on the counter, blood on the label.

She tried to revive him, but he only moaned.

Then she took her phone out and called for an ambulance. She thought it would be good for everybody if Robert Molloy were dead. Just not right now.

SEVENTY-TWO

'Nice place you got here, Ray,' Neil McGovern said, taking a sip of the single malt Richard Sullivan had poured for him.

'I don't know why you keep calling me that,' Sullivan said. 'Raymond Cross doesn't exist. Never has, remember?'

McGovern looked out of the large window in Sullivan's living room, admiring the view through the darkness. The lights in the harbour illuminated a supply ship docked below, while the colourful lights of the casino further along invited him to part with his money. He turned to look at Sullivan.

'Somebody thinks Raymond Cross still exists. That should really narrow it down a bit.'

Sullivan took a long swallow of the whisky. 'It's not narrowing it down quickly enough. People are dying.'

'We're working on that.' He looked at him. 'Why didn't you think I was dead?'

Sullivan laughed. 'Because I know *you*. You always were a slippery bastard. I remember that from when I worked in the department.'

'You should have stayed with us, Dickie. You could have been way up the ladder by now.'

Sullivan shook his head. 'I was already out of the department when I did you that favour. I should have stayed out. *One more time*, you said. *This time, we'll get the bastard*, you said. And you saw the opportunity because of Moira, who was your way in through the back door. I'll live to regret that decision as long as I live.'

'You're not the only one who feels guilty about that, old son. It was supposed to be a simple operation, remember? None of us could have seen that coming.'

'*Raymond Cross*.' Sullivan almost spat the words out. 'I didn't like that name to begin with, and now it's come back to haunt me. Somebody's killing people associated with Robert Molloy, and now they think it's me come back after all these years. None of them know I never went away, or that Raymond Cross never even existed. I thought Raymond Cross was dead and buried after we walked out of that station.'

McGovern looked at him. 'The department did a good job on the nip and tuck. Not even Molloy recognised you when you were representing his men. That must have been the highlight of your legal career.'

Sullivan shrugged. 'Means to an end. It made my name, then I got lucky after that.'

'And now somebody wants to take it all away.' More whisky. McGovern sat down on the leather couch. 'I did wonder if you really killed Carol when I read about her being run down by your car. You didn't think somebody stole your car by coincidence, did you?'

Sullivan sat in a chair and rested one foot on the other knee. 'I did at the time. Nobody knows who I was, or what I did, back then. Obviously I was wrong. Maybe Molloy is being cunning and really knows who I am.'

'I don't think Robert Molloy is that subtle. You'd be out in the Forth by now if he knew about you.' He took another sip of whisky. 'Don't worry, I'll put Frank straight about it.'

'You're not going to talk to Miller, are you?'

'Already have, old son. Frank's not too bad when you get to know him. He's just pissed off that somebody killed his wife.' Once again, McGovern looked Sullivan in the eyes. 'You sure you didn't mow her down, and pretend it had been stolen?'

'Fuck off. I reported it stolen two days before she was run over.'

'Good cover story.'

Sullivan smiled, but there was no warmth in it. 'You wouldn't be in my flat drinking whisky with me with your men waiting outside if you thought for one minute I'd murdered Carol Miller. I think you'd have fed me to the sharks by now, aka, the Miller clan. Frank and his mental father, Jack.'

McGovern raised his glass and drank some more. 'I wouldn't have done that, Dickie; I would have arranged for you to go away on holiday somewhere.'

'With a one-way ticket?'

'Hell doesn't do return journeys.'

Sullivan picked up the remote from the arm of the chair. The TV was on low, and he flipped through the channels, more to give him thinking time than any real interest in what was on.

'Any ideas who could be doing this?' he asked McGovern.

'I told Miller to concentrate on your past, not because I think you did this, but he might find somebody in there we overlooked. At this point, I'm willing to try anything.'

'So that's a "no".'

'That would be a no. And to be honest, since I already knew it wasn't you, I didn't have a clue who it could be. Somebody who hates you enough to set you up.'

'How did you know I wasn't responsible?'

McGovern laughed out loud. 'No offence, Dickie, but you as a serial killer? No, old son, you're a lover, not a fighter. Talking of which, how's the delightful Miss Lopez?'

'You know about her?'

'I know everything about you.'

'If you know, then maybe Molloy knows.'

'Even if he does, he won't do anything. He wouldn't be that stupid. Tai's family are well connected in Columbia. I checked. Somebody would be using his corpse as a coffee table if they messed with her. Besides, I have a team here in Edinburgh, working round the clock. Makes those clowns who work for Molloy look like choir boys. We have a huge arsenal, and it's all legal. More than I can say about daftie Michael Molloy with his Glock.'

They drank in silence for a moment. 'Did you ever have any dealings with Harry Davidson over the years?' McGovern asked.

Sullivan nodded. 'He obviously knew about me and how I was taken care of by the department. I think somebody upstairs told him about me, so he knew my new identity. I met him a few times over the years, but the last time was when he came to me wanting to rip my head off after he thought I'd killed Carol. Did he tell you who'd killed her the night you were both attacked?'

McGovern drank some more whisky. 'He'd already been stabbed by the time I got to those crypts. He was grasping onto life, but he said Frank was in danger. And mentioned Cross, just before he died. Wasn't making too much sense.'

'I wonder why the killer waited over two years to come back after killing those three women.'

McGovern looked at him. 'Somehow, Harry knew who he was, and was going to tell me, and who killed Moira Kennedy. The thing is, I think both killers are one and the same. He started twenty-five years ago, and his first victim was Moira Kennedy.'

SEVENTY-THREE

The ambulance was at Molloy's door in minutes. The control centre had automatically dispatched a patrol car when the caller said the occupant of the house had been attacked.

The paramedics walked into the house behind the uniforms.

'He's in here,' Sienna said. The first officer, an older sergeant, nodded at his partner. *Keep your fucking eyes peeled,* his look said. *This might be a domestic, or she might be a psycho.* It was a rich part of town, but it took all sorts.

'I need you to step back and let the paramedics in,' the sergeant said to Sienna. Then to his partner, 'Go and give the rest of the house the once-over. Just in case he's still here.'

'He's gone. I chased him out of the house,' Sienna said, as the two paramedics came into the kitchen and started work on Molloy.

'Nevertheless. Just so we don't leave any stone unturned. He mightn't have been working alone.' *Although by the looks of you, that wouldn't give you any sleepless nights.* He kept his hand near his Taser just in case.

Five minutes later, the other uniform came back down, shaking his head. Sienna stood watching over the paramedics, her arms folded. The sergeant stepped along to the front door. Made the call. *Bring everything you've got.*

'Well, I never thought I'd see Robert Molloy laid out like that,' Miller said, as he and Tam Scott looked down at the prone body.

Miller had called Kim and asked her to take a detour before she got to his place.

'Is he still alive?' Scott asked, tempted to kick Molloy.

'Robert Molloy's invincible, isn't he?' Kim said.

'He likes to think so,' Miller said.

A paramedic was kneeling beside Molloy, attending to him. Patching him up. 'He's stable right now, but I don't know what damage that wine bottle did to his head.' The other paramedic knelt at the other side with the bag. He was holding the oxygen mask over Molloy's face.

Gary Davidson came in and walked up to Miller. 'I got here as soon as, Frank.'

'I wanted you in on this, even though you're leading the other team.'

'I appreciate the heads-up. What happened?'

Miller took him aside. 'Raymond Cross was here. We think he scudded Molloy with a wine bottle then attacked Sienna Craig, planning to finish off Molloy afterwards.'

'Why didn't he just kill Molloy?'

'I think he enjoys it, Gary. Rushing the job isn't his thing. He wants to take his time doing it. By smacking Molloy first, he could quickly kill the bodyguard, then take his time over Molloy. That's what I think, anyway.'

'You're right. He's a vicious bastard.'

Miller looked at him. 'Do you remember your dad ever talking about Cross and the Moira Kennedy case?'

'Not that I recall. Julie was the one who was always asking questions about Dad's job, but she's ten years older. He'd talk to her about things without telling Carol and me. Why?'

Miller shook his head. 'I just thought it might have given us more insight into how Cross ticks.'

'About earlier, Frank. I was out of order.'

'Forget it, mate. We're all on edge right now.'

They walked back down the hall. Sienna looked at Miller. 'I tried calling Michael. It went to voicemail.'

'He's had a rough day. He's probably well pished by now.'

Sienna shrugged. 'You know him better than I do.'

Paddy Gibb was standing with a frown on his face. He hadn't been pleased to get the phone call from Miller, but when he heard what had happened, it had made his night. 'It's lucky you were here tonight. If not, Molloy might have been killed.'

'Yeah, lucky.'

'You sure there was somebody in here, Ms Craig? Sure you didn't get into a fight with him and decide to clean his clock?'

'Oh, piss off. If I had, I wouldn't have called the ambulance afterwards, would I?'

Gibb looked at her. *You might if you were fucking clever enough.* 'Stick around. We'll want to have another chat soon.'

'I'm going to the hospital.'

The paramedic stood up. 'We're ready to transport him now.'

The first one left for a moment and came back with the stretcher. They got Molloy strapped onto it and wheeled him away, helped by some uniforms. Sienna was right behind them.

Five minutes later, the ambulance left with its siren blaring. 'Jimmy, you and Hazel go to the hospital and talk to Molloy when he wakes up, see if he remembers anything before he was attacked. Keep your eyes on that Craig woman.'

'Sir.' He and Carter left to follow the ambulance as Maggie Parks was coming in with her team.

'What's going on now, Frank?'

'Robert Molloy was attacked by an intruder. We think it was Raymond Cross.' He pointed to the bag in the hallway.

'Molloy's minder fought him off and he left without his stuff,' Kim said.

'Ah. Let's have a look then.' Parks and her team suited up, and a few minutes later, opened the large holdall. She pulled out a plastic crime scene suit. 'He came ready for action I see.'

'That's how he stays clean,' Miller said to Gibb.

Maggie pulled out a dust mask and plastic safety specs. 'Used for DIY jobs. Can be bought in any DIY store. Used to stop blood spatter getting in your mouth and eyes.' She looked at Miller. 'He came prepared.'

'He always does.'

'I wonder where he would get the suit?' Gibb said.

Maggie Parks lifted the suit. Peered inside like a mother might do to a children's dirty sweater before sticking it in the washing machine. 'I know where he got it from.'

Miller, Gibb and Scott looked at the label inside the collar: *Property of Police Scotland.*

'A cop?' Gibb looked at Maggie. 'One of you lot?'

'What? Not one of my crew, Detective Chief Inspector.' There was disdain on her face.

'Well, apparently, it fucking is,' Gibb retaliated.

'Okay, let's calm down here,' Miller said, waiting for Maggie to punch Gibb in the mouth. He looked at her. 'How would he be able to get hold of one of these, Maggie? And are any reported missing?'

She looked at him. 'We take several to crime scenes. We have them on of course, and we also have a box of them in the van.' She looked at Gibb. 'Sometimes, crime scenes are so messy we have to change several times.'

'What about the dirty ones?'

'They're put into another box. Disposed of at HQ.'

'Are they counted?' Miller asked.

She shook her head. 'No. They're disposable. They all come with the Police label on them.'

'So somebody could have whipped one,' Gibb said.

'It couldn't have been just anybody,' Miller said. 'It would have to be somebody close to the investigation.'

'Let's get it up to the lab and get it tested. Get the boys and girls at the crime lab to go over it. I don't care who you have to wake up, it's getting done tonight.'

Miller turned round to look for Gary.

He was gone.

SEVENTY-FOUR

Miller thought about Julie. Thought about Andrea Kennedy's words as they'd interviewed her in her office. *Julie Davidson was there that night. Michael heard her call Harry Davidson "Dad".*

What if Cross now saw her as a threat? What if that was who'd attacked her and he still had her on his hit list?

'Have you heard from Julie at all?' he asked Scott.

'No.'

He tried Julie's mobile number. No answer.

'Maybe she's asleep,' Scott said.

Maybe she's fucking dead, *Miller thought.*

'Do you want me to go round and check on her?' Kim asked.

He shook his head. 'I'll try her home phone.' No answer on that either, his call going to her answering machine.

He walked along Molloy's hallway and into the kitchen. Some of the crime scene guys were still there and probably would be for the next few hours.

He tried Julie's number again. This time she answered. 'Hi, Frank. I was about to call you back. I'm just out of the shower and saw I missed your call. What's up?'

Miller felt a sudden rush of relief. 'I just wanted to make sure you were safe.'

'There you go, worrying again.'

'For good reason. Robert Molloy was attacked in his home, and his bodyguard fought the assailant off.' Miller didn't want to go into details just yet.

'Is he okay?'

'He'll be fine, I'm sure. The paramedics took him away, but I want you to double-check your front door's locked.'

'I already did, but thanks for caring. I'm going to bed early, and I'll make sure the alarm's on.'

'Good. Do you want me to come round?'

'Don't be daft. I'm going to bed to watch some TV. I want to make sure I'm fit for tomorrow.'

'Okay, if you're sure. I'll talk to you tomorrow.'

'See you then.'

He hung up. 'There's nothing much for us to do here, Tam. Crime Scene can stay for a while and wrap things up.'

'I'm away home then, boss. I had company round.' He left the warmth of Molloy's house.

Miller looked at Kim. 'Did you get all your stuff?'

She nodded. 'It's in the car.'

Miller felt like they were going away for a dirty weekend or something. *She's staying over, that's all. Don't get ahead of yourself there, cowboy. You're just keeping her safe, nothing more.* Like two men in a Range Rover, most likely armed to the teeth, couldn't keep her safe.

They left together and went to their separate cars. Miller following Kim in her rented Vauxhall.

The car slipped as it tried to gain purchase on Molloy's street. Then they were off.

Ten minutes later, both cars were parked in Cockburn Street.

They walked through the biting wind, their feet slipping on the slick pavements. Miller grabbed Kim's bag and she slipped an arm through his.

'You can stay as long as you like, Kim.' Miller hoped he didn't sound like a deviant.

Kim smiled at him. 'Thanks, I'll bear that in mind.'

He looked at her, at the glistening snowflakes on the black woollen hat. Just for a moment, it felt like Carol was by his side, holding onto him. He knew Kim wasn't a substitute for his dead wife, hell, they were just colleagues, but it felt good to have a woman hang onto his arm. Just for once, he didn't feel completely alone in the world.

They stomped the snow off their boots on the large mat in the building's hallway and rode the lift up, making small talk.

Jack was watching TV.

'Hey, Kim,' he said, as they walked in after taking their coats off. 'Want a beer, anybody?'

'Sure. I know where they are.' Kim went through to the kitchen.

'Dad, I want you to think back to the Moira Kennedy murder,' Miller said, as they all sat down.

Jack muted the TV. 'I've been thinking about nothing else ever since you said that nutter came back.'

'Do you remember Toni Cooper?'

'Yes, I remember her. She was gorgeous. Poor lassie. I can't believe he killed her as well.'

'She worked for Robert Molloy at the time, didn't she?'

'Yes. She was one of the cocktail waitresses.'

'Did you interview her?'

'No, that was Harry's job.'

'Was she brought in for a formal interview?'

'If she was, I didn't see her. I seem to remember Harry being fond of her. He spoke about her a lot.'

'Did he see her after the enquiry?'

'In what way?'

This is going to hurt me a lot more than it's going to hurt you, Jack. 'Was he sleeping with her?'

He heard Jack take a breath. 'What? Don't be stupid. That's my friend you're talking about.'

'There's nothing stupid about it, Jack. And he was my father-in-law. Harry was covering for Moira Kennedy's real murderer. He covered for him for twenty-five years.'

'What are you getting at?'

'What if Harry and Colin Fleming were a couple of players, back in the day? We know Fleming was, because he married Toni after cheating on his wife. Suppose Colin had tried it on with Moira Kennedy and he killed her accidentally and made it look like a murder, or he went into a frenzy and ripped her open? They were both there that night, keeping an eye on the hotel. What if Harry covered for him for some reason? Maybe Fleming had something on Harry. Then they made Raymond Cross the scapegoat.'

'I don't believe Harry would do that,' Jack said.

'Maybe he was fooling around on his wife, and Fleming black-mailed him. Or asked for his help. Either way, Fleming had a hold over Harry, so Harry couldn't do anything about Fleming being a murderer. They could blame Cross, knowing Cross worked under-cover, and he'd be taken away by McGovern, disappear and you'd be chasing your tails. Cross disappears, and is never caught. The case goes cold and gets filed away, and Colin Fleming gets away with murder. With Harry Davidson's help.'

'That sounds like something out of a movie. Harry was happily married. I can't see him shagging around.' He looked at Kim. 'Excuse the French.'

'It's plausible, Jack,' Kim said.

Silence again. Miller could imagine the wheels turning in Jack's mind.

'You know, Frank, there were times Harry and I were supposed to meet up for a drink and he didn't appear.'

'Recently?'

He watched Jack breathing in and out. 'Not only recently, but over the years. It wasn't something we ever thought about later. There were times when me and the boys would go to the pub, and Harry'd tell us, see you later, but he'd never appear. Whenever I asked him about it, he'd have different excuses, but mostly, he'd tell us he had to meet a contact.'

'Let me ask you this. Was Colin Fleming with you when Harry didn't appear?'

'Yes. He'd been away from his wife for a while, and was going out with this woman. Later on, we found out it was Toni Cooper. Then he got divorced and married her.'

'Did Harry miss going to the pub before Fleming married Toni?'

'Yes. He was at it for years. He didn't miss every piss-up, but there were a fair number of occasions. Then for a while, he just stopped going.'

'And Fleming was with you all the time?'

'Oh yes, Colin liked a good scoop. More often than not, we'd have to throw the bastard into a taxi. The taxi driver would only take him because we were coppers and gave him an extra big tip.'

'So maybe Harry would only fool around when Fleming couldn't see what he was up to. That way, Fleming wouldn't have a hold over Harry anymore.'

'I wonder if Harry's wife ever had an inclination?' Kim said.

'If she did, she kept it to herself. I'm sure Carol would have said something to me.'

'Why did Cross decide to kill Harry now?' Kim asked.

'We don't know what the catalyst was,' Miller said.

Jack got up. Walked over to the living room window and looked down onto the street below. Snow was falling lazily through the air. The wind had died, leaving the snow to fight the battle on its own.

He turned back to face his son and his friend. 'So what now?'

'We'll have to call Gibb,' Miller said.

'What if you're wrong?'

'I don't see how we can be, Jack,' Kim said. 'It all fits.'

Jack nodded. 'I know it does. And that's what hurts – Harry keeping me out of the loop.'

'Dad, it wasn't as if he *could* talk to you. Or me. Or Carol. Or any of us.'

'I can't believe this. Harry; harbouring a fucking killer for all those years until he got it as well.' He looked at Kim as Miller got on the phone to control. 'I never thought Harry used his small brain.'

'That's it done,' Miller said. 'I told Gibb. I want to keep him in the loop.'

He also wanted to call Julie again, not just to see if she was safe. He wanted to ask her if she knew her father had been protecting a killer all these years.

SEVENTY-FIVE

Thursday

Robert Molloy sat back on his couch and looked at his watch; another two hours before he could take more painkillers. His head hurt like it had been trampled by a rhino. When he caught up with Cross, he'd make sure the fucker died in a lot of pain.

He was alone, having sent Sienna away. The house was secure, so he wasn't worried. He'd been putting off calling Michael, knowing his unstable son would go berserk when he found out. He'd go off at a tangent, looking to break Raymond Cross's legs, probably breaking somebody else's when he couldn't find Cross.

He looked across at the overturned TV and wondered if it would still work when it was switched on. He had another, smaller one stuck up on his kitchen wall, so he wasn't going to miss any programmes. His phone rang.

'About fucking time you called.' It was Greg Sampson.

'How you feeling this morning, boss.'

'How do you think I fucking feel?' He took a deep breath and exhaled slowly. The doctor had told him he needed to keep his blood pressure down. 'What you got for me?'

'We're checking private CCTVs from your street, and cameras from nearby stores. There's nothing yet.'

'Just keep looking, Greg. If you find something and I can get the bastard, I'll bring in squads of guys from down south, and we'll deal with him in-house.'

'Miller and his team are desperate to get their hands on him too, boss. We need to be careful.'

'I won't lose any sleep over it. Talking of which, I'm going to bed now. Call me if you make some progress.' Molloy hung up. Thought about calling Michael but let it go.

Thought instead about Cross hanging from the rafters of his warehouse, blood running down his legs from what was left of his throat.

SEVENTY-SIX

Richard Sullivan woke to the sun coming through his bedroom window. For a moment, he couldn't think what day it was. Wednesday? Tuesday? No, it was Thursday. Not that it mattered when you were the boss.

Then he remembered Tai. McGovern had been long gone by the time she got home. They'd made love before falling into a deep sleep, fuelled by exhaustion and wine. He smiled to himself and looked over to her side of the bed.

She wasn't there.

He felt a stab of panic for a moment. She was a spy after all. Wasn't she? She must have gathered details about his flat and gone running to Molloy. He looked at his bedside clock; 7:56 am. He got up and used the en suite. Pulled on his dressing gown before going upstairs to the living room.

Then he heard it; the sound of cooking.

'Good morning,' Tai said, smiling at him. 'I like some bacon and eggs in the morning. I hope you don't mind.'

He smiled back. Felt relief. 'Of course not. I just didn't think I had any in.' He walked over to her and put his arms around her. She kissed him.

'You didn't. I went out and got some.' She looked at him. 'Don't worry, Molloy's boat doesn't open until lunchtime. There was nobody there.'

'You walked past there?'

She laughed. 'Of course not.' She nodded to his car keys lying on the dining table. 'I'm not that silly.'

She dished up the breakfast, while Sullivan poured coffee. They sat at the table and ate.

'I wanted to talk to you about something,' Tai said.

Sullivan wondered if he'd told her he loved her the night before. It wasn't something that was in his memory bank. 'Okay.'

'I'm going to quit my job.'

'Why?'

'I have feelings for you, Richard. I want to put any unease you have about me out the window. I figured if I quit, you'd see you have nothing to worry about.'

You could always quit and still report back to him, he thought, but then regretted it. She'd been honest with him, as far as he could tell.

'I appreciate it, but what would you do with your time?'

'I'll think of something. Besides, my father left me money when he died. It's still in an account, untouched. I didn't want to live off it. I wanted to keep it for a rainy day, as you Scots say. Besides, it's not exactly an account I can declare to the tax man. I can wire some over here so I can live off it while I look for something else. I might even open my own bar.'

'Won't Molloy be pissed off at you?'

'Of course he will, but he won't say anything. He knows it's better to leave me alone.'

Sullivan poured more coffee for them. 'I'll stand by any decision you make,' he said, sitting back down again. For the first time, he could actually see a future with this woman. He thought she felt the same way.

'You know I'm ten years older than you?'

'Yes, of course I do. You told me that up front. I don't care about age. I want to be with you, Richard. I've never felt like this about a man in my entire life. Besides, ten years is nothing.'

And he finally felt like she was telling him the truth.

He wondered if she'd still want to stay with him if she found out the truth.

'I can take the day off,' he said to her. 'I don't have any client meetings and what I do have lined up, I can have one of my assistants do.'

'Sounds good to me.' She got up from the table, and came round to sit on his lap. Kissed him. 'I'm falling in love with you, Richard Sullivan.'

'Me too,' he said, the words sounding strange to him.

'Good. Now, take me back to bed.'

SEVENTY-SEVEN

Miller had a restless night. Cross was getting bolder, attacking Robert Molloy like that. He showered and dressed. Went through to the living room. Kim was sitting talking with Jack at the bistro table in the kitchen. Charlie was sitting close by. Miller felt something inside, an alien feeling, one he hadn't felt in a long time.

He felt as if he was getting up to have breakfast with his family.

'You two are very cosy,' he said, smiling at Kim.

'I slept like a log. The best sleep I've had since my dad died.'

Miller felt a pang of guilt, wanting to tell her, *Your dad isn't dead!* Instead, he poured more coffee for Kim.

Jack declined. 'I'm going out early today,' he said, excusing himself.

Miller sat down at the table and buttered some toast. Charlie rubbed his legs. 'I see you've made a new friend.'

'He's a beautiful cat.' She put her hand down and rubbed her finger and thumb together and watched the cat trot over. She petted him.

'Do you really think Cross will come after me, Frank?'

'You told me a few days ago Cross was coming after me, and he did. There's nothing stopping him coming after any of us.' *Except maybe two guys in a black Range Rover.*

'I feel better staying here. At least we're prepared.'

Miller finished getting ready and they walked together to the station, Miller holding onto Kim's arm. The cold air felt good on his face, helping to wake him up. They grabbed coffees from Starbucks.

The morning rush hour was still in full swing.

Scott was already in the office, talking with Hazel Carter in a corner. He saw Miller come in and they walked over.

'Morning, sir,' he said. 'Hi, Kim.'

'Morning, Tam.' Frank put his coffee down and took off his overcoat. 'Have we heard anything from the lab yet?'

'Nothing,' Scott said. 'I called earlier and they were still processing it.'

'How long does it take them?' Miller shook his head. He knew they'd be going through the crime scene suit thoroughly, wanting to get it right, but it still irritated him. They'd taken it out of the bag Cross had left in Robert Molloy's house, so surely they'd find something on it? He walked over to his office.

Paddy Gibb came in and closed the door. 'Robert Molloy getting a doing. I can't believe it.'

'Neither can I, Paddy. The thing is, if Cross is trying to take out Molloy, maybe he was the last on the list. Maybe Cross will disappear now.'

'Or maybe he'll go back and finish the job.'

'Nobody will get near Molloy now. He'll have somebody with him twenty-four seven until we get Cross.'

'*If* we get Cross. Molloy could be looking over his shoulder for the rest of his life.' He took out a cigarette and lit up, opening Miller's office window for a moment. 'No smoking, my arse.'

'That's it, Paddy, kill both of us.'

'Back in my day, all the team in CID smoked. Not like now.'

'How many of them are still alive?'

Gibb looked at him. Shook his head and flicked the unfinished cigarette out the window where it fell to earth and landed in a snow bank. 'Anybody told Michael Molloy about his old man?'

'No. The old man will want to do it himself. Why should we make it easy for the old bastard?'

'Good point.'

Miller yawned and took a sip of his coffee.

'You need to get to the gym, get yourself fit,' Gibb said.

'*I don't have time to get fit.*' Too many late nights searching for the guy who killed my wife, Paddy, *he wanted to say*. Not enough sleep and too much caffeine.

'That's my boy,' Gibb said, slapping Miller on the back. 'I'll make a smoker out of you yet.' He left the office.

Miller followed and stood at the front of the room. The voices hushed a little. He noticed Gary Davidson was absent. *Did you know your father was covering for a killer? Would you have helped him if you did?*

'Ladies and gentlemen, I want to talk to you about last night.' He looked at them, at the faces hooked on his every word. 'As you all know, Robert Molloy was attacked in his home by Raymond Cross last night. It's lucky his minder was with him. She saved his life. She also scared Cross off, and he ran out, leaving a bag of goodies behind. Including a scene-of-crime suit. We assume he was going to put it on before gutting Molloy.'

'We get anything useful from the bag?' Jimmy Gilmour asked.

'Forensics are going through it now, trying to find some trace. We'll have to wait and see. We need to keep at it. We'll be going back to interview Molloy later, and I've asked Sienna Craig to come to the station for more questioning.'

'Could she be the one who attacked him?' Hazel Carter asked.

'We can't rule anything out, but our first indications are, no. There's no obvious motive, unless she wanted her boss dead. Which does happen.'

'You got that right,' Andy Watt said, and laughter burst out in the room.

'Okay, folks, stay focused. Back to work.'

There was the murmur of voices as they all went back to their desks.

Then the call came in.

Some big name was dead.

'Are you sure nobody followed you here?' Neil McGovern said. He sat at the small wooden table, drinking a strong, black coffee.

'As sure as I can be.' Sienna Craig sat down opposite him with her own coffee. 'Besides, if any of Molloy's men spot me, I'll tell him I'm putting some feelers out to try and track down Cross. You heard about last night, I take it?'

McGovern nodded. His head felt like it was going to explode. He'd only meant to have one with Sullivan, but one turned into two, and the rest was history. 'I was worried about you, Ashley. When I heard, I have to admit I panicked.'

'I'm glad you worry about me, boss, but I can take care of myself.'

'You're in deep with Molloy now, but I don't care about that. I do care about your safety. Remember, all you need to do to get out is make a phone call, and the deal is over.'

Agent Ashley Turner nodded her head. She liked working with McGovern, not feeling like she had to prove herself, which she'd done more than once, but he was a good boss to work for, and this undercover mission was perfect for her.

'I know that, boss, but I want to see this through.'

McGovern drank more coffee, feeling more human with every sip. 'I'm quite happy for you to carry on as long as you don't feel compromised. It would be good to get Molloy, but not at the expense of losing you.'

Ashley smiled at him. 'You say the nicest things, boss.'

'I know I do. Luckily my wife knows you, or she'd kill us both.'

'No she wouldn't. Norma's sweet.'

More coffee. Feeling the heat go down into his gut. 'She says she'll be happier when I don't have to keep changing my hair colour. Or wear any funny glasses.'

'Or wear a big, false nose.'

'You're so funny, Miss Turner. Remember who writes your annual evaluation.'

'I try.' She sipped some of her own coffee then looked at McGovern with a serious look on her face. 'I had to get rough with somebody the other day.'

'Really? Do tell.'

'His name's Ian Powers. He was doing a search on Alamo International, and one of Molloy's IT guys spotted it. So he sent me round with Sampson to have a word. I was rough but I didn't hurt him. Much.'

'Ah, Ian Powers. Yes, I know of him. Haven't met the man, but he's a friend of Frank Miller. He seems to be good around computers.'

'It might be worth bringing him on board.' She looked at her boss. 'Just a thought.'

'Way ahead of you there. If he's as good as Miller thinks, he could be a good asset for us. Not right now, though. I don't want anybody seeing him near us. Maybe after this case is done with.'

'It might give him a shock to see me round at his place without slapping him about.'

McGovern laughed. 'I'm sure you'll win him round.' He stood up. 'I'll get more coffee. Then we can go and see our friend. I'm sure he'd like to be introduced to you.'

He stood up and looked out the window. Saw somebody walking in the distance.

'Uh oh. Seems like that introduction is going to be made sooner than we thought. Let's go.'

SEVENTY-EIGHT

Miller pulled into the private road and braked hard. A patrol car blocked the road. The uniform saw his blue flashers behind the grill and pulled the car aside. The snow that had previously covered Molloy's drive had been annihilated by the convoy of police vehicles. He crept the Vauxhall round the uniform on guard duty and pulled up behind the other vehicles.

'How the hell did Molloy let himself get taken like this?' Miller said.

Scott shook his head. 'With all the money he has, and all the security, he still ends up dead in his own home.'

'This is awful,' Kim said, from the back seat.

They walked into the house past the uniform guarding the door. The inside of the house was warm. Det Sup Paddy Gibb stood in the living room amongst the technicians. He was wearing a forensic suit, and a scowl that would melt wallpaper.

Miller and the others pulled on their latex gloves and overshoes before entering Michael Molloy's last resting place. The last one before he was put in a box.

His corpse had been left just like the others; opened up in front, with some of his intestines laid on top of him. The front of his face had been pulverised, almost like it had taken a hit from a shotgun, but there was no evidence a firearm had been used. Blood had spattered round the room as if it had been fed through a hose into a lawn sprinkler. What was once a beige carpet was now soaked in blood, which had turned the colour of raspberry jam.

'This is turning into a pile of shite,' Gibb said.

'It's not one of our better weeks, I have to admit,' Miller said. 'What have we got?'

'Cross has some fucking stamina. He's obviously unhinged, Frank. I mean, I didn't like Michael Molloy, but look at him.'

Miller saw Jake Dagger working over Molloy. Walked over to him. 'Where's Julie?'

Dagger looked at him. 'She called and said she'd taken your advice. She's having another few days off.'

Miller was relieved. 'For once, somebody's listening to me.' He also knew since Julie was leaving for London, she wouldn't be back on duty again. He nodded towards the corpse. 'What would have done that much damage to his face?'

'A sharp object, like an axe. There are cuts as well as broken bones, so an axe would be my guess.'

'Jesus Christ.'

'Any idea of time, Jake?' Scott asked.

He turned to look at the detectives. 'I told Gibb I'm thinking between seven and nine pm. Before his father was attacked.'

'Who found the body?' Kim asked Gibb.

'The cleaner. This is her day to come in, and when she got here, she found our distinguished friend lying here dead.'

'Any chance she did it?'

'No. She was taken away by ambulance to the Royal. She's being treated for shock.'

'Whoever did this, wasn't taking any prisoners,' Scott said.

'We're assuming it's Cross, but we can't rule out somebody else.

Molloy had a lot of enemies.' Miller didn't believe his own words as he looked down at Michael Molloy's cold corpse.

'Maybe he'll stop killing now he's killed Molloy's son,' said Gibb.

'Or maybe he's just getting warmed up.'

'Your attempts at cheering me up are woefully short, Frank. If you want my job, I'm sure it's going to be available shortly after those clowns in charge find their scapegoat.' He took out a cigarette and put it into his mouth, unlit. Miller thought he looked ten years older than he was.

'Maybe we'll find he's finished, right enough,' Miller said.

Gibb took the cigarette out. 'He can't keep up this pace. Killing Michael and then attacking Robert in the same night. He's either got some fucking stamina, or he's on drugs. Remember Levitt said Cross will continue until he hits his Crash Point. That's what usually happens with these killers; they carry on until they have to rest, so there's time between killings.' He looked at Miller. 'I don't know what I'm more worried about, him keeping on killing or stopping killing and we never find him.'

Miller let out a deep breath. 'We need to go and talk to Robert Molloy. I heard he signed himself out of the Royal.'

'I think we should go heavy handed.'

'Agreed. I don't know how he'll handle this one.'

SEVENTY-NINE

'Maybe hit the Almondvale shopping centre first then have something to eat later?' Tai asked Richard Sullivan as he drove the A5 out of the underground car park.

'Sounds good.' He stopped to let the gate open and it was almost done when somebody stepped into the middle of the lane with his back to them. Sullivan honked his horn but the man didn't move.

His heart was beating faster. What if it was the killer they were looking for? What if he was waiting for Sullivan to get out of the car? He honked the horn again. The man still didn't move.

'Wait here,' Tai said, opening her door. She didn't wear heels; heels were for dancing, flats were for fighting.

'You need to move,' she said, to the man's back. 'I'm not going to tell you twice.'

'Well, well, Miss Lopez,' Jack Miller said, turning round. He smiled at her. 'What if I'd been one of Molloy's men? That wouldn't have looked good on your CV.'

'Who are you?' she said, keeping her distance, ready to take him on if a knife should be pulled.

'His name's Jack Miller,' Sullivan said, getting out of the car. 'What can I do for you, Detective Miller?'

Jack walked up to him, sensing Tai was about to leap, but Sullivan looked at her and shook his head slightly.

'I just wondered if we could have a little chat somewhere,' Jack said, his hands dug deep into his overcoat.

'What about?'

'Listen, son, I'm freezing my balls off here. I'm older than you, and I'm outnumbered. I'm hardly a threat to you. All I want is a wee chat.'

'I'm certainly in demand this week.' Sullivan sighed. 'We can go back up to my flat. If that's okay with you, Tai.'

'Sure. Shopping can wait until later.'

Five minutes later, they were riding the lift back up to Sullivan's flat. Tai offered to put the coffee pot on while the two men talked in the living room.

'I appreciate you seeing me, Mr Sullivan,' Jack said. He was standing looking out the windows over to Fife.

'Everybody drifts over to that window when they come in here. It was this view that sold me the flat.' He walked over and stood beside Jack. 'And you can call me Richard.'

'Or Dick?' Jack looked at him.

'Richard's fine.'

'Coffee's ready,' Tai said.

'Thanks,' Sullivan said. 'How do you like yours?' he asked Jack.

'Milk. No sugar.'

Sullivan poured, and invited Jack to sit on the couch. 'What did you want to speak to me about? Or shall I have a guess?'

'Carol was like a daughter to me. I worked with her father for a long time. And my son was married to her.' Jack took a sip of the coffee and put the cup on the coffee table in front of him. 'We all want to know what happened to her. I'm not here to ask you any awkward questions, but rather to see if you can shed any light on things.'

Sullivan nodded. 'You know Frank and I have no love for each other. But I didn't have anything to do with Carol's death. For all I know, Molloy might have had something to do with it, and now he's trying to frame me. I had an interesting conversation with Robert Molloy. He said if he found out I'd had anything to do with Carol's death, he'd... well, the threat was implied. I don't know why he'd take it so personally, but I can assure you, I had nothing to do with it. If you're here because you suspect me, then you're wasting your time. If I had something to hide, I wouldn't be talking to you.'

Jack drank some of his coffee. 'You know, as a murder squad detective for a long time, you get a feeling about somebody when you're talking to them. I never had that feeling about you. Sometimes Frank can't see the wood for the trees, but I can. Killing a copper's a big deal, and I somehow don't see you doing it. You obviously don't need the money. I don't think Carol got in your face too many times. It was her obsession with Molloy that brought your name into the mix. You do like to take risks though, Richard.' He nodded over to Tai.

She looked over and smiled at him.

'I'm not going to let Molloy get in my way when it comes to Tai.'

'Don't worry, son, he won't hear anything from me. I know what it's like to love a woman. I was married a long time before my wife passed away.' He stood up.

There was a knock on Sullivan's door and he rolled his eyes. There was only one man who could let himself in the building.

A few seconds later, he and Jack heard voices as Tai let somebody in and they came upstairs to the living room. A man and woman walked in.

The short man walked over to Jack Miller. 'Allow me to introduce myself. Neil McGovern.'

EIGHTY

Jack stood in silence for a moment, his thought processes trying to make sense of what he'd just been told.

Neil McGovern had been sent to the psychiatric hospital for being a multiple killer, where he'd died. And now he was here, standing before him in the flesh.

'You want to tell me what's going on?' *Before I hurt you.*

'No, I'm not dead, and I didn't kill Harry. Frank knows all about it. I was working with Harry the night he died. He said he knew who was responsible for killing those three women two years ago but he died before he could tell me.'

Jack realised everything he knew about the Cross case had just flown out the window.

'This is Robert Molloy's new head of security, Sienna Craig. Otherwise known as Agent Ashley Turner. She works for me.'

'More coffee?' Tai asked, unfazed.

'Thank you, Miss Lopez,' McGovern said. 'Come on, Jack, let's get a seat. I think it's about time we let you in on what's been going on.'

Sullivan stood up. 'I think I need something stronger.'

'Didn't you have enough last night, old son?' McGovern smiled at Jack. 'This lad knows how to put the booze away.

They sat down on various seats, Sullivan joining them after pouring himself a whisky.

'Right, let's cut to the chase,' McGovern said, unbuttoning his coat. 'I have a feeling after what happened last night, our killer's coming to an end. Maybe he'll come back to finish off Robert Molloy, maybe he won't. Maybe he'll try for Frank again. We just don't know, but I think he's almost done.'

'Do you know where Raymond Cross is?' Jack asked.

McGovern looked at Sullivan briefly before he carried on. 'He's sitting right there.'

'What are you talking about?'

'Richard is Raymond Cross. He worked for my department a long time ago, but then he wanted to be a lawyer, so he left. I asked him to do me a favour and do another job for me. His undercover name was *Raymond Cross*. You won't recognise the guy who was brought into the station and charged with Moira's murder, and who I took out with Harry's help, but he's one and the same.'

Jack took a coffee from Tai and thanked her. Looked at Sullivan. 'I remember you. Lippy bastard.'

'It was all part of the act,' Sullivan said, sipping on the golden liquid.

'So we're not looking for Raymond Cross, is that what you're saying?'

'That's exactly what I'm saying,' McGovern said. 'Cross didn't exist except in name only. Moira got murdered that night, God bless her soul, and that was the operation over. Richard went back to being a lawyer, but we had his appearance changed a bit. Not even Robert Molloy recognised him.'

'Look, call me sceptical, but how do we know he didn't kill Moira. Hell, how do we know he didn't kill Carol?'

McGovern took his time answering, looking across at Sullivan for a moment, as if asking for permission. Sullivan nodded before McGovern carried on.

'Richard and I catch up on occasion. I worked mostly in London but when I was up here, we sometimes got together for a beer. I was with him the night Carol was murdered. That's how I know he didn't kill her. Somebody wants you to believe he did.

'As for Moira, well, they both worked for me. They were trying to get information about Molloy so we could take him down. It was their last job. Richard and Moira didn't just work well together, they were husband and wife. Richard decided he didn't want to work undercover for me anymore, and went off to be a lawyer instead, with my blessing. However, I needed Moira to do one last job for me. If she wanted to. I didn't pressure her, but she was ever the professional. She persuaded Richard to work with her, and got her sister, Andrea, to introduce Raymond to Michael Molloy and they hit it off. Andrea didn't know Richard. She thought he was some bloke her sister had met.'

Jack looked stunned. 'Carol hated Richard. They were seen arguing outside the court. She arrested him.'

Sullivan spoke up. 'One of Molloy's men struck a deal with the PF. He'd only talk to me, so it was arranged for me to be arrested. It was all a cover. I was in the cells with him, and I took the details. Some drug runner got busted. Then my case was thrown out of court, to maintain my cover.'

'What about when Carol was seen arguing outside the court with you?'

'Again, cover. Harry knew about it.'

'She never told Frank.'

'It had to stay that way,' McGovern said.

Sullivan carried on. 'She also came to me in secret one night. Harry told her I knew who her biological father was. I couldn't tell her, but she kept going on about it. I caved in and told her on the understanding she wouldn't confront him, and she agreed.'

'Who's her father?'

Sullivan didn't look sure for a moment but McGovern nodded.

Sullivan told Jack.

Jack sat in silence again, processing the information. 'Does he know Carol was his daughter?'

'Yes.'

'Where do you fit into this, Sienna? I mean Ashley.'

'We've been trying to get Molloy for years,' she said. 'That's why I was brought in. However, my time's done with him. He was making enquiries about me, and we think my cover's been compromised. Time for me to go soon.'

'So somebody's using the name Cross and trying to make it look like it's Cross who's responsible for killing people.'

'Yes he is,' Ashley said. 'I know it's none of Molloy's crew.'

'What about his son, Michael?' Jack asked.

'We don't think he murdered Moira, but we're not a hundred per cent sure. If he did, then his wife Andrea wasn't privy to the information.'

Jack drank some coffee. 'Somebody wants to get back at Michael Molloy by killing people who are associated with him.'

Ashley leaned forward in her chair. 'We think he pissed off the wrong person, but the obvious one, his wife Andrea, she's dead, a victim herself.'

'But Harry said he knew who it was, nine weeks ago.'

'And he had to be silenced,' Sullivan said.

'I wish he'd come to me,' Jack said.

McGovern took his phone out after it vibrated. 'I just got a text from one of my men; Michael Molloy was found dead in his home this morning.'

'What?' Jack said, disbelief in his voice. 'Michael Molloy's dead?'

'And Robert Molloy was attacked at home last night. Looks like he tried to take them both out.'

'I fought him off,' Ashley said. 'If I hadn't been there, Molloy would have been killed as well as his son. That's why we think Cross, or whoever's pretending to be Cross, is almost finished. And our window of opportunity to catch him is getting smaller by the minute.'

McGovern stood up. 'I need to go out. I'll catch up with you all later.'

Jack Miller watched him go, not knowing the killer had already finished his killing spree.

There was just one loose end he was going to tie up.

EIGHTY-ONE

Kim Smith walked down High Street from the station and went into Starbucks for another coffee. She hated the cold, but she psyched herself up by telling herself they had to get through the winter in order to get to the summer. Her father had told her that once. *You've got to have rain to see the rainbow.*

She took a seat at the window. The snow had stopped, and the forecasters said there was going to be a respite for a day or so. She'd believe that when she saw it.

She took her iPhone out again and looked at the text once more. *Get to Starbucks in the high street. Sit at the window. This will benefit you. Go right now.* Cryptic wasn't the word. So curiosity had brought her here. Without her gun. Her mother had warned her against carrying it all the time, and now it was locked in her desk. She felt naked without it.

Her phone buzzed on the counter. She'd left it on vibrate and now it danced round in a tight circle until she grabbed it. Another text. *It's me, Jack. Frank's dad. Meet me in Hangman's Close. Now. I need your help, Kim.*

Kim picked up her coffee and left Starbucks, pocketing her

phone. Maybe I should call Frank, she thought. But what if she did? Frank would tell her to hang fire, to wait until he got there. He was in Cramond, a good twenty minutes away. Jack sounded as if he was in trouble, and he needed her now. She wasn't willing to take the risk. Besides, she could look after herself.

She walked up to Hangman's Close, a few short steps down from the station. The snow was banked up at the side of the road.

She reached the close. It was narrow and dark, and the wind whipped through it in gusts, stinging her eyes. There was nobody about. Not even Jack.

She stopped. He was nowhere to be seen. Further down, on the left, were the back doors to a pub or some shop. They were closed, with rubbish bins sitting outside. Where was he?

She turned round, looking back the way she'd come. He had said this one, hadn't he?

Raymond Cross was standing ten feet away.

He was dressed from head to toe in black, with a black balaclava. His eyes glinted through the small holes that had been cut for him to see out of. He was pointing a gun at her.

'Hello, Raymond,' Kim said, trying to stay calm. Trying to make a connection.

Cross said nothing. Just stared, the gun unwavering.

She didn't have her gun. Cross had his. There was nothing she could do.

Her thoughts were cut off as Cross moved forward expertly, and pistol-whipped her.

Kim yelled, and fell onto her backside, banging her head on a large green recycling bin. She picked up a black garbage bag and threw it at Cross, where he easily smacked it away.

'Now, now, my friend, that isn't sportsmanlike. Don't you see the girl doesn't have a gun? Why don't you put it away and then have a fist fight? Bit more even then, I should say.' It was said in a posh, English accent. 'Even better, have a fight with me.'

Cross turned to see a man standing watching them. He was about five foot eight, wearing a long, black jacket, and black trousers. He had short hair, black, as if he'd just dyed it. Black-rimmed glasses filled his face. He was smiling at Cross, walking slowly towards him.

Cross said nothing, just grabbed hold of Kim, hauling her to her feet and putting the gun to her head.

'Take it easy. Nobody needs to get hurt,' the man said.

Cross had Kim's hair wrapped in one hand, yanking her head back.

'Okay, okay.' The man put his hands in the air and took a few steps back. 'We can talk about this.'

Cross took the gun away from Kim's head and shot the man in the chest. Kim screamed, as the man was thrown off his feet, the sound of the gunshot reverberating around the narrow close.

Cross started walking backwards, dragging Kim with him. 'Fight me and I'll kill you.'

Still she struggled, but she felt woozy from being hit. He headed for the end of the building where the pathway turned. They went round the corner and were gone.

EIGHTY-TWO

Paddy Gibb and Jimmy Gilmour were waiting in the car outside Robert Molloy's house when Miller turned the corner, blues flashing behind the grill. Miller and Scott got out of the car and walked up to the passenger side. Gibb rolled the window down.

'He's in. We saw him walking about in front of the window earlier.'

'Must be nice, living in a place like this,' Scott said. 'Makes you wonder why we're so law abiding.'

'That was Colin Fleming's philosophy and look where that got him,' Miller said.

They walked through the build-up of snow to the front door of the house, and Miller rang the bell, stamping his feet to try and keep them warm.

They heard the interior door opening, and then the front door being unlocked. 'This had better be bloody good,' Robert Molloy said, swinging the door open. 'Oh, it's you lot. What's up now?' He was dressed in a pair of black trousers with a thick sweater. The state of his unkempt hair suggested he'd pulled it on in a hurry.

'We need to talk to you, Mr Molloy,' Miller said.

'*Mr* Molloy? That sounds ominous.' He didn't look unduly worried. 'And you brought your friends along. Did I invite you to a party or something?'

'Can we come in?'

'Why?'

'We don't want to conduct business on your doorstep.'

Reluctantly, Molloy opened the door wider and let them all in. They walked through the inner vestibule and he showed them through to the living room.

'This must be serious, Miller coming to my house with Paddy Gibb. Has my liquor license run out or something?' Molloy gave a small chuff of laughter. 'Should I call my lawyer now?'

'You might want to sit down, Molloy,' Gibb said. He put his right hand in his coat pocket, and felt the pack of cigarettes sitting there, teasing him. *Come on, smoke us, you bastard.* He took his hand out.

'Did you find Cross? Is that why you're here?'

'No. It's not about the attack,' Gibb said.

For the first time, they could see a shift in Molloy's demeanour, a quick look between Gibb and Miller, as if this was some kind of joke.

'Why don't you tell me what it is you've come to say and then I can have some coffee?'

'Your son's dead,' Gibb said, getting straight to the point, just like Molloy wanted.

The older man looked like somebody had just shoved a gun in his face. 'Dead? What do you mean, dead?' He tensed up, his body going rigid.

'I'm sorry, but Michael was murdered last night,' Miller said.

'What is this, a fucking comedy routine? You and your boss turn up and tell me my son's dead, just for a laugh?'

Miller looked at him, no sympathy in his eyes. This man had caused so much pain to so many people over the years, there was no pity there anymore. 'I know it's hard to take, but if you know anybody who'd do this, you have to tell us.'

'There are too many people to count, you know that.' Molloy sat down, like a balloon that had suddenly deflated. He shook his head. 'You sure it was him?'

Miller nodded. 'We're ninety per cent sure, but we've had the techs take blood. We'll need some of your DNA for the ID.'

'What? You know what he looks, *looked* like. Why do you need my DNA?'

'There was some head trauma,' Gibb said. 'Cross left your son a mess.'

Molloy took a deep breath. 'I want to see him.'

'Molloy, you can't,' Miller said.

'I know my fucking rights. If I want to see him, there's nothing on this earth you can do to stop me.'

'We'll need to give the mortuary time to prepare him.'

'I can wait. But I want to see my son.' He sat even further back in his chair. 'How did it happen?' His eyes were bright now, sparkling with tears he was determined not to shed in front of the police.

'He was stabbed to death. He died before Cross came here to kill you. It seemed he went for a double-whammy, but Sienna stopped him from killing you.'

'Where did he die? He was going home.'

'He was killed in his house,' Miller said. 'We believe Raymond Cross killed Michael. Killed Andrea too. Killed three of the witnesses from long ago. Raymond Cross has come back after all this time, and now he's killing people connected to you, Molloy. We want to know why.' Miller thought about Molloy's story of Cross blackmailing him, and was sure there was more to it.

Molloy hesitated. 'How should I know?' A look passed between them.

Miller called Jake Dagger and gave him a heads-up. Twenty minutes later, he called back.

'We can go to the mortuary now, if you like,' Miller said.

Molloy nodded. 'Give me five minutes.'

The four detectives stood and waited as Molloy went upstairs.

301

Miller started looking around, as Gibb went over to stand by the window, as if he was looking out for somebody.

'Frank, you take him to the mortuary. I'll head up to the station with Scott. He won't want us all there, and to be honest, I don't want to be there with him.'

'Right, I'm ready,' Molloy said, coming back into the room.

'Who's having the pleasure of driving me?' He looked at Miller.

'I'll take you.'

'Fine. Let's go.'

Scott opened the back of Miller's car.

'I think I'll ride in the front this time. I don't want the neighbours to think you bastards have arrested me.'

A tear rolled down Molloy's cheek as Miller drove away.

EIGHTY-THREE

Neil McGovern lay on his back, feeling like an elephant had sat on his chest. Eventually, he rolled onto his side. He wasn't sure how long he'd been down, but it felt like an age. The bullet had hit his vest, which had absorbed the impact, but it was going to hurt for a while.

He struggled onto his side, knowing he had to get to Kim, but the pain was still kicking away at him. His breath was shallow and coming in spurts. He spoke into his cuff microphone.

'Are you two there yet? He's got Kim,' he said, feeling panic starting to get the better of him.

The two men in the Range Rover had sped away after dropping their boss off, heading for the lower end of the close. When McGovern had seen his daughter go down there, he'd had an uneasy feeling and hopped out of the car, telling his two associates to get down to Cowgate and block the exit.

'Less than a minute, boss,' the passenger said.

McGovern wondered how long he'd lain there. It couldn't have been more than a few minutes.

The closes leading off High Street all ran downhill. Hangman's Close ran down towards Cowgate. They were all designed for pedestrians to connect with other streets, and were built hundreds of years ago, before cars were even thought of. They weren't designed for traffic to use.

Cross's plan made sense, McGovern thought, as he got to his feet and struggled to the corner of the building and looked round. The pathway carved its way between the building in High Street and a high wall that bordered an office block. It ran a short distance before turning left and heading back down to Cowgate. McGovern made his way to the next corner, his chest on fire. He was grateful to Frank Miller for giving him a heads-up about the man having a gun. Looked round. This part was steeper and a flight of steps led down to the bottom part of the close that traffic could come into.

He ran carefully down the stairs, and jumped into the street. Maybe Kim could fight him off and get enough distance between her and the killer so McGovern could get a shot off.

There was nobody there.

The Range Rover came screeching round the corner from Cowgate. Stopped near McGovern. The two men jumped out and ran to their boss.

'Where are they?' the driver asked.

'I don't know. How the hell did it take you so long?' He balled his fists up and felt the tension run through his body like a virus.

'Traffic was heavy,' was all the driver had to say. 'Guthrie Street was blocked by a delivery van.'

They looked around. Kim and the killer were nowhere to be seen.

'Look for them. They can't have gone far. Fucking move!'

The men ran back towards the car, checking doorways at the back of the office building Hangman's Close ran round, but none were open.

McGovern ran back up the steps, looking for somewhere they could hide, but none of the snow was disturbed at any of the back doors. Where the hell had they gone?

They'd vanished into thin air.

EIGHTY-FOUR

Jake Dagger was in attendance with Gus Weaver. Molloy walked into the mortuary behind Miller, making a face at the smell of disinfectant. Scott stayed outside in the waiting room. Sienna Craig was there, waiting. Molloy had called her from home and asked her to be there and she'd been dropped off before they arrived.

'Dr Dagger. This is Mr Molloy, here to formally identify his son,' Miller said. He put his phone on silent mode.

Dagger nodded. 'We have him ready for viewing.' He looked at Molloy. 'I'm sorry for your loss.'

'I haven't identified him yet, you arsehole,' he said to him, and for a moment, Miller thought Molloy was going to hit the pathologist.

Dagger turned and walked away with Weaver, going through a swing door that was for staff only.

'Come on, up this way,' Miller said, walking up a corridor to the viewing window. 'Don't be taking it out on them, they're just doing their job.'

'You ever lost anybody close to you, Miller?'

'I have as a matter of fact.'

Molloy looked at him. 'Oh yeah. So you have. You had to look at

305

her through a plate glass window, with disin-fucking-fectant clogging your nostrils, watching some daft bastard wearing a white coat, pulling back the white sheet!'

Miller saw Molloy was losing it and put a hand on his arm. The older man was trembling through his coat, and Miller could see Molloy's teeth chattering with nerves. Molloy looked down at the hand. Miller didn't move it.

'I'm here, Molloy. Keep it together for Michael's sake.'

Robert Molloy nodded to him and only then did Miller remove his hand.

Molloy cleared his throat, and took a deep breath.

The window was set into a wall next to the waiting room. Curtains hid what lay behind, like they were waiting at a circus freak show. Molloy stood staring at the glass. The curtains parted. Act one. Michael Molloy lay on a gurney, only his eyes revealed, but even they were bruised, as if he'd been boxing. The rest of his body was covered by a sheet. Gus Weaver stood back out of the way, waiting to close the curtains again.

'Is that it? That's all I get to see?'

That's all you'll fucking want to see. 'I know it's a cliché, but trust me, you want to remember him the way he was.'

'He tried to kill me, but he killed my son. For his sake, he'd better be out of Edinburgh by now.' He looked at Miller. 'Where do I give a DNA sample?'

Miller took a slender tube out of his pocket that a tech had given to him as they came in, alerted by Paddy Gibb before they got there. He swabbed the inside of Molloy's cheek and put the sample back in the tube.

Molloy turned and walked out of the mortuary. Sienna saw him leave, and hurried to catch up with him.

I just hope this isn't the start of World War Three, Miller thought as the curtains slid together again, taking Michael Molloy away for good.

EIGHTY-FIVE

Hangman's Close was swarming with patrol cars when Scott turned in from Cowgate. He and Gibb got out into the freezing cold and looked for McGovern. Saw him up ahead with two men standing beside him. They were beside a black Range Rover.

Norma Banks was there too, her usually professional veneer crumbling. Husband and wife together, waiting for the bad news.

McGovern's call had been short and simple. Gibb, I can't get hold of Miller. Cross has got Kim. I'm at Hangman's Close. Down by Cowgate.

McGovern walked over when he saw Gibb and Scott coming. 'I tried calling Miller but he's not answering.'

'He's at the mortuary. Probably switched his phone off for a few minutes. You need to tell me what happened here, Neil.' Gibb still thought it was surreal that McGovern was still alive.

'Our daughter was kidnapped, that's what fucking happened,' Norma Banks said, stopping behind her husband.

Gibb remained composed. 'That's why we're here, Ms Banks.'

She looked at her shoes for a moment before looking him in the eyes. 'I don't mean to get snappy, but Kim means the world to us.' Her words caught in her throat for a moment. 'I couldn't bear it if anything happened to her.'

'I know. I have kids myself. We'll do what it takes to get her back.'

'It's all my fault,' McGovern said. 'I was supposed to be watching Kim, but I got caught up in a meeting with some people. By the time we traced the GPS on her phone, I saw her coming down this lane—'

'It's called a close, Neil,' Norma said, putting a hand on his arm.

'Close, and then he was there and he had a gun. When I tried interfering, he shot me. Luckily I'm wearing a bulletproof vest. I'd sent my men round in the car to come up from the other side, but when they got there, the close was empty. The back doors that lead into the buildings are all locked. We checked. There's no sign of them anywhere. They've disappeared.'

'This was obviously well planned,' Scott said. 'Kim didn't just come down here, I assume. She was probably lured here, and Cross wouldn't be able to go far with her at gunpoint, so he'd have a car or a van parked here.'

'Did you two see anybody come belting out of here in a car?' McGovern asked his men.

'Nothing. Only the ambulance,' the driver said.

'What?' Scott said.

'The ambulance. I was about to turn in here, but had to wait while the ambulance came out. He had his blues on, so he was in a hurry.' Suddenly he didn't look too sure of himself.

Gibb was talking to some of the uniforms.

'Come with me,' Scott said to McGovern as he took his mobile out. He made a quick call as they walked to the end of the lane. Hung up. He stopped and looked around.

'What are you thinking, mate?' McGovern said. 'You don't think...'

Scott nodded. 'The ambulance.' He pointed to a huge turning space at the end. 'This is a narrow lane with double yellows. He wouldn't want to attract the attention of a parking warden by sticking a car on the yellows. Nobody would think twice about an ambulance with its blues on.

'He'd want out of here as quickly as possible. However, he didn't count on you turning up, but that didn't disrupt his plans. He still came down here with Kim. Probably had the ambulance parked there, ready for a quick getaway.'

Scott's phone rang. He answered it and then hung up. 'I asked control to check. There was a treble nine call for Hangman's Close twenty minutes ago. They haven't had a report back since.'

'What was the call for?'

'Heart attack. Nothing the police would be called for. They assumed the technicians were still working on the patient.'

'Do you think he took them with him?'

Scott shook his head. 'No. Too risky. Too time consuming. He'd get the ambulance to come here with a false call, but then he wouldn't risk leaving them in the ambulance while he went up the close.'

'He killed them,' McGovern said, quietly.

'I think so.'

'Where would you dump them?' McGovern asked the question, but knew the answer. Two blue communal business dumpsters sat against a wall. Scott lifted the lid on the first one. Saw some blonde hair below some garbage bags. Pulled some bags aside and saw a female lying amongst the garbage with her throat slit. Dressed only in her underwear. She'd had her paramedic jumpsuit removed. Or had been made to take it off before being killed.

'I have one here,' he said, to McGovern, who lifted the lid on the second dumpster. Let it slam down. 'Bastard. There's a young guy in there.'

'He got his uniform on?' Scott asked.

'Yeah. Why?'

'The female hasn't.' Scott looked at the dead paramedic; he was a big man, with a big build. Unlike the female. Why would Cross take the woman's and not the man's?

Scott shouted for some uniforms to come up. Then he radioed in for Maggie Parks and her forensic team.

EIGHTY-SIX

Miller caught Dagger in his office. 'Sorry about that.'

'Don't worry about it, Frank. Grief always make people act strangely. I'm used to it.'

Dagger stood up from behind his desk and walked over to a coffee machine, which sat on another table. Poured a cup and asked Miller if he wanted one. Miller didn't.

They walked out to the loading bay where Molloy had gone. Sienna was standing behind the freight doors, looking out.

'He wants some peace for a minute,' she said. 'Just let him be.'

Miller gave her a *Fuck you* look and walked out into the freezing cold air. Gusts of wind toyed with the snow that lay against the side of the grey building. The sky was clear and a weak sun was showing through.

The older man was standing looking skyward. 'Do you believe in Heaven, Miller?'

Miller looked up at the sky. 'I do. In this job, you have to believe that there's a better place after dealing with all the shite down here.'

Molloy looked at him. 'I believe that thing in there's just my son's shell, that his spirit is gone now. He's probably up there laughing his head off seeing me like this. Wee bastard.' He put a hand on Miller's right arm. 'Come, walk with me for a minute.'

Miller turned and looked at Sienna peering through the doors. Miller hunched himself into his overcoat.

Molloy stopped when he judged they were out of earshot. 'Sorry about losing it in there. Dagger's a good bloke from what I hear.' He looked at Miller. 'Where's your girlfriend, by the way?'

'If you mean Kim, she's not my girlfriend. She's a colleague.'

Molloy took in a deep breath and blew it out in a plume. 'I miss Sean so much. I'm heartbroken about Michael of course, but Sean was my *wee* boy. I've never forgotten you saved my son. He would have died years ago if it weren't for you. You gave me another, what, ten years with him? Something like that. Years I wouldn't have had.' He looked Miller in the eyes. 'I loved that he stood up to me and went his own way in life. He thought he was hard, but deep down, he was a softy.'

'I remember the first day I saw him in high school. He was standing alone, and I could see he was wanting to make friends, but nobody went up to him. I think they knew who he was and nobody was sure of him. So I went up and we started talking. Turns out he liked building Airfix planes too.'

Molloy laughed. 'I remember him telling me that.' He dug his hands deeper into his pockets. 'He could have gone to George Watson's or Heriot's like Michael did, but Sean was different. He wanted to go to a "normal" high school. Never missed a day of school. And he found his best friend there, even if that best friend's old man was a copper.'

Miller looked at him. 'I know this isn't the right time, but I wanted to ask you a question.'

'Private or business?'

'Private.'

'Fire away.'

'How well do you know Richard Sullivan?'

Molloy gritted his teeth and shook his head. 'Total fucking

weasel. Once he won that case with the actor who was suing that newspaper rag, he didn't want to be associated with me. Why you asking?'

'I'm guessing he had some information on you that could have been harmful to your empire,' Miller said, ignoring the question.

Molloy blew out a long chilly breath. 'You guess wrong. First of all, I'm a law-abiding citizen, and secondly, if he'd started any of that shite, I'd have asked him politely to stop.'

'You would have had him dumped out at sea, you mean.'

'I mean nothing of the sort.'

'Don't worry, I'm not wired for sound.'

Molloy gave a small laugh. 'I don't care if you are. I've nothing incriminating to say.'

'My question is, why would Carol's wallet be in a house he bought and is only now renovating?'

'Somebody took it from her, remember? They obviously dumped the wallet in there.'

'When we checked over every pub she'd been sent to that night, we searched within a half mile radius of each call, just to see if anything would jump out. Lamb's House was derelict, but it was boarded up. I asked a colleague of mine to check the place out that night, because I knew it was empty. He went round and looked at all the boards on the windows on the ground floor, all the boards on the doors. They were all nailed tightly shut. Nobody could have come along that night and gone inside.'

'So what are you saying?'

'I'm saying, whoever had that wallet kept onto it for a while and dumped it in the house after the renovations started.'

'I don't have the answer then, Miller.'

'Was Sullivan into anything illegal that you know about?'

'Not that I know of. He's just a slimy bastard.'

'I'm going to do some more digging into him.'

'I think you're barking up the wrong tree. He knows what would happen to him if he'd killed Carol that night.'

Molloy's BMW pulled into the car park, Greg Sampson at the wheel. 'Anyway, it's cold, and I have a funeral to arrange.'

Sienna walked out of the receiving bay and over to Molloy. The car stopped beside Molloy. Sienna opened the back door for her boss. Molloy climbed in. The window slid down. 'Just so we're clear on one thing, Frank, if I find Cross before you do, you'll never find out what happened to him. And you can take that to the bank.'

Miller watched the car leave, then he felt his mobile vibrate. Took it out of his pocket and answered the call.

'Frank? It's McGovern. Cross has taken Kim. I don't know where they went, but he took her away in an ambulance.'

'How long ago?' Miller felt his heart racing.

'Ten, fifteen minutes. Cross killed the paramedics after he shot me. He's lost it now.'

'Are you okay?'

'I'm fine. I wasn't hurt. I need to find Kim. I don't know where he's taken her.'

'I think I might know where they are,' Miller said, running for his car.

EIGHTY-SEVEN

Miller hammered the car along the snow-covered road in Warriston cemetery. There were tracks from other vehicles and he followed them, diverting off to the left at the last minute. He was going back to the crypts where he'd been with Kim just a few days before, only this time, her life depended on him getting there.

He stopped the car on the top road, on top of the crypts and ran through the snow towards the hill at the side. He slipped going down and fell backwards, getting back up again and reaching the bottom without cracking his skull on a gravestone.

He saw the ambulance as he reached the bottom road. No exhaust coming from the pipe at the back, no blue flashers going. There was no way he could creep up on it, so he ran at it, hoping he wasn't going to be gunned down.

It was empty.

He took the LED flashlight from his pocket and walked up to the main entrance, looking at the confusion of footprints in the fresh snow. His rapid breathing was blowing plumes into the cold air.

Miller switched on his torch, the light shining bright in the darkness. He swept the light around, but there was no sign of anybody. He hurried up the central passageway, shining the light around him, constantly turning around. *Devil takes the hindmost.*

He stopped and listened, but the wind whistling through was the only sound. Up ahead, the gate was still open to the crypt where Harry Davidson had died. Back to where it all started. He went in, walking carefully, aiming the torch like it was a light sabre, but it was obvious from the flickering, one of the oil torches had been lit in the crypt. He turned left from the entrance corridor into the crypt itself. There was no sign of Cross. He shone the torch around.

Its beam picked out Kim sitting in the corner, the oil lamp causing shadows to dance. 'It's me, Kim,' he said to her. She was dressed in a green jumpsuit he assumed had been taken off a paramedic. Her hands were tied behind her back and she had tape over her mouth. He pulled the tape off and untied her.

She stood up, rubbing her wrists and then threw her arms around Miller. 'I thought I was never going to see you again, Frank.'

He had a strange feeling inside right then, a feeling he hadn't felt in a long time. He held her tightly.

'Where's Cross?' he asked.

'I don't know. He left.'

Miller swung the flashlight around. Near where Neil McGovern had sat that night over nine weeks ago. Then they heard feet scuffing the hard earth behind them. They turned round.

The figure stood in front of him, dressed in black, wearing a balaclava. He could make out the mouth and eyes. And the gun.

'Why don't you make yourself more comfortable,' Miller said. 'You can start by taking the balaclava off. Julie.'

He saw the mouth break into a smile and she quickly whipped the woollen mask off. 'You're clever, Frank. Did you know it was me, or was that just a guess?'

'Let's call it an educated guess. When I got a call saying Kim had been abducted, it all fell into place.'

Kim looked shocked. Her eyes wide. 'Julie? What the fuck?'

'Kim? Meet Raymond Cross,' Miller said. 'Or the woman who's made us think Cross has been going on the rampage all this time.'

'I don't believe it.'

'Believe it, dear.' Julie looked at Miller. 'What made you think I'd be here?'

'Lucky guess. There's not many places in Edinburgh where you can hide a stolen ambulance for long. Not when you have a prisoner in tow who you don't want anybody to see. So I took a guess.'

She gave a quick laugh. 'My dad always said you were a good detective. So tell me how you knew it was me and not Raymond Cross.' The unwavering gun was pointed at Miller's stomach.

'Believe it or not, it was something you told me that made me think. You see, Harvey Levitt, the psychologist, said the killer was hurrying through this because time was running out for him. Of course, I didn't think about you at the time, but later on I did. You told me you had another job to go to. Unfortunately for you, I called St Luke's in London. They hadn't heard of you. Which wouldn't have mattered if I'd called, say, next week, because you would have been long gone.'

Julie shrugged. 'Doesn't make much difference if you know now. You and Kim will both be dead in a minute.'

'Why the crypts though, I thought?' Miller said, continuing. 'When I was with Harry as he died, I looked at the names on the markers. They all had the same last name. This is an old family crypt. I got a friend of mine to do a search – this belongs to your stepmother's family. Although it hasn't been used for years, it's the perfect place for hiding somebody.'

'It still doesn't explain how you figured it was me, Frank.'

'I started to think maybe Harry was protecting somebody all these years. Andrea Kennedy told me you were at Moira Kennedy's murder scene with your father. Then I got to thinking, who would Harry be protecting if Cross was innocent?'

'Who says Cross was innocent?' Julie asked.

Miller smiled. 'Let's not play games, Julie. Your father was protecting you all these years. *You* killed Moira Kennedy. And he covered it up.'

EIGHTY-EIGHT

She drew in a breath and looked at him. He could see the change in her eyes, turning her into a version of Julie he'd never seen before. 'Believe me when I tell you I didn't want it to end this way.'

'I don't want to believe it, but now you've shown me just what you're capable of.'

'I'm capable of a lot more than you give me credit for,' Julie said, smiling.

'Like faking being attacked on your doorstep?'

She laughed. 'I was pretty convincing, wasn't I?'

'Yes, you were. I wondered why my cat wasn't acting scared just before I was attacked in my flat. He knew you.'

'That's right. When you called me, I was in your flat, not in the mortuary like you thought. I just went downstairs after that, and changed jackets in my car.'

'What if Kim and Tam Scott had come upstairs with me?'

'I'd have killed them where they stood.'

'Jesus, Julie. Don't do this.' Miller felt a mixture of fear and sadness.

'It's a pity you turned up, Frank. I was going to let you live, now I'll just let you both have it.'

'Like you were going to let me live when you set Lamb's House on fire?'

Her smile dropped. 'I don't want to kill you, Frank. That was meant to scare you. To make you think Sullivan was involved.'

'Why don't I believe you?'

'I could have shot you when I was pointing the gun at your face in your living room if I wanted you dead.'

'Why did you kill Moira Kennedy?' Miller asked, trying to keep her talking. 'You murdered her that night. At least tell me why. You didn't even know her, did you?'

Julie shook her head. 'Never met her before in my life. But she was Raymond's girlfriend and she was taking him away from me.'

'He wasn't really your boyfriend though, was he?'

She waved the gun at him. 'You don't understand! My dad introduced me to him. Brought him round to our house. I thought he was an informant. I fell in love with him as soon as I saw him. He came round quite a few times. He was handsome, he made me laugh, flirted with me. We had a great time. Shared a few beers together. I thought he was going to ask me out. I fell head-over-heels for him. I was so in love. I'd had boyfriends before, but this was different; this was the real deal.

'Then my dad told me I should stay away from Ray. He didn't want me going with boys, no matter who it was. So I went to the opening party of Robert Molloy's hotel. I'd heard Ray and my dad talk about it. I told you the other day I got invited there, but I didn't. They weren't my friends, but I blended in anyway. Nobody knew the difference.'

'You saw him there with Moira?'

Julie looked right into his eyes as the smile dropped from her face. 'I didn't set out to do it, Frank. I saw Ray come from the hotel into the car park and got in the back of the car. It nearly drove me mad. Then Ray got out of the car for whatever reason. Moira got out and went

319

and sat in the front. I couldn't help myself after that. I got in the car with Moira and told her to leave Ray alone. Then she started in on me. Fucking bitch slapped me. So I took my knife and stuck it in her throat. I was in the back and she was in the front. Blood spattered out, but I didn't get any on me. I couldn't help myself.'

Miller quickly looked over at Kim as Julie took her eyes off him for a second and started to pace. He nodded his head slightly, hoping she got the meaning: *If I can wrestle with her, get out and run like fuck.*

'So what happened next?' Miller asked her, knowing it was important to keep her talking. He put himself between Kim and Julie. *When you're marching, you're not fighting.* More talking equals less shooting.

Julie gave him her full attention again. 'I went into the hotel lobby and called the bar, asking to speak to Robert Molloy. When he came on the phone, I told him there was somebody outside who was going to put him in jail. Then I hung up. Then I called the police. Said I saw a man kill a woman in a car.

'Then I watched Molloy come out, but he wasn't alone. Michael was with him. They saw Moira in the car and Michael lost it, shouting and screaming. He grabbed Moira but there was nothing he could do. He and his father had blood all over them, and if my dad had been on time, he would have caught them red-handed. He could have arrested them, and I'm sure they would have made the charges stick.'

'Clever,' Miller said, 'but they didn't get caught.'

'No. My dad got the call. I knew he was close to Molloy's hotel. I'd heard him talk about it on the phone. Then Ray came out. Saw what was in the car. Then my dad turned up with the cavalry. Ray and my dad talked for a bit. I didn't know what they were saying, but then my dad put Ray in handcuffs. The place was swarming with uniforms.'

Miller kept his eye on the gun. 'But Molloy didn't get arrested. He had three witnesses who would swear they were with him the whole time and he never even stepped outside. The three women you killed two years ago.'

'That's right. So I told my dad what I'd done. I think I wanted to see if he loved me or not. He had little Carol and little Gary now. He'd married that bitch after my mum died, and they couldn't have children. So they adopted a little girl. Why the fuck would he want another girl? He had me.' She poked herself in the chest. 'Me. His own flesh and blood. So now was the time to prove he loved me more than Carol. My dad *did*. He protected me.'

'I don't think you had to resort to murder to see if your dad loved you.'

Julie gritted her teeth. 'It wasn't that simple. I thought me telling my dad might have made sure Ray was in the clear so we could be together. Again, my dad told me I should stay away from Ray, that he wasn't what he seemed to be. He'd been working undercover with my dad. I was excited. I thought Ray would come round and get me. Ray was smuggled out of the station by another agent pretending to be a fucking copper from London. I never saw him again. Turns out Moira was Ray's wife, so he was never interested in me in the first place.'

Kim moved slightly towards the exit. Julie pointed the gun at her. 'You take one more step, and I'll finish you before Frank gets to hear my side of the story.'

Kim moved back a step.

Julie's eyes were bright and ferocious in the light from Miller's flashlight. 'My dad and I had a tumultuous relationship after he married that bitch. I thought things would be different when she died, but no. I often complained about Carol, and he verbally lashed out at me one night after he'd been drinking. Said Carol was the better daughter, and she was the best detective on the force and she'd climb high. I was so jealous I looked at Harry's old case file and saw the list of witnesses who'd given Robert Molloy an alibi the night of Moira's murder. And I started killing them. Neither you nor Carol could figure out who'd murdered them. I won the challenge. I made a comment to Harry, that Carol couldn't be that good if she couldn't track down a killer. He said Carol was still the better daughter.'

'I don't think Harry saw a difference between you and Carol,' Miller said.

'If he didn't, then he should have!' Her voice was getting louder. 'I was flesh and blood. It didn't matter, at least *I knew I was the better daughter*. It would have stayed that way as well if Carol hadn't poked her nose in.'

Miller's eyebrows narrowed. He felt a shiver of cold crawl down his neck. 'What do you mean?'

'If Carol hadn't gone looking for stuff in my dad's attic the day she died, she'd still be alive today.' She looked at him and smiled. 'You've always wondered who killed her, Frank. Now you know. I killed her!'

EIGHTY-NINE

Miller felt a ringing in his ears, like he'd been slapped hard on the side of the head. 'What did you say?'

Julie laughed, like a person who'd lost all grip on reality. 'I stole Richard Sullivan's car that night. It was an old classic Jag, easy to hotwire. Harry taught me how to do that a long time ago in case I ever lost my own keys. I knew Carol had been having problems with him and I thought it would be fun to divert attention to him. I used his car to kill Carol.'

Kim glared at her. 'How could you have killed her? How would you know where she was? Don't listen to her, Frank. She's playing games with you now.'

'Why don't you tell her how I knew where Carol was, Frank?' She smiled at Miller.

Miller looked round at Kim. 'I told her where Carol was.'

'That's right. Detective Miller here told me. In fact, he kept me informed of how everything was going. You know why? Because I asked him to. I was playing the worried sister. I simply called, and Frank told me. Then he told me she'd had to throw her radio away but she'd put a throwaway phone in her boot. She called him and told

323

him she was heading for a pub in Leith. The Admiral's Rest. Convenient for me, but it wouldn't have been a problem if she was going somewhere else. Frank kept in touch with me.'

'You haven't told me why you killed her.'

'I was getting to that.' She pointed the gun at the uneven floor. 'When I killed those three women, I took their IDs. Just to make it harder for you lot. I put them in a box of photos that were in my dad's attic. Little did I know they were Carol's photos.

'Then one day, Carol was round and found the box when she was looking for something. Saw the bank cards and the driving licenses. She called me, in a right tizzy. Crying and getting hysterical. She thought Harry had killed those women and was going to confront him, but I told her not to do anything rash. Keep it to herself, and I'd go with her and talk to him. She didn't want to talk to you about it, Frank, not at that point. Harry was her dad after all.'

'And you couldn't have her confronting Harry because he'd know he himself didn't kill those women, and that would leave only one person who could hide those things in his attic: you.'

Julie was silent for a moment before answering, as if her mind was taking her back to that time. 'That was the night she went on the ransom drop. You told me she was doing it, remember?'

Miller nodded. He was starting to feel very cold now. Shivering inside his overcoat. He remembered Carol had told him the night she was doing the ransom drop she had bad news for him and was scared. That must have been what she was scared about.

'I knew I had to silence her, so I put the plan into action. It wasn't much of a plan, and I originally thought about calling to tell her all about it, then I'd have killed her somewhere else, but the whole kidnap drop thing was perfect. I had to give it a try. And it worked. I stole Richard Sullivan's car and ran her down with it. I knew there was bad blood between them, and the suspicion would fall on him.'

Miller couldn't believe what he was hearing. His sister-in-law had killed his fucking wife. No matter how many times he repeated it in his head, he still found it hard to believe, like it was a dream.

'Things couldn't have gone more smoothly. Nobody knew exactly who killed Carol, and Sullivan had an alibi, albeit a shaky one, but nobody could prove he did it. Then life went back to normal.'

'For you, maybe. My life was never the same again after I held my wife's funeral.' He looked at her. Had to keep her talking if he was going to get out of this alive. 'What did you do with the ransom money?'

'I didn't take it. I just ran her down.'

'You expect me to believe you didn't take the money?'

'I don't care what you believe. I know I left her dead in the middle of the road.'

Miller was trying to read her face, but couldn't. 'Why did you get your father and McGovern here that night nine weeks ago?'

'I was arguing with him, which we did a lot. He said he missed Carol. She was more like a daughter than I was. So I told him I was the one who killed those women and killed her. He said I had to be stopped. I heard him talking to McGovern, asking him to meet him in the catacombs. I figured he thought I'd never find him there in the family crypt. I didn't figure on him bringing you into it.'

'So you thought nobody would ever find them.'

She nodded. 'I couldn't let him put me in prison. I tried to kill them both, but McGovern didn't die. And he got the blame for killing my father. Except he died in the hospital. Then when Kim and I got chatting, she told me McGovern was really her father. Since I was robbed of killing him, I thought I'd kill his daughter instead.'

Miller shook his head. 'You don't have to do this. We can get you help, Julie. They'll be lenient with you.'

Julie laughed. 'What, because I'm a sicko? Is that what you're saying?' She looked Miller in the eyes, and they were the eyes of somebody who was unhinged.

'I still don't understand why you wanted Molloy to take the fall for Moira's murder. Or why you targeted Molloy after all this time. Why you killed innocent people associated with him,' Miller said, trying to buy time.

'You really don't know?'

'Know what, Julie?'

The laugh and smile again, spittle forming a chain between her top and bottom lips. 'As I said, my father and his wife adopted Carol and she became the baby of the family. I'd been pushed aside by a baby who wasn't even flesh and blood. I hated her. So let me tell you who your wife's real father was: Robert Molloy! And that bitch I killed in the pub, Jennifer Wilson? That's her mother. I wanted to kill people associated with Molloy so he'd feel pain.'

'Robert Molloy?' Miller said, incredulously.

'That's right. When I was arguing with Harry one night, he told me Molloy was Carol's father. So you see, Frank, I'm not sick; I'm angry.'

'I can see you've been harbouring this hatred for years, and I can understand that, but—'

'You understand nothing. You have no siblings. You couldn't even begin to understand, you patronising bastard.'

Julie turned to look at Kim. 'I'm going shoot you right in the head. After I've shot him. Murder-suicide. Then I'll be away and they'll be chasing Raymond Cross for years. But they'll never find him.'

They heard shouts coming from far away. Miller looked at her.

'It's over. I didn't come alone. They're not looking for Cross any more, Julie; they're looking for you.'

Julie was fast. She moved the gun and shot Kim.

NINETY

Miller didn't have much chance to stop her but he lunged anyway. His hand knocked her arm a fraction and the bullet hit Kim in the side.

Kim screamed and fell over sideways. Blood mushroomed on the front of the green jumpsuit.

Miller had hold of Julie's sleeve, but she managed to pull her arm back. She brought the gun round in an arc, connecting it with the side of his head. He reached out and blindly grabbed at the weapon. His fingers wrapped round the barrel as he fell. He hit the floor, rolled and got a proper hold of the gun, taking it from her. As he lay prone on the floor, he saw Julie's legs disappear round the corner.

He got up on shaky legs, checked on Kim. 'I'll get you help. They're here. They'll help us.'

'This hurts, but I'll be fine. Go after her. Don't let that bitch get away. Go!'

He nodded and ran the same way Julie had done.

Outside the crypt, the main passageway was dark, the light from the oil torches diffused to a dull glow. He looked the way he'd come in and didn't see Julie. More voices, louder this time, coming from the direction of the entrance. Lights dancing about in the dark.

'Down here!' he shouted. 'Bring a medic. Officer down! Gunshot wound.' Where was Julie? The ventilation shaft. In the opposite direction. He started running as fast as he could, the pain shooting through his head. He held his torch in one hand, the gun in the other. Turned right, the same way Kim had showed them before. Then left. There was no slowing down this time, no wondering if there was somebody round the corner waiting with a gun.

Up ahead, light from the ventilation grate shone down into the passageway, bathing it in a dull light. Snow had fallen through, making the floor slippery.

Julie was standing on the pile of gravestones that provided a makeshift ladder to the iron grate above. She was pushing the grate, but it wasn't moving.

'I parked one of the front wheels of my car over it,' Miller said.

Julie stopped pushing. Turned to look at him and smiled. Then she climbed back down. Stood looking at him.

'Keep your hands where I can see them,' he said. It was much colder here, making him shiver. Blood trickled down his neck from where she'd hit him with the gun, and his legs were starting to shake.

'You don't want to shoot me, Frank,' she said, breathing heavily.

'You're under arrest, Julie.' He pointed the gun at her.

'That's something you don't want to do. You wouldn't find the answer if you arrested me.'

Miller looked into her eyes and saw something there; not fear, but amusement. For some reason, she looked like she had the upper hand although he was the one with the gun. 'What answer?'

And in that instant, she smiled. 'Who I was working with.'

'What are you talking about?' He was starting to sweat, despite the cold. Could it be true? Or was this just a madwoman talking? *Don't listen! Don't listen! Don't listen! Ignore her!*

'You don't think I did all this on my own, do you? I told you I didn't take the ransom money, and that was the truth. *He* took it.'

'The kidnapper?'

Julie shook her head. 'No, the man I was working with. He thought we were only going to rip Carol off for the money. When he saw I'd killed her, it was too late; he was in as deep as I was. Too late for him to turn back.'

'Were you lying about Richard Sullivan? Was he involved?'

'No, he doesn't know anything. He was just a false lead.'

'So tell me who it is.' Miller kept the gun on her, but he could feel the tremors creeping into his hand.

'I'm not telling you everything just now. We're bargaining, Frank. Let me leave. There are other ventilation shafts I can get out of. Nobody will ever know, remember that. I'll be away from Edinburgh. I've finished killing. You can go about your life again. Then when all this has died down, we'll meet again, just you and me. Then I'll tell you everything you want to know.'

'What's to stop you disappearing and never contacting me?' Stop asking her fucking questions! his mind screamed. His head was buzzing now. What was he thinking? He couldn't bargain with this woman. This was crazy. She was a psychopathic killer. *She just said she was going to shoot you and then Kim. Murder-suicide.*

'You'd have to trust me. I could have shot you, but I didn't. I wasn't going to shoot you, Frank. I could have killed you in your flat, but I didn't. You're not part of the plan.'

They both heard the shouts getting closer.

Miller wavered. 'We both know you're lying.'

Julie was still smiling. 'Time to make up your mind. Let me go, and I can meet you somewhere after all this dies down. I'll tell you who he is. You can go and get him and all this will be over. You can get on with your life and I can too. We'll both get what we want, Frank. I'll contact you. Nobody will ever know.'

'I'll know.'

Julie looked past him. 'This is a one-time deal and you know it.'

'You killed my wife, and a lot of other people. You know I can't let you go.'

'You'll spend the rest of your life wondering who he is, and he'll still be out there, free as a bird.'

'I think you're making all this up.'

'That's a dangerous road to start going down.'

'You're full of it, Julie.'

'Am I? I can tell you who he is. It's very interesting.'

'Tell me.'

'I can't tell you everything. I will though, if you let me go.' She stepped closer. He kept the gun pointing at her.

'You won't shoot me.'

'Go ahead and try me.'

So she did.

Maybe it was the darkness that threw him off. Maybe he was distracted too much. Maybe Julie was right; he *couldn't* shoot her in cold blood. Whatever the reason, his guard was down long enough for her to throw herself at him.

She was fighting with the strength of someone on drugs. In that moment, he understood how she could overpower men stronger than herself. How she could overpower somebody like Michael Molloy.

He could feel her left hand grab the gun as she tried to wrench it from him. Then the gun went off. He fell backwards onto the hard-packed dirt floor.

Miller felt pain like he'd never known before. His shoulder felt numb as the agony exploded through him. He couldn't move, except to look up at Julie holding the gun.

The voices were getting closer.

'Were you lying about working with somebody?'

'Of course I was. Or was I? Make up your own mind.' She looked down at him lying helpless on the ground. Smiled at him.

Miller shook his head. 'You won't get away.'

'Drop that fucking gun!'

Miller could make out a man standing in the dim light, pointing a gun at Julie. A sharp beam of light from the weapon illuminated Julie's face. She was smiling down at Miller.

Despite the pain, he recognised the face, recognised the voice, the Cockney accent reverberating around the subterranean catacomb. 'Julie... you remember Neil McGovern, don't you?'

'What? You're lying!'

'In the flesh, as we speak, princess,' McGovern said.

Then she swung the gun up, and in that moment, Miller knew she'd never get a pinpoint on McGovern.

He heard a crack, deafening in the confines of the catacombs. Watched as Julie fell on top of him, blood spreading across her chest.

He tried to scream but couldn't.

The sound of running feet and voices shouting.

Then hands grabbing Julie's lifeless body.

Then total darkness.

NINETY-ONE

Two Weeks Later

'You ready?' Neil McGovern said, walking into Miller's hospital room.

Miller looked over at his friend. He still shook his head at the thought of McGovern being his friend, but that was the best description he had.

'Yeah. Just finishing up.' His left arm was in a sling and he winced at the pain as he moved.

McGovern moved forward and helped Miller on with his jacket. He looked at the cut on Miller's head. It had healed well, but the gunshot wound would take a bit longer.

'You're lucky she missed your head,' he said.

'I know.' It was something Miller thought about almost every waking moment. 'If it wasn't for you, she would have shot me dead.'

'You saved my little girl. We're even. Has the doc been in yet?'

'The nurse said he'll be along shortly. He's doing his rounds.'

McGovern looked at the clock on the wall.

'You been in to see Kim yet?' Miller asked.

'Yeah. I went there first. She asked where you were. Said you usually go in to see her in the morning but she hadn't seen you today. I told her you were busy packing.'

'Has the doc spoken to her yet?'

McGovern smiled. 'He has. He said she'll be in here another week. The infection in her wound took a lot out of her.'

'I've noticed a difference though, Neil. I'm glad the bullet went right through.'

'Listen, Frank, I want you to meet somebody. Ash?' He turned to the door and Sienna Craig walked in.

Miller looked at her, confused.

'Frank, this is Agent Ashley Turner. She works for me.'

Ashley smiled at him and walked forward. 'We haven't been formally introduced before.' They shook hands.

'Did Molloy find out you're undercover?'

Ashley shook her head. 'No. He won't see me again. I'm heading off to New York tomorrow to work in our US office for a while.'

'New York?'

'We have an office in the British Consulate in Manhattan,' McGovern said. 'Molloy won't know Ashley's left until she doesn't turn up for work. He'll wonder where the hell she went, but he'll think she just skipped out on him.'

'That's the second time I know of that you failed to get inside Molloy's organisation.'

'We were closer this time,' Ashley said. 'There'll be other times.'

'Talking of Raymond Cross... did Jack tell you about him?' McGovern said.

Miller shook his head.

'Maybe he thought it better I tell you; he worked for us back then as you know. However, he retrained as a lawyer and we helped him change his identity. A little nip and tuck, new name. Nobody ever figured out who he really was.'

Miller shook his head. 'Don't fucking tell me: Richard Sullivan.'

McGovern looked at him. 'That's how I knew he couldn't be the man you were looking for. He was over the Atlantic, flying back to Edinburgh, the night Colin Fleming was murdered for a start.'

'Carol hated him.'

'No, she didn't. She worked with him on a few cases and that was part of the cover. Sorry for the deception, but it was part of the job. He's not a real bad guy, but he wanted to stick it right up Molloy, that's why he took work from him. Then he lucked out and made a fortune. Molloy hates him now, and he would have him topped if he found out about his past life.'

'And Jack knew?'

'I introduced him to Sullivan. Don't stress over it now though. We'll have a beer one night and I'll tell you all about it.'

There was silence for a moment as Miller let this fact settle in.

Ashley spoke first. 'I'd better be off, boss.'

McGovern put a hand on her shoulder. 'Take care. You'll have a team with you all the way to New York. Let me know when you've settled in. I'm having somebody ready your apartment in Brooklyn now.'

'I'll call you.' She looked at Miller. 'Get well soon. It was nice meeting you, Frank.'

'You too.' He watched as Ashley left. 'You're a dark horse, McGovern.'

'In my line of work, you have to be.'

The doctor came into the room. 'Inspector Miller. Glad to be going home now?'

Miller nodded. 'There's only so much excitement I can take, doc.'

The doctor smiled. 'I have a prescription for you.' He handed it over. 'Painkillers. Follow up with your own GP. And take care of the shoulder. You'll have to go to physiotherapy for a few weeks, but the wound has healed well. No infection there, and we got the bullet out. Once again, you were lucky. Straight in and out.'

'I don't feel lucky.' Miller knew Julie would have overpowered him if the gun hadn't gone off. Then she would have killed him before McGovern got there.

'Take care of him,' the doctor said to McGovern.

'My wife's cooking him dinner tonight. And my daughter will be staying with us for a while when she gets out, so they'll both be looked after.'

'Ah, yes, Miss Smith. She's making a good recovery.'

'I'd like to see her before I go,' Miller said, standing up and putting the prescription in his pocket.

McGovern grabbed Miller's holdall and walked into the corridor. 'I'll see you down in the car, Frank. We'll be at the front door.'

'Aren't you coming to see Kim?'

'I've just seen her. Believe me, she doesn't want to see her old man twice in twenty minutes.'

Miller nodded and left the room. He walked out into the main spur, heading for another ward. Trying not to think of Sean Molloy in his death bed.

There were two armed officers standing outside her room, and there would be men there twenty-four seven until they could determine the level of the threat. In case what Julie said about not working alone was true.

I wasn't working alone. He could still hear Julie's voice when he thought about it.

Kim smiled when she saw him walk into the room.

'Hey, I was wondering where you'd got to this morning.'

'How you feeling?'

'Sore. As if the bullet didn't do enough damage to me. Still, the infection's almost gone and no vital organs were hit. Thanks to you.'

'I was just in the right place at the right time.'

'You're too modest.' She smiled at him, then winced as she changed position. 'I hear my mother's cooking dinner for you tonight. You and your dad.'

'Yeah, Jack won't pass up a free meal. It'll be a change for him to eat real food instead of my defrosted dinners.'

She laughed and winced again. 'Don't make me laugh, Miller.'

Miller looked at the drip still attached to her arm. 'More antibiotics?'

Kim nodded. 'Shut the door, Frank.'

Miller got up off the bed and closed her door. Sat back down again. She had the same view into the car park, just further along.

'I wanted to thank you again for saving my life. If you hadn't knocked Julie's arm, the bullet would have killed me.'

'Now you're giving me a beamer.' Miller could feel his cheeks getting red.

'Don't be silly. I owe my life to you. And when I get out of here and I'm on my feet again, I'd like to buy you dinner.'

He reached out and squeezed her hand. 'Just concentrate on getting better.'

She nodded. Yawned. 'I'd like to get a little bit of sleep before my mother comes in. She fusses like an old mother hen.'

'It's what mothers do.' He stood up. 'Call me when you're ready to get out.'

'I will. They said next week after the infection clears up. I'll be off work for a while.'

'Will you be back with your dad's department?'

'No. Norma wants my dad to be based up here permanently, and she wants me to be a full-time investigator with her office. Nobody knows my mother's Norma Banks and I certainly won't be telling anybody.'

'I'm glad you'll still be around.' He kissed her on the cheek. 'I'd better go. Your dad's downstairs waiting to drive me home.'

She watched him walk to the door and stopped him. 'Frank, do you think Julie would have killed you?'

He nodded. 'I think so. She wanted to kill people related to Moira Kennedy's murder. I was in her way.'

He said goodbye and left. Downstairs, the black Range Rover was at the door.

McGovern was sitting in the back waiting for him. The driver and passenger looked straight ahead as the car pulled away from the hospital entrance.

'You know, you saved my little girl's life, and there's nothing I can do that will ever fully repay that debt, Frank. You know that, don't you?'

'Kim and I were working together. We were part of a team. She's one of us and we do anything for our own.'

'And her mother insists she stay working up here. For her department this time, not mine.'

'And you're staying too, I hear.'

'My wife always gets her own way.' He smiled. 'Seriously, if there's anything you ever need, or if there's anything I can do for you, you only have to ask.'

Miller sat in silence. The car turned into Old Dalkeith Road. 'Well, Neil, there *is* something...'

NINETY-TWO

'Do you want me to wait here?' McGovern said to Miller as they stopped outside Julie's house.

Miller shook his head. 'No, I don't know how long I'll be.'

'I can come in if you like, Frank.'

Miller took a deep breath and let it out slowly. 'This is something I've been dreading, but I have to do it. One last time.' He looked up at Julie's townhouse. 'Maggie Parks and her team went through here and found nothing?'

'They were looking for evidence that she had an accomplice after what she told you, but there was none. She could have just been saying that to wind you up, Frank. She was literally negotiating for her life.'

'I know. I just had to make sure. Thanks, mate. I'll catch you later.'

Miller took out the spare key he had for the house. A quick phone call to the station confirmed all the forensics had been done and he could go in. Now, there was no evidence the whole place had been gone through.

Miller felt like a lead weight had dropped from his chest into his stomach as he turned the key in the lock. Walking into the house brought back memories of better times. Like the first time he and Carol had come here.

'This is a nice place you have here,' Miller said, handing over the bottle of wine they'd brought.

'I love it,' Carol said, hugging her sister.

'Thank you,' Julie said. 'Come on up, the rest are here.'

They followed her up to the first floor living room. They could hear the buzz of conversation as they walked into the living room. Julie introduced Miller and Carol to her work colleagues. Jack was there with Helen, Miller's mother.

'Hey, kids,' Jack said. 'Have a drink.'

'Are you sure there's any left?' Miller said, with a grin.

'Cheeky wee bugger. Mother, have a word with your son.'

'He only calls me "mother" in front of you, I'll have you know,' Helen said, hugging her son. 'Come on, Carol, let's leave the boys to insult each other. Leo Chester's here.'

Chester had been Julie's boss for years and was as charming as ever. One of the old school who still wore a bow-tie.

Harry Davidson was there with his wife, Ann. They were talking to Chester, and Harry came over when the women got in a group.

'Nice place,' Miller said, to Harry.

'Yes. She's done well for herself.' He looked around conspiratorially. 'Between you and me, I wish she'd find a man. Somebody to share this place with. She's knocking on the door of forty and no man in her life. It's a crime, Frank. I'm glad Carol's got you.'

'I'm sure she'll find somebody one day,' Jack said, not quite believing his own words.

'Well, somebody has to make me a granddad one day. You too, Jack. I'm sure you and the missus can see a little nipper running around your house?'

'I hear nothing else, Harry. Now Helen's retired, she wants nothing more than to hear the sound of little feet running about our place. I *told her we could look after Frank's cat now and then to satisfy her cravings.'*

Harry sucked in a breath. 'You're a brave man, Jack. Most women want to become a grandma, and that's not a thing to joke about. Am I right, Frank?'

Miller nodded. 'I'm with Harry on this one, Dad. You're on your own there.'

'Well, if you and Carol get married soon and produce a little Frank, then I won't have to keep putting my foot in it, will I?'

'We're happy living together.'

'I'm sure you are, son, but a woman always wants a gold band on her finger, and I can't blame Carol for wanting one. Why she doesn't pester you to death is beyond me.'

'Well, it was nice chatting with you, Dad, but I'm going to have a chat with Gus Weaver.' Miller walked away from his father and over to the mortuary assistant, glad to be away from the talk of marriage.

That had been five years ago. It would be another two before Miller and Carol got married. They'd been husband and wife for six months before she died. Sometimes he thought getting married had been a curse.

Now, Julie's house felt not only quiet, but empty.

He walked past the laundry room and the door leading to the garage. Up the stairs and into the living room. Everything had been gone through carefully, and put back as best they could, but it still looked messy.

Miller tried to picture that house warming party, imagining where Carol had stood. Where his mother and father had stood. Tried to hear the laughter again. Then a thought occurred to him; at the party, it was all family and colleagues who'd been there. None of Julie's friends had been there.

Did she have any friends?

He didn't have the answer. He'd never heard her talking about any close friends. No boyfriends, no girlfriends that she went out drinking with. She'd been a very lonely woman. *Or had she?* Maybe the madness kept her entertained.

He looked through some of the private papers and bills that had been piled on the floor. He didn't know where they'd come from, but they obviously hadn't been put back. He wondered if Julie had left a will, and whether Gary would be in it. *Wondered if Carol would be in it.* A lawyer would have to wrap up her estate.

He carried on looking around for a while longer and then walked down to Julie's laundry room. Then through to her garage.

That's where he found what he was looking for. It all fell into place.

He went back upstairs.

Now all he had to do was sit back and wait.

He didn't have to wait long.

NINETY-THREE

The front door clicked shut softly.

Miller was sitting on the couch facing the living room door when Gary Davidson walked in.

Gary stopped as if he'd hit a brick wall when he saw Miller. 'What are you doing here?' he said to Miller, through gritted teeth.

'Take it easy, Gary.'

'Who the hell said you could come in here? It wasn't good enough that you killed my sister, you have to come back and rake around in her things?' His face was red, as if he was about to explode. 'How did you get in?'

'Julie gave me a spare key a long time ago,' Miller said. 'What are you doing here?'

'Me? I'm her fucking brother! I have every right to be here. I come by every day to try and sort this mess out. I'm on compassionate leave, remember? I'm seeing a fucking therapist. It's not every day you find out your sister's a fucking serial killer! And she murdered my other sister and my father.'

Miller's brother-in-law was losing control but he couldn't risk going over to him in case he got hit on the shoulder.

'Gary, this isn't going to be easy. I'm going to make a call and get you help. You shouldn't be here.'

'It's none of your business. I'm doing fine, and if people leave me alone, I can get on with this.'

'I'm not going to leave you alone.'

'Yes, you fucking will!' Gary said. Then he made his move.

Miller moved fast, grabbing Gary round the neck, pulling him backwards. Gary struggled, grabbing hold of Miller's arm, but to no avail.

Then he passed out.

When Gary came round, he didn't know where he was for a moment. 'What... what happened?' he asked, when he saw Miller standing watching him.

'Drink that glass of water,' Miller said, sitting down beside him. 'You're just stressed out, Gary. I don't blame you. It can't be easy, but you're getting help. I'm here for you.'

'I don't know what came over me.'

'That's alright, mate,' Miller said. 'Sorry about choking you, but I just applied enough pressure to let you rest for a moment.'

'Sorry about that. I feel like a real fool now.' He took the glass from Miller.

'Don't be daft. It must have been a shock seeing me sitting there. You want some ice for that?' Miller said.

'Thanks.'

Miller left the living room, going through to the kitchen. When he came back, he threw the small, ice-covered package into Gary's lap. 'Is that what you came looking for today?'

'What the hell is this?'

Miller wasn't sure if Gary meant the package or the situation. Probably both. 'I found the packets of money in her chest freezer in the garage. It was hidden in all the bags of frozen peas and carrots.'

'I know nothing about this,' Gary said, sweeping the thawing bundle onto the floor.

'It's some of the money Julie took from Colin Fleming the night he died. She was blackmailing Robert Molloy. You knew Julie had the money, didn't you?'

'What? How the fuck would I know what she did?' The calm demeanour was gone again.

'You came here looking for it.'

'If that was the case, then that makes me an accessory to Julie's murder spree. I didn't know anything about that.'

'Don't start lying to me now, Gary.'

'Okay, okay. Molloy told me about his money being missing. Fleming had it last, and he wanted me to keep my ears open. If Julie had pretended she was Cross, then I figured she had it.'

Miller stood a few feet back from his brother-in-law, in case he made a sudden move. 'Why would he come to you, Gary?'

'I owed him a lot of money a couple of years ago. I paid it back, but I keep gambling at his private den. A group of us get together, and I can't help it. I get carried away, looking to make a fortune.' He looked up at Miller. 'You don't understand; I'd have had to sell my house to pay off the debt.'

'So what now, you were going to get him his money back and all bets were off?' Miller thought about things for a moment. 'Wait; you said you'd have had to sell your house, meaning now you don't. But you didn't use this money. You paid him back. Where did you get the money before? I mean, if you needed to sell your house, it must have been a hell of a debt. We're not talking a couple of thousand.'

'It doesn't matter.'

A thought slammed into Miller's brain like a freight train going a thousand miles an hour. Julie's words to him in the crypts when he'd asked her about the ransom money: *I didn't take it.*

Now he knew who did. And who'd really killed his wife.

NINETY-FOUR

Gary Davidson sat in the unmarked Mondeo at the foot of Constitution Street, the engine running. The heat was on low, but he felt the sweat running down his body. Dare he do this? More to the point, could he pull it off?

Thoughts were exploding through his mind like the fireworks bursting up above.

Terry White. The image of the little boy looked back at him. A little boy, Gary! he mentally screamed. He grabbed the steering wheel and shook it back and forth. What to do.

You're going to make us homeless, the way you're going, Rosie, his wife, had said to him one night. Claire will be living on the streets with us and then they'll take her away. Is that what you want?

It wasn't. Gary saw a quick fix to his problem. He could pay off his debts to Robert Molloy virtually overnight. He'd tell him they were on a drugs bust and somebody overlooked a black holdall in a wardrobe. He slipped back in and got it. If Molloy didn't believe it, then so what? Gary didn't see a problem, as long as Molloy got his filthy lucre.

He'd told Miller since he was Carol's brother, he wanted to be the first shadow car. The whole team were spread out like ripples in a *pond, but he was at the epicentre. First contact should it go haywire. Miller agreed.*

They'd been going full tilt when the call came through from Miller. "I got a call, Gary. Admiral's Rest, Leith."

There was no GPS in her car, now the kidnapper had forced her to use another vehicle. Whoever he was, he was very clever.

There was no direct communication with him now she'd had to dump her radio, and he was relying on Miller to be his eyes and ears.

He'd taken a direct route to Leith and was waiting for the red Nova to make an appearance. He knew he'd have only minutes to carry out his plan if he was to be successful. He thought about his wife, Rosie, and his daughter, Claire. Thought about how all their troubles would be over if he could just pull this off. He didn't give another thought to Terry White.

He was slouched down in his seat. The Admiral's Rest was on the corner of Constitution Street and Maritime Lane, the latter being one-way leading towards him. He saw the Nova pull up and Carol get out, carrying the holdall. She went into the pub.

In the days and weeks after that night, Gary Davidson had run this scenario in his mind over and over again, to see if there had been any other way he could have pulled it off, but each time, it was the same result.

"Gary, Carol called me on her hidden phone. She's to go up Maritime Lane. You got her?"

Gary watched as Carol came out of the pub minutes later, still carrying the black bag.

'Got her, boss.' He also saw the box truck coming down the lane towards him. He wanted to stay with the car. 'I'm going round the back way. Maritime Lane is one-way against me.'

'Roger. Go now. I don't want her out of your sight for longer than necessary. Backup shadow crews on their way.'

Gary drove round the long way. He didn't know how long it took him but it felt like a lifetime. His plans changed in an instant.

Maritime Street crossed Maritime Lane, each section a one-way, going in opposite directions.

The Jaguar had its full beam on, blinding him, as it sped away up the part of the lane that led to the shore. Dazzled for a moment, Gary didn't see Carol at first, lying on the road.

The black bag was lying further away from her.

This part of the street was filled with office staff during the day but was deserted at night. Nobody else was near her. Then she got to her feet.

He shot the car across the junction and got out. 'Carol, you okay?'

'Gary. Go... get him. That car.'

He could see there was a horrendous fracture in her leg. Her face was scraped and there was a trickle of blood running down her cheek.

He felt himself start to panic. Looked around. There was still nobody here.

He looked into her eyes. They were still sharp. For now. 'I thought you were just going to dump the bag and leave.'

'What... do you mean?'

He reached out and grabbed the nylon holdall.

'Gary... what are you doing? Follow the car. I'll... call Frank. Oh shit... I think I broke a rib as well,' she gasped.

He stood with the bag. Turned to the Astra and opened the boot and slung the bag in. Like a miracle, Carol was on her feet, leaning against a car.

'You're not taking... that money.' Her breathing was raspy now, and he realised a rib had probably punctured a lung.

'You don't understand. I'll leave. Then I'll make the call.'

What followed happened in a flash. She grabbed the sleeve of his jacket. A firework exploded overhead. Gary, his nerves taut, thought she'd taken a gun out and fired it. He pushed her hard. She fell backwards and the back of her head cracked against the edge of the kerb. Carol lay there with her eyes open, blood flowing through her hair onto the pavement.

Oh fuck, no.

Gary had no more than two seconds to make a decision, and then he went into autopilot. He knelt beside Carol and took his radio out. 'Officer down! I repeat, officer down!' He gave the location just as the first of the other shadow cars pulled up.

He felt arms pulling him out of the way. The other members of the team knew he was Carol's brother, and could see he'd frozen. They needed to help her, and right now.

Gary didn't know how much time passed between knocking Carol down and the ambulance getting there. Frank Miller was brought down in an Alpha Victor armed response unit vehicle.

Gary heard voices shouting, probably heard Miller talking to him, but his head felt like it had been dunked in syrup.

He remembered seeing Miller get in the back of the ambulance and telling somebody – he didn't know who – he was going to the hospital. Patrol cars were on the lookout for the Jag.

He parked in the Royal Infirmary with the blue grill lights going. Walked into the hospital in a daze, one half of him hoping somebody would look in the boot of his car and find a bag with a hundred grand in it, but nobody did.

He walked into the A&E, not taking in all the noise and activity as doctors rushed about, dodging police officers. Both in uniform and in plainclothes.

'Please, no,' he said, in his head.

It seemed as if Carol had been behind the curtain in the emergency bay for days, but it turned out she was in there for forty-five minutes. Being a copper, they tried longer than they normally would. She didn't regain consciousness in the ambulance somebody told him.

'Fuck, no!' he heard a voice cry out, and in that instant, he knew.

The doctors and nurses came out. Gary didn't even know what time it was. Didn't want to know. He felt this night would go on and on forever. That he'd relive this night, this exact moment, over and over, in a never-ending cycle.

'Nurse? I'm her brother,' he said.

'I'm so sorry. You can go in.'

Frank and Harry were in there. Tears were flowing down Harry's cheeks. Frank was slumped over Carol, holding her hand, his shoulders heaving. He looked up when Gary walked in.

'She's gone, Gary. She didn't make it.'

Then Gary cried like a child, screaming in his head. He covered his face, unable to look at anybody.

Later on, in a small, private room, the doctor sat them down and said Carol had a broken rib which had pierced her lung. Her leg was shattered. Her skull was fractured, from hitting the windscreen the doctor said. They found glass in her hair.

'What was the cause of death?' Gary asked.

'Severe trauma to her head,' the doctor stated, matter-of-factly.

'So the fracture from the windscreen killed her?'

The doctor shook his head. 'No, I don't think that was fatal. It was a fracture, and I can't say for sure of course, but I've seen people come in with a similar fracture and live. It's hard to say, and it will be the determination of the pathologist, but if it wasn't fatal, then the back of her skull hitting the kerb definitely was a fatal injury.'

The rest of the night was a blur. Being the first officer on the scene, Gary would have to give a witness account. They'd see he was emotionally distressed and give him some time, but they'd come knocking.

And by the time they checked his car over, the money was long gone.

'So you killed my wife? Over a bag of fucking money?' Miller didn't feel the pain in his shoulder now, such was the adrenaline rush.

'It was an accident, Frank. I swear to God. I just wanted the money. I was in so much debt. Taking that money would have solved everything for me.'

'The brass upstairs thought because she was on foot the kidnapper was watching, waiting for her to put the money down. That the car which killed Carol was driven by a drunk driver. They didn't think the kidnapper would kill her for it, so they dismissed the idea.'

'I know, I know, I work for them too, remember.'

'Were you working with Julie on this?'

'What? No! I never knew what that mad cow was doing.'

'We never heard from the kidnapper again. The money was gone, and we thought he'd killed the little boy. We still don't know his fate.'

Gary hung his head.

Life as he knew it, was over.

NINETY-FIVE

One week later

The cheers went up when Miller walked into the investigation suite. Jimmy Gilmour, Andy Watt, Hazel Carter and the others were clapping and whistling.

Miller held up his one good hand, the left one still in the sling. 'Thanks, folks, but it's unnecessary.'

'My arse,' Andy Watt said. 'You caught one of the worst serial killers this country's seen in a long time. Good on you.'

They came to see him one by one and asked how he was feeling.

'Good to see you, boss,' DS Jimmy Gilmour said. 'Please come back soon. Andy Watt thinks he's in an episode of *The Walking Dead* and he's taken over.'

'I'm working on it, Jimmy.'

'Hey, you show a little respect,' Watt said.

'See what happens when you're away, boss?' Hazel Carter said. 'The boys start fighting.' She gave Miller a peck on the cheek. 'Good to see you on your feet again.'

They'd come in to see him in hospital, but seeing them in the office meant much more to Miller.

'So, you springing for the coffees at Starbucks?' Watt said.

'Andy, you're the one making serious dosh in overtime since I've been away. Make mine black.'

'Oh, what? I can see you've not lost your sense of humour anyway.'

Nobody mentioned Gary Davidson. Nobody wanted to talk about his arrest.

After a little while, it became too much and he excused himself. What nobody took into account was Julie had been his sister-in-law. Another family member was dead. And Gary was now in remand.

Paddy Gibb came into Miller's office. 'Creeping about in the dark? Got some scuddy books on the go or something?' He walked over to the window and raised the blinds.

'You wish.' The sun streamed in. They hadn't had a snowstorm for a couple of weeks and spring was only a couple of days away.

'How you feeling?'

'I'm okay,' Miller said. 'I'm not officially back on duty yet. I'm just here to see the team.' He looked at Gibb. 'How's the team in there? They don't secretly hate me behind my back for arresting Gary, do they?'

'Behave yourself. They loved Carol. She was a fantastic member of the team. They miss her almost as much as you, and to think her brother killed her over money, well, they'd like five minutes alone with the bastard downstairs in a cell. Me included.'

'I wonder if Julie really would have killed me in the crypts?'

'Who knows what goes through the mind of a mad person? However, she could've killed you in your flat, so I'm leaning towards saying, no, I don't think she would've killed you. You said yourself the gun went off when you were fighting her.' He took out a cigarette and lit it.

'By the way, Dennis Friendly and David Elliot want to see you upstairs.' The divisional commander and the head of CID.

'Is this for my commendation? I thought that was scheduled for next week. I can't be arsed with it all anyway.'

'Who knows?'

'Nothing new then.' He stood up and grabbed his jacket from the back of his chair. Put it on carefully, tucking his left arm inside. 'I'll go now.'

'Let me know what they want.'

'What if they want me to tell them all about you? That would put me in an awkward position.' Miller grinned at him.

'Just get up the fucking stairs. I'll be here, raking about in your desk.'

'I keep my scuddy books at home.'

He walked up the two flights of stairs and along to the management suite. He stopped at Dennis Friendly's office and knocked. Waited to enter.

The office was a lot lighter than Miller's with a view of the street. 'Sit down, Miller,' Friendly said. He was a heavily-built man in his fifties, with brown hair that looked like it came out of a bottle. David Elliot sat on a leather couch on one side.

The door opened and Neil McGovern walked in and smiled. 'Good morning, Dennis, David.'

'Good morning, Mr McGovern.'

'How you feeling, Frank?' McGovern said, sitting next to him.

'I'm getting there. Tackling Gary didn't do my shoulder much good, but nothing permanent.'

'Good. Dennis, would you mind being mother? A little milk and sugar in my tea, and pour one for the rest of us, would you?'

'Certainly.' Friendly got up, and walked over to a couple of catering pots on a side table. 'Frank?'

'Coffee, thanks.'

McGovern smiled again as they took their drinks. 'Saving our daughter hasn't harmed your career in any way, Frank. Has it, Dennis?'

'It most certainly hasn't. I always said you're a rising star, Frank.

353

That's why I was only too glad to accept Paddy Gibb's recommendation for your commendation.'

'That's very good of you to say so.'

'Now,' McGovern continued, 'I've just come from a meeting with Norma. She's going to throw the book at Davidson: murder, theft, perverting the course of justice, plus a load of other little bits. He's pleaded not guilty of course, especially on the charge of murder, but fuck 'im, he meant to push Carol down, and it resulted in her death. And knowing my wife, when she gets her teeth into a case, well, let me just say, it isn't pretty.'

Friendly looked at McGovern like a man might wait for a noose to be placed round his neck. McGovern put him out of his misery.

'There's no attributable blame in this department. Nobody could have known what Davidson did. He was first on the scene that night, and everybody thought the kidnapper had run her down and stopped to take the money. Gary had been given the word to follow Carol. Everything slotted into place. Davidson's not talking, but from Frank's statement, he told him it was just an idea, and he carried it out because the opportunity presented itself. We don't believe he was working with Julie. She thought she'd killed her sister by running her over. Turns out it wasn't her after all.'

'That's good news,' Friendly said, relief obvious on his face.

'Yes, that is good news,' Elliot chirped in.

'Now, gentlemen, my wife would like to have another interview with Frank here, an informal one this time.'

'Certainly.' The two officers stood up. Friendly shook Miller's hand. 'Take your time coming back, Frank. Take all the time you need.'

'Thank you, sir, I will.'

McGovern walked out of the office with Miller in tow.

'What happened to the EastEnders accent? You were talking all posh there, McGovern.'

'I've still got it, Frank, me old cock.'

'Did you see their faces? They saw their pensions disappearing down the toilet.'

'They were crapping themselves. Norma said they're a pair of useless wankers, but I omitted that little bit. Every cart needs a horse to pull it, and they're our horses right now.' They started walking down the stairs.

'What does Norma want to talk to me about?' Miller asked.

'Nothing. My car's waiting downstairs and we're going to lunch. Nice meal, a few drinks. It's on Norma.'

'Your wife's a good woman.'

'I know. Just don't tell her.'

NINETY-SIX

'It's an old family plot,' Robert Molloy said to Frank Miller.

Snow still lay on the edges of the driveway in Warriston ceme-tery, and it was freezing cold, but spring was knocking on the door. Miller nodded as he looked at the other gravestones with the name "Molloy" on them.

'I know,' Miller replied. He wasn't wearing the sling anymore, but the physiotherapy sessions made him wish he were.

There was a big turnout and Miller knew some people would wonder why he was standing next to Molloy on the day of Michael Molloy's funeral. It was sanctioned, so he wasn't worried.

Miller looked over at the hearse. There were flowers lined round the edge of the coffin. One wreath spelled out the word "SON" in big, yellow capital letters. Miller turned his head back to Sean's grave. Wondered what his friend would have thought of all this.

'I had an interesting conversation with Julie before she died.'

Molloy turned to look at him. 'I hope the officers who are video-taping this don't have the lens pointed at your mouth. They have forensic lip readers nowadays.'

'They're behind us. They're more interested in who's getting out of the cars than they are in taping me.' Miller looked around anyway. He didn't recognise any undercover officers, but they were in the distance, hiding and trying not to look like they were.

'Tell me then.'

Miller stared off into space for a moment. 'She told me you're Carol's father.'

'This was obviously before she took the gun off you and shot you.' Molloy shivered under his overcoat.

They stood in silence as the coffin was brought across from the hearse.

'Is it true?' McGovern had already confirmed it to Miller, but he wanted to hear it from Molloy's mouth.

'I couldn't keep her, obviously. I was married with kids. I also didn't want her to go to some scumbag either. Harry Davidson and his wife couldn't have kids, so I told him to take care of Carol. I arranged the adoption.' He looked at Miller. 'Simple as that.'

'You were that close to Harry that you'd trust him with your daughter?'

'Yes, I was.'

'It must have stuck in your throat that she wanted to become a police officer like her father.'

Molloy gave him a brief smile. 'She failed the entrance exam. I had one of my contacts take care of it.'

'What?'

'That's right, Miller, my daughter couldn't have become a police officer if it wasn't for me.'

'Did Harry know?'

'Of course he did. I have a lot of fingers in a lot of pies.' He shook his head. 'Fat lot of good that did though; I've lost all my children.'

Miller didn't have an answer.

Molloy looked at him. 'We both lost her that day. I was convinced Sullivan had something to do with it. I didn't think Gary Davidson would have the guts, but he knew how to gamble. He cleared his debt and I didn't question where he got the money. I didn't think for one second he killed my little girl for it.'

'He's going to prison for a long time.'

'I'm saying nothing, Miller.'

'I hope they throw away the key. I hope nothing happens to him inside. Oh, and by the way.' He put his hand up to his mouth as if he was rubbing his face. 'He told them about your money, that I found it in Julie's freezer.'

Molloy looked at him. 'Did you?'

'I did. I was looking for evidence of Julie having a partner-in-crime. That's when I came across your money, hidden. That's why Gary was there too. He was trying to find it, but I got there first. I thought if the department knew about it, they'd take it into evidence where it would sit for a long time. They figured he was making it up.'

The coffin was put down on planks of wood over the open grave. The snow was mostly gone, leaving the grass hard and wet in its wake.

'You know what's underneath us, don't you?'

'It's where that woman shot you, if I'm not mistaken.'

Again, the hand at the mouth. 'It's also where your money is.'

'What?'

'It's your money, Molloy. I wasn't going to keep it, neither was I going to let Gary have it.' He told him where the crypt was, and how light the lid on the sarcophagus was.

Molloy took in a deep breath and let it out slowly. 'I owe you one, Miller.'

They stood in silence for a few minutes. 'Again, I'm sorry for your loss,' Miller said quietly, and walked away.

Just outside the cemetery gate, Paddy Gibb and Tam Scott sat in an unmarked car. Miller got in, grateful to be back in the warmth again.

'What did you say to him?' Gibb said.

'I told him if I ever catch him stepping over the line, he'll be the next one being lowered into the ground.'

Gibb smiled. 'Good job, Frank.'

If you only knew, Miller thought as they drove away. *If you only knew.*

NINETY-SEVEN

It was the first time Miller had been in Kim's house. A mews flat on Circus Lane in New Town. He remembered her telling him she'd got a good divorce settlement.

She'd invited him over for dinner, and now here he was, standing on her doorstep, a bottle of wine in one hand, a small bunch of flowers in the other. *As if I'm on a date,* he'd said to Jack.

Well, isn't that what it is? When a woman offers to cook for a man?

We're colleagues, Jack.

His father had shaken his head and left to go to the pub with his mates. Now Miller felt a buzz inside, his guts churning. *What am I doing here?* He pictured Carol's face; it felt like he was cheating on her.

It's been almost two and a half years, his father had reminded him one night when they were talking about Kim.

He knew Jack was talking sense, but it didn't make things any easier. Yet he felt more at peace, as if finding out who'd killed Carol, and having it acknowledged that she'd been murdered, meant he could finally mourn her properly. He'd gone back to her grave and laid some flowers. Told her he'd love her forever, no matter what.

Now he was shivering from the cold. He turned away from the door, about to walk back along the lane to catch a taxi back up the road when the front door opened.

'Frank!' Kim said, as if she hadn't seen him for months. *As if she'd known him for years.*

He turned back. 'Hi, Kim. You're looking good. Glad to see you're feeling better.' And she did look good, Miller thought. Dressed in black trousers that weren't jeans and a classy white blouse.

'Thank you. Come on in.' She stepped aside, and he walked into the warmth of the house.

The living room was surprisingly large, with a couch and two chairs facing a gas fire. A TV sat in one corner, turned off.

'How's your side?' he asked her, giving her the wine and flowers.

She smiled. He'd forgotten how good she looked when she smiled. 'I'm okay as long as I don't laugh.' She took his coat from him, closing the door behind him. 'Getting it infected was a real bummer though. It floored me.'

'I bet you thought you'd never get out.' He followed her through to the living room after she hung up his coat.

'I've never been so glad to see the back of a place. Don't get me wrong, they do a brilliant job, but I'm not one for sitting about in bed all day.' She looked at him. 'Can I get you a drink?'

'Beer if you have any. Thanks.'

'I do. Sit down and make yourself comfortable.'

Miller sat down on the leather couch. Kim came back with a bottle of beer for him. He opened it and put it down on the small side table.

'I'll get you a glass for that,' she said.

'No, no, don't be daft.'

She sat on a chair opposite him. There was already a glass of wine there. 'I asked you round here tonight to thank you again, Frank. You saved my life. I owe you everything.'

'No, you don't. We work together, and we all look out for each other. Besides, your dad saved me. Julie was standing with a gun pointed at my face, just before she tried to shoot *him*.'

'He heard what she'd said to you, about wanting you to let her go. You don't know for sure she was going to shoot you.'

'In the crypt, she said she was going to shoot us both, remember? Murder-suicide, she called it.'

Kim nodded. 'I remember.'

'So I think she would have shot me in the head. Your dad's a bloody good shot and he got her before she killed me. We're even. No more talk about you owing me anything, okay?'

She nodded and smiled. 'I hope you're hungry?'

'Famished.'

'Good. I learnt a lot from my mother, and one thing she's good at is cooking. I've cooked some chicken.'

'Sounds good. It has to be better than Jack's cooking; if it has heating instructions on the back of the packet, then we won't starve.'

She laughed. 'What about you? Do you cook?'

'I'm a dab hand with a tin opener, if that counts.'

'Well, when I come round to your place, you can open me a can of beans and put them on toast.'

'I can do that.' He took a sip of the beer. 'This is a nice place you have here.'

'Thanks. It needed a lot of work when I bought it, but my dad knows a lot of people who helped.'

'I've always loved New Town. These mews houses are great. I can imagine what went on here when they were carriage houses for the toffs across the street.'

She stood up and picked up her glass of wine. 'Come on through to the kitchen. Dinner should be ready.'

The kitchen was large, with a round table at the far end. Kim pulled the blinds down on the two back windows, keeping the dark out, then served the dinner and Miller tucked in, impressed. They made small talk, Kim telling Miller about living in London.

'What about your ex?' he asked her.

'He's in the army. He moves around a lot.'

She didn't expand on it and Miller didn't push the subject.

Kim took a breath and let it out. 'You'll never know how grateful I am, Frank. You see, I have a little girl. Her name's Emma and she'll be six in May.'

'Really? You kept quiet about that. Where is she?' Miller smiled at her, seeing Kim in a new light.

'She's with my mum and dad right now. She's been staying there since all this stuff kicked off with Cross. Two of my dad's men were staying here while I was in the hospital, then when I was at Mum and Dad's after that. I wanted to make sure I was completely on the mend before Emma came home. To be honest, I can't wait until we get our life back to normal.'

Miller leaned forward. 'That's brilliant. I want to meet her.'

Kim smiled. 'You can meet her. Maybe we can go to KFC along the road or something.'

'That'll be good.' He drank more beer. He was still on his first, and wanted it to stay that way. 'Wait 'til I see your dad. Keeping that from me. He's more secretive than Jack, and that's saying something.'

'He loves his granddaughter. He and my mum had been at me for a long time to come back home. I have custody of Emma, and Eric and I get along fine, but he's her dad, and I didn't want to do that to him. Then one day, I ran it past him, and he said he was fine with it. He got remarried anyway. As I said, he moves around a lot with the military.'

Miller wondered if Neil McGovern had told Eric he'd *better* be okay with it.

After dinner, Kim put the gas fire on. The darkness had brought a chill with it. He felt comfortable here but felt the heat was starting to get to him.

Miller smiled. 'I'm glad you're sticking around.'

'I'm now officially an investigator with the PF's office. I have to liaise with Serious Crimes. So there'll be no getting away from me.'

'I can live with that.' Miller yawned. 'Sorry. I think I should be going. I don't have the same energy levels just now.'

'I'm glad it's not me boring you.' She laughed.

He put his jacket back on, and she stood facing him. He felt a connection to her, and not only because he'd saved her life.

'Thanks for dinner. Next time it's on me, but maybe we'd better go to a restaurant.'

'I can live with that.' She stepped forward and kissed him. He held her for a moment before taking a step back.

'I'll see you soon.'

He smiled at her as he let himself out. Then a car came blazing along the road and stopped next to him.

NINETY-EIGHT

The passenger window wound down and Miller ducked down to see who was driving.

'Get in, me old son.' Neil McGovern.

Miller smiled and got in. 'What are you doing here?'

'I'll always be paranoid about me little girl, Frank. Besides, when she mentioned you were visiting tonight, I wanted to come down. Give you a lift home. You like it?'

Miller nodded. The heated leather seats felt good. 'What is it?'

'Yours.'

'What?'

'It's an Audi A6, but it's yours.' He drove away fast along the lane towards St Stephen's Street, turning up Frederick Street, heading for Miller's flat.

'You know I can't take this.'

'Sure you can. Officially, it's Jack's. Registered in his name, insured with you as a named driver. He bought it.' He smiled and winked.

Miller held on as McGovern gunned the car up the hill. 'I still can't take it.'

'Frank, relax, old son. It was seized under asset forfeit. It belonged to a drug dealer on the South Bank. Then it was ours and now it's yours. It's almost brand new.'

'It's a nice car, but still...'

'Too late. All the paperwork's been taken care of.' They turned onto George Street and McGovern pulled in behind the black Range Rover.

'Did Sienna Craig get away okay? I mean, Ashley.'

McGovern laughed. 'Yes. She's in New York now. We'll catch up when we go over for our hooly.'

'What?'

'I cleared it with the commander of Police Edinburgh. You're coming with me to New York on official business.'

'I don't think he's going to believe I'm going there on business.'

'If he knows what's good for his career, he'll not give it a second thought. Besides, Ashley's looking forward to us coming over. The tickets are booked already. I need your input on something that's a matter of national security.'

'Once again, you never cease to amaze me.' He saw McGovern grinning at him. 'Does Kim know about this?'

'She's having coffee with her mother tomorrow. She'll find out then.'

'How did Ashley get away from Molloy?'

'A note was left in his office telling him she had a better offer. He won't try looking for retribution. He's a lot smarter than that. If he does, his operation will be closed down overnight, proof or no proof, I promise you.'

'Will you try and infiltrate Molloy's empire again?'

'Who knows? Not for a while though.' There was silence between them for a second before McGovern carried on. 'You'll hear about it tomorrow, but I just received a call from a colleague. I'm sorry to tell you your brother-in-law Gary took his own life tonight. He hung himself with a sheet.'

Miller felt cold inside. Suicide? Really?

'Do you think...?'

'Robert Molloy? Don't overthink it, Frank.'

Miller changed the subject. 'Kim told me about Emma.'

McGovern smiled and opened the door, letting the cold in. 'And now she's still got her mum. And more importantly, my missus has still got her little girl. So if you ever need me for anything, you just ask. Now get your arse in the driver's seat and I'll call you about the trip details.' He got out and climbed into the Range Rover.

Miller got behind the wheel. Watched the black SUV pull away. He'd always wonder if Gary did take his own life. Maybe McGovern was right though.

Sometimes it doesn't pay to think too much.

AFTERWORD

Thank you for buying a copy of Crash point. I hope you enjoyed the book.

I want to thank some people for helping me on this journey. My late mother Margaret, a retired police officer, for her behind-the-scenes stories of police life, and for never letting me think I didn't have a story in me.

Thanks go to Thomas, my former agent, for helping me shape the book into what it is today.

Special thanks go to my friend and fellow writer, John Walker, for batting ideas back and forth with me over the years and for giving me the benefit of his wisdom. It's been a great journey, buddy, with many more to come. Remember, keep the faith!

Thanks to my daughters, Stephanie and Samantha. Love you both. And thanks to Mo for all her support.

Finally, thank you, the readers, for all your support. You all make this worthwhile.

If you could please leave a review of this book, that would be fantastic. Each and every one helps.

John Carson
New York
February 2016

ABOUT THE AUTHOR

John Carson is originally from Edinburgh, Scotland, but now lives in New York State with his wife and family. And two dogs. And four cats.

website - johncarsonauthor.com
    Facebook - JohnCarsonAuthor
    Twitter - JohnCarsonBooks
    Instagram - JohnCarsonAuthor

Made in the USA
Las Vegas, NV
20 February 2022